# DON'T LET ME GO

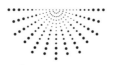

## KELSIE RAE

Don't Let Me Go
Cover Art by Cover My Wagon Dragon Art
Editing by Wickedcoolflight Editing Services
Proofreading by Marjorie Lord
Published by Twisty Pines Publishing, LLC
September 2022 Edition
Published in the United States of America

*To my readers...*
*Here we go again. :)*

# BLAKELY

"**C**olt's gonna kill me," I mutter as I tug at the hem of Mia's tight black dress. It barely reaches my ass, but she insisted I wear the damn thing before curling my hair and doing my makeup. Pretty sure I'm her own personal Barbie. Not that I'm complaining. Growing up with three older brothers didn't exactly encourage femininity. I was just...one of the guys.

Until I moved in with my new roommates.

Ashlyn grabs my hand, stalling my fidgeting. "Stop. You look cute."

Ashlyn's dating my brother, Colt. She's also the mastermind behind my new living arrangement. When she offered to let me move in with her, Mia, and Kate after finding out I was transferring to LAU, I felt like I'd won the lottery. She's also one of the reasons I'm standing in front of this house currently thumping with music. Colt lives here with his best friend, Theo.

Apparently, the girls aren't only fanning my femininity. They're also showing me the ropes of college life, including--but not limited to--parties with hot guys.

I smooth out the front of the dark dress again, another wave of indecision pulsing through me. "I look like——"

"A gorgeous girl?" Mia offers.

I puff out my cheeks, and let out a sigh. Maybe I should've stayed home with Kate. She's our third roommate. She's also the anti-partier of the group. Part of me doesn't blame her. The other part? I look up at the massive house again. It reminds me of the movie *Home Alone*, complete with red bricks, rows of windows, and music thumping through the open front door.

Well, I guess I can see the appeal of coming tonight.

"Besides. Colt's not the one you have to worry about," Mia adds, stealing my attention from the daunting house in front of me. "Theo's gonna shit his pants."

Theo.

Also known as Theodore Taylor.

He might be my brother's best friend, but he's also LAU's hockey captain and my arch-nemesis.

Kind of.

We used to be friends when we were little, but as soon as he saw me wear a dress, it was like a switch flipped, and he's despised me ever since which, ya know, was great for a fifteen-year-old's self-esteem.

His name alone causes a lump to lodge in my throat, but I choke it back and paste on a fake smile.

"Greaaaat," I drag out while eyeing the front of the Taylor House like it's straight out of a horror movie.

"Seriously. You look awesome," Ash tells me. "Why are you freaking out?"

"Because this"——I wave my hand at the house literally thumping with rap music——"is not where a girl like me usually hangs out. Especially when looking like this." I wave my hand around again, this time showcasing the dress that feels like it's practically painted on me. "Or this." I pick up a wave of perfectly styled red hair and flick it over my shoulder. "Or this." I motion to the smokey eye shadow Mia painted on my face before we left our townhouse.

To say I'm a tomboy would be an understatement. But I think it's par for the course when you're raised with three older brothers and have a penchant for sports.

"You're in a new place now," Mia reminds me. "You get to start over. Be who you want to be. Look how you want to look. Attract who you want to..."--she winks--"*attract.*"

The girl saw me one time--one. time--with Theo. But apparently, that's all it took. She's convinced the guy has a thing for me. It doesn't matter how much I've tried to explain the truth since then. It's like I'm talking to a wall.

I glare back at her. "I don't want to *attract* anyone. I just want to fit in and have fun without being yelled at by a certain--"

"What the hell are you wearing?" Theo barks, rushing toward us on the front lawn from his porch.

*Speak of the freaking devil.*

He's practically throttling a bottle of beer in one hand as he grabs my arm with his other. Not roughly but with a possessiveness causing my breath to hitch.

He's always been this way, though.

Overly protective while detached and bossy at the same time. Like I'm a nuisance. A pariah. Someone he wishes would simply...go away. Yet anytime I try to, he reels me back in.

It's annoying.

And confusing as hell.

"She's wearing *my* dress," Mia interrupts, yanking me from the opposite side like I'm in some twisted game of tug-of-war, though I appreciate her protectiveness. I'll take anything to distract me from drowning in my feelings for a guy who will never feel the same.

"Doesn't she look hot?" she adds, scanning me up and down.

Theo's nostrils flare, but he lets go, clenching his hand at his side and glaring at me. A weaker girl would crumble under the weight of such a look, but I hold his gaze.

"You really think Colt's gonna let you inside looking like this?" he demands.

"Pretty sure it's my decision," I remind him. "And even if it wasn't, you would *still* have no say in the matter. I'm not a little girl you can boss around anymore, Teddy Bear."

I say the nickname through clenched teeth, well aware of how many buttons I'm pushing right now. But I refuse to back down. Not with anyone, let alone Theodore Taylor, asshole extraordinaire. He made it clear when I first transferred to LAU how much I wasn't wanted. Thankfully, it isn't his decision. And I've never been afraid of going head-to-head with the bastard.

His jaw ticks as he towers over me, two seconds from having an aneurysm.

*Good.*

"I thought we discussed you calling me that," he growls.

With a syrupy sweet smile, I answer, "Must've slipped my mind."

"O. M. G," a gorgeous brunette interrupts as she stumbles into Theo. I flinch beside him. One of her heels is caught in the grass, and she's laughing like a hyena, clutching at his bicep like he's her own personal savior.

My hackles rise, and it takes everything inside of me to keep from sneering at her.

"Oh. Hi, Theo," she purrs when she recognizes him. "Good to see you again." Her hand brushes against his exposed forearm, a coy smile curling at the edge of her dark red lips. Clearly, they know each other. And clearly, it isn't in a *we-share-the-same-class* kind of way.

My cheeks feel like they're on fire as I mutter under my breath, "Of course, she knows him."

Without another word, I march into the Taylor House with my head held high, trying to ignore the frustration boiling in my veins. But I can't help it. Theodore Taylor seems to have that effect on me.

He *always* has.

I'm too pissed off to appreciate the energy pulsing through the main floor of the Taylor House as I slip inside and dart straight toward the kitchen where I assume the booze is located.

After all, attending my first college party should have at least a few perks, right? One of which is free alcohol. Since I'm only nineteen and can't purchase the stuff myself, I plan on taking full advantage. Hell, I'm gonna need it after my little run-in with Theo.

And why does he care what I'm wearing anyway?

I twist the cap off the clear liquor bottle, slam it against the surface, and reach for the stack of red Solo cups in the center of the table. After grabbing the top one from the stack and inspecting it for cleanliness, I scoop some ice into it from a large, plastic bowl, then add a generous splash of liquor followed by some Orange Crush soda.

Which I regret instantly.

Orange Crush will always remind me of him.

Theo.

Teddy.

The boy next door who happened to be my hero.

Once upon a time, anyway.

With a frown, I shove the memory of warm summers and drama-free childhoods away and shoot the entire drink back, keeping my throat open so it slides down without protest before almost choking on an ice cube.

"Whoa there," Mia interrupts. She sidles up next to me and pats my back. The girl looks like a badass. Someone who's a little on the intimidating side but has a heart of gold. She has tattoos on her left arm, piercings lining the shell of her ear, and a past rough enough to make even the most numb, heartless bastard weep. She hasn't opened up to me about it, but I've picked up a piece or two. Something about her father being a drug addict who was murdered a few years ago, though I haven't asked for details. Not yet, anyway.

She's also insanely good at reading people, and I hate knowing it's exactly what she's doing to me at this very moment.

With a quick side-eye toward her, I grumble, "Don't judge."

"No judgment," she clarifies as a few hockey players join us in the kitchen and start reaching around our bodies to make their own drinks. Keeping her voice low, she adds, "Wanna talk about it?"

"Nothing to talk about."

"Are you sure?" She watches as I splash some more vodka into my cup and top it off with Sprite while glaring at the Crush soda as if it offended me.

I chug this drink down, too, clearing my throat to relieve the burn.

*Okay, that one was a little stronger than the last.*

Mia frowns. "Blake--"

"I'm fine," I rush out.

With a sigh, she touches my shoulder. The same shoulder left bare thanks to her dress I'm wearing. The dress that somehow caught a certain someone's attention as soon as we walked up to the infamous Taylor House belonging to the devil himself.

I shrug out of her grasp and pour another drink, making a mental note to pace myself after this. Heaven forbid I end up shitfaced in my brother's best friend's house.

Well, technically, I guess it's Colt's house, too, since he lives here. But he doesn't have quite the same stick up his ass a certain someone else seems to have, so I'm not sure if he counts.

So. Fucking. Annoying.

Once the players have their drinks, they disperse, giving us another ounce of privacy.

"Seriously, Blake. You sure you're okay?" Mia asks. "Do you want me to get you some water or something?"

"Look around, Mia. It's a party. A *college* party. And what does one normally do at college parties?" I tip my cup in her direction, then lift it to my lips. "Drink, of course."

"Drinking at a party is fine as long as it's to have fun and not to erase a certain brother's best friend from your mind."

My lips purse, and I take another small-*ish* sip. So sue me. "Who said I'm trying to erase a certain brother's best friend from my mind?" I lift my hand and stop her from replying. "You know what? Don't answer that. Because it doesn't even matter. I'm not going to do this anymore," I decide, more to myself than anyone else. "It's like you said. This is the perfect time to turn over a new leaf. Be who I want to be, attract who I want to attract, and I'm not going to play his game again. I'm done."

"So, what are you going to do?" she asks.

"I'm going to…" I bite my lower lip as my gaze catches on a group of people cheering in the backyard. A pair of French doors are propped open in the kitchen, probably to let in the fresh air. They lead to the back of the property where a patio table is set up. It's littered with red Solo cups, and there's a concrete pad beneath it. My smile widens when a Ping-Pong ball bounces off the surface and into the grass. "I'm gonna play a game of Beer Pong. Wanna join?"

She frowns. "Blake, are you sure Beer Pong is a good idea?"

I'm not sure if it's the copious amount of alcohol streaming through my system or my newfound desire to move on with my life and make a new name for myself. But at this point, I don't really care. Besides, if there's anything I'm good at, it's being one of the guys. It's all Theo ever saw me as, anyway. And the guys outside? It looks like they're having fun. I'm in desperate need of something fun.

"Seems like an excellent idea to me," I announce, keeping my head held high. "You wanna come?"

With another sigh, she looks out the open doors leading to the backyard and turns to me. "I'm gonna go use the ladies' room first. I'll meet you out there." She points her finger at me. "Don't get bombed."

"Who said I'm gonna get bombed?"

Her gaze narrows as if she isn't convinced. "I'm serious. I really don't want to clean up puke tonight."

I laugh and head toward the exit as I call over my shoulder, "I'll be fine! See you in a few."

I walk over to the Beer Pong setup a few feet away, the cool wind kissing my cheeks and bringing an ounce of clarity with it. There's a small crowd––most of them are guys––and they're laughing as a Ping-Pong ball plops into a cup. The person closest to the cup groans and downs the warm beer inside. Once he's finished, he raises his hands in surrender, slightly stumbling to the left. "All right, man." He laughs and tosses the cup onto the grass. "You win."

"Any more takers?" his opponent calls, searching the crowd huddled around the table. Apparently, I'm not the only one who finds the game interesting.

Stepping forward, I announce, "I'll play."

All eyes turn to me.

Clearly, most of the guys are hockey players. There's something about the way athletes carry themselves. Confidence bordering on arrogance. An aura screaming they're on top of the world, even when they're drunk off their asses. They also like to stay together. Like a pack of wolves or something. It's rare to find one on their own out in the wild. And tonight isn't any different.

They each take their turn scanning me up and down, probably wondering who the hell I am since they've never seen me before. Most of their mouths turn up into smirks as one of them––the previous winner–––motions to the now-empty space across from him.

"Be my guest."

The guy's cute. Or at least I think he is. There's only one of him so far, so I don't think my beer goggles are skewing his features, but the night's still young. Dark, curly hair cropped short to his head. Dark skin. Dark eyes. *Kind* eyes. And his smile? Hello, handsome. His straight white teeth are freaking perfect and only add to his chiseled jaw and attractive features. He's balancing himself on a set of crutches. His boyish grin is showcased as he laughs at something one of the other players is saying, though I don't hear what's said as I close the distance between us.

"Hi," I greet him, offering my hand. "I should probably introduce myself before I beat your ass."

He grins, looking like the perfect candidate to distract me from a certain someone I want to banish from my mind. A pinch of guilt spreads in my chest as I check out the stranger, but I shove it away. I don't need to be loyal to Theo. I don't owe him anything except maybe a dead leg for all the shit he's put me through.

Besides, I'm here to turn over a new leaf. Meaning I should *not* be pining over someone who looks at me like I'm a little kid, thank you very much. And who better to distract me than the man in front of me?

The stranger chuckles and takes my offered hand. "Hey. I'm Burrows. Shawn," he clarifies. "But everyone calls me Burrows."

"Blakely," I return. "Most people call me Blake. Nice to meet you."

His eyes are curious as they slide down my body. The inspection doesn't leave me feeling skeevy or anything. Only…curious.

"You too," he replies. "You ready to play?"

"Yup." I grab the Ping-Pong ball from Burrows' grasp and toss it a few inches into the air. But as it comes back down, it misses my hand entirely and bounces off the ground, pulling a chuckle from the guy beside me.

"Are you usually this uncoordinated or have you already had a few drinks tonight?" Burrows asks.

My lips pull into a thin line. "No comment."

His chuckle is warm and inviting as he grabs another Ping-Pong ball from the table, tosses it into the air, and successfully catches it. "Do you know the rules?"

"Yup." *Okay, I most definitely don't, but it can't be too hard, can it?* "I bounce the ball, and if it falls into a cup, you have to drink it, right?"

"Yup. Pretty much sums it up." He motions to the table. "But we're gonna play on the same side of the table."

"Why?"

"'Cause I'm afraid you might fall over after a round or two. Gotta keep you within arm's length so I can catch you in case you pass out."

I laugh. "You're that confident you're gonna win?"

He turns to me again, the same boyish grin turning my insides into melted butter as his eyes crinkle in the corners. "Yeah, Blake. I'm *that* confident."

"Care to make it interesting?" I ask. I can't help it. Even when the ground is spinning, I'm a competitive person, and he's thrown down the gauntlet.

Burrows leans closer, balancing on his good leg while sidling up next to me. "Maybe. What're the stakes?"

"If I win––"

"Blake!" Colt calls from the open French doors. My neck snaps in his direction, and I paste on a smile. "Yes?"

"You good out here?"

My grin widens. "Yup!"

He points his finger at Burrows. "She's my little sister, man. Keep that in mind, all right?"

Burrows dips his chin. "Yeah, Colt. I got you."

With a slow nod, Colt turns back to me, adds, "Don't puke," and disappears into the house.

A bout of silence rolls over us while Burrows realizes my not-so-well-hidden secret. His interested gaze makes me twitchy as he looks at me again, this time with a new wave of curiosity. I keep my head held high and quirk my brow, as if to say, *Is there a problem?*

I shouldn't be surprised. I've grown up in Colt's shadow for as long as I can remember. Between him and my two other brothers, Knox and Garrett, people have always looked at me this way. Like they're curious what the youngest Thorne can bring to the table or if her vagina makes her weaker and less significant.

Fun fact: It doesn't.

Being taken seriously or looked at like I'm my own person, however, has definitely been a challenge. But I don't see it changing anytime soon, especially not with the guy in front of me.

"So, you're Colt's little sister?" Burrows confirms, continuing his examination of me with his head cocked to one side. He's probably searching for any resemblance between Colt and me, though I doubt he'll find it. I have red hair, freckles over every inch of skin, and am basically a walking stick while Colt has dark hair, olive-ish skin, and muscles. The only things we have in common are our potty mouths and obsession with sports.

That same sugary-sweet smile spreads across my face as I fake curtsy. "The one and only. Now where were we? Oh, yes. I believe we were discussing the terms of our bet. When I win, you can buy me dinner."

"*When?*" he challenges, hobbling closer to me.

I tilt my head up but don't back away from him. "Did I stutter?"

He snorts. "All right, I'll take the bait. And if I win?"

I shrug one shoulder. "What do you want?"

"A date with you."

"So I...still get dinner?" I verify.

"Apparently."

My eyes light up. "Deal."

"Deal," he agrees, handing me another Ping-Pong ball. "First to five?"

"Five?" I question. I realize how stupid I must sound right now, but I'm also drunk off my ass thanks to the Crush and vodka, so it's not exactly my fault.

"First to land five balls in the cups wins," he explains.

"Oh. Deal."

He nods. "Ladies first."

I blink slowly, attempting to concentrate and toss the small white ball onto the table. It bounces once but misses the cups by a long shot and lands on the ground, pulling a dark chuckle from the man beside me. Following suit, he grabs a second ball and bounces it onto the table. With a wet plop, it lands in a cup, and the crowd around us cheers.

"Drink up, Blake," he urges, his mouth tilting up while his triumph rolls off him in waves.

I laugh and drink the warm beer. My nose wrinkles as it spreads across my tongue.

*Gross.*

Once I've gagged it down, I grab the still-wet ball from my cup and bounce it off the table toward my targets.

It misses. Again.

"This is gonna be a quick game," Burrows jokes, landing another ball into the row of cups across from us.

I groan and swallow more stale beer back. "How are you so good at this?"

"'Cause I start the game sober. Leaves me a little more wiggle room than my opponents," he informs me and waves his hand toward the table. "Your turn."

My vision is blurry at best, and my tongue feels swollen in my mouth as I take the ball from Burrows' fingers and attempt to throw it at the table. I swear the ground is moving beneath my feet. As the Ping-Pong ball slips from my fingers, I lose my balance and stumble into Burrows' rock hard chest.

*Oops.*

His hand slides around my waist, keeping me from face-planting on the concrete when a low voice barks, "Blake!"

I flinch and turn toward the familiar voice, but the back-yard continues spinning.

*Aaaand it's official. I've had too much to drink.*

A pair of hands wrenches me away from Burrows, and before I can even register what's happening, I'm plastered against a solid chest. It's warmer than Burrows'. More famil-iar, though I'd never admit it out loud. It takes everything inside of me to stop myself from snuggling against it, but I keep my spine straight and my muscles from melting into Theo's grasp.

"What the hell are you doing, man?" he growls, the sound vibrating from his chest and against my palms firmly planted on his pecs.

"Calm down," Burrows replies. "We're just playing a game."

"This is Colt's little sister!"

"Yeah. I know." Burrows' tone is calm and level-headed, unlike the man who's holding me hostage. "He saw us playing and was fine with it."

"Did he know you were gonna get her wasted too?"

"I wasn't--"

Smacking Theo's chest, I wiggle out of his arms and nearly fall on my ass. His grip tightens around my bicep, keeping me upright, though I refuse to thank him for it.

"He wasn't doing anything, you big neanderthal," I argue. "We were just playing--"

"Yeah, well, you're done."

"Who do you think you are?" I demand. Or at least, it's what I'm trying to demand. My tongue isn't exactly working at top speed. Nope. Instead, my speech is slurred, and I'm pretty sure I sound like an idiot. But it isn't my fault. It's Theo's. He shouldn't have pissed me off as soon as I walked up to his house. He also shouldn't be smelling this good. What is it? Cologne? Or is it his own natural scent? If it is, it isn't fair. That's for sure.

"Look. I've already had enough shit go down for one night," Theo growls, though I have no idea what he's talking about. He glares down at me, shaking his head. "I don't need to deal with you too."

"Then don't," I argue. "I'm fine."

Without bothering to tear his gaze from mine, Theo yells, "Everyone! Out!"

I flinch at the sharpness in his tone. He isn't usually an angry guy. Most of the time, he's laid back and--dare I say it--almost jovial. Like Santa Claus. Except sexier and without the massive belly.

Well. Unless I'm around. Then, he's the Grinch with a

side of Jack the Ripper. And with the way he's looking at me right now? I might as well dig my own grave next to the massive trees in the backyard, 'cause I'm not walking out of here tonight.

"Now!" Theo snaps.

*Welp. Apparently, the party's over.*

## 2

## BLAKELY

A collective groan rolls through the backyard as people start heading inside and toward the front door, repeating Theo's order to those who hadn't heard him yet. I'm surprised no one protests though.

Nope. Just me.

Smacking at Theo's chest——again——I spit, "Who said you get to end the party? They were having fun. *I* was having fun!"

"Yeah, I can see," he grumbles. "Can you walk, or do I need to carry you?"

I blink slowly as I register his question. My mind feels like it's stuck in quicksand, making every thought, every decision feel like it's happening in slow-motion. Like I can't catch up. Like I'm always a beat or two behind.

Impatient, Theo bends down, grabs the back of my thighs, and hauls me over his shoulder like I'm a sack of potatoes. It isn't sweet or romantic. It's tainted with annoyance. Obligation. Like he'd rather be anywhere else than holding me against him. And it pisses me off.

"You should let me down," I slur, hating how good he

smells. Seriously. It's delicious. Like aftershave and sweat. But not gross sweat. Good sweat. I didn't know there was good sweat until this moment. But it's official. There's such a thing as good sweat. Clean sweat. And I want to wrap myself up in it. Not to mention the view. Hello, tushy, tush. I kind of want to pinch it, bite it, and smack it all at once. Maybe if I do, he'll even put me down.

Now that's what I call a win-win.

"Well, this is just great," a familiar feminine voice announces as Theo steps inside the Taylor House. "I swear I only left her for five minutes. But then Colt punched Logan and--"

"I get it," Theo replies as I turn my head toward the voice and find a very upside down roommate staring back at me.

"Mia! My mama Mia!" I snort. "Get it? *Mama Mia*? It's such a great movie."

"She's totally gonna puke in Ash's car," Mia mutters. She turns on her heel toward the front door. "Come on--"

"I need to pee," I announce.

Pinching the bridge of her nose, the keys dangling from her other hand, Mia sighs while Theo takes a sharp turn toward the bathroom on the main floor.

My legs feel like overcooked noodles as he sets me down on the gray tile. I grab his arm to keep from falling over, vertigo practically assaulting me. Seriously. It's official. This is the most drunk I've ever been, and I'm gonna be miserable tomorrow.

*Nice move, Blake.*

"Can you pee on your own?" Theo grumbles. I swear, the bastard isn't even trying to hide his annoyance.

Rude.

Although, it *is* an excellent question.

*Can I pee on my own right now?*

17

I gulp, my stomach knotting as the alcohol settles inside of me, then nod at him.

Unconvinced, he stays close, eyeing me like I'm a ticking time bomb. "You sure?"

"Yup," I lie, giving him a thumbs up with my hand not currently digging into his arm to hold myself upright.

He grabs my wrist and removes my death grip on his bicep but makes sure I have my balance somewhat steady before he lets me go and steps away from me. "I'll be outside."

The door closes behind him with a quiet click.

I don't know how long I'm in the bathroom, but I do know it's spinning. Round and round, like I'm on a carousel, when I'm most definitely sitting on the toilet with my thong around my ankles and my dress pooled around my waist.

*Classy, I know.*

I shouldn't have had the last drink.

*Damn you, Burrows. You're too good at Beer Pong.*

"Bad idea, Blake," I scold myself, resting my head in my hands with my elbows perched on my knees as I close my eyes.

A soft knock echoes from the door, and my head lolls to the side.

"Who is it?" I sing.

"Blake," a familiar low voice barks.

"Who is it?" I repeat a little louder this time while dropping the song.

"Unlock the door, Blake. Now."

*I locked the door?*

Not gonna lie. I don't even remember closing it.

Too. Much. Alcohol.

With a frown, I push myself onto my feet, pull up my underwear, and stumble to the sink. The cool water feels good against my hands as I wash them. The towel feels gross, though. Like it hasn't been washed recently.

Or maybe it's because there were so many people at the party.

I guess it makes sense.

A loud, jarring knock vibrates against the door again, and I jump in surprise.

"Now, Blake," the low voice warns.

*So bossy.*

Grumbling under my breath, I unlock the door. The handle twists on its own, and the door is shoved open to reveal a very pissed off Theo.

"What's your problem?" I slur.

"Mia and I have been trying to get you to open this door for five minutes."

My brows furrow. "What?"

"We thought you'd passed out."

"Blake!" Mia calls, squeezing past Teddy's massive body through the doorframe. She pulls me into a hug.

"I'm sorry. Why are you hugging me?" I ask against her blonde hair. She smells good too. Like shampoo. I grin and take a giant whiff. "Girl. Why do you smell so good? You should let me borrow your shampoo next time along with this kickass dress."

With a laugh, she pulls away from me. "Deal. But for now, let's get you home, okay?"

"Cool." I sway on my feet, and my stomach churns. "First, I gotta puke."

The tile is cold against my knees as I collapse in front of the toilet and vomit like there's no tomorrow. My chest heaves. My stomach twists. My throat burns. And my eyes water.

It freaking sucks.

I hate throwing up. The lack of control. The bitter, acidic taste. It's seriously the worst.

Hands are in my hair, holding it away from my face as I

hurl my guts out until there's nothing left in my stomach but the realization I just vomited in front of an audience.

*Fan-freaking-tastic.*

I want to go home.

I want to go to sleep.

I want to erase this entire night.

Especially those last couple of drinks.

Man, I'm so embarrassed.

How can this be happening right now?

I rest my head against the hand cupping my temple while the other one keeps a firm grasp on my messy hair. It feels nice. The hand. It's warm. Calloused. Gentle.

"You good?" a low voice murmurs.

*Theo.*

Yup. Theo just saw me puke.

And act like an idiot at my first college party.

No, not an idiot.

*A child.*

He saw me act like a child.

The same thing I've been trying to change for years.

*Dammit!*

I rub beneath my nose with the back of my hand as Theo helps me to my feet in silence. The room is still spinning but not quite as badly.

He doesn't let me go as he leads me to the sink to clean up. And boy, do I need it. When I catch a glimpse of myself in the mirror, a lump clogs my throat.

My dark, smokey makeup is smudged, making me look like a raccoon instead of the sexy goddess I'd been channeling. Not to mention my naturally curly red hair. It's sticking up in every direction like I just rolled out of bed. I don't look sexy anymore. I don't look put together.

I look like a freaking train wreck.

Like Merida from Brave. Except without the Disney Princess filter. Just pale and pasty and…a mess.

I want to go home.

My attention shifts from my own reflection to Theo's as embarrassment floods my cheeks, turning them red. Then again, maybe it's from the vomiting. He's standing behind me, his brows pulled low and angry. And it hurts. To see him mad at me. To see him disappointed.

"I don't want a lecture," I whisper. My voice echoes in the otherwise silent bathroom, and the ensuing quiet is almost eerie. Like he doesn't know what to say or how to express how much of a screw-up I am.

Fun fact, Theo: I already know.

With a soft curse under his breath, he leans down and grabs something from beneath the sink.

*Mouthwash.*

I take the bottle from his grasp and swig a little of it, the minty flavor a welcome change from the taste of acid and alcohol.

After a solid thirty seconds of swishing, I spit it in the sink and twist the cap back onto the bottle, setting it onto the counter while Theo simply…watches me.

He's always watching me. Even when we were little, I would catch him staring. Studying. I always wanted to know what he was thinking. If he was as fascinated with me as I've always been with him. But not today. Not in this moment. Tonight, I think I'd prefer to be left in the dark. No need to add salt to the wound and all that.

Avoiding his gaze, I tuck my hair behind my ear and murmur, "I should probably get home."

"I told Mia to leave."

I crane my neck toward him and look over my shoulder, meeting his gaze with my own as he stands behind me. "What?"

"She shouldn't have to clean up your puke."

*Ouch.*

His sharp words shouldn't hurt, but they do. I'm not surprised. Everything hurts when it comes to Theo. My heart. My pride. My confidence.

Why would tonight be any different?

But I refuse to let him see it. How much it hurts to be around him.

I turn and face him fully, crossing my arms over my chest. "She won't need to clean up my puke. I already hurled everything out."

He scoffs. "For now. Who's to say you won't throw up again? It's not her job––"

"So, what? It's yours?" I challenge.

With another scoff, he takes his beat-up baseball hat off and scrubs his hand over his face like he doesn't know what to say, then he mutters, "Apparently."

I step to the side, leaving some space between us. Some much needed space. "I'm not a little girl––"

"Then stop acting like one," he growls, closing the distance and covering his wavy hair with his hat again. It shields the bathroom light from hitting his eyes, making them darker and more intense than usual. They're almost animalistic, lacking any humanity or softness at all. Only bitterness. And it's all directed at me.

I shake off the realization and argue, "You shouldn't have embarrassed me when I was playing Beer Pong."

"You shouldn't have been playing in the first place."

"Why? Because I don't belong here?" The question slips out of me before I can stop it, laced with vulnerability and a sharp accusation I've been too scared to voice aloud until this moment. But it's out in the open now, and I want to know if I'm right. If it was a mistake to come here. If he'll always look at me like I'm a burden––like I'm a little kid––or if he'll ever view me as the adult I want him to see. I've been asking myself if it was a mistake to come to LAU since the moment he moved me in with Ash and the girls. And apparently, buzzed Blake wants to know too.

Theo pulls back, confused. "You don't belong where? At my place?"

"Why stop there?" I demand, my frustration finally boiling over. "Not only the Taylor House but LAU too. You don't want me here at all," I tell him. "Am I right?"

"It's not my fault any of those guys would love to chew you up and spit you back out."

I frown. "Burrows is nice."

"He's a hockey player, Blake. None of us are nice. Not to girls like you."

"What's that supposed to mean?" I demand, reaching onto my tiptoes to close a bit more of the distance between us. Because I don't like this. Feeling small. Weak. Inconsequential.

"It means you're too innocent to be here," he growls.

"Who says I'm innocent?"

His gaze slides down my body, and for the first time ever, there's a glint of heat in it. Not much. Hell, it's barely a spark. But it's there. Tempting me. Testing me. My resolve. My self-preservation. My restraint.

I lift my chin and meet his gaze with my own. "Maybe I'm not so innocent anymore." I let out a shuddered breath, our lips so close I can practically taste him. "You haven't seen me for over a year, Teddy. You don't know where I've been. Who I've kissed. Who I've fucked."

His upper lip curls. "If Colt heard you say––"

"Colt isn't here," I remind him with a dry laugh. "It's just me and you. And I'm tired. Tired of this…responsibility you've decided to put on yourself. To be my surrogate brother when all I ever wanted was a friend. You've decided

23

it's your responsibility to boss me around. To make sure no one touches me, when guess what, Teddy? No one asked you to take on those responsibilities. And here's the real doozy, my friend." I pat his chest, ignoring the feel of his tense muscles beneath my palm. "I *want* to be touched. I *want* to be kissed. To be fu--"

He slams his mouth against mine. I gasp, and he shoves his tongue between my lips. It isn't soft or sweet. It isn't innocent. It's freaking dirty. And selfish. Like I'm being used. Like he's proving exactly what it's like to wind up with a hockey player instead of the sweet and caring gentleman he thinks I want.

*Oh, how wrong you are, Teddy.*

I like the way he takes what he wants without giving a shit about me or how I feel. It's like he's trying to prove a point, though he's far from successful. Because *this* is what I've been craving. I don't want to be treated like a child. Like a breakable doll.

*Fucking break me, Theo*, I want to beg. But I don't. I let him kiss me. Let him take what he wants. Let him try to prove it isn't what I want, when it's the opposite.

I've craved him for years.

And now…here he is.

Kissing me.

## 3

## BLAKELY

W ith his hands on my waist, Theo guides me backward until my back hits the wall with a quiet thump. It takes my breath away but makes my pulse go wild.

"Shit," I whimper between kisses.

I need more.

He nips at my bottom lip. Probably to keep me quiet when we both know it'll only spur me on. The feeling shoots straight between my thighs. He tears his mouth away and presses his forehead against mine. But even that isn't gentle. It's rough. Bruising. Forceful.

"This is what it's like to kiss a guy like me––a guy like anyone you meet at these parties," he grits out. "It isn't soft and sweet and shit. You should remember that."

The warning in his voice is loud and clear, but I ignore it.

Maybe it's the remaining alcohol in my system. Maybe it's the taste of Theodore Taylor still clinging to my tongue. Maybe it's the girlish dreams that've been taunting me over the past five years since I looked at Theo with rose-colored glasses. Whatever it is, I can't put my finger on it, but I don't want this moment to disappear. I also don't know what to say. I liked the kiss. I liked it a lot. I kind of want to keep doing it. In thirty seconds or less, he blew apart every fantasy I've ever had about another guy. Honestly, the bastard obliterated them.

"But guess what, Blake?" he adds, his hands gripping my waist, his fingers flexing.

"What?" I breathe.

"I think you're full of shit." He laughs dryly. "About your *experiences* over the last year."

My experiences?

I blink slowly.

*Oh. Right.*

"What about my experiences?" I ask, my voice nothing but a whisper.

"You don't kiss like an experienced girl."

*Aaaand, there's the dagger to the chest I'd been expecting.*

I pull away slightly, reality crashing into me like a freight train. "Excuse me?"

"I said, you don't kiss like an experienced girl," he repeats, his gaze darkening.

"And how do I kiss?"

His Adam's apple bobs up and down in his throat as his attention dips to my bruised lips for a split second. "Like an innocent little virgin."

If he'd have slapped me, it would've hurt less.

But I don't let him see it. I refuse to.

Because he's right. Compared to the puck bunnies I know he's had sex with, I *am* innocent. Hell, even without them as a comparison, I'm still innocent. Truth be told, he hit the nail on the head, describing me perfectly.

An innocent little virgin.

But it isn't fair for Theo to throw it in my face or to make me feel self-conscious for my lack of experience.

*Screw him.*

"And it's a bad thing?" I volley back. "That I kiss like an innocent little virgin?"

He shrugs one shoulder. "Not necessarily. Does make it a little difficult, though."

"Make *what* difficult?"

"Hooking up," he clarifies with a devilish smirk. "Watching an innocent little virgin fumble to figure out what they're doing isn't everyone's thing."

*Did he seriously just go there?*

He's going to pretend he's not turned on? Pretend he didn't like our kiss? Don't get me wrong. I'm not naive enough to think I'm the best kisser in the world or anything, but there's no way a kiss can be so good for one person and so terrible for the other.

*Bullshit.*

With a dry laugh, I call his bluff and slide my hand down his body, brushing against the swell in his jeans I knew would be there. "Funny. If I didn't know any better, I'd say it's *your* thing. Do you have a penchant for innocent little virgins, Teddy Bear?"

"Are you an innocent little virgin, Blake?" he counters.

"It's none of your business."

"When your hand is on my dick, I think it *is* my business."

I bite my lip, barely able to withhold my grin because of how frustrated he looks in the bathroom light. How sexy he looks. How unhinged he looks. Like I've finally managed to burrow under his skin the same way he has mine.

"You're right," I whisper. "I'm a virgin. An innocent. Little. Virgin." I squeeze him again through his jeans. I'm not sure if it's the liquid courage swimming through my veins or the years of pent-up frustration spurring me on, but I'm not going to question it. Not when I've finally had a taste. "The question is… What are you going to do about it?"

I shouldn't be goading him. Not when he looks so close to snapping. But I can't help it. This is how it's always been with us. The way we push each other. Competing against each other. Calling each other out when someone's acting like a piece of shit. And if he honestly thinks he can get away with lying to my face and saying he wasn't invested in the kiss the same way I was? He's delusional. And I'm not above rubbing his nose in it.

He grabs my wrist and pulls me away from the front of his pants, twisting my arm behind my back until my front is pressed to his. "If you were innocent, you wouldn't touch my dick through my jeans."

"So now I'm *not* an innocent little virgin?" I question, my head tilting to one side. "I think you should get your story straight, Teddy."

"And I think you should remember I'm your brother's best friend, and if he knew your hand was on my cock a second ago, he'd kill us both."

"But what a way to go, am I right?" I quip.

His nostrils flare as his attention drops to my lips. Again. It makes my core tighten, but I don't move a muscle. I wait. Blame it on the alcohol left in my system. The empty hallway separating us from the rest of the world. Hell, maybe it's the dress's fault, and the way it hugs my slender hips. Whatever it is, I'm not going to question it. Because I just kissed Theodore Taylor. I felt his erection in my palm before he pulled my hand away from it. I can still feel his chest brushing against my sensitive nipples as he takes a deep breath. And it's addictive. Consuming.

He lets me go and steps back. "You're annoying when you're drunk."

Whiplashed, I blink slowly, my gaze tracing his steps as he puts more distance between us. "Excuse me?"

"You should get some sleep."

"Who says I'm still drunk? Buzzed, maybe. But drunk?" I snort. "I think it's a reach, Teddy Bear."

Ignoring me, he reaches for my hand and tugs me toward the hall. "Come on. You can sleep it off in my bed."

"And where will you sleep?"

"On the couch."

"Or you could always sleep with me," I offer.

"I'm not gonna fuck you, Blake."

"Who said I wanted you to?" I counter, disguising my hurt with annoyance as I wrench my wrist away from him. "I said sleep, not fuck. Those are two different things."

"I don't sleep with girls."

"Especially not innocent ones, am I right? Let me guess. You don't usually kiss them, either."

He grits his teeth and turns back to me. "I was proving a point."

"What point?" I demand with a laugh. There isn't any humor in it, though. I'm too pissed off. Too sexually frustrated to enjoy our banter. Honestly, I kind of want to deck him.

"My point," he spits, "is a girl like you doesn't belong with a guy like me––or with any other guy you'd run into at these parties. You should stay away next time."

"Why? So you can enjoy your party and hook up with whoever you want instead of babysitting me?"

"Exactly."

"Fine." I slip past him and head toward the front door, unable to stay in his presence for a second longer.

I'm sure there's an Uber close by. It's Friday night in a college town. There has to be. If not, I'll call Colt. Or maybe I'll just walk. Maybe the cool air will finally clear my head. Honestly, I don't know. But I need to get the hell out of here.

I hate this. This rollercoaster. I feel like I've been on it with Theo since the moment I turned fifteen and he saw me in a dress on my birthday. A freaking dress. It was the first one I'd worn since I was a toddler and decided shopping in the boys' section was more fun than anything pink or frilly on the girls' side.

But the stupid dress changed everything, and until tonight, I hadn't worn one since. He saw me differently that day. It was like I'd popped the proverbial *one-of-the-guys* bubble I'd been wrapped in for years. Which is what I thought I'd wanted. Maybe not fully. But a little bit. Unfortunately, it had the opposite effect I'd been hoping for. Afterward, I was *Colt's little sister* instead of *Blakely Thorne, girl next door*, and I couldn't erase the title no matter what I did.

Seems tonight isn't any different.

His heavy footsteps follow me down the hall before he twists me around, his silence more telling than any words he could utter in this moment. His gaze is frustrated but impenetrable, his protective walls higher than ever as he glares at me. Like I'm the problem. The one who ruined his night. Who forced him to kiss me. In reality, he's the one who leaned in first and crossed the line. *Him.* Not me.

"What do you want, Teddy?" I demand, ignoring the warmth from his hand or the way his calloused fingertips tickle the inside of my arm, causing goosebumps to spread along my flesh.

"I want you to stop calling me Teddy and to walk your ass up the stairs so we can both get some sleep."

"And I want you to drive me home," I counter.

He lets me go and pinches the bridge of his nose. "I knew this would happen. I knew you'd be a pain in my ass if you decided to come to LAU. I fucking knew it."

Arms crossed, I spit, "You wanna talk about being a pain in the ass, Theo? All I want is a normal college experience without you babysitting me the entire time. Because guess what? It isn't your job. I'm allowed to get drunk. I'm allowed to lose my virginity and to have sex with random guys. Including hockey players, I might add, and it's none of your business." I jab my finger at his chest. "None. Of. Your. Business. Do you understand?"

"Fine."

"Fine."

He stares at me, his molars practically cracking. "Now, get your ass upstairs and go to bed before I make you."

He's serious. I can see it in his eyes. Feel it in his tense muscles. Hell, it's tainting the air around us. Stealing all the oxygen in the room until I'm lightheaded and dizzy.

Without a word, I turn on my heel and march up the stairs toward his room. I don't say anything when I slip beneath his bedsheets. I don't utter a single syllable as his scent rolls over me, tickling my senses and making my mouth water.

I don't say a damn word.

Because he doesn't deserve them. Not my voice. Or my thoughts. Or my feelings.

After tonight, he's made one thing very clear.

He doesn't deserve a single piece of me.

Not anymore.

And I'm too stubborn to ever forget it.

4

# BLAKELY

*Two months later*

Sweat drips down my back as my feet pound against the pavement while Eminem blasts through my AirPods.

*Push it,* I remind myself. *Almost there.*

I race around the corner and down the sidewalk toward my street, my muscles burning in the most exhilarating way possible. I mean, yeah, it hurts. But exercise is a *good* hurt. It makes you feel alive. Like you can do anything. *If* you're willing to put in the work.

Sure, there's the bad kind of hurting. When you work too hard and have to stop pushing yourself so you can recover. Sometimes there's a fine line between the two, and if I learned anything from my kiss with Theo, it's that I'd gone too far. I'd crossed the line.

*He* crossed the line.

And I haven't seen him since.

Not really.

We've crossed paths a time or two, but other than a head

nod or a forced smile, we've been silent. And I refuse to have it any other way.

Which is why today is terrifying.

I cross my imaginary finish line in front of the fire hydrant by our house and place my hands on top of my head as I catch my breath.

In. Hold. Out. Hold. In. Hold. Out. Hold.

My legs ache, and there's a slight twinge in my knee thanks to blowing it out during my sophomore year of soccer. But otherwise, I feel good.

Or at least I should.

If only my nerves would settle.

After taking the steps to the front porch slowly, I open the door and find Kate, Ash, and Mia surrounding the kitchen table with bowls of cereal in front of them.

"Hey!" they greet me.

"Hey." I round the small kitchen island and fill a cup with water from the fridge as they continue the conversation I must've interrupted when I came inside.

"So you like him, then?" Ash asks Kate.

"I think so," she hedges, tucking her dark hair behind her ear. "He's really nice and funny, but..."

"But what?" Mia probes.

"Pause," I interrupt, taking a quick sip of water. "Who are we talking about?"

"Wes," Ash answers. She turns in her chair until she's partially facing me in the kitchen along with everyone else at the table. "As you know, they've been dating for a few months now, and Kate knows she likes him, but..." She drags out the word and gives Kate a pointed look.

"But he wants to take things to the next level," Kate admits.

"And it's a bad thing?" I ask.

"Kind of?" Pushing aside her half-eaten bowl of Cheerios, she mutters, "I haven't told him about my condition."

*Condition.*

Also known as epilepsy, though Kate refuses to use the word. Pretty sure she treats the e-word the same way the wizards in Harry Potter treat he-who-must-not-be-named. I wouldn't even know what she's referring to if it weren't for Mia explaining the situation. After I moved in, she informed me of the giant elephant Kate likes to avoid at all costs. Including keeping it from her casual boyfriend.

*Yikes.*

"Why haven't you told him?" Mia prods. "It doesn't have to be a big deal."

"It *is* a big deal." Kate's spoon clatters in her cereal bowl as she lets it go and shakes her head, too frustrated to eat. "I finally found someone good in my life. I don't want to ruin it."

"It's not going to ruin anything."

Running her fingers through her hair from roots to tip, Kate flips it over one shoulder until it cascades down the side of her face, shielding her for a moment. Then, with a weak-ass smile, she bites her thumbnail and murmurs, "You have no idea. I can't drink alcohol. I can't see movies with flashing lights. I can't have kids, or at least, I shouldn't thanks to the medicine I'm on. I..." She lets out a soft, shuddering breath. "I can't do anything."

My heart cracks, and a silence fills the room as my attention shifts from Mia to Ash. But none of us know what to say. None of us know what she needs to hear or what we can do to help. Because...shit. Epilepsy sucks. And until this moment, I had no idea how much it affects her. The realization makes me feel heartless. Like I'm a shitty friend for letting her down, completely oblivious.

"Kate," I breathe out. My glass makes a soft clinking

sound as I set it on the counter. I rush toward her and pull her into a big, sweaty hug. It's all I can do. All I can give. Because I don't have advice for this situation. I'm the furthest thing from an expert. But I can be here for her. I can show her she's cared about. I can prove she isn't alone. And I'm sure as hell not going anywhere.

She laughs, only waiting a quick second before wrapping her limp arms around me. "I'm fine, Blake."

"Liar," I mutter against her as Mia and Ash join in, creating a Kate sandwich.

"We're sorry," Mia mumbles against the crown of her head. "Seriously."

Kate sniffs again and wiggles out of our hug, wiping beneath her eyes. "It's fine. Really. It is. It just makes relationships...tough."

"But you like him, right?" I ask.

She puffs out her cheeks, letting the air out on a sigh. "I think so, yeah."

"And he likes you?" I prod.

She nods.

"Then, give him a chance. You might be surprised by how he reacts."

Digging her straight white teeth into her bottom lip, she scratches at her temple, giving in with a shrug. "We'll see."

Ash, Mia, and I exchange worried glances but don't say a word because no one knows what to say.

"So." Ash nudges my shoulder. "Are you excited about your first day?"

Gratitude shines in Kate's eyes at the subject change, while mine dim with anxiety.

It's an excellent question. If only the answer was cut-and-dry.

"Blake?" Ash prods.

"Yeah, I can't wait," I lie, heading back to the kitchen like a woman on a mission. I grab some fruit and kale from the fridge so I can whip up a quick smoothie and keep myself distracted from the current interrogation I feel building around me. Unfortunately, it does shit to prevent the anxiety welling in my stomach.

As I add a scoop of protein powder to the blender, Ash interjects, "Coach Sanderson wouldn't have given you the position if he didn't think you deserved it."

These girls know me too well.

Turning toward them, I rest my hip on the counter and cross my arms. "I'm not worried about Sanderson. He's usually a pretty level-headed dude."

"Then, what are you worried about?" Mia asks.

My nose scrunches, and I let out a sigh and turn back toward the blender, ripping off a few pieces of kale and tossing them in with the strawberries and blueberries while the girls wait in silence.

"Oh, Blake," Mia sings.

I add a splash of almond milk and a handful of ice. "Fine. I'm worried the guys won't take me seriously 'cause I'm a girl."

"Of course, the guys will take you seriously," Kate argues. "If they don't, I'm pretty sure your brother will beat them up."

"Him or Theo," Mia adds with a smirk.

I ignore her and turn on the blender, letting the loud whir cut off any more asinine comments.

Unfortunately, after I turn it off, Mia keeps poking the bear like it's her job. "Speaking of Theo, have you seen him lately?"

"Nope," I answer. "And I don't plan to if I can help it."

"You mean, other than practice," she counters.

"Or games," Ash adds with a smirk.

Through gritted teeth, I remind them, "He's as healthy as

a horse. I'm sure he won't need any physical therapy or anything."

"Burrows will, though," Mia argues.

"Aw…I love Burrows," Ash gushes, clutching at her heart. "He's such a sweetheart."

"A hot sweetheart," adds Mia with a grin.

"Ooo, is he the guy who was on crutches a couple months back?" Kate asks. "He comes into the restaurant sometimes. Good tipper."

"Yup. That's the one," Ash confirms. "He got hurt during last season and went home to have surgery on his knee. But the coach is planning on playing him this season as long as he's ready, which means Blake will have plenty of time to help him feel better. Won't you, Blake?"

Mia's brows bounce up and down as I pour my smoothie into a to-go cup and head down the hall like a bat out of hell. "Aaaand, I'm done talking to you guys. Wish me luck today."

"Good luck!" they call as I retreat to my room.

*Boy, am I gonna need it.*

# 5

# BLAKELY

Toying with the red and black lanyard around my neck, I scan the rows of lockers in the hockey facility. After arriving for my first day at the internship, I was given a badge with my picture on it, along with a keycard for after hours, and a quick introduction to Coach Sanderson and my mentor, Russell Trist, aka Russ. He's the athletic trainer for the hockey team and is older than my grandpa. But he's nice in a snappy, take-no-shit kind of way. I like him immediately.

"As you can see, Sanderson's office is over here," Russ motions to a closed door off the main locker area. "And here's the team's lockers." He waves his hand again. There are rows and rows of black and red lockers with wooden benches lining the front of them. Pictures of LAU hockey alumni are hung on the walls, showcasing players in their most memorable moments on the ice. There's also a black framed display of every previous player who was recruited to the NHL. Their jersey numbers, athletic stats, and which team they played for are all there too. It's crazy and shows exactly how prestigious LAU's program really is.

My chest swells with pride as I take in the names.

I'm not related to them or anything, but it's still cool. To see some of the greatest professional hockey players' origin stories. Their history. And now, I share a piece of their history. It's freaking amazing.

Epic, actually.

I trace a name with my finger, a smile gracing my lips.

This.

This is why I want to go into athletic medicine. So I can help some of the future greatest players of all time *stay* great. So I can help prevent and mend injuries. So I can keep the players healthy and on the ice instead of on the bench before they reach their full potential.

Like I did with soccer.

Sure, some are a bunch of big babies, and it'll probably feel like babysitting half the time, but it's still worth it.

*Isn't it?*

"My office is down the hall past the showers," Russ says behind me. "Have you ever seen a dick before?"

I nearly choke on my own spit as I twist on my heel and face him. "I'm sorry, what?"

"I'm just saying." He shrugs and tucks his hands into his front pockets. "You're the first girl we've hired. I think you have what it takes to excel in this field, but there were a lot of people chomping at the bit for this internship, and you're gonna be around a lot of guys. They like walking around naked. You okay with it?"

An image of Theo in nothing but a towel comes to mind. I shove it away.

"Not a problem," I lie, praying my cheeks aren't as red as they feel.

His bushy white brows rise on his weathered face. "You sure?"

"Definitely. Yup. Positive." I bite my tongue to keep from rambling even more.

His gaze narrows, and he mutters, "All right. Good. 'Cause I don't work with dandies. If you're gonna be here, you're gonna see shit. Broken bones. Bloody mouths. And a few naked men. I'm not gonna say something to the team or ask them to act differently 'round here just because we hired a girl. The locker room is their safe space. I'd prefer to keep it that way without making them bend over backward for the new intern. We clear?"

I nod and clear my throat. "Crystal."

"Good. Now, most of the players are good guys, but if you ever feel unsafe or any of that shit, reach out to me. Sanderson and I already talked about it. Bringing a girl into the locker room can be a sticky situation, but we're trying to be progressive. As long as you aren't stupid, we want you here, and if the guys give you any trouble, you can talk to us."

"I'll keep it in mind."

"Good. Also, I'm not your babysitter. I expect you to be here when I tell you and to follow orders when I give them."

"I can do that."

"Figured." He winks then checks the time on his watch. "Shit. I lost track of time. I have a phone call I have to take, and until you finish the HIPAA training, you can't be included." He glances at the head coach's closed door and frowns. "You can shadow Sanderson as soon as he's finished in his office with your brother. Once I'm done with the call, I'll come find ya, and we'll go through some massage techniques on one of the players in my office. Sanderson should be done any minute. Just hang out in here. We'll introduce you to the team as soon as they're done cleaning up."

Practice ended about ten minutes ago, before I was led into the training facility, so I haven't seen any of the players yet. I can hear the showers running, though, along with their deep voices. Part of me wants to ask if Russ really thinks it's a good idea to leave me alone in the locker room when the entire team is showering less than thirty feet away. But he already asked if I'm comfortable being here, and if I bring up the showering tidbit, it'll prove the opposite.

I can't let that happen.

"Sure thing. I'll just wait here." I rock back on my heels, hooking my thumbs into the back pockets of my dark jeans and wait, though I have no idea what I'm waiting for.

"Good," he returns. "I'll be back in ten."

He heads down the hall, disappearing through the steam billowing from the shower area as he passes it while leaving me completely and utterly alone.

*Great.*

Fidgeting with the lanyard around my neck, I peruse the black billboard showcasing the hockey alumni again and search for any familiar names.

Barely a minute passes when a bunch of boisterous male voices echoes behind me. Fisting my sweaty palms on the bottom of my T-shirt, I try not to freak the hell out and remind myself to breathe.

Apparently, they're done with their showers.

I squeeze my eyes shut even though I'm not facing anyone and prepare for the inevitable.

*Please don't be naked.*

## 6

## BLAKELY

The hair along the back of my neck stands at full attention since, you know, I'm standing in the men's locker room where a few players are possibly––*probably*––naked. And they have no idea I'm here. Or at least, not yet. I count down from ten, curious to see how long it takes until I'm spotted. But I don't turn around. I won't. Not until they have a chance to notice a girl's in the locker room and realize they need to cover their junk. Or at least, *hopefully*, they'll realize they need to cover their junk. Honestly, hockey players are known for being hit in the head, so who knows if they'll put two and two together. But a girl can hope, can't she?

*Ten.*

*Nine.*

*Eight.*

"You lost, beautiful?" a low voice asks, the rest of their chatter ceasing.

*Well, would ya look at this? Apparently, I've been spotted.*

Sucking in my cheeks until they're hollow, I turn around, steel my shoulders, and smile, making sure my line of sight is angled toward the ceiling instead of anyone's nether regions. When I catch a glimpse of fluffy white towels wrapped around their waists, I breathe out a sigh of relief. There are three of them. And even though they're covered from hip to calf, their massive builds are still on full display as their attention drifts down my body.

They don't even have the decency to hide their curiosity. Nope. They're checking me out openly and without an ounce of shame. Can't say I'm surprised.

"Gentlemen," I greet them. "And no, I'm not lost."

I've watched enough games to recognize each and every one of them. Quin Graves. One of the goaltenders on the roster. A little hot-tempered but good at protecting the net. Winston Depp. Defenseman. A little weak in the skating department but pretty freaking awesome at stealing the puck. And a new guy. Austin, I think? Greg Austin? He hasn't had any time on the ice yet, but he played well in high school. Sanderson was smart to recruit him.

"Aw, you guys got me a present for my first practice," Austin jokes, sauntering toward me like he owns the place. "Hey, baby girl. I'm Greg––"

"Careful, Austin," Depp warns him. A grin teases his lips as he holds my gaze but keeps addressing the new guy. "That's Baby Thorne."

Austin turns to Depp. "*Baby* Thorne?"

"Yeah. As in Colt's little sister," Graves explains. I'm not sure how he knows me. We've never been formally introduced. Maybe he was at the Taylor House not so long ago?

"Although, she obviously got the good looks in the family," he continues.

I laugh as Austin steps closer to me, his buddies flanking his sides. "I think I've seen you around a time or two," he notes, analyzing me a little more carefully. "You ever come to the Taylor House?"

"Last time she came, Burrows beat her fine ass at Beer Pong," Graves interjects, confirming my suspicion. He scratches his dark jaw already sporting a five-o'clock shadow and looks me up and down again. "Although, if you're looking for someone to teach you the ropes and show you how to actually beat the bastard, I'd be happy to--"

I roll my eyes. "I'm good, thanks."

"Maybe you can cheer me on while I defend your honor myself," Austin suggests. "I could take down Burrows."

"Again, I think I'm good," I repeat, more amused than annoyed by their boldness. Growing up around hockey players has taught me a few things.

One. They hang out in packs.

Two. They're cocky as shit.

Three. They're always looking to hook up.

And four. They're flirty little buggers.

*That's* for sure.

With a dark chuckle, Graves suggests, "Or maybe you and I can--"

"Graves!" Colt barks, standing in the doorframe of Coach's office with his arms crossed and a warning in his eyes.

Graves raises his hands into the air as if to prove his innocence and takes a step away from me like I have *Don't Touch* tattooed across my forehead. "Hey, man. I didn't touch her."

"Good. 'Cause I doubt Sally would appreciate you hitting on my little sister," Colt warns.

"Sally and Graves broke up--again--last week," Depp informs my older brother. He turns to me and lifts his chin. "But what's up, Baby Thorne? Is there a reason you're hanging out in our locker room?"

"She's here because she'll be shadowing Russ for the season," Coach Sanderson informs them. Raising his voice, he adds, "I have an announcement! Everyone in the showers, get your asses in here!"

The pipes groan in protest as the showers shut off, and the rest of the team files into the locker room. Most have towels wrapped around their waists, but as the room becomes more crowded with half-naked bodies, I'm blocked from view. A few of the stragglers slide off their towels and start getting dressed by their lockers, oblivious to the fact a girl is standing less than ten feet away.

When a sliver of space forms between the mass of bodies, a few birthday suits come into view, and I gulp, dropping my gaze to the ground.

Yup.

That was most definitely a penis.

Or four.

"All right, guys." Coach's booming voice bounces off the walls, demanding everyone's attention, including mine. Thank goodness. I do my best to ignore the tan, wet skin on full display in my periphery––although it's freaking diffi-cult––and stare at Coach Sanderson instead.

"You did well at practice today. I think we're gonna have a good year. As always, we have some shit to take care of, and some wrinkles to smooth out, but I know if we put in the work, we're gonna make it to the playoffs."

The team cheers, spreading their enthusiasm like wild-fire. And just like that, it doesn't matter that I'm here anymore. They have their eyes on the prize, and there isn't a single distraction––including a woman––who will keep them from getting it. I grin and clap my hands while Sanderson waits a solid three seconds, then quiets the team down.

He continues. "I know I introduced the rest of the new members before practice, but I want to make one final intro-duction." He clears his throat and motions for me to step forward. Depp and Graves had managed to sandwich me between them when the rest of the team ambled in from the shower. I squeeze myself out from between them and head toward my brother and Sanderson at the front of the room.

Once I'm by his side, Coach announces, "This is Blakely Thorne. She'll be shadowing Russ throughout the season. Don't give her any shit, all right?"

The guys laugh, each and every one of their focuses shifting from Coach to me. If I hadn't been raised with three older brothers, I might be intimidated by the amount of testosterone wafting throughout the room, but I'm used to it.

In fact, I thrive in it. It's familiar. Comfortable, even. Which is weird but true. I'm used to being one of the guys. Once they realize I'm not like other girls they've met––and I have no intention of jumping into bed with any of them–– they'll stop looking at me like I'm a piece of meat, and we'll get along just fine. But until then, I'll have to put up with the snide remarks and flirtatious comments. Thankfully, I have thick skin. Well, unless Theo's involved. But I digress.

Wiggling my fingers in a small wave, I say, "Hey, guys! Thanks for having me."

Tukani, one of the goalies, says something in a low voice to his buddy, and the guy chuckles, his gaze flicking over me from head to toe. His mouth curves up on the side.

My eyes hurt from keeping them in place when all they want to do is roll like a damn bowling ball at Tukani's attention, but I stay strong. When a shadow from the entrance to the rink comes into view, I'm grateful for the distraction.

That is, until I recognize who it belongs to.

Theo stops short, realizing he's interrupted one of Coach's speeches and squeezes the back of his neck.

"Sorry, Coach. I was taking a few extra laps."

"Taylor," Sanderson acknowledges. "I was just introducing the newest member of our staff." He motions to me with a quick wave of his hand. "Blakely will be shadowing Russ during the season."

I haven't seen Theo since his party. I've been avoiding him––and what happened––at all costs. But now, he's less than ten feet away, and the reminder of our kiss hits me square in the chest.

I still can't believe it happened. But the memory's richer than any fantasy I've ever whipped up, and boy have I whipped up a few doozies over the years. If I close my eyes, I'm pretty sure I can still taste the bastard. Feel the way he grabbed my waist. The way he took what he wanted without giving a damn about the consequences. The way he felt in my hand when I reached down and––

I snap myself out of it, digging my nails into my fisted palms. But I'm too much of a coward to meet his gaze. Instead, my attention bounces around Theo's face while attempting to look indifferent in his presence when it couldn't be further from the truth.

How the hell does a guy look this attractive? It isn't fair.

All sweaty and lickable. His soft, curly hair clings to his forehead as he rubs the back of his hand against it, wiping away the moisture. The guy isn't as big as Shorty, one of the defensemen from last year who went pro, but he's definitely the largest member on the offensive side. And boy, those muscles do him good.

He must drink a lot of milk.

That's a lie. He's only ever been a sucker for Crush and protein shakes, but, apparently, I need to give the sugary drink another go––sans vodka, of course––because the guy's a freaking babe. My gaze finally meets his. He's staring at me. His jaw is tight and his brow pulled low, showcasing the stubborn, unreadable ass who only really comes around when I'm in the vicinity with him.

And I'm not crazy.

Even Mom noticed when we were in high school. How he changes when I'm around. How he can go from fun-loving, bullshit-talking Theo, to broody, overprotective asshat in two seconds flat as soon as I enter the room.

It's ridiculous.

And with me shadowing the team, I'm sure his friends will *love* it.

*Great.*

"All right, I think that's it," Sanderson concludes. I force myself to stop checking Theo out and turn back toward the coach, though I can feel Theo's hot stare on the side of my face. Clearly, my presence caught him off guard. And clearly, he isn't a fan of it.

Coach claps his hands together and adds, "Now, get dressed and get outta here. I'll see you tomorrow for practice."

The team gets back to work, dispersing and dropping towels in some kind of twisted game to see who can make me uncomfortable first because they sure as hell aren't rushing to get dressed.

I roll my eyes, unable to hold it back any longer while pretending being given front row seats to a dozen penises is just an average Tuesday afternoon for a girl like me. In reality, it couldn't be further from the truth, though I'd never admit it out loud.

When Colt catches onto his teammates' game, noticing the fact the majority of them are taking their sweet time in covering up their birthday suits, he scoffs, but he doesn't give them any shit for it.

He knows as well as I do it'll only egg them on. He also knows I can take care of myself. One swift knee to his groin in middle school was all it took to prove to him––and everyone at my school––I can handle myself. Colt hasn't overstepped his bounds since.

"Hey, big brother," I greet him while pretending to be oblivious to the penises around me.

"Hey, Baby Thorne," he teases before deciding, "I like the nickname."

Theo sidles up next to Colt, practically towering over us in his skates and quips, "Fitting too. Like she's a thorn in our side."

"Clever," I note. I pat his pec like he's a good dog while refusing to fawn over just how hot the bastard is or how good he feels in the palm of my hand. And that's through the thick material of his pads and practice jersey. The idea of touching his actual skin?

*Swoon.*

Lips pursed, I drop my hand to my side and rub my palm against my jeans.

"You done for the day?" Colt asks me. "Wanna ride home with me?"

"Russ said I should wait––"

"Thorne!" Russ yells. Our heads snap toward the back office. Russ cringes and points to me. "Girl Thorne!"

"Baby Thorne," Theo suggests with a wry grin.

Nodding, Russ repeats, "Baby Thorne. Got it."

"Thanks a lot, Teddy," I mutter, tossing a quick glare at my nemesis. Raising my voice, I reply, "Yes, Russ?"

"I just got off the phone with Burrows' doctor. He's been cleared for the first game, but I want you to come with me. I'm gonna show you some things we can do to help with mobility before and after the games."

"Yeah. Sure. Whatever you need," I answer.

"Burrows, introduce yourself," Russ adds. "Then meet me in the office."

He disappears down the hall as Burrows approaches, his hand outstretched.

Ignoring Theo's hot stare on the side of my face, I take it and smile. "Hey, Burrows."

"Hey, Blake. Long time, no see."

"Yeah, it's been a while," I admit, refusing to look at Theo, the culprit for why I've been so absent since the first night I met him.

Burrows looks good, though. No crutches this time. Same boyish grin. And lucky me, he isn't wearing a shirt.

*Hello, pectorals.*

"We'll have to have you at the Taylor House again soon," Burrows adds, watching me as I blatantly check the guy out. His mouth is tilted in a knowing smirk as my gaze snaps to his. "I think I owe you a rematch."

"You mean when you aren't cheating?" I tease.

He laughs. "Cheating?"

"You already told me your secret, remember? Start sober. Pick an opponent who's already buzzed. Very sneaky, my friend."

An annoyed huff interrupts our friendly banter, and Theo storms back toward the rink without a word.

*What the hell?*

I exchange a confused look with Colt and Burrows.

Burrows shrugs, and Colt calls out, "Where are you going, man?"

"Gonna work on sprints," Theo yells back, but he doesn't turn around.

"Sprints?" Colt's nose wrinkles.

"Chop, chop, Baby Thorne," Russ orders from his office. "Burrows, you too. Let's go!"

Well, all right, then. Apparently, the bee in Theo's bonnet is going to have to stay *his* problem.

Which is good.

It's none of my business, anyway.

# 7

# BLAKELY

Once Russ was finished showing me the motions for a proper leg massage, he went to his small desk in the back corner and has been flipping through paperwork ever since.

"That's enough," he says without bothering to look over at us.

I stop touching Burrows' knee and rub my hands together. "Uh, I guess that's it for the day. Thanks."

He slides off the black-cushioned table similar to one you'd find at a doctor's office. Once he's on his feet, he asks, "For what?"

You'd never know the guy had knee surgery. He's strong. Athletic. Practically indestructible. You can see it in the way he carries himself.

Well, *carried*, since I kind of put him through the ringer during our PT session. He bends down and rubs at his knee gently while I bite the inside of my cheek to keep from ogling him. The guy's good looking. So sue me.

Once he's back to his full height, he looks at me, waiting for an answer.

*Oh. Right.*

I meet his gaze and smile, clarifying, "Thank you for being my first patient."

Burrows digs into his pocket and offers me his phone. "Glad I could be of service. Any chance you'd give me your number in exchange for my glowing review?"

I snort but take his cell and plug in my number, handing it back to him. "Only so you can let me know if your knee starts hurting or something."

"I'll be sure to keep you in the loop. Maybe I can even give you an update during dinner? I believe I owe you after our Beer Pong game."

"Pretty sure the offer expired," I tease.

"Then, I guess I really will need another rematch." His brow arches with a silent challenge.

"Maybe some other time."

"All right," he returns, clearly unperturbed by my dismissal. "See you around, Blake." He walks out of the PT room with a slight limp, and I watch him leave.

He's cute.

Safe.

I should want safe.

"It's normal," Russ says.

Tearing my attention from Burrows' backside, I clear my throat and turn back to Russ. Shit. I'd almost forgotten he was here.

"What's normal?" I ask.

"The slight limp."

"Oh." I nod and cross my arms. "Gotcha."

"You did good today," he notes, standing up and heading toward the door.

"Thanks."

"After you put away the foam rollers and bands, wipe down the table with some cleaning wipes. Then, you can go."

"Okay."

"And don't forget to turn off the lights," he adds.

With a salute and a cheeky grin, I reply, "Yes, sir."

He watches for a few seconds as I gather up everything into my arms before he strides out of the room. Once everything is organized in the large metal cabinet at the back of the room, and the massage table is sanitized, I dig out my cell from my back pocket to check the time and find a message from an unknown number.

**UNKNOWN NUMBER: So, when I leave this glowing review, do I mention the part where I couldn't take my eyes off you, or should I focus on the way your hands felt against my leg?**

A breath of laughter slips out of me. The guy's a flirt. I'll give him that much. Innocent flirting, I can handle. It's the broody stares and snarky comments made by a certain someone that have a habit of getting under my skin.

The thought annoys me, so I shove it aside and begin typing my response as I head toward the exit when I smack against a hard, wet chest.

*What the--?*

My phone clatters to the floor as a pair of strong hands reach out and steady me. The grip is soft but firm against my elbows as I peek up at who they belong to.

It's Theo.

A jolt of electricity inches up my limbs, making my heart beat faster and faster as I attempt to process what the hell just happened.

"I--" My fingers flex against his damp and *very naked* chest before I realize my hands are against Theo's damp and very naked freaking chest.

I pull them away as if I've been shocked.

*This is so embarrassing.*

Avoiding his gaze, I look at the ground, and my jaw drops.

His towel is on the floor, and his penis is——

*Holy. Freaking. Shit.*

My head snaps toward the ceiling, my face the shade of cherry flavored Kool-Aid as the image of Theodore Taylor's massive dick is imprinted into my memory for the rest of eternity.

"Oh my hell," I mumble under my breath. Embarrassment and want and surprise and every other freaking emotion filter through my system like I've been given a dose of crack and it doesn't know how to metabolize the stuff.

*Is this seriously happening right now?*

"Shit," he growls.

As the curse slips past his lips, I can't help but look at it again. His penis. It's like it's a damn lighthouse, guiding me to it. Demanding my attention. And boy, does it deserve attention. Theo's hands drop from my arms, and he bends down, tearing the towel from the ground and wrapping it around his waist. But it's too late. The damage is done. I've already seen plenty.

And I mean *plenty.*

Dazed, my gaze stays glued to his crotch when he finally looks up at me, his jaw tight. Like I'm the one in trouble, and he has every right to be pissed at me.

"I didn't…" My voice trails off, the lie tasting bitter on my tongue.

I didn't…what? *See anything*? Oh, boy is that a load of shit.

I didn't…*stare*? I guess it's partially true, but only because I was too shocked to make a closer inspection.

I didn't…*mean to*? To what, exactly? I did nothing. I was just walking and——

"Why the hell weren't you paying attention?" Theo growls.

"Excuse me?" I lift my chin and stare him straight in the eye. "Paying attention to what? Your dick?"

"I meant where you were going," he barks.

The bossy tone sends my frustration into overdrive as I glare up at him, refusing to back down. "At least I had my phone as a distraction, *Teddy*," I spit. "What's your excuse? Did the steam get to your head and make you woozy? Or maybe your stinky aftershave was the culprit. Is that it?"

His aftershave isn't stinky. It smells like heaven, but I refuse to let him know that. Not when he's looking at me like I'm the problem in this scenario when it's clear I'm just as innocent as he is. Although, I also refuse to let him know I'm not blaming him after he's thrown down the gauntlet.

Still. It was a mistake. A mistake that led me to seeing my brother's best friend naked while also getting a chance to touch his naked chest.

No big deal.

Nope.

Not one bit.

I swear I can almost see the wheels turning in his big, stupid head as the water clings to his curly hair. The moisture lingers on it for a split second before a droplet falls onto his skin and rolls down the side of his face, leaving a trail of liquid my fingers itch to wipe away.

I fist my hand at my side.

"You think I smell *stinky*?" he asks, his voice laced with sarcasm and condescension. Neither of which do anything but pour gasoline on my annoyance.

Ignoring him, I continue, "Or maybe you're self conscious. Is that it? Does Baby Taylor have a"--I lift my forefinger into the air, then crook it toward the floor--"wittle problem?"

He chuckles and steps closer, making me feel like a little mouse thanks to the height difference. "I almost forgot."

I drop my hand to my side but crane my neck up, forcing myself to hold his gaze. "Forgot what?"

"I almost forgot my dick is the first one you've ever seen up close." His laugh turns darker. Richer. Sharper. Making my belly tighten. "I almost feel sorry for you now."

"Because it's so pathetic?" I offer.

"Nah, because whatever guy takes your cherry is only gonna be a disappointment if you think any of them will live up to the beast between my legs."

I snort. "For your information, your dick isn't the first I've seen up close."

His eyes darken, and his nostrils flare, all amusement dissipating from his stupidly handsome features. The heat from his bare chest seeps through the thin cotton of my T-shirt. When the hell did he get this close?

*And is it hot in here?*

"Oh?" he challenges.

"Yup."

"And how many have you seen?"

"Three?" I pause, tapping my finger against my chin. "No, wait. Four. Definitely four."

"Four? In two months?" His brow arches, and he steps even closer, all broody and broad shouldered. "Someone's been busy."

I laugh but stand my ground, refusing to back away or let him intimidate me with his massive size. "Says the biggest whore I know."

He looks lethal right now. Like he could rip a car to shreds with his bare hands. His bare hands currently caging me in on both sides. How the hell did I get in this position? I swear, it's like anytime he's around me, I'm in some kind of weird haze and things just…happen. Like the kiss not so long ago. Like the way we're alone in the men's locker room. Like how my back is pressed to the smooth brick wall behind me, and how his breath is fanning across my cheeks as he bends down, compensating for our height difference. "You still a virgin, Blake?"

I gulp, my bravado swallowed up by the intensity in his gaze.

He just had to mention the v-word, didn't he?

*Asshole.*

I still can't believe I told him I was a virgin. Not sure what I was trying to prove, or how I allowed myself to confess something so embarrassing and intimate right after kissing him, but somehow, I managed to do exactly that.

*Good one, Blake.*

"Answer me," he pushes.

I dip my chin. It's a subtle nod at best, but my voice isn't working. Not right now. Nope. It's too busy catching in my throat, leaving me desperate for air. Or maybe Theo. Whichever works.

"Then, whose dicks did you see?" he demands.

My attention drops to his mouth, my tongue wetting my bottom lip as the memory from our kiss rises to the surface.

I still can't believe I kissed him. That he kissed me. That I've tasted those lips. That I know what they feel like. Hard. Demanding. Dominating. Addictive.

"Answer me," he growls.

I flick my gaze up to his again. "It's none of your business."

"I'm not playing around, Blake," he warns.

The only penis imagery rising to the surface belongs to the guy in front of me, but I refuse to admit the not-so-little tidbit, so I shake my head to dispel it and keep my head held high. "I said it's none––"

57

He grabs my throat and angles my head up at him, demanding my full attention. I gulp but hold his gaze.

*Holy crap on a cracker, Batman!*

He's never touched me like this. It's possessive. And commanding. And so freaking hot. The pressure is gentle but deliberate, proving he means business as he stares down at me. "Whose dicks did you see?"

"Theo--"

"Tell me."

I shake my head again, but he doesn't let me go.

"You think I'm playing, Blake?"

"It isn't any of your business," I remind him.

There's a storm in his eyes. An angry and turbulent storm, transforming the dark blue to a deep gray, one matching his emotions.

He's beautiful like this. He'd hate me for using the word, but it's true. All worked up and frustrated. It's sexy as hell.

I could tell him the truth. The only dicks I've seen have been in this very locker room, and I have no idea which appendage belongs to which player since I didn't exactly see their faces. I could tell him I was avoiding said dicks because I've never even wanted to look at one until about two minutes ago when the bastard dropped his towel. I could tell Theo a lot of things. But I won't. Not when he's assuming he's earned the right to care. To know about my sex life or lack thereof. He hasn't earned anything but a solid place on my shit list, and I don't see the particular tidbit changing anytime soon.

Now if I could just figure out how to not be turned on when his hand is on my throat and he's standing over me, that'd be great. Especially when his minty breath is kissing my cheeks, and his stormy gaze is daring me to give into him.

"Blake," he warns.

My phone buzzes against the ground as another text is delivered, breaking the tension between us like a glow stick cracking. Theo's hand drops to his side, and he takes a step back, giving me space to breathe. To let out the oxygen I'd been holding in my lungs as if it had the power to ground me when I was oh so close to floating away a moment ago.

Without a word, he turns around, his back muscles tightening as he bends down and grabs my iPhone from the polished concrete floor.

He faces me again, his eyes even harder, and he hands me the phone.

"There a problem?" I ask.

"Burrows texted."

Then he walks away.

# 8
# THEO

Practice should start any minute, but Coach is taking his sweet time today, giving the rest of the team way too much free time to talk to Blake for my liking. You'd think she's a shiny new toy by the way the team is surrounding her next to the bench along the side boards, but I keep my head down, forcing myself to ignore them. It doesn't block out her light laugh, though, or the way her freckled skin heats anytime Burrows skates toward her.

*Fucking Burrows.*

I actually like the asshole, which only makes it worse. He's a decent guy most of the time and doesn't sample the puck bunnies quite as often as the rest of us. Well, the rest of the team, anyway.

After being fucked up enough to kiss Blake at my place a couple months ago, it felt weird to touch anyone else. Wrong, maybe. Which is messed up on a whole other level since it's not like I plan on making the mistake of touching Blake again.

Especially after the locker room incident.

My dick twitches at the memory, but I push the thought aside.

I've fantasized about the moment for days. What she looked like. The way her breath hitched and her lips parted as I leaned closer to her. What I wish I could've done––and *would* have––if she were any other girl but my best friend's little sister.

Russ calls for Blake from the arch leading to the locker room, and she waves goodbye to the team, heading down the tunnel and out of sight.

The rest of the guys watch her leave as Depp says something to Graves, but I'm too far away to hear what he's said. The bastard laughs as I skate toward them, braking at the last second until a plume of icy mist blankets their calves and skates.

Depp looks down at the slush on his legs, then cocks his head. "There a problem, Theo?"

"You guys need to stay away from her."

Tukani laughs, his elbows on his knees and ass still resting next to the spot Blake had been sitting. "Come on, man. We were just talking––"

"So, you don't want to get in her pants?" I argue, my attention shifting from one asshole teammate to the next.

Austin, who'd been sitting on Tukani's opposite side, stands up and rests his hip against the partition separating the ice from the bench. "Coach didn't say she was off-limits."

"It's Colt's little sister."

"Yeah, we know," Depp reminds me, fiddling with his glove. "And he doesn't have a problem with us talking to her, either."

"'Cause he's too busy hanging out with Ash to see you guys fuck anything with two legs on the weekends," I counter.

"We're just talking to her," Graves argues. Logan adds, "Why's a stick up your ass, man?"

My brows raise in surprise as I turn to him, throttling my hockey stick while attempting to keep my temper in check. Logan and I have been on shaky ground ever since Ash broke up with him and started dating Colt. Afterward, Logan decided to shove her nose in a bunch of shit in hopes of breaking them up. Unfortunately, it backfired. Colt decked Logan for being a dick, and I politely asked him to move out of the Taylor House, despite us being roommates and best friends since we were kids. I'm not one to pick sides--I've *never* been one to pick sides--but after the shit Logan pulled, I had no choice. It seemed like the perfect time to clean house, so I told Shorty and Graves to find a new place to live too.

It was the best decision, even though it made things a little more tense on the ice and in the locker room. But overall, it needed to be done, and I'm not the only one who knows it. However, unless it's hockey related, Logan and I haven't spoken since. Guess I shouldn't be surprised he's being a dick about this, though, especially since it involves a Thorne.

"I don't have a stick up my ass," I answer. I keep my tone light, but my muscles are tight and begging for a fight. "I just think she deserves a little more respect--"

"You like her or something, Taylor?" Burrows interjects, skating toward us from the opposite side of the rink.

My molars grind together, then I clear my throat. "She's not some puck bunny."

"Never said she was," Burrows returns. "Doesn't mean we aren't allowed to talk to her."

"Fine. You can talk. But as your captain, I expect all of you to keep your junk covered when she's around from now on, including in the locker room. We clear?"

Tukani laughs as Depp points out, "Dude, it's a men's locker room. We gotta get dressed somewhere."

Graves adds, "And it's not like she hasn't seen a dick before. She isn't the Virgin Mary or some shit."

"Yeah, well, maybe she is," I offer, cutting him off.

Silence.

Fucking silence.

Their eyes widen as they exchange curious glances with each other, the energy in the arena twisting with testosterone. And interest.

The blood drains from my face, but I keep my expression indifferent, well aware I'm on thin ice and even the smallest wrong move could send them spiraling.

"Are you saying she's a virgin?" Logan asks, voicing the question they're all wondering. Then, his mouth lifts in the corner as he glances toward the tunnel where she recently disappeared. The bastard's practically salivating.

My tongue slides between my upper lip and teeth as I realize just how much I screwed up. But I don't answer him. If I do, it'll only put a bounty on her head.

Tukani slaps his knee and lets out a laugh of disbelief. "Dude, how's a girl like *her* still a virgin?"

"Just stay away from her," I order. My attention shifts from one player to the next, my blood boiling in my veins at the idea of *any* of them touching Blakely or being her first.

"Nah, man. You can't tell us she's a virgin then expect us to drop it," Graves says. I knew the guy was dense, but I didn't think he was *this* stupid.

Shifting my stick to my other hand, I point my index finger at him. "Especially you, asshole. You just broke things off with Sally. You really think hooking up with Colt's little sister is the way to go? Stay away from her."

Tukani raises his hands in the air. "Sorry, Theo, but if she's interested in getting a slice of the Tukani Tsunami--"

"Dude, she was talking to *me* the whole time, not you," Depp reminds Tukani.

"Nah, I'm pretty sure she's got a thing for rookies," Austin jokes from the edge of the group.

The rest of the team laughs as Graves slaps Austin's shoulder. "Sure she does, little man. Sure she does."

"Oh, you think I'm wrong?" Austin argues. "Then, let's make a bet. Hundred bucks says I can sleep with her first."

"Shut the fuck up, Austin," I bark, skating closer until the toes of our skates are touching and I'm looking down at the bastard. He's still trying to find his place here, but if he thinks this is his opportunity to show the team what he's got, he has a death wish. He's shorter than me by at least three inches, but he's got balls. I'll give him that much. Because he doesn't cower. Maybe it's because he knows he has four other guys backing him right now, but I'm not afraid to take them all on if I have to. Not when it comes to Blake.

"Let me make one thing clear, Austin," I warn through clenched teeth. "You are *not* going to make a bet on Colt's little sister's virginity."

"You might be the captain on the ice, but you don't control shit off it," Graves reminds me. He skates closer until he's standing next to Austin. You'd think he's the freshman's right-hand man or some shit. My upper lip curls in disgust as I turn to him, ready to throw a punch on my own teammate without any regret if he dares to say one more fucking word to me about Blakely Thorne and her virginity.

A loud whistle cuts through our conversation like a hot knife through butter as Coach Sanderson strides toward us from the hallway leading to the locker room.

"I'm sorry. I thought I told you to warm up," he calls, dropping the whistle from his lips and letting it rest against his sternum from a black piece of string hanging around his neck.

My nostrils flare as I shift my gaze from Graves, to Austin, to Logan. But I don't back down. I don't move first. I just wait. Like we're in a game of Chicken, and the first to crack loses. Graves grumbles something under his breath and backs away from me as the rest of the team disperses and lines up to start sprints from one side of the rink to the other, following his lead.

"Taylor," Sanderson calls.

My head snaps toward him, my anger threatening to suffocate me.

"You good?"

Tongue in cheek, I force myself to nod and line up with the my teammates on the far goal line.

And even though I'm grateful Coach broke up the conversation, it doesn't stop Austin's smartass remark from niggling the back of my mind for the rest of practice.

He wants to place a bet on Blake's virginity?

I'll fucking kill him.

# 9

# THEO

y muscles groan in protest as I shove the bar's door open. I've been pushing myself too hard lately, but hockey's the only thing keeping me sane since Blake transferred to LAU. Besides, a small part of me thinks I deserve the grueling torture. Lusting after your best friend's little sister while knowing it's a bad idea does that to a person. And fantasizing about kissing them again is even worse.

I adjust the hat on my head and force the thought away, heading into SeaBird. We haven't spoken since the shower. But I've still noticed her. At practice. Surrounded by the team. Laughing. Chatting. Flirting. Being her usual untouchable self. I haven't heard any rumors involving her with anyone on the team, though. It's been my only saving grace. Pretty sure if it changes, I'll lose my damn mind, and I've already felt insane enough since she moved here.

No need to fan the flames.

Now, if I could just stop thinking about her when she isn't around, that'd be great.

I scratch the scruff along my jaw and head toward the bar

on the right side of the building. A band is on the stage on the back left side of the establishment. They're covering a Broken Vows song, and the dance floor in front of them is packed with people. Most of them are classmates or locals around town. The scent of coconut and lime wafts through the air as I order my drink from Sammie, the bartender and owner of SeaBird. A minute later, she sets a tall glass of amber liquid in front of me, and I thank her before searching for Ash and Colt.

They invited me to come out. And because I was driving myself crazy at home and didn't feel like throwing a party, I agreed to be the third wheel for the evening.

I scan the dance floor and booths lining the side walls for my best friend and his girl, but a different couple grabs my attention. My heels dig into the ground, and I stop short, nearly spilling my beer.

*What. The actual. Fuck?*

My fingers grip the glass with so much force, I'm surprised it doesn't crack as I zero in on Colt's little sister.

Blake is on the dance floor with Burrows. Her lithe body is pressed against his, and she sways back and forth. With a smile, she lifts her half empty glass at the stage, mouthing the lyrics to the song. She owned up to her long, curly red hair in elementary school when Colt and I threatened to beat the hell out of anyone who made fun of her for it. Now, it almost reaches her lower back, and even though it's usually piled on top of her head in a messy bun, tonight it's hanging around her shoulders, making her look even more wild and free than usual.

I want to wrap my fingers in it, tug her head back, and drag her to the nearest corner so I can kiss the shit out of her, but I restrain myself…barely. She turns around and faces Burrows, tilting her head up and smiling. Like she's having the time of her life with him. Standing on her tiptoes, she says something in his ear, then hands him her tumbler and heads down the hall toward the bathroom.

My feet move on their own as if possessed by a jealous asshole as I follow her through the crowd. There's a line wrapping around the corner leading to the bathrooms. You'd think Sammie would've invested in expanding the bathrooms since there's only two, but she insists it would only create more toilets for her or her employees to clean. I guess she has a point, but it makes using the restroom at SeaBird a bitch.

Oblivious to my presence, Blake takes her place at the end of the line and starts chatting with the guy in front of her as I approach. When the stranger finally gets a glimpse of her, his smile widens, and he turns around to face her completely. Like she has his full attention. The same way she has mine. And Burrows'. And the whole fucking team's. With his shoulder against the wall, he tilts his head closer to her and says something else, but the music's too loud for me to hear.

*Seriously, does the girl have no boundaries?*

I stalk closer as she laughs and shakes her head, still unaware of my presence.

It's time I change that.

"Hey, Baby Thorne," I greet her.

She glances over her shoulder at me, does a double-take, then covers her surprise by rolling her eyes. "Please tell me you're not going to start calling me that."

"It's fitting, though," I remind her. "Where'd you get the fake ID?"

Her eyes widen for a split second, and she starts searching the rest of the bar like the cops are hiding in the shadows. "Will you *please* keep your voice down, asshole?"

"Just sayin'. How the hell did you get in? Did the bouncer not check––"

She grabs the edge of my leather jacket and drops out of

the bathroom line, dragging me further down the hall and into a dark corner where we have a bit more privacy.

Once we're both hidden in the shadows, and the head-pounding music is more muted, she lets my jacket go and seethes, "What the hell is your problem?"

"No problem. Just curious how you got in."

"It's none of your business."

"Does your brother know you're here?"

She glances around me again, making sure we're still alone as she hisses, "Yes, as a matter of fact. He most definitely *does* know I'm here, and he most definitely does *not* care." She looks up at me. The heat in her eyes does her fiery personality and redhead stereotypes justice. It also makes my blood rush south, no matter how much I try to fight it.

She's so fucking...infuriating. But gorgeous too. Like a tornado. Or a storm. A tsunami, maybe.

I squeeze my hands into a ball to keep them in check when all I want to do is reach out, tug her long red hair into my fist, and slam my mouth to hers.

But I can't.

I won't.

"Do you want to know why my brother doesn't care, Teddy?" she adds, her voice laced with sass.

I press into her, my nostrils flaring as her perfume taints the air surrounding us. "Don't call me Teddy."

"It's because he knows I'm an adult and I can make my own choices."

I scoff. "You mean like getting drunk again and making a fool out of yourself?"

Her eyes narrow into a glare, and I know I've crossed a line. But I'm too pissed to care.

"I know you're not talking about tonight," she spits, "because I've only had one shot of Fireball, and I'm sipping my other one."

"You mean the one being held by your little boy toy on the dance floor? Yeah. I saw."

She pulls back, surprised. "Are you following me, Theo?"

"I was invited," I growl.

"By who?" she taunts. "One of your puck bunnies?"

The sarcastic little brat has her hip popped out and her tiny fist pressed against it. It's adorable as shit and gets under my skin more than I'd like to admit, but I shake off the feeling and push her a bit more. Because seeing those green eyes flare to life? It's like a drug. And I'm ready for my next hit.

I keep my voice low but step closer, suddenly feeling guilty for being in the hall with my best friend's little sister. But what I feel even more guilty about? The way I want to push her up against the wall and taste those sassy lips like they're my dying meal. Especially when I know what they taste like.

"Your brother, Baby Thorne. He invited me. I haven't touched a puck bunny since last season. You, however, seem busy with my teammate. There a reason for that?"

"You mean, other than the obvious?" She lifts her dainty little hand and starts ticking her fingers up as she rambles off a list. "He's good looking, and respectful, and is one hell of a dancer?"

I grab her wrist, her pulse jumping against my thumb as I squeeze softly. "You shouldn't be here."

"Why?"

"Because you don't belong here."

"Why?" she repeats, her voice laced with a challenge. A dare. One I desperately want to fulfill. But I'm not an idiot. And I'd have to be one if I leaned down and kissed her again. Especially in public. Because despite how laid back Colt is, the only reason he trusts Blake is because he knows she only looks at guys like they're friends. For a while, he even wondered if she was into girls, but those assumptions were quickly doused when he tried to set her up with Laura Christensen for her prom date in high school.

Yeah. It didn't go well.

When he asked why she hadn't dated anyone, she told him she's picky. His response? *"Keep being picky. 'Cause no matter who you bring home, he won't be good enough for you. And we both know me and your other brothers will have no issue reminding him."*

And he's right.

The girl likes sports. Has a kickass body. And isn't afraid to put a guy in his place.

She has every right to be picky. She can have anybody she wants. But if that's the case, why is she with Burrows?

The guy's nice, sure, but he's also too soft for her. She'd barrel over him within a week of dating. A pit forms in my stomach.

*Are they dating?*

And if they are, did he take Austin's bet at practice the other day? Did anyone take his bet? Is *she* a bet? Is Burrows only with her so he can pop her cherry and win some cash? The guy's here on scholarship and doesn't have much money, especially after his knee surgery. Would he cross the line with Blake?

He wouldn't.

*Would he?*

The questions roll around in my brain, one after the other until I feel like I need to hit something. Namely someone from the hockey team.

"Theo?" Blake murmurs, cutting through my fury with her soft voice and worried expression.

If she wasn't here, she wouldn't be messing with my head. If she wasn't here, she wouldn't be making me question things. If she wasn't here, I wouldn't be jealous of Burrows or

Tukani or even a fucking freshman who's had zero time on the ice this year.

I grit my teeth but drop her hand. "You need to leave."

Her bright green eyes harden with contempt, her worry twisting into frustration. "And you need to keep your nose out of my business."

I shouldn't be surprised she isn't willing to listen. She's never been willing to listen. But if she wants to push me, fine. I'm not afraid to get my hands dirty. Not tonight. Not when it comes to her.

I hold her glare for another second, then grab her wrist again and drag her toward the front of the bar. My adrenaline and frustration are like gasoline on the precarious situation, but I shove aside the tiny voice of reason telling me this is a bad idea and I'm about to cross a line I shouldn't.

Too bad I don't give a damn.

"What are you doing?" Blake demands as she races to keep up with me so she doesn't fall on her ass. The girl has long legs, but they aren't long enough to keep up with my lengthy stride. Not when I'm this pissed off.

"Sammie!" I bellow at the top of my lungs as we turn the corner into the main area. The music is still thumping from the stage, but Sammie's head snaps toward me from behind the bar.

Apparently, she heard me.

With a white dishrag in one hand, and an empty glass in the other, she says, "I'm sorry. Is it polite to yell at your bartender?"

"This girl's under twenty-one."

"What the hell?" Blake screeches, punching my chest and wrenching her opposite arm away from me.

I rub at the sore spot. It'll definitely be bruised tomorrow. Ignoring her outburst, I repeat, "She's under twenty-one."

Sammie almost looks apologetic as she turns to Blake, her lips pulled into a thin line. "How'd you get in here?"

"He's lying," she argues. "And I walked through the door like every other customer––"

"She has a fake ID," I interrupt.

Blake glares at me, the look almost branding me with its heat, but she doesn't say a word. She can't anymore. She doesn't have a leg to stand on.

She knows it.

Sammie knows it.

And I know it too.

I also know I was right. I've crossed a line. I've pissed her off––more than ever. But I'm too angry to care. She needs to get out of here. To go home. To get away from me and from every other player on the team, including Burrows. It's for her own good. It's for my sanity. It's for my friendship with Colt. It's for a lot of things. I need to remember that.

With a frown, Sammie outstretches her hand toward Blake with her palm facing up. "Can I see your ID again, miss?"

"There a problem?" Burrows asks as he approaches Blake from the dance floor. But she doesn't answer him. She's too busy imagining all the ways she's going to kill me for this.

I don't know why, but it makes me feel better. That she's ignoring him. That she's too busy looking at me instead, even if it's because I pissed her off.

*Guess what, Baby Thorne. You pissed me off too.*

The menacing scowl on her face could make a damn lion cower in fear as she stares at me. But I don't meet her gaze no matter how much I feel it burning against my cheek. I turn around and head toward the exit without a backward glance.

"Fuck you, Theo!" Blake yells as she watches me go.

I keep my head down and ignore her, shoving the door

open. It bounces off the rough red brick outside, and I hang my head as I walk back to my car before remembering why I showed up at SeaBird in the first place.

Pulling out my cell, I send a quick message to Colt.

**Me: Going home. Headache. We'll talk later.**

His response is almost instant.

**Colt: Way to piss her off, then ditch her. She's gonna kill you.**

Without bothering to reply, I slide into my car, toss my phone onto the passenger seat, and rest my head against the headrest, defeated.

Colt's right. She's gonna be the death of me. But what he doesn't know is she's been killing me for years.

Long before tonight.

Why would my future be any different?

# 10

# THEO

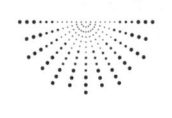

"Dude, what the hell?" Burrows demands as he stalks into the weight room. It's late morning, and most of the team hasn't arrived at the rink yet. But I got here early and have been kicking my own ass in here for the past twenty minutes.

When the angry words echo through the otherwise silent gym, I set the weights back into their place and sit up on the bench press, stretching my already tired muscles over my head as I watch Burrows' approach.

Apparently, the last twelve hours wasn't enough time to calm him down after the shitstorm at SeaBird.

Twisting my baseball hat backwards, I stare at Burrows with a bored expression. "There a problem, man?"

"Why'd you have Blake and me thrown out of SeaBird?"

I laugh, dryly. "I didn't get *you* thrown out––"

"I invited Blake. You really think I was just gonna let her catch a ride home with a stranger or something?"

My annoyance spikes. I don't know if it's because I feel guilty that it wasn't me who drove her home, or if it's because he was a nice enough guy to make sure she got home safely, *or* if it's because he got some extra time with her when I didn't. None of it even matters. I don't want time with her. What I want is distance. But the girl won't go away.

"You in on the bet, Burrows?" I blurt out, my voice sharp and unyielding as I voice the question that's been on a constant loop since I saw them at SeaBird last night.

He pulls back, and his eyebrows pinch. "Excuse me?"

"I wanna know. Are you in on the bet with Austin, Tukani, and everyone else?"

"I liked Blake before––"

"So you are," I surmise, but it doesn't make me feel any better. If anything, it only frustrates me more.

At least the bastard has the decency to look sheepish as he squeezes the back of his neck and mutters, "It doesn't matter."

"Yes, it does."

"No, it doesn't," he argues. "I liked her before. And if I was pursuing her anyway, what's the harm in cashing in on it? Besides, I'm here on scholarship, and after my knee injury––"

"Tell me, Burrows," I interrupt. "How much money is Blake's virginity worth?"

His jaw flexes. "I don't care about––"

"You had to have put something on the line to participate, didn't you?"

The silence is tense and heavy, but the bastard stays quiet, his posture stiff.

"Tell me," I order.

He clears his throat but avoids my gaze. "The entire team chipped in a hundred bucks each."

"And winner takes all?" I ask.

He looks at me again, his dark eyes sparking with determination. "It isn't about the money."

With a dry laugh, I fish my wallet out and slap a crisp,

one-hundred-dollar bill onto the bench press. "Yet you just admitted you could use the cash."

"I was interested in Blake before any money was on the table," he reiterates, glancing at the hundred dollar bill between us. "Why are you putting anything into the pot?"

"Since apparently you and the other assholes need it, I might as well do my part to help you guys out, right?"

"So, you're not gonna try to sleep with her?"

I laugh darkly and stand up. "She's my best friend's little sister."

"That isn't an answer."

"I wouldn't touch Blake if my life depended on it."

"Well, at least the feeling's mutual," a strong, feminine voice interrupts.

Our necks snap in its direction.

Blake's standing at the entrance of the gym, her arms crossed over her white LAU tank top. I don't know how long she's been standing there. I don't know if she heard about the bet, or if she only caught the part about me not wanting to touch her. Neither option makes me feel any better, though. Especially not after the shit I pulled last night.

"Blake, " Burrows starts.

She lifts her hand and cuts him off. "Whatever weird pissing contest or…whatever it is going on between you two needs to stop. Burrows, I know I've already said it, but I'm really sorry my age and Theo's neanderthal behavior got in the way of us having a good time last night." She turns to me, and whatever warmth had been in her expression morphs into a damn ice storm. Angry. Frigid. And sharp as shit. "Teddy. For someone who likes to remind me I'm a child, you sure as hell acted like one last night, and unless I get an apology––a *sincere* one––I don't want to hear a damn word out of your mouth. Are we clear?"

I open my mouth to reply, and her eyes narrow in a silent warning.

Tongue in cheek, I close my mouth again and lift my chin, acknowledging I've heard her loud and clear.

"Good," she snaps, her voice just as sharp as before. "Now, if you'll excuse me." She turns on her heel and marches down the hall. A glimpse of her tight ass in her jeans tattoos itself into my mind as she walks away. I shake my head and stare at the floor instead, grappling for images of Grandma Taylor in a bikini, but it does shit to erase how good Blake looks when she's feeling particularly spicy like this morning.

I swear the girl is trying to kill me.

A few of our teammates enter the gym, stopping short when they feel how charged and tense the room is after Blake's interruption.

And combined with Burrows, who's glaring at me like I kicked his puppy? Well, at least I'm not the only one feeling the animosity directed at me.

Colt chuckles as he scans the space, approaching me with a crooked half-smirk. "I assume Blake's here already?"

"So, you could feel the chill of the Ice Witch too?" I counter, my tone thick with sarcasm.

Colt's attention shifts to Burrows. "Did he apologize for last night yet?"

Burrows shakes his head. "Not sure he knows how to form the words."

With a laugh, Colt picks up the hundred dollar bill and sits next to me, keeping the money raised in the air. "What's this?"

"Theo's apology," Burrows mumbles, taking the cash from Colt's fingers and slipping it into his pocket. "Good chat, Theo." He turns on his heel and heads toward the locker room.

The rest of the team follows Burrows, leaving me alone with Colt in the weight room. I don't blame them. I wanna get the hell out of here too. Especially when I know Colt well enough to guess he wants to have a little chat. I also know him well enough to guess where he wants the conversation to go.

Scrubbing my hand over my face, I stay seated on the bench press and wait.

Colt folds his arms, watching me, but he doesn't say a word.

Guess he doesn't have to.

I already know I screwed up.

A pool of guilt collects in my stomach. Scratch that. The guilt's been sitting in my stomach since last night. Maybe even before then. Now, it's rising. Churning. Mixing with regret and attraction and indecision and anger and frustration and––

Taking off my hat, I slap it onto the bench press and snap, "Just say it."

"Say what?"

"Whatever you're wanting to say."

Colt scratches at his temple with his index finger but stays silent for another second, then mutters, "Can I ask you something?"

With my elbows on my knees, I stare at the flecks of gray in the white laminate floor and mumble, "Sure."

"Why are you an ass to her?"

Frowning, I look up at him. "I'm not––"

"You are. And I wanna know why. It's been worse since she moved in with Ash and the girls."

*Yeah, it's been worse*, I think to myself. Because I haven't been able to escape her since she moved here. I haven't been able to get her off my mind. I haven't been able to think straight. I can't even come to practice anymore without seeing her. It's messing with my head and my resolve. It's driving me fucking crazy.

Picking up my hat, I fidget with the brim, dragging my thumbs along the edge, muttering, "Blake and I have never exactly been close."

"And I call bullshit." Colt laughs. "She always liked you 'cause you were nice to her. You didn't care when she tagged along with us or wanted to play whatever we were playing when we were kids. But when we went to high school, you started acting like an ass—"

"It isn't my fault I want to keep her safe," I say through clenched teeth. I force my jaw muscles to relax and glance back at him. adding, "Just like you do."

He shrugs one shoulder. "I dunno, man. Feels different with you two."

I force a laugh, but there isn't any humor in it. "Not sure what you mean."

"Me neither," he admits. "But I don't like seeing my sister hurting. And I really don't like how it's you who's hurting her."

"I'm not—"

"Last night was a dick move, and you know it," Colt says. "I need my best friend and my sister to get along, especially when my sister lives with my girlfriend. I need you to fix this."

"Colt," I groan. "She's underage. She shouldn't have been at SeaBird—"

"Says the guy who's slipped more than one of his puck bunnies a fake ID so they could sneak past the bouncers."

"I haven't done it in forever," I mutter, well-aware of how much I sound like an ass right now. But I can't help it. Can't stop it. Can't control myself when it comes to Blake.

Colt shrugs. "Yeah, but I've heard the stories. Not to

mention what I've seen firsthand at the Taylor House. It's a mighty high horse you like to ride on, Theo."

"Do you even care about her?" I spit. The words roll off my tongue before I can stop them, followed by another wave of regret.

Colt pulls back, surprised.

*Fuck me. Why the hell did I say that?*

Of course, he cares about her. He loves her. But he also respects her and her decisions. I know I should do the same, but it's hard with Blake. The girl knows how to get under my skin and piss me off more than anyone I've ever met. But still. Insinuating Colt doesn't care about her because he knows how to keep his head out of his ass? It was a dick move, and he deserves better.

Pinching the bridge of my nose, I let out a sigh. "Fuck, Colt. That was uncalled for. I'm sorry."

"I do care about Blake," he tells me. "And I'm here for her in case she needs me. But she's a big girl, man. And she was raised with three older brothers who taught her how to bring a guy to his knees if he ever tried anything she didn't want."

The imagery brings a small smile to my lips as I imagine any guy making a move Blake doesn't want. She'd drop him like a sack of potatoes. Hell, it's been a while, but I even witnessed it firsthand in high school once or twice.

He's right.

She's stronger than I give her credit for.

Doesn't make it any easier for me, though.

"Don't get me wrong. It's hard for me too," Colt continues as if he can read my mind. "She's better than every guy on campus. She deserves a fuckin' prince. But it isn't my job to determine which guy is shitty versus the ones I deem good enough for Blake. It's her job. But Burrows? He isn't so bad, man. Blake could do a helluva lot worse than him. And Ash says Blake likes him."

Blake told Ash she likes Burrows?

*Fuck.*

I dig my fingers into my thighs to keep from rubbing at the ache in my chest. I should be happy for her. Colt's right. There are a lot of worse guys at LAU for Blake to fall for. But Burrows?

*Come on, Blake.*

"It isn't my place to stand in the way of what Blake wants," Colt adds. "It isn't yours, either."

"I'll keep it in mind," I mutter.

"You will," he agrees, though I can hear the undertone in his voice. The warning. The order. "You'll also make last night up to her."

With a scowl, I face him. "Colt..."

"I'm serious. It was a dick move, and she deserves better. You know it. I know it. And you're going to make it up to her, *and* you're gonna do more than slip her a hundred bucks like you did with Burrows. We both know money doesn't fix everything, especially not with Blake."

He thinks I really just tried to throw money at the situation in order to fix it? My stomach churns and is only heightened when the reality of the matter sinks in. Colt doesn't know about the bet involving his baby sister. If he did, he'd put an end to it, no matter how much he's trying to give Blake the space to make her own decisions.

But is it my place to tell him about it? Or will I come off like even more of a controlling asshole if I intervene? And if I *didn't* have a thing for the star of the bet, would I stick my nose where it didn't belong in the first place? Probably not. The team has made shitty bets in the past, and I never cared or bothered to put a stop to them. So why is this time any different?

I look down at the worn material on my hat as I continue rubbing my thumb against the brim, indecision warring with regret.

I care about Blake. And the shit the team is pulling is exactly that. Shit.

Before I can talk myself out of it, I say, "Listen, Colt. About the money––"

"Thorne! Taylor!" Coach Sanderson yells from the entrance of the weight room. "Enough talking. Practice starts in five."

Colt holds my gaze for one more second, then calls back, "We'll be right there."

I put my baseball hat on, wipe my palms against my thighs, and stand up.

Practice. Right.

## 11

## BLAKELY

Everyone else went to SeaBird tonight, including Kate the introvert, and since I'm officially banned until I turn twenty-one, I'm stuck at home. Alone. The girls offered to stay and hang out with me, but it's not like I'd actually take them up on it. They deserve to have fun and to not be held back by their youngest roommate.

Stupid Theo and his stupid nosiness.

I already hit the gym, ran home after lifting weights, and showered, which leaves me all alone, throwing a pity party for one while ignoring Burrows' texts. He's been super sweet and even offered to come over, but I can't accept his suggestion without feeling like a wet blanket for ruining his Saturday night with the rest of his team. I prop my sore legs on the coffee table and grab the remote, scrolling through Netflix for my next binge since there are only so many other forms of entertainment when you're home alone on a Saturday night.

I could probably hit up the party at the Taylor House just to piss Theo off, but I'm not ready for another fight. I'm too drained. Especially after walking in before practice and hearing his comment about touching me...er *not* touching me.

*Asshole.*

I still can't believe he said it, let alone to the guy I've been hanging out with lately.

Like, who does that?

Controlling, bossy, motherfu––

A soft knock echoes from the front door, interrupting my useless analysis of today's earlier event. Which, I guess, is a good thing. I've already spent enough brainpower on the matter. No need to beat a dead horse.

I unfold myself from the couch, tossing the remote back onto the cushion. Running my fingers through my still-damp hair, I rise onto my tiptoes and peek through the peephole to see who's here.

I'd recognize the old, worn baseball hat just about anywhere. It's turned backward as an uninvited Theo looks down at his phone, giving me a perfect, shameless view of his strong forearms. The weather's been warm enough so he hasn't needed to wear a jacket, and boy is he taking full advantage. He's wearing a white T-shirt that hugs his biceps along with a pair of dark jeans. The combination makes him look effortlessly sexy. So much so, I can only imagine how many girls eye-screwed the bastard when he went about his daily routine before coming here.

It's annoying. How attractive he is. And he knows it too. The guy could have any girl he wants. Hell, he *has* had any girl he wants. And each and every one of those girls knew exactly what they were signing up for. One and done. That's it. Why, you might ask? Because Theo's an adamant believer in "spreading the love." And the fact I want a piece of that particular pie? Even after all the shit he's put me through? After I full-blown heard him talking to Burrows at practice?

After he said he would never touch me? It's absolutely ridiculous.

Aaaand I'm doing it again. Incessantly over-analyzing every single exchange I've ever had with the guy.

*Get a grip, girl.*

Maybe I should go for another run. Not that the first one helped get a certain someone off my mind. But still.

Theo lifts his hand and raps his fist against the door again. I jump back in surprise and clear my throat. I should go back to my show and ignore him. I should pretend I'm not home and hide away in my room so he can't hear the television flip on. I should do a lot of things. What I shouldn't do is actually consider opening this stupid door, which is exactly what I'm doing right now.

*Come on, Blake!*

I fist the hem of my sleep shorts into my sweaty palms.

*Don't do it. Don't open the door.*

"I know you're in there!" Theo calls out. "Already saw Colt and Ash––"

I wrench the door open and fold my arms, leaning against the doorjamb with a scowl.

"Oh. Hey," he offers, taken aback.

"You mean you saw them at SeaBird? You know, the place I was thrown out of because of you?"

The bastard has the decency to look sheepish. "Look, I'm sorry––"

"Bullshit. You didn't want me there."

"It's not that I didn't want you––"

"Don't lie, Teddy." I dig my fingernails into my arms, letting the crescent shapes mar my flesh as another wave of frustration and embarrassment settles into my bones. "It was a jerk thing to do, and you know it."

His sigh is soft but still hits me square in the chest as he holds my gaze, tearing apart my defenses with a single look.

"You're right," he confesses. "It was a dick move, and I shouldn't have tattled on you. Half the people in the bar were as young as you. I shouldn't have thrown you under the bus."

I blink slowly, surprised by how easily he caved. He's the most stubborn person I've ever met. Admitting he's wrong is rare as hell. But I'm not ready to give in and forgive him. Not yet.

Lifting my chin, I demand, "Then tell me why. Why'd you do it to me?"

He hesitates, scratching the scruff along his jaw. A grocery sack hangs from his arm, but I don't ask what's inside. I'm too anxious to hear his explanation about why he was such an ass in the first place.

"It's complicated," he starts.

*And we're back to square one.*

Before he has a chance to finish his stupid excuse, I grab the edge of the door, ready to slam it closed when Theo's hand slaps against it, keeping it open.

"Come on, Blake," Theo grumbles. "Will you just listen——"

"I don't want to hear your bullshit excuse."

"It isn't bullshit."

"That's exactly what it is. You don't want me around because for some messed-up reason, you still look at me like I'm the scared little eight-year-old who fell and scraped her knees while trying to keep up with her older brother and his friends who were playing roller-hockey on the street."

I gulp and pull away slightly, surprising myself with my assessment just as much as it surprises Theo.

*But damn, it felt good.*

To admit my feelings. To call him out for his bullshit. I bite the inside of my cheek, stopping myself from steam-rolling over him with another monologue. Instead, I wait. For him to deny it. To tell me I'm blowing things out of proportion. To tell me I'm pouting and acting like a child. A child he *still* sees me as.

He shifts the bag from one hand to the other and rocks back on his heels. "You're right."

My eyes widen in surprise. "Two concessions in a row, Theo? Are you growing soft on me?"

His mouth lifts, but he doesn't answer me as his warm gaze rolls over my body, starting at the top of my head and drifting down my front. Which is when I realize just how little clothing is covering me. Nothing too crazy or anything, but I'm only wearing a baby blue crop top––no bra since I'm flat as a board––and a pair of black sleep shorts.

And yet here he is, my kryptonite, staring at me. Oh, what I'd give to read minds. To read his mind. Especially in this moment. When it's only the two of us. When he's been open and honest with me for the past few minutes. When I've been given a glimpse of the boy I fell in love with. The one without a stick up his ass.

*What are you thinking, Theo?* I want to ask, but I don't. I won't.

Instead, I ignore the swell of butterflies in my stomach from Theo's wandering gaze. Gathering my proverbial armor, I pop out my hip, plaster on a grin, and say, "Eyes up here, Teddy."

He chuckles, as shameless as ever, and meets my gaze again. "Mind if I come in?"

"For what? So you can lecture me about the importance of modesty in my own home?"

Without waiting for an invitation, he steps inside, mumbling, "Once a smartass, always a smartass."

"That isn't an answer."

"Since when do my lectures get me anywhere with you?" he counters.

*The man has a point.*

I watch from the doorway as he saunters into the family room, taking in the used leather couch, dark wooden coffee table, and bookshelf beside the television.

He hasn't been here since he helped me move in a few months ago. And it's weird. To have him in my space. Even when we were kids, he never went into my room or anything. And even though the family room and open kitchen floor plan are technically shared with the rest of my roommates, it still feels intimate somehow.

Because I don't share this space with my brother. It's just mine. Which means, if he's here, standing smack-dab in the middle of my family room, it's because he wants to see me. Not Colt. *Me.*

The question is... Why?

"Do you remember when we were kids?" he asks, still studying the space like it's the surface of the moon.

I snort. "I think you're gonna have to be more specific."

He continues his perusal, reading the book titles on the shelf as he clarifies, "When your mom got mad at me and Colt for teaching you how to swear."

With a grudging laugh, I mutter, "Yeah?"

"Do you remember what we taught you after? To get around it?"

"You mean like Cheese and Rice for Jesus Christ?" I ask, watching him carefully.

Why does his butt have to look so good in those freaking jeans? And his biceps in that shirt?

*Kill me now.*

"Yeah, and uh, vacuum beach for fuck you, bitch," he adds, his hands in his pockets and the grocery sack still dangling from his wrist, hanging limply against his thigh.

My mouth quirks up on one side as I tear my attention from his killer body, trying to keep my amusement in check. "My mom was so mad at you guys."

"Yeah, I know." He glances at me over his shoulder and smirks. "She even called my mom and got me grounded for it. Didn't help when you'd mouth it to us on the ice during our hockey games."

"To be fair, I only mouthed it to *you*," I point out. "Colt got olive juice."

"Yeah, I know," he returns, his eyes losing a bit of the happy crinkles framing them. "I got fuck you, bitch, and Colt got I love you. How's that for fair?"

"You wanted olive juice too?" I question, convinced the guy's full of shit as I cross my arms and raise my brow.

"I wanted a lot of things, Blake." He sighs, his attention dropping to my mouth for a split second from across the room, then he clears his throat and turns back to the messy bookshelf, taking it in like it's a foreign country.

"Like what?" I prod, unable to help myself. "What do you want?"

His shoulders lift into a shrug, and he faces me again. "Like wanting us to get over this bullshit feud."

*Feud.* If that's what he wants to call it, sure. Personally, I think it has more to do with his overbearing personality grating on me like sandpaper. But what do I know?

"From what I remember, you're the one who started it," I remind him. Actually, I'm positive. All it took was one stupid dress on my fifteenth birthday to turn our friendship into some kind of messed up bodyguard protection program. And it sucks. Royally.

His mouth lifts up in the corner as he looks at the used brown couch taking up the majority of the family room. "You're probably right."

I stare at his stupid biceps again and the way the material stretches over them. Like seriously. Does he shrink his clothes on purpose or does he need to start buying a bigger size?

Annoyed, I huff, "I'm still mad at you."

"Yeah, I know," he mutters, turning and facing me again. "What show are we watching?"

"We"––I wag my finger between us––"aren't watching anything. You"––I step closer and jab my finger against his chest––"were just leaving."

"It's like you said. I still picture you as the cute little neighbor girl who liked to keep up with the boys. It's time we change it."

"And how do we change it?"

"By hanging out. Letting me get to know you. The *new* you," he clarifies. "Who apparently likes to wear tiny clothes and no makeup."

"Is there a problem with tiny clothes and no make up?" I cross my arms and cover my braless chest, daring him to say yes.

"Nope. I like the freckles." He steps closer and boops my nose with his calloused finger, turning back toward the modest family room like he didn't rock my world with a simple compliment. Next to the couch, there's a fake house plant since Mia has a habit of killing live ones, and an orange and brown floral cushioned chair. It's the ugliest thing I've ever seen. Kate informed me it was a gift from Ash's parents a few months ago, so we can't get rid of it. But it's still home. And I'm still not sure how I feel about him being in it.

Stomping toward him as he examines the tall, skinny bookshelf littered with old textbooks and a few romance novels, I remind him, "The freckles aren't new."

With a knowing smirk, he looks at me over his shoulder. "I know. That's what I like about them. Come on." He rounds the edge of the worn leather couch and collapses onto it, perusing the grocery sack like it holds goodies belonging in the Cave of Wonders.

"What do you have in there?" I ask.

He sets a brand new blu-ray case on the coffee table, and I laugh when the title comes into view. "*Happy Gilmore?*"

"It's a classic," he says without bothering to look up.

To be fair, he isn't wrong, but I can't help but poke the bear. "Can't believe you used to think it was a hockey movie."

"It *is* a hockey movie."

"Just because one of the most iconic scenes happens on the ice doesn't make it a hockey movie."

"Iconic?" he asks, his curiosity piqued. "I thought you hated the scene."

"When Happy brings Virginia Venit onto the ice, and they dance to a Diana Ross song? It's adorable and probably the closest example of romance I ever witnessed as a kid, thanks to you boys always stealing the controller and never letting me watch any girl shows."

"Would you have watched them even if we let you pick the movie?"

I bite the inside of my cheek, refusing to acknowledge he has a valid point. I thought I hated all things romance, especially the cheesy or overdramatic stories. To be honest, I still do. But Happy and Virginia on the ice?

*Swoon.*

Convinced he's won, Theo adds a pack of cinnamon gummy bears to the table, and I bite my lip to stop the grin from splitting my face in two.

"Who says I still like cinnamon gummy bears?" I challenge. Heaven forbid I let the bastard know how thoughtful he is for remembering my favorite treat.

"You drank Fireball last weekend. *Cinnamon*," he clarifies as if he's speaking to an idiot. "Just a hunch, but I figured it stemmed from your addiction to these." He picks up the bag and wiggles it back and forth.

I stare at the familiar package, refusing to let him win.

"To be fair, I'm pretty sure you're the one who got me addicted."

"You're the one who found my stash." He sets the candy back onto the coffee table and continues his perusal of whatever else is in the grocery bag.

"You're the one who should've hidden your stash better," I point out.

He stops rummaging around in the grocery sack and looks up at me. "They were in my room."

"On the *nightstand*," I counter. "You really think it's a good place to hide your cinnamon bears?"

"From my buddy's nosy little sister who had a habit of breaking into things––"

"I didn't break into things," I screech.

"Such as her older brother's friend's room so she could steal his cinnamon bears?"

"Whatever." I snatch the Blu-Ray from the coffee table and put it into the Blu-Ray player.

Apparently, Theo's hijacking my night, and there's nothing I can do about it.

At least he brought snacks.

## 12

## BLAKELY

Once Happy and his grandma are chatting on the screen, I plop onto the couch and rest my feet on the coffee table, determined to ignore Theo's presence even if it kills me.

Until he grabs my big toe, and I tug my foot away from him.

"Hey!" I tuck my feet under my butt. "What was that for?"

"Just getting to know the new Blake. Since when do you paint your nails?"

"Since recently," I argue. "What? Is there a problem with purple nail polish?"

"No problem." He opens the bag of cinnamon bears, pops one into his mouth, and offers me one.

Grudgingly, I take it while studying him from the corner of my eye. Seriously. What is up with this guy?

"I actually like the purple, by the way," he adds. "It suits you."

"Oh, really?"

"Yeah." He pops another cinnamon bear into his mouth.

I raise my brow. "The new me or the old me?"

His gaze softens as it bounces around my face while he chews slowly. Thoughtfully, if it's even possible.

*Who. Is. This. Guy?*

"Just you," he decides. "Whoever you want to be."

My breath catches softly in my lungs, but I stay quiet.

Seriously. Who is this guy, and what has he done with the Theo I've known for the past four years?

I'm too caught in his stare to form a snarky response. Hypnotized almost. Like I'm in some sort of twisted reality. The one I dreamt about when I was in high school. The one I wished for every year on my birthday. Where Theo finally looked at me like I was more than Colt's little sister. Like I was my own person. Like I was someone worth knowing. Worth seeing.

I don't know what to do about it. About the situation, let alone the guy in front of me. Because he isn't being a jerk at this moment. And I'm not sure my armor's strong enough to battle Sweet Teddy when I'm so used to the asshole persona.

When he realizes I don't know what to say, he clears his throat and announces, "So. Twenty questions."

I blink and nibble on the cinnamon bear's ear, forcing myself back to reality. But even the spicy goodness doesn't bring any clarity, so I shake my head and ask, "Twenty questions?"

"Yeah. Let's play."

"Why?"

"So I can get to know the new Blake," he answers as if it's the most plausible thing in the whole world. "Favorite color?"

He can't be serious.

My eyebrow arches as he stares back at me, patiently waiting for my answer.

He is.

He's actually serious.

95

*All right, Teddy Bear. I'll play.*

Letting my curiosity get the best of me, I settle further into the couch cushions and answer, "Green."

"So, the same as the old Blake," he jokes. "Noted."

"You?" I counter, refusing to acknowledge how adorable he is when he's teasing me.

"Purple."

With a laugh, I repeat, "Purple?"

"Yeah. It's a recent realization. Favorite animal?" he continues.

"Lioness."

He quirks his brow. "Not lions in general?"

"Nope. Only the girls."

"Well if that isn't the most sexist thing I've ever heard." His eyes crinkle at the corners as he waits for whatever asinine response he knows I have locked and loaded. And even though I know he's egging me on, I take the bait without hesitation.

"Not sexist. True. The girls are badass hunters. The guys are lazy assholes."

Another laugh rumbles out of him as he tosses his arm along the back of the couch and turns to face me head-on. "Come on. The guys aren't so bad."

"Uh, yes they are. They're terrible."

"How?"

"For starters, they're lazy. All they do is sit on their asses and eat the food the females bring to them."

"And who's fault is that? The lions? Or the females for doting on them?"

"The only thing males are good at is protecting the lionesses from other male lions, and even then, they're only successful like half the time." I reach for the bag of cinnamon bears in his lap and pop another one into my mouth, adding, "Oh. And that's *if* they decide to fight in the first place. If not, they get up and walk away from their pack, leaving the women to deal with their new entitled guy lion who's just as lazy as the last one."

"Seems like you know a lot about lions."

"Ash may have convinced me to watch a documentary or two," I mutter, bringing my knees to my chest as I make myself more comfortable on the couch. "But how 'bout you? What's your favorite animal?"

"Lions," he answers without hesitation.

I laugh a little harder, way more amused than I should be, and shake my head. "Seriously?"

"Come on. They're king of the jungle. Waited on hand and foot. Surrounded by badass women," he reminds me, bouncing his eyebrows up and down. The same arrogant grin is plastered on his face as if he's God's gift to women and he knows it.

If only he didn't look so good while he was at it, that'd be great.

Studying him, I decide, "I think you're trying to piss me off."

"And I think you have a chip on your shoulder when it comes to the opposite sex," he counters.

I fold my arms. "Not all of them."

"Oh?"

"Yeah. Some are nice guys."

"And you want a nice guy?" He laughs, but there's a hint of condescension in it.

My hackles rise, and I sit up a little straighter. "Is there something wrong with wanting a nice guy?"

"Not for most girls. You, however..." He shrugs one shoulder and pulls out a red Vitamin Water from the grocery sack on the coffee table. Apparently, he remembers I'm not usually a soda girl. Unless it's Crush.

*Stupid Crush.*

He tosses the Vitamin Water to me and twists the top off the second bottle, bringing it to his lips. I watch in fascination as he swallows a quarter of the drink, then twists the cap back on. As if he's already won. As if he's proven his point, when he hasn't even made it yet.

"And who do you think I want?" I demand, attempting to focus on the conversation instead of how much I want to kiss his stupid lips to see if they taste like his Vitamin Water.

"I think you want a guy who pushes you. A guy who eggs you on. A guy who doesn't let you barrel over him. Someone who looks at you like an equal. Someone who challenges you."

I pull back, surprised by his assessment. "Oh, really?"

"Yeah. It's why you haven't had sex yet."

"Because I haven't found a guy who challenges me?" I laugh, but he doesn't join in.

"You want a guy who can break you, Blake," he rasps, his voice low and gritty and shooting straight to my core. "One who grabs you by the throat and squeezes as he enters you. One who treats you like you aren't made of glass. You're different than other girls."

My inhale is sharp but shallow as I hold his gaze for a split second too long, his words rolling over me as my thighs tighten at the imagery. Because one, holy shit it's hot. And two, he's right. I've never been like most girls. I've never wanted to be like most girls. Even growing up, I liked boy things. Ninja turtles. Indiana Jones. Football. I hated My Little Pony, Barbies, and American Girl dolls.

It's probably because I looked up to my brothers so much and wanted to be included in all their shenanigans, and thankfully, my parents took it in stride. They let me be who I wanted to be.

But I never wanted to be treated like a doll. I never wanted to be put on a pedestal or looked down upon simply because I had a vagina instead of a penis. I wanted to be an equal. A rival. Someone taken seriously. Someone who could give as good as they got.

And all I want in a partner is exactly that. Someone who accepts me. Someone who looks at me like I'm sexy and feminine even when I'm covered in grass stains from a quick game of football in the quad.

Is that so hard?

Actually, yes. Yes it is. Because other than my brother's best friend, I haven't found anyone who's even remotely close to giving me those things.

But the fact Theo's calling me out on it? Saying he knows what I really want in a guy? Especially when I've yet to find it myself?

It hits a little too close to home.

"Am I wrong?" he teases, the same cocky smirk tugging at his mouth, finding way too much amusement in watching me squirm.

"I think it's rich coming from you," I counter.

"Oh?"

"Yeah. How could you know what I want?" I laugh again, but it feels forced. "Honestly, I don't even think you know what *you* want."

"Oh?" Curiosity piqued, a slow smile builds on his lips. "And what do you think I want?"

"I think you like messing with girls who don't matter to you because you won't ever be rejected by them. Instead, you keep them at a distance under the guise of"––I lift my fingers and do air quotes––"spreading the love."

His chuckle is cool at best, hinting at just how close I am to hitting my mark. "Is something wrong with spreading the love, Blake?"

"Not at all. But do you really think it'll get you what you want in the long run?"

"A shit ton of orgasms and a memorable college experience before I go into the NHL?" He laughs a little harder and cups his hands behind his head, making himself more comfortable on the couch. "Yeah. I think that covers it."

"You forgot about a plethora of STDs with a side of accidental pregnancy," I quip.

He laughs again. But this time it's warmer, deeper, more genuine. He grabs my knee and squeezes. The heat from his palm feels like the sun in the middle of summer. It's hot. Almost scalding. So much so, my muscles tense beneath his touch, but I don't pull away. Because I like being close to Theo. I always have.

Even when it hurts.

Like right now.

He didn't deny it.

A shit ton of orgasms and a memorable college experience is all he wants.

And yet, here I am, fawning over the bastard.

I mean, I already knew the truth, but the confirmation is a harder pill to swallow.

Then again, maybe he's onto something.

Maybe it's what I need too. I'll pass on the whole STD and accidental pregnancy part. But meaningless sex? It's gotta feel better than this. This...rejection that isn't even rejection because he was never mine in the first place.

"You know what? I think you may be onto something," I decide. I stretch my legs out and rest them on the coffee table, hooking one ankle over the other.

He slides his attention down my legs, letting it land on my purple toenails. "Oh, you do?"

"Yeah. Meaningless sex definitely feels like the safer option compared to putting your heart on the line, right? I might have to give it a try."

His gaze narrows as it slides back up my body and meets mine again. "Not sure you're meaningless sex material."

"Oh, I'm not?"

He shrugs but stays quiet, holding my gaze. But there's something in his stare. Something simmering just beneath the surface. A dare? A warning? A challenge?

"Tell me this," I prod. "If I weren't Colt's little sister, and you didn't know I was a virgin, would you *still* think I wasn't meaningless sex material?"

Shifting on the cushion, he moves his hand from my thigh and runs it over his face, breaking our little staring contest while giving me the upper hand. Or at least, it sure feels like it.

"I, uh, I don't know," he answers. "I don't look at you like anything but Colt's little sister, so…"

"So." I click my tongue against the roof of my mouth and reach for the bag of cinnamon bears. "I guess I'll have to find someone who *does* see me as more than Colt's little sister."

I don't even bother hiding my shameless smile as I turn back to Happy Gilmore and watch him shatter glass with a hockey puck. Or at least, I *pretend* to watch. The man beside me is still one hell of a distraction despite my best efforts to keep from showing it to him, and he's stiff as a board.

*Good.*

Let him stew. Let him be uncomfortable. Let him regret bringing up this conversation in the first place. Because it definitely wasn't me.

"Not sure it's a good idea," he mutters, not even bothering to fake like he's invested in the movie. Nope. The poor bastard is much more interested in my sex life…er, lack thereof.

"Maybe not. But it also isn't your problem, remember?" I look up at him again. "And don't forget why you showed up on my doorstep tonight. You came to make amends for being an overprotective ass. I suggest you don't screw it up before the night's even over. Besides. You're the one who pointed out I need a guy who can break me. Who better to do the job than a man with a penchant for meaningless sex?"

"I didn't mean——"

"Promise me one thing, though," I interrupt. Because I know him. And I know if I give him an inch, he'll take a mile.

He scrubs his hand over his face and closes his eyes. "What, Blake?"

"Promise you won't stick your nose where it doesn't belong——especially in my sex life."

"Blake," he murmurs, the tone bordering on annoyance and pain, though I don't know which is more prevalent.

"I'm serious," I tell him. "I don't want to ruin all the progress we made tonight by you overstepping your bounds again. And call it a hunch, but I don't think you want to ruin it, either."

His eyes open, and he holds my stare but stays quiet.

"I've had fun so far, and I don't feel like strangling you, which is a definite plus," I add, my mouth lifting with amusement. "Seriously. Don't ruin it."

"I won't," he promises, more somber than I've seen in a long time.

"Good." I shove his shoulder and snuggle into the cushions a bit more. "Now, enough talking. We're almost to my favorite part."

## 13

## BLAKELY

The bass is thumping as we pull up to the Taylor House. It's exactly like I remember it from a few months ago. Same red brick. Same dark shutters. Same ominous feeling as I stare up at it. Unfortunately, the familiarity does nothing to ease the anxiety pulsing through me. If anything, it only amplifies it.

Which is ridiculous. After my chat with Theo, things have calmed down. He doesn't get mad at me at practice. Doesn't give me shit for talking to the other guys. Doesn't get all bossy and broody.

It's been nice.

Refreshing.

I think?

Honestly, I can't tell. But I've tried not to focus on it. I've tried to distract myself. With running. Classes. And free coffee from Tukani. Free lunch from Depp. Along with copious amounts of texts with Burrows…and Austin, though I have no idea how he got my number.

Seriously. The team has bent over backwards to make me feel wanted. Even Logan complimented me the other day.

But that one was weird. Because it's Logan. And I know what he did to Ash and Colt. I almost kneed him in the balls for even talking to me but decided against it when I realized Coach would've seen the whole thing. Regardless...overall, it's been nice. Being noticed. If only I could ignore the angry glare Theo likes to pass out anytime he witnesses said hospitality.

*Asshole.*

Then again, he's held up his end of the deal and has let me do my own thing for the most part, so I can't exactly complain.

He's not supposed to be here tonight, which is the only reason I accepted Burrows' invitation to tag along. Colt mentioned he's visiting his older brother, Mack. It's not any of my business, and I most definitely don't care what he does or who he's with in the first place, but still. I officially get a night at the Taylor House without the one and only Taylor being here to ruin it for me.

Okay, maybe I'm being unfair on that front.

Or maybe I'm not.

Honestly, I don't even know.

I let out a slow breath and focus on the positive.

Yup.

Everything's great, grand, and wonderful.

"Hey. You ready?" Burrows asks from the driver's seat. He looks good. With a dark red T-shirt, light-washed jeans, and the same boyish smirk any girl would swoon over, he's every girl's fantasy.

And here I am.

His official plus-one for the evening.

"You know you didn't have to pick me up, right?" I ask. Burrows has invited me to multiple parties over the past few weeks, but I've always declined. Which is stupid. I'm allowed to do what I want, and Theo promised he wouldn't intervene.

But running into Theo at practice is one thing. Seeing him in his element at a party, or heaven forbid, with a girl who isn't me? Yeah, it's a whole new level of torture. One I'm not strong enough to handle, despite me throwing down the gauntlet and saying I was interested in meaningless sex with a guy who wasn't him.

But tonight isn't about Theo.

It's about moving on.

It's about me and Burrows.

*Maybe.*

*It. Is. Not. About. Theo*, I remind myself for the thousandth time.

I swear, the dude knows how to cockblock me even when he's *not* trying, and it only frustrates me more.

"I *wanted* to pick you up," Burrows reminds me. Tilting his head toward the house, he adds, "Come on. Let's go inside."

He tangles his fingers with mine, leading me into the house and through the throng of people packed into the space like sardines in a can. My wingwomen aren't here tonight. Colt and Ash are visiting her parents for the weekend, and Mia's working at SeaBird while Kate is being Kate, aka the anti-partier with a side of *I-have-to-be-up-early-tomorrow* locked and loaded for whenever someone invites her out for the night.

I huff out a sigh, grateful when Burrows leads me to the kitchen.

"You want anything?" he asks.

"Depends."

"On what?"

"Whether or not we're playing Beer Pong tonight," I quip.

With a low laugh, he splashes some Fireball and Coke

into a plastic cup, handing it to me. "And lose my winning streak? Nah. I think I'll keep the bragging rights. Thanks, though."

He hands me the cup and mixes another for himself as I watch.

"I thought you said you wanted a rematch?" I point out.

"That was before I got to know you. Pretty sure our first game was a fluke, and I don't wanna lose my undefeated title." He winks. "Not yet, anyway."

"I have an idea," a guy pipes up next to me.

My drink splashes over the rim of my cup and onto my hand as I jump in surprise.

"Dude!" I shift the cup to my other hand and wipe off the excess Coke and Fireball against a napkin on the table as I turn to LAU's rookie. "Austin, you scared the shit out of me."

The guy is unapologetic as he tosses his arm around my shoulder and leans in closer, trusting me with the majority of his weight while his whiskey-laced breath tickles my nostrils. The guy is bombed.

"Some of the guys are wanting to play a game," Austin slurs. "Maybe Strip Pong or something. You should join."

Austin and Burrows share a look, though I can't put my finger on what's exchanged when Burrows replies, "I think we're good."

"Come on, man," Austin argues. "At least play fair."

"We were just gonna keep things low-key tonight," Burrows returns, his eyes narrowing with a silent warning as he tugs me away from Austin's grasp.

*What the hell is this about?*

Ignoring Burrows, Austin turns to me. "Come on, Blake. I heard you're a fan of healthy competition. Come hang out with the rest of the team. You're one of us now, remember?"

My attention shifts back to Burrows as the hair along my nape stands on end. Seriously. Something's up. Austin has always reminded me of a golden retriever puppy or some-thing, always looking for attention or a chance to show off, never wanting to leave my side unless he has no choice. But tonight's different. He's more...desperate almost. And I can't figure out why.

"Yeah. The team wants to play a game or something," Austin answers. "Or if not, we could always dance. Do you like to dance?" He hooks his thumb over his shoulder toward the makeshift dance area in the center of the family room.

"I—"

Burrows puts himself between Austin and me. "Sorry, man, but Blake's my date tonight, so I think we're gonna do our own thing."

*This is a date?*

"Yo, Baby Thorne!" Tukani calls from outside. The French doors leading from the kitchen to the backyard are propped open again, like the first time I visited, giving a clear view of half the team scattered along the patio.

I wave at Tukani who must've lost his shirt since the party started. With his tribal tattoos on full display, he waves back at me like a lunatic, his massive biceps bulging as his arm sways in the air.

"Come hang out with us!" he yells. "We're playing a game!"

The guy looks like he's about to fall over, but he also has a habit of making me laugh harder than anyone I've ever met, so I cup my hands around my mouth and yell back, "What game are you playing?"

"Strip Pong! Now, we're getting naked *and* getting drunk!" he slurs with a big, dopey grin.

"Oh, 'cause that sounds promising," I mutter under my breath, unable to hide my amusement. The guy's a handful on a good day, and apparently, tonight isn't any different.

Burrows snorts and hooks his arm around my shoulder, using his body to block Austin from getting too close to me.

"He's already bombed," I point out to Burrows.

Tilting his head toward the backyard while continuing to hold my gaze, Burrows says, "And that's why I'm the undefeated champion at Beer Pong."

I glance at Tukani, who's chugging from a red Solo cup while pumping his opposite fist in the air and bite back my laugh. "Yeah, since you've divulged your little secret, it seems pretty obvious about how easy it is to gain the upper hand."

Burrows chuckles and drops his voice low. "Just don't tell Tukani my secret."

"Or Austin," I return, my attention darting toward the freshman who's mixing rum with a can of sugar-free Redbull.

He follows my gaze, then grins down at me. "So, what do you think? Do you want to challenge them to a game of Beer Pong, or do you want us to do our own thing tonight?"

"I'm always up for a challenge."

"Yo, Baby Thorne!" Tukani yells, interrupting us again. "You comin' or what?"

"We're coming!" I call back to him as Burrows presses his hand to my lower back and leads me outside.

However, when a certain childhood friend of Colt's comes into view, my heels dig into the ground.

*Bloody hell.*

I thought he wasn't supposed to be here tonight.

# 14
## BLAKELY

**B**urrows looks back at me as I stop short on the back patio, my heart racing.

"You okay?" he asks.

"Yo, Tay-looooor!" Tukani bellows, cupping his hands around his mouth. It doesn't matter that Theo's only a few yards away from the patio table. Tukani's hell-bent on getting the guy's attention. "What's up, man?"

Understanding flashes in Burrows' eyes. He wraps his hand around my waist and pulls me against him.

I should like it. His touch. Instead, my spine feels as straight and unmoldable as a freaking two-by-four.

Theo doesn't answer Tukani. His attention is glued to Burrows' arm wrapped around my waist.

And I feel like I'm caught in a trap. Like I'm prey. Like the damn lion in front of me isn't afraid to pounce and rip me to shreds. Or maybe it's Burrows he's planning on tearing apart.

We haven't spoken since our impromptu movie night. Other than the death glares he likes to toss at his teammates anytime they're near me, he's given me a wide berth. Which is exactly what I want.

*Isn't it?*

If only it made me feel better or erased my attraction to the bastard.

Fun fact: It hasn't.

"We were gonna play a game of Strip Pong," Tukani adds, oblivious to our little stare down. "You in?" He ambles closer to Theo and cuts him from my view. Well, partially, anyway. Theo's stupid forearms are still in perfect sight, looking all tight and muscular as they lead to his clenched fists at his sides.

*Someone's grouchy.*

"Who's 'we'?" Theo demands.

Tukani waves his arm toward Burrows and me on the patio next to the French doors, then motions to the handful of other people chatting near the patio table. Most are hockey players, but there are a few puck bunnies mixed in.

Burrows bends closer but keeps his voice low. "Wanna go back inside?"

Tearing my attention from the impending shit show in front of me, I look up at Burrows. There's worry in his eyes. Trepidation. Anxiousness.

Is it because Theo is here? Can he see right through me the same way Theo always does? Am I so easy to read? The thought eats at me as I force a smile. "I'm good with whatever--"

"*Blake's* playing Strip Pong?" The condescension in Theo's voice rings loud and clear from all the way across the patio. It's like our conversation about him not inter-vening in my life didn't even happen. My hand clenches around my drink. I swear, it's always one step forward and two steps back with the bastard, and it's getting on my nerves.

"We should go," Burrows starts, but I shake my head.

"Is there a problem with me playing Strip Pong?" I call

back to Theo, interrupting his conversation with Tukani the same way he interrupted mine.

Tukani turns on his heel and steps aside, giving me a perfect view of the tick in Theo's jaw.

The guy is pissed.

Good.

"You sure you wanna wind up half-naked in front of the team?" he challenges.

"Sounds like a party to me." I lift the Fireball and Coke to my lips, taking a slow sip as I hold Theo's dark gaze. "Unless you don't want me to," I finish.

I stay quiet but tilt my head, daring him to say yes. To tell me he has a problem with me playing Strip Pong. That he has a problem with me being here in the first place when he promised he'd back off.

*Now's your chance to put your money where your mouth is, Theo*, I silently goad.

His muscles are tight, and his biceps are bulging as he stares at me, his arms crossed over his chest. The kitchen lights from behind me cast a glow against his chiseled, stern features. And I'm not the only one who's curious to hear his response. I swear, everyone in the backyard is waiting with bated breath. Wondering if he's going to throw everyone out of his house the same way he did after my first party, or if he'll take a chill pill and let us have some fun. I can feel their curious stares. The way their attention is shifting from Theo to me and back again.

Waiting.

Guessing.

Hoping.

Analyzing.

But I hold my ground, daring him to go back on his word.

After a few seconds, Theo growls, "You're an adult, right, Blake?"

I lift my chin. "I am."

"Then, I guess it's not a problem."

"Yeah, no problem," Austin interjects next to the table. He slaps Depp's shoulder and looks at me through glazed eyes. "Come on, Blake. Let's play. It'll be fun."

Theo glares at the rookie but keeps his feet planted on the cement as Burrows and I head toward the patio table.

The night air is warm against my skin as I do my best to ignore my brother's best friend a few yards away. Then again, maybe it's his angry stare causing my skin to heat. Regardless, I'm ready to shed some extra layers to keep from sweating my brains out. It's not even hot, but I still feel flushed. Naked. Like my protective layers have already been peeled away, and we haven't even started playing the game yet.

If I was smart, I'd turn around and head inside.

But I'm not smart.

Not when it comes to Theo.

"So, what are the rules?" I ask while ignoring an angry Theo who still hasn't left the patio. "I've only ever played the traditional version of Beer Pong, so..." I rock back on my heels and tuck my thumbs into the back pocket of my jeans.

"Yeah, what are the rules?" Theo chirps as he walks closer to the patio table.

"You never play Pong," Burrows argues when he sees him.

"Guess I'm feeling like mixing things up. That a problem?" Theo returns indifferently.

Seriously. Could we have any more testosterone flowing through this place?

My nose wrinkles as I answer for Burrows. "It's no problem."

Burrows slides his arm around my waist and tugs me against him. "Yeah. No problem, man."

"All right, the rules are simple," Depp interjects, oblivious to the pissing match as he finishes filling up the plastic cups with beer. "We cut the players into two separate teams and cycle through both sides. Essentially, you're playing against one opponent until the person on the opposite team decides to drop out. Last team with a player standing, er, not entirely naked, wins. Any questions?"

"Do I have to put my shirt back on?" Tukani asks. He flexes his pecs one at a time, causing them to dance on his chest as he bounces his eyebrows up and down.

Gwyn, one of the puck bunnies, laughs and hooks her arm through his while Depp answers, "Not unless you want to give the opposite team a leg up."

"More clothes means more chances to win," Gwyn clarifies. She rises onto her tiptoes and bites his earlobe. "Or *lose*, since the sooner we get naked, the sooner we can go upstairs."

Tukani chuckles then plants a loud smacking kiss on her cheek. It's more playful than sensual and eases a bit of the tension in my chest from Theo's close proximity. I take a sip of my drink, and Tukani looks at me, lifting his chin while giving me a come-hither stare. "Ya know, if you're interested in the Tukani Tsunami, there's plenty to go around."

"Tukani!" Gwyn smacks his bare chest--hard--and I nearly spit out my drink.

"Ouch." He rubs at the spot with a frown and tugs her back to his side. She melts almost instantly while Depp rolls his eyes and finishes setting the table up for Strip Pong.

"When the opposite player gets a ball in the cup, do we drink *and* strip?" I ask.

"Yeah," Depp answers. "Theo, you're on this side." He tilts his head toward the opposing team and adds, "Tukani, you're with Burrows and Blake."

"Ooo, a threesome." He lets Gwyn go and stumbles to our side of the table. "I'm game."

The scent of whiskey taints his breath as he smacks a kiss to my cheek, the same way he did to Gwyn's less than two minutes ago. My nose wrinkles, but another laugh slips out of me. Seriously. Who is this guy?

When he tosses his arm around Burrows and me, swaying on his feet, I purse my lips. "Really, Depp? 'Cause this is fair?"

"You and Burrows haven't been drinking, and Burrows is Beer Pong champ. I'd say it's an even game. Now, line up." He rubs his hands together. "Let's get this party started."

# 15

# BLAKELY

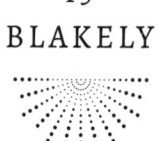

Three rounds later, I've already seen Tukani's penis and Gwyn's boobs. Apparently, she thinks bras are overrated, and once she'd slipped off her shirt, Tukani dragged her to the hot tub like it was his last night alive, leaving Burrows and me against Depp, Austin, and Theo.

Well, for a minute anyway.

Austin sucks ass and dropped out once he'd been stripped to his underwear, while Depp struts around in nothing but a pair of jeans with a sliver of gray boxers peeking from the waistband.

Burrows' little trick about playing sober has done wonders for me, though. So far, I've only lost my shoes and Apple Watch. But Burrows? Well, the poor bastard has been matched up with Theo, leaving him with about as much clothing as Depp. Less, actually. Only a pair of dark gray boxer briefs are standing between me and my first official introduction to the man's junk.

Not that I haven't enjoyed the view.

Theo, however, is still fully clothed. Well, almost.

Burrows managed to get Theo's left shoe added to the pile of discarded clothes, but that's it.

Apparently, he's as sober as I am.

And just as competitive.

I'm not sure why Burrows keeps choking anytime it's his turn to play, but he has. Then again, maybe he wants to lose. Maybe he wants me to see him naked. I peek at his massive shoulders and bulging biceps. If that's the case, his plan is working.

"Depp!" Theo yells. My attention snaps away from Burrows and toward the opposing team. Theo's gaze is dark as he stares at me, slapping a ball into Depp's hand.

Depp rolls it between his hands and winds up to throw it. If it lands in a cup, I'll be in my bra and jeans. If it doesn't, I'll get to keep my shirt for another round and have a chance to knock off his pants. I gotta give him credit, though. He's definitely buzzed. But the guy's still pretty coordinated considering how much stale beer he's had to swallow so far.

With a deep breath, a very serious Depp tosses the ball onto the table. It misses the cups on my side, bouncing onto the grass as the crowd around us cheers and groans simultaneously.

"Close, but no cigar," I note, grabbing a Ping-Pong ball from the grass a few feet away.

I rub it against my jeans as Burrows cheers, "Come on, babe."

"Yeah, come on, *babe*," Depp taunts, framing his hands on the opposite side of the table as he leans down and tries to throw me off.

The pet name caresses my skin like sandpaper. Part of me wants to lie to myself, insisting it only irked me when Depp mimicked Burrows. But the truth is, I'm not sure how much I liked it coming from my date, either. It feels...off. I'm not sure if it's because of Theo's hard stare or my own reservations. Regardless, I don't think I like it.

Then again, now isn't the time to overanalyze something as trivial as being called babe. I have a game to win, and a hockey player to destroy.

"Someone's excited to get naked," I note.

"Someone's excited to strip me down," Depp volleys back. "You curious what's under these boxers, Baby Thorne?"

With a cocky smirk, I bounce the Ping-Pong ball against the surface. It lands with a wet plop, and Depp's eyes narrow as I meet his gaze from across the table.

"Drink up, *babe*," I say, my voice syrupy sweet.

He drinks the beer, tugs at his jeans, and shoves them past his knees. "One more layer to go, and you'll get front row seats to my dick." He bends at the waist to pull them off his ankles and attempts to look...seductive? Too bad the guy's *this* close to falling on his ass thanks to the alcohol filtering through his system.

I snort and cover my mouth as he starts wiggling his butt back and forth, turning the awkward display into some kind of warped striptease.

"Wait. Are you twerking?" I ask on a laugh. Apparently, he's more drunk than I gave him credit for.

"All right, enough of that." Theo shoves him in the back, and Depp tumbles onto the lawn, his jeans still wrapped around his ankles as everyone cracks up around us.

"Hey," Depp whines, rolling on the ground.

"Depp's out. I don't wanna see his dick," Theo interjects, ignoring his teammate's half-assed protest. He lifts his chin at my date. "Burrows, you're up."

I step aside and give Burrows some room at the edge of the table. He rubs his thumb back and forth along the white ball in his grasp, looking more serious than I've ever seen.

Then, with a soft flick of his wrist, he tosses the ball onto the table, and it lands in a cup closest to Theo. The small crowd cheers, and Theo reaches for his other shoe when a brunette––who's been watching the game and eye-fucking him all night long––cups her hands around her mouth and yells, "Take off your shirt!"

My gaze flicks up toward the dark sky, and my lips pull into a thin line as I almost choke on my scoff.

*Is she serious right now?*

Theo catches the movement, hesitating for barely a moment before he plants his shoe-clad foot back onto the ground. Curious, I look back at him to find his gaze on me, making my skin hotter with a simple freaking look. He sets his baseball hat onto the table, reaches for the collar of his T-shirt, and tugs it over his head. There's a silent dare in his gaze, though I'm not sure what it means. Then again, I'm not sure I want to know. This game between us, the push and pull, has been going for so long, it's hard to know what the terms are anymore.

But one thing's for sure. The man's as much of a health nut as I am. Either that, or his god-like genes have been even more blessed than I'd anticipated.

*Holy crap on a cracker, Batman.*

I've seen the guy without a shirt more times than I can count. I even got to touch those bad boys in the locker room a little while ago. But it doesn't matter how many times I get front row seats to the Adonis in front of me. The sight never gets old.

Sunkissed skin. Tiny nipples. A small dusting of hair on his pecs. And a blonde happy-trail leading from his belly button to his jeans. Not to mention his broad shoulders and chiseled abs.

My mouth waters as they come into view. He drops the cotton material onto the ground, his gaze never leaving mine.

Hot damn.

*Is it hot in here?*

The brunette whistles and picks up a stray Ping-Pong ball from the grass. Then, she strides closer, taking his compliance with her suggestion as some sort of twisted approval to approach him. Her dark red lips pucker as she holds Theo's gaze and blows on the Ping-Pong ball like it's the head of his dick or something before she offers it to him.

"Wow," I whisper under my breath.

*Subtle, girlfriend. Really subtle.*

Theo's attention shifts to me again for a split second as if he heard me. I'm not sure what he's looking for, but his eyes spark with…something as he pastes on the fakest, most arrogant smile I've ever seen. His chuckle is low as he winks at the girl, takes the ball from her talon hand, and lobs it toward the table without even bothering to look at his target. It bounces once in the center, then lands in a cup on our side.

"You been practicing?" Burrows jokes as he reaches for the cup, drinks its contents, then tosses it over his shoulder onto the grass. Then he turns to me and smiles, hooking his thumbs in his boxers.

I look up at the sky, ignoring the curiosity buzzing in my veins or the fact I can most definitely still feel his gaze on me, along with another pair of eyes from across the table.

"You're out, Burrows," Theo calls, his tone brooking no argument. "And that's game."

My head snaps toward him. "Excuse me? I believe I'm still playing."

"I think we're done here."

"And I think I'm still pretty much clothed," I point in, my not-boyfriend naked but forgotten beside me. Because right now, I don't care. My competitive instinct is in full-blown overdrive, and if Theo thinks he won because he knocked Burrows out of the game, he's got another thing coming.

"Then, we'll call it a tie," he decides.

"No. We'll keep playing until one of us loses."

"I'm not gonna lose, Blake."

"Pretty cocky for someone who's missing his shirt."

"Pretty confident for someone who's missing both shoes," he counters.

"Then, I'd say we agree, and this game is far from over."

"Fine. Claim the title." He pushes himself away from the makeshift Ping-Pong table. "You win."

I pause, my mouth falling open as the truth dawns on me. *No. Freaking. Way.*

"You don't want to see me naked, do you?" I accuse.

The crowd falls quiet, their attention shifting from Theo to me and back again.

A beat of silence passes, and Theo announces, "Good game, everyone. Burrows, get your pants back on. Depp, you too."

He's ignoring me. Acting like I'm a petulant child. Which means, whatever effort he'd been putting into looking at me like I'm an equal is a bunch of bullshit.

Marching toward the bastard, I jab my finger against his bare chest. "Is that what it is? Gwyn can show her boobs to everyone, and Tukani can hang out in your hot tub without a swimsuit, but I'm not allowed to play a simple game of Strip Pong all because you might catch a glimpse of my chest?"

"Blake--"

"The only reason you decided to jump in was so you could end the game as quickly as possible. Am I right?" I demand.

A vein in his forehead throbs as he finally gives me an ounce of his attention and turns his heated gaze on me, staring me down. The rest of the party is silent. Or maybe they aren't, and I'm too invested in the conversation to notice. Regardless, in this moment, it's only me and Theo.

Going head-to-head over something so stupid, yet so important, it's mind-boggling.

"Am. I. Right?" I repeat.

"Good game, Theo," Burrows interjects, sidling up next to us. His jeans are back on, but he's clutching his T-shirt in his hand as he slides an arm around my waist.

Theo's gaze drifts to Burrows' grasp on my hip. It stays glued there until he shakes his head and steps around us. "Good game, guys."

I watch the muscles along his back bunch and flex as he walks a few feet away. I yell out, "Teddy!"

He stops.

"Teddy!" I call again. "Look at me."

As if in slow motion, he turns around and faces me. And while I have no doubt I look about two seconds from ripping his head off, he looks...indifferent. Cold. Detached. Like an asshole.

I hold his stare with my own, blindly reaching for a red Solo cup on the table. I'm not sure why I do it or what's spurring me on. It's like I'm looking down at my body from up in the clouds but have no control over what I'm doing or how stupid it is. But it doesn't matter. Because I don't stop. I lift the beer to my lips as Theo's eyes narrow. It tastes bitter and warm as I throw the drink back, all while staring at him a few feet away. Then, I grab the hem of my shirt, yank it off, throw it on the ground, and pick up another cup of beer.

"What are you doing?" Theo growls.

"Playing the game."

Theo's gaze darkens as I pick up a second cup and shoot down the alcohol, then reach for the button on my jeans. Burrows stops me with a gentle hand on mine.

"Blake," he warns. It isn't harsh or commanding. It's soft. Hell, it's the only voice of logic swimming in my brain, and yet I *still* don't want to listen. I don't want to be logical. I

121

want to be pushed. I want to be dared. I want to take back an ounce of the power Theo manages to strip every single fucking time he's around me.

My fingers drag along the denim fabric, toying with the button, my stomach pooling with warmth. Theo's gaze drops to my fingers. Watching. Waiting. His molars grind as he digs his fingers into his thighs. Like he wants to reach for me. To touch me. To make me stop. To make me keep going.

I drag my finger in a circular motion over the button, playing with it for one more second just to see if his eyes can darken a shade further than they already are. His lips part, and his breathing turns shallow. But he doesn't move. He just...waits. To see if I'll push him any further, and fuck, do I want to push him further. I grasp the heavy material between my thumb and forefinger, ready to undo the button when--

"Blake," Burrows murmurs beside me.

I drop my hands to my sides.

He's right. What the hell am I doing? Giving the entire hockey team a strip tease?

Snap. The hell. Out of it.

"Good game, Theo," I tell him.

I strut toward the house, leaving my shirt on the stupid ground while ignoring the stares from everyone at the party.

As I slip past Theo, who still hasn't bothered to move a muscle, Burrows murmurs, "Come on. Let me take you to my room."

"Sounds like a great idea," I return.

And it does.

Because I'm desperate. To erase Theo's harsh words and the way he lied to me about giving me a real chance to be his friend. The way he lied when he promised to let me do my own thing. The way I actually believed him.

I'm a fool.

16

THEO

Throwing on my T-shirt, I pour myself a drink, and stare at the door to the basement as if it's offended me. I didn't want to throw a party tonight, but when you're known for being the party guy, certain expectations are harder to break than I'd like to admit. And having a party every Friday night at the Taylor House is one of them.

Pretty sure I should get a reward for that shit. But what do I know?

"Hey, Theo," Missy purrs, dragging her hand along my bare arm.

I can't believe she dared me to take off my shirt during the game. I can't believe I actually listened. Now, she has the wrong idea about us, which is the last thing I need. She's one of the newer puck bunnies who likes to come around. I haven't slept with her, though. I do have *some* standards.

Or at least, it's what I tell myself.

Thanks to Blake's observation about my love life the other night, it's been harder for me to talk to women, let alone sleep with them. Not that I've slept with anyone since I kissed Blake a few months ago, but it's beside the point.

The point is, I shouldn't have taken the bait during the game. I shouldn't have taken off my shirt just to see if Blake's eyes would flair with jealousy. They did, but that's beside the point too. I should've never agreed to Strip Pong. I should've never allowed them to start the game in the first place. I should've never thrown this party or agreed to look at Blake like she's a friend when she's still very clearly my best friend's little sister.

But the cherry on top of my clusterfuck? I should've never seen Blake in a white, lacy bra. Or let her disappear with Burrows downstairs—where his bedroom is—five minutes ago.

Five. Fucking. Minutes. And as the seconds slowly tick by, I'm driven more and more insane.

My attention darts to the door leading to the basement for the hundredth time.

"So, do you wanna dance?" Missy asks, pressing her tits to my arm.

No. I don't want to dance. I want to see if Burrows and Blake are still holed up in his room. I want to see if he's kissing her or if she finally realized he isn't the guy for her. I want Missy to realize I'm not interested instead of pawing at my arm like a bitch in heat.

Yeah, I want a lot of things.

And none of them are on the main floor.

"Come on," Missy prods. "We should dance."

I shrug her off and disappear through the basement door without a backward glance. It's a dick move. I could've at least lied and made up an excuse. But I don't have time to make a puck bunny feel better about me ditching her, and I can't take it anymore. I pissed Blake off. And a pissed-off Blake is capable of anything. Including sleeping with a guy just to prove she can, knowing it'll get under my skin.

*Fuck this.*

In the basement, there's a pool table, a dart board, and an entertainment center where the guys and I like to play *Call Of Duty* or watch movies, but the screen's off for now. A few people are scattered around. Some are playing a game of pool, while a few others are dry humping on the couches and sticking their tongues down each other's throats.

None of them are Blake, though. And I almost wish they were. Because if she were out here, she wouldn't actively be losing her virginity, and I wouldn't be seconds from barging into my buddy's bedroom in order to stop that exact thing from happening.

There are three bedrooms in the basement and one bathroom all of the guys share. It's why their rent is cheaper. It's also why the players who room down here are all invested in winning the bet for Blake's virginity. Most of them don't have as much cash to spare and would love to win the pot.

The idea makes me feel like little bugs are crawling along my skin, leaving me itchy and uncomfortable.

This is a mistake.

Fuck my promise to stay away from her.

And fuck my loyalty to my teammates for keeping her in the dark so they could get away with popping her cherry for money.

My hand clenches at my side as I stride toward the last door on the right and shove it open. It flings against the wall with a heavy thud, followed by a screech.

"What the fuck, man?" Burrows shouts.

He's still shirtless as he glares at me over his shoulder near the wall on the opposite side of the room. His torso covers the Thorne in my side from my view, which only makes shit worse. Is she naked? Was I too late? Did I just walk in on my best friend's little sister getting fucked for the first time?

"Get the hell out," I order.

Burrows turns around and faces me fully but keeps using his body to block me from seeing Blake. His jeans are unbuckled, and his chest is puffed out while a pair of green eyes peek at me from behind him.

"This is my room," Burrows reminds me. Cooly. Calmly.

I tear my gaze away from what little I can see of Blake and look back at one of my good friends. Or at least, he used to be. Right now, I want to beat the shit out of him.

"Yeah, I know this is your room. And if you don't want to end the lease early, I suggest you leave it so I can have a chat with Blake."

"Are you threatening me?" Burrows' hands tighten as he stalks closer.

"Yeah. I am," I reply. "Get the hell out of this room. Now."

Blake snaps out of whatever reverie she'd been in and rushes after him, grabbing his arm. "Uh, bullshit. He's not leaving," she argues.

"Yes, he is," I growl.

She steps around him, her lacy, white bra and dark jeans leaving little to the imagination as relief pools in my stomach.

I'm not too late.

Sandwiching herself between Burrows and me, she seethes, "What the hell is your problem, Theo?"

I step closer, and Burrows does the same, practically squishing Blake between us as our nostrils flare.

"My problem?" I laugh. "Why don't you ask your friend what my problem is?"

"Oh, so now he's my friend and not yours?" she counters. "Since when?"

"Since he put a bet on your virginity," I spit.

Her breath hitches, and the blood drains from her face. Like it's finally sunk in. Like she's realized I'm not the enemy anymore. Like she's realized I'm trying to protect her. The vice around my ribcage eases, giving me a second to breathe before she replaces her surprise and hurt with a look of indifference. One that fucking chills me to the bone.

"Is it true?" she asks no one in particular. Dazed yet controlled. No tears. No anger. Nothing but the same dose of cold indifference.

"Blake, I can explain," Burrows starts.

She looks up at him, her upper lip curling and her messy red hair covering half her face, though she doesn't bother to push it away. The combination makes her look even more wild, more unpredictable, than ever.

"Get out of this room," she orders. "Now."

"Blake--"

"I'm not kidding, Burrows. Leave."

He holds her stare for another second, his expression twisting with shame. Then, he walks out the bedroom door and slams it behind him. Her shoulders flinch slightly at the sound, but other than that, you'd think we were discussing the weather instead of a bet involving her virginity.

Guilt builds inside of me. Whether it's from me barging in and breaking them up, my slipup during Strip Pong, or maybe it's from my involvement in the first place, I'm not sure. But I feel like a piece of shit, and I hate how she was caught in the crosshairs.

It doesn't matter that the bass is still thumping throughout the house, we're in the eye of the storm in this room, and the silence is so tense, so charged, I'm surprised I'm still left standing. Her eyes are hazy as she looks straight ahead, almost disoriented. Numb.

I wish she'd yell. Wish she'd throw something. Wish she'd storm out of here and call everyone out for being assholes, vowing to never speak to any of us again. *That* Blake I can handle. The one in front of me, though? Silent and in

127

control? She's a wild card, leaving me helpless and feeling more on edge than I've ever felt in my entire life.

"Blake…"

"Are you in on it?" she whispers.

Convinced I heard her wrong, my brows lift, and I ask, "What?"

"Are you in on the bet?" She blinks and looks up at me.

"You think I'd bet on your virginity?"

"It's the only plausible reason why you'd come in here and stop me from hooking up with Burrows."

With a bark of laughter, I argue, "You're shitting me, right?"

"If that's not the case, you should probably tell me why you felt like you had *any* right to come in here and stop me from having sex with Shawn."

Shawn.

The name sounds more intimate as it slips past her lips, twisting the dagger in my chest.

I open my mouth, but she crosses her arms and glares at me. The sight only makes my heart beat faster and leaves my hands itching to tug at her fiery hair so I can bring her closer and kiss the shit out of her. So I can make her feel better. So I can fix this.

*Give me your fire, Blake. Give me everything. Just don't be numb.*

"Tell me something, *Teddy*," she spits. "How'd the team know about my virginity in the first place?"

My expression falls, and I take a step closer to her, but she backs away.

"Blake," I start.

"You told them. Didn't you?"

My chest feels tight. Like I can't breathe as my gaze takes in the most stubborn woman in the entire world standing in front of me who's going head-to-head with her brother's best friend.

She's beautiful like this. Angry. Pissed, actually. And wound up with nowhere to go.

Well, that's a lie. I can think of a few places I could take her anger, especially when she's looking at me like this. Where I could wield it. Teach her how to channel it into the best sex of our lives. But I won't. Because she's Colt's little sister. And I might be lusting over the woman, but I won't cross that line.

Ever.

Teasing her, though? To snap her out of whatever's swirling in her pretty little head? That, I can do.

"You mad at me, Blake?" I murmur, inching closer to her.

She stands her ground. "Furious."

"Wanna take it out on me?"

Her mouth twitches, surprising me more than anything, her eyes practically glowing in the dim light. I figured she'd deck me in the face or knee me in the balls––both of which I deserve––but instead, she's...amused?

Suspicion flares in my chest, but I stay quiet, my curiosity leading me to the slaughterhouse without any hope of stopping it.

As if realizing the ball is still in her court, she tilts her head to one side and asks, "Are you gonna fuck me now or what?"

My head jerks back a few inches, a flush of adrenaline surging through my body.

*What did she say?*

There's no way I heard her right. Not a chance. I guess I need to have my ears checked. Either that or a CT scan because I'm definitely going crazy. I make a mental note to check into a psych ward as soon as I muster up the discipline to walk out of this room. Clearing my throat, I scratch at the scruff on my jaw, stalling. Because I don't know what I'm supposed to say. I don't know how I should react or if I hallucinated in the first place. This is Blakely Thorne. Baby Thorne. Innocent Blakely. The little girl who used to tag along with her older brother anywhere he went. The girl who snuck into my room and stole cinnamon bears from my secret stash. The kid who kept up with the guys just to prove she could. There's no way she just asked if I'd have sex with her.

"I'm sorry, is that a no or…?" Her voice trails off, and she bats her lashes, looking innocent yet tempting at the same time. Like she has all the time in the world as she waits for my brain to stop short-circuiting.

"W-what did you just say?" I rasp, sounding like I've gargled gravel or some shit.

"I asked if you're going to fuck me, or if I need to find Burrows again. Or hell, maybe Austin will do."

I rush toward her, shoving her back against the door as the players' names slip past her pink, pouty lips. A soft whoosh of air slips out of her, but the bullshit she'd been spewing ceases as she glares up at me.

"You're not gonna sleep with anyone on the team," I grit out.

"I'm gonna do whatever the hell I want because you don't own me, Theodore Taylor. You didn't own me when we were playing Strip Pong, and you sure as shit don't own me in this room, either. Right now, you're nothing more than a means to an end, and you have something I need."

"Something you need?" I scoff. "And what's that, Baby Thorne?"

Her chin dips toward my dick straining against my jeans. It's been standing at full attention ever since I saw her in the damn white, lacy bra. Taunting me. Torturing me as all the thoughts of what it would be like to take it off the girl in front of me. How smooth her skin would feel in my hands. How tight her little nipples would be as I sucked on them. My balls tighten at the thought.

"I need the thing between your legs," she clarifies.

I chuckle and step even closer, framing her feet with my own as she leans her upper back against the door and looks up at me, more confident and sexy than I've ever witnessed. She's so small like this, though. So fragile.

"You want my dick, Blake?" I ask.

"Yours. Burrows." She shrugs one freckled shoulder. Her bra strap slips down, though she doesn't bother to fix it. "Hell, I'll take Austin's right now if I have to," she adds, her tone dripping with sarcasm. "I'd say Tukani might be a good fit, but the guy's massive and would probably rip me apart, so…" She clicks her tongue against the roof of her mouth like she's actually considering her options. "I might have to pass on him. For now, anyway."

My frustration burns as I lean down, closing a bit of the distance between our heights. "So any dick will do, huh? I thought you'd want a good guy--"

"You assumed I'd want a good guy. But what I *really* want is to get rid of this stupid thing so I can move on with my life and so can everyone else around me."

"You want me to take your virginity so you can get on with your life," I repeat, reeling that we're even having this conversation. Her familiar scent of cinnamon tickles my nostrils as I take a slow, shallow breath. She's standing so close. So fucking close. With my elbows resting against the door, I cage her in, the last of my restraint seconds from snapping. "Am I hearing you right?"

Her eyes dance with determination as her fiery traits spark to life in front of me. "What I want is to *not* question whether a guy really likes me based on a bet he made with his friends in regards to my freaking hymen, which, thanks to you, they all know about." Her chest heaves, brushing against my own. "So, yeah. I want to get rid of it."

"I'm not going to pop your cherry, Bla--"

Her dry laughter cuts me off. "Then, I'll find someone who will. It'll take me what? Two minutes? Maybe five?" She twists around and reaches for the door handle, ready to put her money where her mouth is.

I press my chest to her back and pin her against the door, refusing to let her walk away. Not after her bullshit comment.

Fuck, she feels amazing against me. Her skin like silk. Her body heaving as she sucks in shallow breaths. Like every nerve in her body is aligning with mine. I haven't even touched her yet, but if I slipped my fingers between her thighs, I have no doubt she'd be dripping. And it wouldn't be for Burrows. Or for Austin. Or for fucking Tukani. It would be for me.

Leaning closer, I touch the shell of her ear with my lips and growl, "You think I'm gonna let a random guy touch you, Blake?"

She rests her forehead against the closed door, her body practically humming beneath me. "I think if you're too much of a coward to do it yourself, then yeah. I can find another guy who will fit the bill just fine."

I grip her slender waist, my fingers flexing against her supple flesh. "So, I'm just a dick to you?" My cock hardens against the swell of her ass, and it takes everything inside of me to keep from grinding it against her.

"It's exactly what you are," she breathes out, a tremble racing down her spine. "Now, are you gonna fuck me or not? Because I won't ask you again."

## 17

## THEO

*N*ow, *are you gonna fuck me or not? Because I won't ask you again.*

The words snap something deep inside of me. Something I've been keeping in check since her fifteenth birthday. And now? The damn flood gates are open, and there's no going back.

I twist her around and grab her throat, tilting her head up and kissing the shit out of her. It isn't sweet. It isn't soft. It's angry. And demanding. And so fucking charged, I'm surprised we're both still standing when I pull myself away from her.

"On the bed," I order.

Her straight white teeth dig into her lower lip as she glances at the rumpled sheets on the bed. "In Burrows' room?"

Fuck. She's right.

Without a word, I grab her wrist and tug her away from the door. It flies open and bounces off the wall as I drag her through the doorway and lead her to the room that used to be Graves' across the hall. Now, it's an empty bedroom with a bare queen-sized mattress. Blake falls into it, and I follow right after, making sure the door is closed and locked behind us. I don't want to wait. I don't want to second-guess myself. I want to give in. To stop overthinking shit out of my control. Like who her brother is, and how many lines I'm crossing by feeling her lithe body beneath mine.

Instead, I savor her, ravaging her mouth with my tongue. She tastes like cinnamon. Fucking cinnamon. The spice has haunted me since we were kids, and I've refused to taste it until the last time we kissed in my bedroom. Since then, I've been chewing Big Red and sucking on cinnamon bears anytime I'm off the ice. I even caved and bought a cinnamon car freshener, hoping the scent would be enough to put me out of my misery. You know, like exposure therapy. Maybe the more I surrounded myself with all things Blake, the easier it would be to keep the real woman at arm's length. Apparently, it only fed my addiction.

I skim my hands down her slender hips and hike her thighs up around my waist. She moans softly as I grind against her, unable to help myself. She feels fucking amazing, so I do it again.

"Theo," she breathes out, her breath hitching softly as her fingers rake down my back, causing a zing of anticipation to race down my spine.

I suck on her neck before trailing kisses down her body to her small breasts. She squirms beneath me like she can't help herself, and it only turns me on more. Dragging my nose along the lacy fabric of her bra, I breathe her in deep and press my lips to her cleavage as I grab her breast and squeeze. She fits perfectly in my hand. Fucking perfect. I groan and bite her small cleavage, anxious to suck her into my mouth, aching to see if she tastes as good as I've imagined.

Her eyes shine with hesitation as she looks down at me while I pull her bra down and suck her pert little nipple into my mouth. It peaks against my tongue. I nibble softly, then lick away the slight sting.

She's nervous.

Screw that. More determined than ever to erase the pinch in her brows, I swirl my tongue around her nipple again and suck a little harder, my gaze never leaving hers. With a gasp, her hips raise to meet me, and her hands tangle in my hair, keeping me close against her as she arches her back.

*That's my girl.*

"Theo," she repeats, her voice still breathy.

I continue my journey south, unbuttoning her pants, my desperation taking over. She lifts her hips again and wiggles out of them, the same tinge of vulnerability shining down at me in her green gaze as she watches me, her lips parted and her chest rising and falling in shallow breaths. She's nervous. Scared.

I dig my fingers into her ass and ignore the ache in my cock as I stop and ask, "Still want this?"

She rubs her thighs together, her hands dragging down her sides. "What do you think?"

I think she's wanted this for about as long as I have, despite this being her first time, and if she isn't going to protest, then I'm sure as shit not going to question her on it anymore.

In nothing but a white thong, she lays beneath me, her fiery red hair splayed against the mattress. Before she can overthink how messed up this is, I grab her hips and yank her toward the edge of the bed, drop to my knees, drag my nose along her slit, and blow hot air against her damp panties.

Fuck, she's wet.

"Theo." Her breath hitches, and I push the material aside to dip my tongue between her folds.

Her hands grab onto my hair again, this time with more force as I lick her, kissing her core the same way I had her mouth. *Almost.* The tiny whimpers in the back of her throat spur me on, causing my cock to throb in my jeans. I swirl the tip of my tongue against her clit, and she rides my mouth, arching her back and rolling her hips against me. The movements are tiny. Hell, they're barely there, but it's the little things telling me I'm exactly where she wants me. I dip my finger into her center and pump my finger back and forth while focusing my mouth on her clit and lips, lapping at her folds while listening to her little hums of appreciation.

She tastes so fucking good.

"Shit, Theo." She pushes me away from her, and I sit back on my haunches, my brows pinched in confusion as she stands up from the mattress.

*Fuck, is she leaving?* I reach for her, my heart pounding in my chest and regret washing over me. Did I push her too far? Did I not make her feel good?

"Blake…"

She points to the bed. "Lay on your back."

I shake my head. "What?"

"Just do it," she orders.

"So, we're good?" I ask.

"Of course, we're good. I just want to try it in a different position. Now, will you stop talking, Mr. Chatty Cathy so I can orgasm, or what?"

*Shit, she's hot when she's bossy.*

I laugh dryly but do as I'm told, the knot in my stomach slowly releasing. I didn't screw this up. I didn't scare her off.

With my back against the mattress, I tuck my hands behind my head and wait, my gaze flaring with interest as her lips pull into a Cheshire grin.

Apparently, someone likes what she sees.

Wearing her confidence like the damn badass she is, she slips off her underwear, climbs back onto the bed, and straddles my face, her toned thighs framing both sides of my head. Then, she freezes, keeping herself propped up a few inches above me. Like she's not quite sure how she got into this position and is starting to second-guess herself.

*Be confident, Blake*, I silently urge. But she doesn't move.

"Hands on the headboard," I order.

She grips the edge for balance but snaps, "I'm sorry, who's in charge, here?"

I nip at the inside of her thigh, and she yelps softly as I grip her ass and pull her down. Not against my mouth like I want. But close enough I know she can feel my breath against her core, using it as a reminder for how good I can make her feel if she gives me the chance. She smells fucking amazing, and I want her on my mouth. But she needs this. The control.

Her dark red hair is a mess around her shoulders as she looks down at me, still unmoving.

It only turns me on more.

*Don't be scared, Blake*. I want to say the words aloud, but I won't. Because they aren't what she needs to hear. What she needs is normalcy. Someone to push her, not to coddle her. And I damn well won't be the latter.

Licking my lips, the taste of her making my mouth water, I tease, "Any day now, Blakely," hoping it'll be enough to spur her on.

"Shut up and lick me." She lowers herself onto my face, and I laugh against her center, gliding my hands up to her slender waist. If this wasn't her first time, I'd take her control, if only to mess with her, but tonight's different. It's about Blake. About making this moment whatever she wants it to be. Besides, it's one of things I love about her. Her bossy-ass personality. The way she isn't afraid to speak up and tell you what she wants. The way she doesn't take anyone's shit, including my own.

"Yes," she breathes out as I use the tip of my tongue to circle her clit from this angle. One of her hands moves back to my scalp while the other rests behind her on my chest, balancing against me. My mouth waters, and my cock fucking throbs as another gasp slips out of her.

"Shit, that feels good, Theo. Keep doing that."

I flick my tongue against her clit.

"Yes. *That.* Oh, fuck. I'm close."

Her little whimpers spur me on, and my grip tightens around her waist. I tug her closer, kissing oxygen goodbye as I nibble her clit. She comes against my mouth and arches her back, her hair hanging down and around her shoulders as my name rolls off her tongue on a moan.

I drink it up. Her taste. This moment. The feel of her on top of me. The sounds she makes. The way her breath is unsteady and her skin is damp. I soak it up like a dry sponge, knowing it'll be the only time I'll see her like this. Feel her like this.

When she's finished, she scoots down my body and fumbles with my jeans until my cock springs free. My brain is still caught up on the taste of her, and it takes me a second to catch up to the present. When I do, I lift my head and look down at those bright green eyes peeking up at me, her mouth tilted up in a coy smile. The same coy fucking smile that's been haunting me for years. My dick twitches in her hand, and without hesitation, she fucking licks the tip of it, her tongue teasing the top as she deep throats me like a champ.

And suddenly, I'm jealous. Of the guys she must've practiced with. Because there's no way this is her first time. She's greedy. And deliberate. And fuck, I'm so deep.

"Stop it, Blake," I order. "If you want me to pop your cherry, you're gonna have to slow down."

She smiles around my cock but doesn't stop sucking me, and shit, is it the hottest thing I've ever seen. Her head bobbing up and down, her hands wrapped around the base of my cock.

I'm not gonna lie. I've imagined this moment. I've pictured her green eyes looking up at me as she sucks my dick between her sassy pink lips. But the real thing is something else, heightening my feelings and every messy obstacle along with them as I pump myself into her mouth. Over and over again. The feel of her tongue causing my balls to tighten.

She gags slightly, tears gathering in her eyes, and I pull her away from me, refusing to give in. This isn't about me. This is about her. What she wants. What she needs. And it isn't my cum down her throat. She needs more.

I push her messy hair away from her face, cupping her cheek with my hand as I rub my thumb back and forth against her soft skin. She's so beautiful. So untouchable, even now. My chest pinches. "Fuck, Blake. You have no idea how good it feels."

"Yet you made me stop."

"'Cause I wanna finish inside you." The words cause my heartbeat to skip, but I shove the feeling aside and growl, "Lay on your back."

She does as she's told while I take off my pants, and search my pockets for my wallet. Once I find it, I pull out a condom and roll it onto my dick, opening her thighs and dragging her back to the edge of the bed. I stand up and look down at the girl splayed out beneath me. She looks like a dream. One I've had for years, despite my best efforts to keep them at bay. But it was inevitable. Blake and me. Our attraction. Our collision.

Every inch of her is perfection. I'm not surprised. After all, it's Blake. She's *always* been perfection. I shove that thought aside, too, determined to keep this physical and *only* physical. My thumb circles her clit as I watch her slit collect with moisture, more turned on than I've ever been in my life.

I finger her slowly, attempting to stretch her, my dick practically weeping at the feel of her hot center gripping me. She's so tight. So little...everywhere. I'm afraid I'll rip her in two.

"Stop looking at me like that," she orders.

My gaze flicks to hers. "I'm not––"

"Like I'm breakable," she clarifies. "Stop looking at me like I'm breakable. Use me, Theo. Because we both know it's what I'm doing to you."

*Fuck.*

If she wanted to stab me in the chest, it would've hurt less.

But she's right. She *is* using me. And I refuse to let this be anything more than what it is. I'm the fuck boy. The good time. The no-strings-attached left wing who isn't looking for anything more.

And I'm not about to start now.

I grab her hips and line myself up with her entrance.

"I'm gonna make this quick," I warn her as I run my hand along her pretty little neck.

She lifts her chin and holds my gaze, a smile toying the edge of her lips."That's what she sai––" Her jaw drops, and her mouth opens wide as I thrust into her and squeeze her throat.

I play with the pressure, mirroring her heat clenching around me.

"Fuuuuck," she chokes out.

I don't move another muscle. I stay still, firmly seated inside her, focusing with every ounce of willpower to keep from thrusting into her over and over again when I know it's the last thing she needs right now.

"Sorry," I mutter.

"I should've picked a smaller dick," she jokes, though her brows are still pinched as she breathes out a slow breath.

"*Not* sorry," I reply, though this time it's laced with amusement.

She meets my gaze and laughs, reaching for me. "Come here, Teddy."

The sentiment makes my chest ache, and I bend down, letting go of her slender neck and cradling her head between my arms, while resting my weight on my elbows to keep from smashing her.

"You okay?"

She drags the tips of her trimmed fingernails against my back and beneath my shirt as she nuzzles her face against my head and nods. The intimacy is almost more than I can bear. The trust. The gift she's given me.

"Yeah, Teddy. I'm good. You can move now."

"You sure?"

Her laugh tickles my throat as she nods against me. "Yeah. Positive."

I pull out a few inches then push into her again. Her hips meet mine, and she wiggles beneath me.

"Keep doing that," she whispers.

I thrust again, softly, and feel her lips stretch into a smile against my neck. "Yeah. Like that."

She drags her hands to my ass and pulls me down harder, hooking her ankles around my waist and moving her hands along my spine, wrapping them around my neck. We find our rhythm, chasing our orgasms. And she clings to me the whole time, refusing to let me go while refusing to look me in the eye, either. It's the latter that gets under my skin.

As her core clenches around me, her pace becomes more

frantic. I love the greediness in her movements, the race to fall over the edge. The way her breath fans across my neck and her fingers dig into my back.

Every thrust carries us closer to oblivion, and even though I'm as anxious to reach it as she is, I slow my movements and rasp, "Look at me, Blake."

With a jerky shake of her head, Blake burrows closer. "Keep going, Theo."

"Look at me first."

Another shake of her head. "I'm close."

"Which is why I want you to look at me." I tangle my hands with hers and unhook her arms from around my neck.

Her eyes are squeezed shut as her chest rises and falls, taking every slow, deliberate thrust while meeting it with her own.

I push away the hair clinging to her damp forehead and cup her cheek while continuing our pace. "Look at me, Blake."

"Let me enjoy––"

"Now." I smack the outside of her thigh just beneath her ass.

Her eyes snap open, and her lips part on a moan as she looks up at me, her stare glazed with surprise.

"You're with me, Blake. Not some random dick. Not Burrows or Austin or fucking Tukani. *Me*."

Her hair is wild, splayed across the bare mattress like a halo of fire as she touches my cheek and whispers, "You."

Satisfied, I dig my fingers into her ass and thrust harder. With her green eyes focused solely on me, I push us over the edge.

"Theo," she whimpers, coming around me and tearing the last of the barriers I'd put between us in two.

I pulse into her and press my forehead to hers as we catch our breaths.

DON'T LET ME GO

*Fuck.*
Well that was...something.

## 18

## BLAKELY

Holy shit. I just had sex. And not only did I just have sex, I had sex with Theodore Taylor. No, no. Teddy Taylor. My Teddy Taylor. Scratch that. He isn't mine. He's...Colt's, I guess? Honestly, I'm too wound up to really grasp anything other than the blanket of euphoria wrapped around every single nerve of my body as I lay on the mattress like a melted candle. What I *do* know is Theo's taking off the used condom.

Because it's what you do when you've just had sex.

Which was great, definitely, but what the hell am I supposed to do now?

Being a virgin less than an hour ago means I'm less than educated on the whole after-sex etiquette. Do I leave? Shake his hand and say thanks? Do we snuggle? No, that would be weird. Especially with Theo, the one-and-done extraordinaire.

Hell, we're not even in his room. We're in a random one in the basement.

Classy, I know.

Also fitting, considering who I let take my virginity.

But it's weird. Grappling with the connection I could've sworn I felt when he was inside of me with the realization of *who* I felt said connection with.

It's Theo.

Not Teddy.

Theodore Taylor.

He's done this a hundred times. With who knows how many women.

Does he always feel the connection we shared or am I alone in the feelings department and he got exactly what he wanted out of it? A solid orgasm and another claim to someone's v-card?

Maybe it's why he stopped and forced me to look at him right before I came. Because he wanted me to remember who I let claim said v-card, and it sure as hell wasn't any of his teammates.

*It's because of the bet*, I remind myself.

Hell, I'd almost forgotten.

Chewing on the inside of my cheek, I watch Theo's toned ass flex as he bends forward a bit and drops the used condom into the trash can by the door.

*Naturally.*

I pull my bra back into place, making sure my boobs are covered. I find my underwear lying on the edge of the mattress and slip them on too. Because, ya know, I've already been vulnerable enough in front of the guy to last a lifetime, so…

Numb. The euphoria has officially turned into numbness. I think I preferred the euphoria. I also feel overwhelmed. So freaking overwhelmed it's not even funny, and it isn't exactly a picnic, either. My mind feels like it's going a million miles per minute, and I can't get it to slow down.

I just had sex with Theo.

Now what?

I clear my throat. Who's room are we even in? And where are the rest of my clothes? I think my shirt's still in Burrows' room. And my jeans? Where are my jeans? A lump on the floor catches my eye, and I sit up, touching the scratchy carpet with my bare feet.

Theo turns to me and smiles, but it looks forced as I slip on my pants. Like he's unsure. Like he's as lost as I am.

Rubbing my hands up and down my bare arms, I offer, "Well that was…something."

He chuckles and buckles up his jeans. "I was just thinking the same thing."

Awkward.

This is *so* awkward.

"I should probably get going," I announce.

I pause before going anywhere. Burrows drove me to the party, and I don't exactly want to see him. Not tonight. Not after how everything happened. So, how am I going to get home?

"Everything okay?" Theo asks.

"Uh, yeah." I fold my arms over my bra, and he hands me his shirt since, apparently, mine is still missing.

As I slip it over my head, he suggests, "I can kick everyone out. We can watch a movie––"

"I can't," I lie as my head pops through the neckline. Although, I guess it isn't entirely false. I'm not sure my emotions can stick around after the night I've had. I need to clear my head. I need to remind myself of the parameters of my relationship––or lack thereof––with Theo. Because I'm not naive enough to think sex automatically means a relationship. Especially not with the man of the hour. I know this. But knowing it and feeling it are two very different things. I need…a minute. Or an hour. Or a lifetime. Not that I'll get it. Theo is Colt's best friend. He isn't going anywhere. Not in the long run.

*Ooo, a run.*

A run sounds good. That's what I need. I need a solid run. Yeah. A solid run sounds perfect, actually. Abso-freaking-lutely perfect.

"You okay?" Theo asks, eyeing me carefully. Like he wants to know what I'm thinking. Like he wants to hold me again. To quiet my racing thoughts.

Does he look at every girl this way after he's had sex?

Not that I care. Because I don't. Nope. I'm just peachy. Hell, I'm better than peachy. I just had incredible sex. Sex most girls would dream about. And I wasn't an idiot when I asked him to sleep with me. I knew the deal. I understood the terms. He doesn't get attached. So neither should I.

I nod, my head bobbing up and down. "Yup. Just great. Thanks for…taking one for the team." I force a smile, pick up my shoes from the ground, and head toward the door. "I'll see you around."

"Blake…"

I slip out of the bedroom before he has a chance to stop me and make my way upstairs. I can feel people's eyes on me. Probably because my shoes are dangling from my fingers, but what do I know? Maybe people have a weird sixth sense when they're exposed to someone who recently lost their virginity. Maybe it's why they're staring. I don't know? Anything's possible, right?

Thankfully, Burrows isn't around as I sneak through the house and toward the front door. The cool concrete feels good against my bare feet. Refreshing almost. Cathartic. Like I'm alive. Like I'm not caught in a dream world where the love of my life is my brother's best friend, and he didn't just take my virginity because I twisted his arm, but because he wanted it. He wanted to be my one and only. The same way I've always wanted him to be.

Which is a freaking joke when I really think about it. I'm

147

not entirely delusional. It's Theo Taylor. The skanky, one-and-done hockey captain we all know and love. He only slept with me because I backed him into a corner. Tomorrow, he'll act like it didn't even happen.

And so will I.

Dodging between cars parked along the road, I head toward home. And once I've rounded the corner, I slip my shoes on, grateful I'd chosen a pair of white Nikes, and run along the dark street, soaking up the solitude. The endorphins. My lungs expanding and retracting in rhythm to my footsteps. And the promise that tomorrow's another day.

I can do hard things.

Even if it includes facing the guy who took my virginity with zero intention of claiming my heart with it.

Yup. Piece of cake.

Cool.

Cool, cool, cool, cool, cool.

# 19

# BLAKELY

**W**ith my feet tucked under my ass, I sip cinnamon tea from my mug. The dark settles around me like a warm blanket as the silence in the quiet house engulfs the space.

It's peaceful.

Comforting almost.

Which is a stark contrast to the chaos inside my head.

I can't sleep.

I can still feel the ache between my thighs.

Every time I move, my muscles twinge slightly.

It's evidence, I guess.

I didn't make it up.

I didn't imagine it.

It was real.

It actually happened.

I had sex with Theodore Taylor.

And I have no idea how I'm going to look him in the eye ever again.

Keys jingle on the opposite side of the front door. The

lock turns, and the hinges squeak lightly as Mia comes into view.

When she sees me on the couch, she flinches and clutches at her chest, her eyes wide with surprise.

"It's me," I rush out.

Her shoulders relax almost instantly, and she drops her arm to her side, giving me a tired smile. "Oh. Hey."

"Hey. Sorry if I scared--"

"You're fine." She locks the front door behind her, then faces me again. "What are you still doing awake? It's late."

"Or early," I counter.

She nods, hooking the strap of her purse on the coat rack next to the front door.

"How was work?" I ask.

"Good. Long," she clarifies,"but good."

"That's good." I clear my throat and sip a little more tea.

Sensing something's off, Mia rounds the edge of the couch and tilts her head, eyeing me warily. "You okay?"

"Yup."

"You sure?"

"Yup," I repeat.

Her gaze narrows. Then, she sighs and collapses onto the worn cushion next to me. "Okay, what happened?"

"Nothing happened."

"Dude." She pauses, giving me a look that would make my own mother proud. "I'm tired. I just got off my shift--"

"Then go to bed," I offer. The words aren't sharp. They're...defeated. And laced with the same exhaustion painted on Mia's tired face.

She frowns and touches my knee. "Not what I meant. Come on. Tell me what's bugging you."

"Nothing's bugging me. I just can't sleep."

"You know you're allowed to like...feel stuff, right?" she asks.

150

"What?" I laugh.

"I mean…" She pauses and tries again. "You're allowed to feel stuff. You're allowed to talk about it. It doesn't make you a bitch or a gossiper to express yourself."

I pull back, surprised. "Where is this coming from?"

"You're allowed to tell people what's on your mind. You don't have to bottle it up or shove it down like most guys do."

"Who says I'm bottling anything up?"

She arches her brow, daring me to argue with her.

And dammit. The girl has a point.

Pursing my lips, I take another sip of cinnamon tea and let out a groan. "Fiiiine. I'm bottling shit up because it's not a big deal. Nothing's bothering me. Well"––I press the brim of the cup to my lips again, then pause––"other than the usual."

"Theo?" she assumes.

I dip my chin and take another sip of tea. The liquid is almost cool now, like the memory of Theo's kisses, but I drink it down anyway.

"What happened?" Mia prods.

Memories of Theo's hands on my body rise to the surface, and my face heats up like a sinner in church.

Man, his hands. The way I freaking rode his face. Like, who does that? I don't know how I'm going to look him in the eye ever again.

Mia's jaw drops, the streetlight's glow from the window lighting up her surprised features when I stay silent too long. "No freaking way."

I blink and curl further into the cushions, pressing the mug to my chest, but I don't say a word.

"No. Freaking. Way," she repeats.

"Stop saying it like that," I whine, finally giving in.

"You slept with him?" Her voice is pitchy and way louder than anyone's should be at four o'clock in the morning.

My attention darts to the dark hallway where Kate is

still--hopefully--blissfully asleep. "Dude," I scold. "Keep your voice down."

"Sorry." She follows my gaze and looks down the still dark hallway, confirming she hasn't woken Kate up. She turns back to me and lowers her voice to a whisper. "But seriously. You slept with Theo?"

*Technically, there was no sleeping,* I think to myself then mutter, "Maybe?"

"Maybe?" She laughs. "You either did or you didn't. There's no in between."

"I mean, there could be, right? He could've passed out mid thrust or--"

"Blake."

"Okay, fine," I snap. "Yes. I slept with Theo."

"And?"

"And...I'm still trying to wrap my head around the whole thing, I guess?"

"Well, yeah. It's kind of a big deal, Blake."

My lips purse, and I gulp more tea. "Duh. But at least I came to one conclusion."

"And what's that?"

"It will never happen again." My spine straightens with determination.

But the pride I expect to see on Mia's face is absent. Instead, she simply frowns and asks, "Why not?"

*Well, for one, there was a bet involved, and second, I had to twist the bastard's arm,* I think to myself, but I bite my tongue, refusing to admit it out loud because it sounds so much worse than acknowledging the truth in my head.

I can't believe I was so stupid. And desperate.

*Man, why did I act so desperate?*

"Tell me," Mia pushes.

"It was for a bet," I mumble, staring at the dark contents in my mug like it's the most fascinating thing in the world.

She blinks slowly, her eyes gleaming with confusion in the glow from the streetlight outside our window. "I'm sorry...a bet?"

"Yup."

"What kind of bet?"

"Between him and the rest of the guys on the team."

"What kind of bet?" she repeats, her tone sharper, though it's easy to see she already knows. "Don't tell me it involved who could sleep with you first."

I glance back at her, then back at my almost empty cup. "Technically, it was a bet to see who could take my virginity, but toe-mae-toe, toe-mah-toe, so..."

She gasps. "They didn't."

"Oh, they most definitely did."

"Blake," she groans and puts her arms around me, pulling me into an awkward hug, the mug sandwiched between us.

Within a millisecond, my muscles melt into her, and I accept the hug, resting my temple on her shoulder as I soak up her warmth. Don't get me wrong. I love having older brothers. But sisters who watch your back? After moving in with these girls, I can definitely see the appeal.

"How did you find out?" she whispers.

"He told me."

"Before or after he slept with you?"

"Before," I mumble, another wave of shame flooding my system.

Her perfectly plucked brows nearly reach her hairline as she pulls away from me and gives me a look that says *are you crazy?*

"I'm sorry. What?" she asks.

I laugh and take another sip of tea. Pretty sure it's a stalling tactic, but I'm too stressed out to overanalyze my behavior.

"Blake," Mia prods.

"I was in Burrows' room, and we were making out when Theo kind of...barged in, told me about the bet, and forced Burrows to leave the room."

"And then?" she pushes.

"Then I asked Theo to sleep with me."

"You *asked* Theo to sleep with you *after* you found out there was a bet involving your virginity?"

"Yup," I confirm for what feels like the hundredth time.

"W-why?" she asks, clearly exasperated and just as confused as I am.

And boy, am I confused.

It was stupid.

So. Damn. Stupid.

But I couldn't help myself. I've wanted Theo for as long as I can remember. When the opportunity presented itself, I kind of...took it. Admitting it to myself is one thing. But voicing it aloud to Mia is another.

Tongue in cheek, I let out a sigh and finish the rest of my tea. With a soft clink, I set the mug onto the coffee table and shrug at Mia. It's half-assed and pathetic at best, but I'm too exhausted to explain my logic when we both know there wasn't any in the first place. Not when it comes to Theo.

"Well...how was it?" she prods. "Are you okay?"

"It was amazing. And I'm fantastic but also like...super sore. Is that a thing?"

She covers her mouth, hiding her amusement before she sobers slightly and nods. "Yeah, Blake. When the guy's big, and you've had a solid roll in the hay, it's a thing."

"Damn." I shift on the cushions, the ache ever present between my thighs.

"How else are you feeling? Like...emotionally?" she prods.

"I'm fine, I guess. I knew what the deal was when I agreed to it. It's Theo we're talking about here. He's the one-and-done king, remember?"

Her gaze fills with pity. "Oh, honey…"

"I think I'm just exhausted from trying to figure out what I'm supposed to do now."

"Well…did you guys at least talk after?"

"Nope. We most definitely did not. As soon as he took off the condom, I made like a baby and headed out."

She snorts and rubs her hand over her face. "At least you used protection."

"I'm not that dense."

Side-eyeing me, she lets the silence around us speak for her.

"Okay, maybe I *am* that dense," I concede. "But you don't get it. I've wanted Theo for forever. The idea of actually having him? Even if it was only for one night?" I shake my head. "I couldn't help myself."

"I get it. I would've been the same way if the guy I was in love with fell into my lap––even if it was only for one night. The problem is the *afterward* part."

"What about it?"

"You left."

"Yeah." I scoff. "I was there. I know."

"Which means you didn't even give him a chance to ask you out or to make something more out of it."

"You know we're talking about Theodore Taylor, right? The guy *never* makes something more out of his one night stands. It isn't in his DNA. Besides, I don't want anything else, either. Why waste my time on a relationship doomed to fail? It isn't worth the effort, especially when my plate's already as full as it is. And now that I'm away from him and his stupid pheromones that like to drive me crazy, I think it's for the best."

"Why?"

"Because it's Theo," I repeat. "He's my brother's best friend. Not to mention, he's been scouted by multiple teams for next year. Honestly, the offers have probably already started rolling in. I know they have been for Colt." The realization makes me twinge, but I stop myself from rubbing at the ache in my chest. "Theo's not going to stick around. And he's not one to be in a relationship period, let alone a long-distance one. Why give my heart to someone when I already know it'll wind up torn to shreds in the process?"

"Oh, Boo," she pouts, pulling me into another hug. "I'm afraid it might already be too late."

And even though I don't admit it aloud, I have a feeling she might be right. I gave my heart to the bastard a long time ago. Before I knew what love was. Before I knew how easily it could be ruined. Before I understood how much it sucks to have it unrequited, let alone the importance of self-preservation.

Yeah, love's a bitch.

And *so* overrated.

"What are you going to do?" she asks.

"Pretend like everything's great, grand, and wonderful while I die a little inside."

"Ah, so you're gonna take the sarcastic way out, eh?" She bounces her eyebrows up and down. "I approve."

"Oh, you do?"

"Yeah." She laughs, though it's laced with sadness. "How do you think I survive every single day of my life, Blake?"

I hesitate, my attention bouncing around her gorgeous face as I take her in. *Really* take her in. The soft bags under her eyes are covered by day-old makeup. Her half-smile is fake at best. She looks like she's unraveling. Burning the candle at both ends. Like she's being torn in two, and I had no idea. Okay, I did know, but it's Mia. She never lets anyone get close. Not to her. Sure, she's managed to wiggle under my own protective barriers, but hers? They're stronger than ever, and it's going to take a special kind of person to scale those walls.

Doesn't make me any less of a shitty friend, though.

"How are *you*, Mia?" I ask.

I'm so used to her being my own personal sounding board, I sometimes forget how well she hides her own problems from the world. And boy, does she have her own problems. From a murdered, drug-addicted father, to an abusive ex, to money issues out the nose she refuses to let her famous uncle help her with. It's one thing after another, and I hate how I've been too self-absorbed to notice.

But it's what Mia does.

She keeps people at arm's length, somehow managing to be reliable while refusing any alliance when the tables are turned. Honestly, she's a ninja, dodging emotional help while delivering blows to anyone who dares to hurt the people she loves. If only she'd let us return the favor.

"I'm fine," she answers. "Let's get to bed."

"Mia..."

"Seriously. I'm fine," she says, avoiding my gaze.

"You know, for someone who likes to help others, you sure do like to keep your friends at arm's length."

"Speaking of friends who like to help," she deflects seamlessly. "My Uncle Fen's band is sponsoring a new program for little kids."

My forehead wrinkles. "Huh?"

"It's really cool. They want to do weekly activities for children who come from not-so-great homes. Obviously, he has enough connections to keep the musical activities under control, but he was looking for someone to volunteer on the physical side. Teaching kids how to shoot a basketball, hit a baseball, serve a volleyball, maybe even set up some mock scrimmages. That kind of thing. I thought you might be interested."

"In teaching kids how to play sports?"

"Yeah. Since you're always dragging me to the gym and making me want to puke my guts out from pushing me so hard, yet *still* have the energy of a five-year-old hopped up on sugar afterward, I thought it might be a good fit. What do you think?"

The idea sounds like an absolute blast. Part of me always wanted to get into coaching, but the pay is shit unless you have an MVP under your belt, and since my knee exploded in high school, I didn't exactly hit the milestone before my career was obliterated.

"And it's a volunteer position?" I ask, though I don't know why. It's not like I can help. I'm hella busy as it is. Adding something else to my plate? Well, I've never been the brightest crayon in the box.

"Yes and no," Mia answers. "There's a full-time position available with a pretty decent salary, but like I said, it's full-time, and a shit ton of work. Basically, they'd be the head of organizing all the activities as well as some hands-on stuff, but we need volunteers too."

"Where did this even come from? I didn't know your uncle was into philanthropy."

She rolls her eyes. "After the whole, *my-ex-is-abusive-and-is-stalking-me* debacle earlier this year, Fender decided to start the organization in hopes of keeping me preoccupied. Not that I needed it. Between waitressing at SeaBird and school, my hands are plenty full, but I think he wanted another avenue for keeping an eye on me. Not that he isn't already friends with everyone at SeaBird, but...I think finding out about Shorty freaked him out, ya know?"

Uh, yeah. I would say so. Most of it happened before I moved in, but I've heard the stories. Saw the faint bruises from the aftermath. She'd been dating an asshole hockey player named Shorty. When she broke up with him, he didn't like it and started stalking her. Coming to SeaBird to talk to her. Trying to convince her to give him another chance. He even grabbed her at work in front of Colt. When he saw this, Colt intervened and pretended to date Mia, using himself and their fake relationship to keep her safe. And it worked... for a while. Until he refused to hide his real relationship with Ash any longer. Then Mia came clean. To everyone. Including her uncle and aunt. Still, it must've freaked her uncle out. And I don't blame him at all for trying to find a solution. A way to keep a closer eye on her and make sure she's taken care of.

"I get it," I reply. "I'm surprised he decided to create a charity organization, though."

"With my past and less-than-amazing childhood, I think he hoped I could connect with some of the kids who might be in similar situations to what I grew up in. You know, heal and all that shit."

I laugh and bump my shoulder against hers on the couch. "I think it's really cool, Mia."

She shrugs, looking sheepish. "Might as well put the trauma of your father being murdered to good use, right?"

Amused by her dark humor while blown away over how she's a fully functioning adult after her messy past, I say, "I guess so."

"Which means you might as well put your trauma"--she pats my knee--"to good use, too. Am I right?"

The idea sounds amazing. But I'm not stupid. And with everything going on? I'd have to be an idiot to agree to help.

Resignation mingles with regret as I let out a soft sigh. "I can't."

"You sure? The kids are all ten and under, and for most of them, this would be their first real experience with sports. Fender wants to start the program relatively small and work out all the kinks, then expand. He was thinking about maybe taking twenty to thirty kids and splitting them into three groups and rotating them between art, music, and athletics."

"It sounds amazing, Mia, but the internship is crazy busy, and we're not even halfway through the season, not to mention the semester. My schedule's insane. I know I like to bite off more than I can chew but..." I shake my head. "I don't want to let Fen down. I'm sorry."

"You sure?"

I sigh. "Yeah. I don't have enough time in the day. I really am sorry, though."

"It's okay," she concedes. "Figured I'd ask. Door's always open," she adds. "Like seriously. You'd be a perfect fit. Come on. Let's go to bed. I need sleep, and so do you."

Even though I know sleep won't be happening for me tonight, I let Mia off the hook. I stand up, head toward the kitchen, put my mug in the sink, and go to my room. All the while, I ignore the memory of tonight while knowing it'll tease me for the rest of my life.

Then again, it's Theodore Taylor.

The guy's been teasing me since grade school.

What else is new?

20

# THEO

The locker room is louder than usual. Or maybe it's my imagination. I guess I could always blame my splitting headache. My skull has been pounding ever since Blake walked out the door after we had sex. I've tried texting, but she hasn't responded. I even called once, but it went straight to voicemail. Not that I would've known what to say if she'd picked up, but I still feel off. Guilty. Like I took something that didn't belong to me. But would I take it back--would I *not* touch her again--if given the chance?

Fuck, no.

She's been running through my thoughts on a constant loop--has been for years--but after sleeping with her, it's been even worse. Like she's haunting me. Taunting me. Wracking at my guilt. Tainting even the smallest things. Like breakfast--I started craving Cinnamon Toast Crunch this morning. Or the gym--I decided to run on the treadmill instead of hitting up the weight machine because the girl's a sucker for jogging. Even SeaBird's tainted. I don't wanna go in because I know she won't be there.

*What the fuck is wrong with me?*

I want to know how she's doing. I want to talk to her. Ask about her day. If she hates me. If she thinks about me the same way I think about her.

But I can't do anything because she left. She fucking flew out of the house like a bat out of hell after we had sex, and if that isn't a sucker punch to the nuts, I don't know what is.

Today's the first day I'll see her, and I've been anxious to find out if she'll actually show up to shadow Russ at the game or if she'll call in sick or something. If she weren't such a determined little shit, I wouldn't put it past her. But there's a reason she earned her internship. When she wants something, she gets it. Regardless of the obstacles, such as running into me, she fights for the things she wants. And this internship? She wants it more than anything. Of that, I have no doubt.

I scan the unread messages from me to her again.

**Me: Hey. Did you get home okay?**

**Me: Hey. You ran off pretty quick the other night. You doing okay?**

**Me: Hey. Cinnamon bears are on sale at the store. Want me to grab you a bag?**

Nothing.
No response.
No, *I'm good. Thanks, though.*
Nadda.
It's driving me insane.

I shouldn't be thinking about Blake. Not right now. Not in the locker room before a big game. I should be getting ready. I should be focusing on the plays we've been working on or the offers buzzing around the locker room for all the seniors, Colt and me included. But instead, I'm distracted. So fucking distracted.

As I shove my phone back into the locker and grab my gloves, Austin slaps ten crisp hundred dollar bills against my chest.

"Congrats, man. Didn't know you had it in ya."

I look down at the cash, acid pooling in the back of my throat.

Resting his shoulder against the locker next to mine, Austin adds, "Burrows doesn't think you should get it because of how things went down, but the rest of us agree. You might've played dirty, but you earned it fair and square."

"What the hell?" Colt's locker is on the opposite side and he slaps it closed, eyeing the cash like it's foreign currency instead of US certified hundred dollar bills. "How come I don't get any, Rookie?" he asks Austin.

Austin snorts, but I glare at him, then turn to Colt and search for an explanation.

How the hell am I supposed to explain this to him? That I slept with his little sister. That the team had a bet to see who could do it first.

This is so messed up.

But it's not like I'm gonna lie to him. We're brothers. We don't have secrets.

Scratching my jaw, I choose my words carefully, all too aware of how quiet the room has become, but I don't acknowledge it.

"So, listen," I start. "There was a fucked-up bet going on––"

"And Theo won," Austin finishes for me. He slaps my shoulder like we're best buds. "We didn't think he had it in him."

My hands clench at my sides, throttling my hockey gloves while imagining they're Austin's throat.

"What kind of bet?" Colt's attention shifts from me, to Austin, to the rest of the team in the locker room. They're silent. Staring at us. The hairs on the back of my neck stand on end and an ominous feeling gathers like static electricity. All it will take is a catalyst to set it off, and I'm fucked.

Most of us are already suited up and ready to get on the ice. Some of the guys had been chatting amongst themselves, but as soon as Austin handed me the cash, their conversations stopped. Because they knew as well as I did how it would open a can of worms.

Logan smirks in the corner and makes a smartass comment to Graves, though it's too low for me to hear what it is. He probably paid Austin to come over in front of Colt to stir up shit. Not that it matters. Clearly, it worked.

Now, everyone is watching Colt. Because everyone knows he was out of town last weekend. And they also know he had no idea about the bet or his little sister's part in any of it.

I'd hoped I could sweep what happened with Blake under the rug since Colt had been out of town––or at least until I was ready to tell him––but apparently, fate hates me even more than normal.

And I think Colt can feel it too.

"What kind of bet?" Colt repeats, an edge to his voice.

Austin's eyes are wide, but he doesn't answer Colt. He turns to me, looking like a deer in the headlights. Apparently, Austin *does* have a sense of self-preservation after all.

"I, uh," Austin clears his throat. "I should probably get my head in the game…" He books it back to his locker on the opposite side of the room.

Colt isn't an idiot, though. His eyes glaze with scrutiny as he scans the room, assessing everyone's expressions like a seasoned detective. Like he knows he's being left in the dark on purpose.

"What's going on?" he demands in the otherwise silent locker room.

Another beat of silence passes, then Logan chirps, "Oh, no one's told you?" He slides his hands into his gloves, sitting on the bench in front of his locker.

"Told me what?" Colt demands.

They haven't spoken since the night at my house when Colt decked him, so this doesn't exactly give me any warm fuzzies.

"Logan," I warn.

But he ignores me.

"Everyone had placed a bet about who could take Blake's v-card. Don't worry, though. I'd never cross that line with your baby sister. Hell, she's like my own little sister." Logan's smirk widens, and his gaze flicks to me. "Theo, on the other hand..."

*Mother. Fucker.*

The asshole has hated me ever since I kicked him out of my house. Not that anyone would blame me. In fact, the bastard looks downright pleased with himself for fucking me over.

With a dry laugh, Colt asks, "You really think I'm gonna believe you, Logan?" The air grows more tense around us. "After all the shit you've pulled?"

Logan joins in, his amusement low and condescending. He stands up, striding closer as if the fight at the Taylor House wasn't enough to satiate either of their hate for each other all those nights ago.

"Sorry, Colt, but apparently, you don't know your friends as well as you think you do. Then again, neither did I," Logan adds with a shrug.

I storm closer and seethe, "You're twisting things--"

"Logan's telling the truth," Burrows interjects from the

corner of the locker room. The room falls deathly quiet, and Colt folds his arms over his jersey. Waiting. Listening.

And fuck Burrows if he says anything else.

"Burrows," I seethe, my eyes narrowing with a silent warning. "Not the time."

"Theo screwed your little sister at a party when you were out of town last weekend. If you have a bone to pick, you should take it up with him and leave the rest of us out of it. Including Logan." He glares at me. "Maybe he can even buy you a nice juicy steak with his winnings and tell you all about it. Ain't that right, Theo?"

Screw him. My only saving grace is Blake is holed up in Russ's office, or I'd be even more pissed at the way he's talking about her. Like she's a thing. An object. Something to be conquered. Taken. Used.

But as far as Colt's concerned, the damage is already done, and Burrows isn't the asshole for talking about his sister like she's a thing. I am. And there's no going back.

Colt looks at me again. Only this time, he's looking at me like I'm a stranger. Nah, even worse. Like I'm an enemy. Like I'm Logan.

"Colt," I start.

Through clenched teeth, he cuts me off and grits out, "Is it true?"

"I can explain."

"You serious, man?"

"It's not what you think."

"After everything we've been through?" he argues, stepping closer until we're chest-to-chest and eye-to-eye. "You've known her since she was a kid."

"It isn't like--"

"All right, guys. Game's on in two," Coach interrupts from the doorway of his office. He usually hangs out in there before a game, mocking up trick-plays while watching the opposing team's footage. Then, about five minutes before the first buzzer rings, he comes into the locker room, says a few words, and leads us through the tunnel to the rink.

Apparently, today isn't any different.

Until he reads the room and sees the team captain going head-to-head with the star player.

Rocking back on his heels, Coach adds, "Usually, I'd give a motivating speech, but it looks like Thorne, Taylor, and Burrows already beat me to it." He crosses his arms, hugging his clipboard to his chest as his gaze zeroes in on me. "Taylor, you wanna add any words?"

I shake my head, the cash all but forgotten in my tightened fist. Because now isn't the time to give some bullshit speech about hockey when it's the furthest thing from my mind. But I can't exactly pull aside Colt and explain what happened when we're expected to be on the ice, either.

My hands are tied.

Fuck.

"Good," Coach decides. "Remember, Hawks. When we're on the ice, we're brothers."

Colt holds my stare, his gaze darker than I've ever seen it. But I don't blame him. Because if the roles were reversed––if anyone else touched Blake––I'd be right next to Colt, ready to hunt the asshole down.

Sensing our animosity, Coach adds, "One more thing. If you have something personal that needs to be addressed, do it *off* the ice. We clear?" He pauses, waiting for us to acknowledge him.

After a brief second, I dip my chin and so does Colt.

"Good," Coach says. "Let's go beat the Razors."

Depp gives a shout, and the team files out of the room, their excitement pushing them forward. But I don't move. I need a minute. To get my head on straight. To focus. To figure out how I can fix this.

I catch a glimpse of Blake hanging out near Russ's office as the locker room empties. Her hair is pulled up into a ponytail, wisps of curly red hair framing her face and a massive LAU hoodie practically swallowing her tiny frame whole. The combination reminds me of the girl I used to know. The *friend* I used to know. Before we grew up and learned what attraction was. Before I saw her as someone more than my best friend's little sister. Before I tasted her for the first time and realized just how well we fit together or how much I knew I'd crave her for the rest of my life.

I don't know how much she heard or if she knows she's the reason behind the testosterone-filled air, but it doesn't matter. Because she isn't running from me. She can't. At least, not right now. I plan on taking full advantage.

I step aside, giving the last of the players some room to slip past me while throttling the cash in my hand as if it's offended me. When Blake finally spots me through the sea of players, she glances over her shoulder, but Russ isn't in sight.

Nah. It's only me and her.

And she can't avoid me anymore.

I approach her carefully, well aware of how little time we have to chat but unable to help myself. Besides, I don't know if she's planning on avoiding me for the rest of her life or not, and if this last week has been anything to go by, it's a definite possibility. Might as well take advantage of the opportunity in front of me to talk to her while I have the chance.

"Hey," I start.

"You should be on the ice."

"I know. But you've been ignoring my texts. I wanted to talk about--"

"There's nothing to talk about."

"I think there is," I argue.

She looks around the empty locker room again and whispers, "I asked you to take something off my hands. You obliged. That's it."

"But you left."

"And why wouldn't I?" She laughs, though I can see the hurt shining in her gaze. "What else was I supposed to do? We'd both gotten what we wanted, didn't we? End of story."

"Not the end of story, Blake."

"It is for me."

"Don't say that," I growl.

"Look." She licks her lips, her gaze darting around the space like a baby deer. Like she can't even look at me. "Whatever guilt you're holding onto, you can let it go. You don't owe me anything."

I ignore the pang in my chest and offer her the money. "Here."

Her brows furrow as she looks down at the not-so-crisp cash. "What's this?"

"It's the money." I offer it to her again, but she doesn't take it. She just stares at the bills like it's a den of venomous snakes ready to strike at any second.

"What money?"

Glancing over my shoulder to make sure we're still alone, I step closer and drop my voice low. "From the bet."

Her eyes widen in understanding as she gives me a slow, knowing nod. "Aw, the virgin money. Gotcha."

Ignoring her sarcasm, I offer it to her again. "Take it."

"No thanks."

"Blake…"

"I don't want my whore money."

The flippant way she says it gets under my skin and feeds my frustration. "You're not a whore," I growl, offering the money again.

She pushes my hand holding the stack of cash away and

shoves it into my chest. "Look. You earned it fair and square––"

"Blake––"

"I don't want it," she snaps, taking a step away from me. And I hate the distance. The walls I can feel being erected around her. The strength she has to push me away when I know I'm not capable of doing the same.

"Well," I look down at the cash, my stomach flooding with shame. "Neither do I." I look up at her again and offer the money another time, desperation flooding my system, leaving me queasy. "Please, Blake. Take it."

"Seriously. Keep it," she orders. "Burn it for all I care. I gotta go."

She turns on her heel and walks back into Russ's office, closing the door in my face.

*Fuck.*

## 2 1

## BLAKELY

I t's a home game, so I've been able to hide in Russ's office. But if I stay holed up in here any longer, people will start asking questions, and those are the last thing I need.

I should've come out before the team even left the locker room, but I didn't want to see Theo again. Didn't want to give him another chance to talk to me after everything happened. Not only the actual sex part, but seeing the cash? The evidence behind why and how we happened? My stomach churns. I figured running home and waking up at the ass crack of dawn to hit up a High fitness class would be enough to clear my head after our little sexcapade, but it's only made things messier.

Or maybe Theo's offhanded texts were the final nail in the coffin. Regardless, I'm not stupid enough to think I can avoid him forever, but if I receive one more concerned look from Russ, it might be the death of me.

Steeling my shoulders, I walk through the tunnel and toward our team's bench across from the penalty boxes. A familiar silhouette catches my attention.

171

"Mack?" I murmur.

Macklin, Theo's older brother, turns around, his mouth pulling into a grin. "Blake?"

"Hey!" I race toward him and throw my arms around his neck. He returns my hug for a brief second and sets me back on my feet.

The guy's as strong––and as hot––as I remember. If I weren't in love with his little brother, and he hadn't married his high school sweetheart, Macklin would definitely have been my first choice. The guy's sweet, responsible, smart, and looks hella good in his paramedic uniform.

"How are things?" I ask.

And just like that, his enthusiasm from seeing me seeps into something else. Something more guarded and somber as he squeezes the back of his neck, avoiding my gaze. "Uh. Same old." Clearing his throat, he looks at me again and adds, "What are you doing here?"

"I'm interning," I reply. "Trying to get some experience in sports medicine and physical therapy."

"Sports medicine and physical therapy, huh?"

"Yup. Is it surprising?"

He shrugs one shoulder. "Kind of figured you'd do something with kids, but this is great, Blake."

"Yeah. I mean, I think it would be a blast to hang out with kids all day, but this has always been the plan, so…"

"Well, I'm sure you'll kill it, and I'm glad at least *someone* can go into the medical field," he teases. He'd been considering going to medical school before he got his girlfriend pregnant in high school. Obviously, the baby curveball threw him for a loop, and he decided to become a paramedic instead.

I tug at the Star of Life emblem on his shirt. "Seems like you found a pretty decent alternative."

"Yeah, I guess so," he hedges.

The whistle blows, signifying the start of the first period, and I grimace, hooking my thumb toward the team's bench. "I should probably get out there. Good to see you, though."

"You too, Blake."

Tiptoeing around a few LAU personnel, I sidle up to Russ and pray he doesn't notice I've been absent in the first place. Not that I think it'll work. I swear the guy has eyes in the back of his head and sees everything. The good. The bad. And the ugly.

"You good?" Russ asks. His arms are crossed, and his eyes are glued to the players as Colt, Theo, and Logan skate across the blue line and into enemy territory. But I can tell Russ is watching me from his periphery. Studying my mannerisms. Reading me better than I can read myself.

"Yup," I reply, ignoring Theo as he skates past me. "Doing great."

"Good."

I watch as Colt shoots the puck toward the goalie, but he blocks it with his leg pads. The crowd groans. Theo catches the rebound and passes the puck back to Colt, but he misses it, and the Razors advantage, chipping it off the board toward their left wing on the other side of the ice.

"Come on, Colt," I mutter under my breath. He shouldn't have missed the pass. He never misses a pass. His head isn't in the game. The question is...why? I didn't hear what the team was talking about before they made their way onto the ice, but clearly, it's gotten into Colt's head and is messing with him.

*Does he know?*

There's no way. Theo wouldn't've told him. He doesn't have a death wish. But Theo had the cash, which means he had to have been paid by someone, right? And if he was paid in the locker room, there's a chance––a good one––Colt saw the exchange. Would he have asked about the money?

Honestly, I don't know. Guys are kind of oblivious some-times, aren't they? The questions swirl in my brain, making me sick to my stomach as my attention shifts to Theo. He looks pissed. Anxious. So does Colt. Logan, however, looks right as rain. And Burrows? The guy glares at me on the bench, causing my stomach to flip-flop all over again.

*Shit.*

I fold my arms and force myself to find the puck on the ice, desperate for a distraction, for something to take my mind off the pressure in my chest or the way the world feels like it's closing in on me.

The Razors' center dodges a distracted Depp and skates right past him, passing the puck to number 42 on the opposing team. Before Tukani, LAU's goalie, has a chance to stop him, the right wing smacks the puck into the top left side of the net, scoring a goal.

Curses erupt in the arena, along with a few cheers from the Razors' fans scattered in the seats.

Colt's head hangs, and he skates back into position at the center of the rink, preparing for another shot at scoring. Once he gets the puck, the opposing team rushes him, leaving Theo wide open. Colt ignores him, going head-to-head with two defensemen but loses the puck at the last second.

Again.

"What the hell are you doing?" Sanderson yells while boos echo throughout the stands.

"Come on, Thorne! He was wide open!" someone in the audience screams.

*The man has a point.*

Coach benches Colt a few minutes later after another screw-up, and Burrows takes his place as center. With a loud crack, Colt chucks his helmet against the half-wall separating the bench from the ice and collapses onto the stretch of seats. Clearly, the guy's upset. Which isn't like him. He's usually pretty levelheaded, especially when he's on the ice. He isn't known for fighting or spending a lot of time in the penalty box. But right now? He looks seconds from punching someone, and his sights are set on his best friend. Colt throttles the hockey stick balancing between his bent knees, his hair damp with sweat as he glares at Theo on the ice. My attention shifts between them a few more times, my pulse thrumming faster and faster.

*He knows.*

He has to.

Depp steals the puck from the Razors' left wing and passes it to Burrows. He skates over the blue line but snubs a wide-open Theo, too, passing it to Logan instead. Within a millisecond, Logan is slammed against the glass by the Razors' defenseman who was right freaking next to him.

*Good one, Burrows.*

The puck is chipped off the board fast as lightning, gliding across the blue line and back into enemy territory.

"Come on! Get your head in the game! Theo was wide open!" Coach yells. With his face red and angry, he waves his clipboard toward the team captain who's been completely ignored since the first whistle blew. Meanwhile, Theo looks like he's about to blow a gasket as he skates toward Burrows, the game forgotten. When they reach each other, they both start talking, their postures practically feral. The crowd is so loud it's blocking out whatever's being said between them, but it doesn't take a genius to figure out it isn't good. Burrows slams his stick against the board, and pushes off the ice, skating even closer while Theo moves a couple of feet back, keeping distance between them without actually retreating. Nope. The guy is about two seconds from losing his shit in front of everyone and is just waiting for Burrows to throw the first punch as Burrows flings his gloved fist toward the bench.

"Not sure what's going on between twenty-one and thirty-three on the home team, but--whoa! Looks like there's a fight about to break out between teammates," the announcer says over the speakers.

Burrows shoves at Theo's chest, and Theo grabs onto his jersey, ready to throw a punch when Depp and Tukani intervene, tearing the two apart. The referee blows his whistle and announces a delay of game penalty on LAU.

Theo and Burrows head to the penalty box on the opposite side of the rink, leaving Logan to fend for himself as our only offensive player for the next two minutes. The combination only makes Coach more frustrated. He paces back and forth in the small space behind the players, cursing under his breath as the opposing team scores another goal on Tukani a minute later. Sanderson calls for a timeout, and the players on the ice skate toward the bench.

When everyone's gathered, Coach slams his clipboard against his thigh and seethes, "What the hell was that about? Do any of you know?"

"Ask Blake," Logan suggests, tilting his head toward me. "Or Colt," he adds, but the bastard's smart enough to not look at him. Pretty sure if he did, there'd be two more Hawks in the penalty box.

*Screw you, Logan*, I think to myself as Sanderson turns around slowly and stares me down. Not gonna lie, the guy's intimidating on a good day. He has to be to keep the players in line. But having his astute attention solely focused on me? I break out into a cold sweat in two seconds flat and fist the long sleeves of my gray LAU hoodie into my palms while feeling like a helpless baby gazelle.

"There a problem, Baby Thorne?" he demands, his tone laced with accusation.

I shake my head. "No problem."

Unconvinced, he orders, "Wait in the locker room. Once the game is finished, I think I need to make an announcement."

An announcement?

The blood drains from my face.

Like what? Is he firing me?

"Now, Thorne," he grits out through clenched teeth.

Dread pools in my stomach, but I force myself to nod. "Yes, sir."

My legs tremble as I turn on my heel and walk back to the locker room, every possible scenario swirling around in my brain until I'm pretty sure I'm gonna puke.

I screwed up. Well, not only me, but I am the catalyst. Okay, it's not entirely true, either. My stupid virginity was the catalyst. Which is ridiculous. But it doesn't change anything. Because of me, there was a fight on the ice during our first game. And now, my head's on the guillotine. I pace the locker room back and forth, tossing around every possible announcement Coach could make, but none of them ease the knot in my chest. If anything, it only tightens, making me lightheaded and more anxious than ever.

I can't lose this internship. Not after everything I've sacrificed to get here. There were countless applicants. Countless. But I was the one who made the cut. I was the one who clicked with Russ. I was the one who worked my ass off, bending over backward at my last school. Studying. Kissing up to the right people. Biting my tongue in spite of the asshole comments people would make because I have a freaking vagina instead of a penis between my legs. I've dealt with all of it and managed to keep my head held high the entire time. And there isn't a chance I'm going to let Coach take it away from me all because of a stupid one-night stand with a stupid boy who will never see me as anything but his best friend's stupid little sister.

Nope.

Not a chance.

The buzzer sounds a few minutes later, and the team piles into the locker room for their break before the second period. Next to the last row of lockers, I shift my weight from one foot to the other with my arms crossed over my chest and a dull hum in my ears.

Waiting.

Suffocating.

Anxiety gnawing on every inch of my confidence with the knowledge of how quickly things can spiral out of control if Coach feels like pulling the final thread.

From the tunnel, a low growl reverberates off the cinder block walls before Theo meets my gaze, stalking into the room with his helmet hanging from his clenched fist, frustration rolling off him in waves. He's followed by a raging Colt, who's sporting a fresh bruise on his left cheekbone, although I have no idea who put it there.

Sanderson slams his hand against his clipboard as he enters the room, glaring at the team and barking, "What the hell was that out there? Huh, Taylor? Thorne? Burrows? Fucking *everyone*? Refusing to pass to your fellow player, then roughing with your own teammates? Not to mention the score or the fact we're zero to three after the first period in our first game. There are scouts on those benches, gentlemen, and you're doing a bang-up job of making the other team look good." He turns to Colt and shakes his head. "And the sucker punch on the opposing team in the final three seconds of the period, Thorne? What were you thinking?" His nostrils flare, and he folds his arms, waiting for someone to answer him. "What the *fuck* is going on?"

The locker room is like a cemetery. Silent. Almost eerie.

Not a single person moves a muscle as we wait with bated breath. Only a fool would pipe up right now and put themselves on Coach's radar. And no one's a fool.

Clearly, Coach is upset.

And he has a good reason to be.

It's easy to see how messed up this situation is. The question is, who's going to own up to it? 'Cause it sure as hell shouldn't be me. I did nothing wrong. I've done nothing wrong. Sure, I slept with someone on the team, but they're the ones who set up the bet. The ones who kept Colt in the dark. *Them*. Not me.

But everyone stays quiet, exchanging glances like they're volunteering for a lobotomy with an icepick instead of answering a simple question. I can't really blame them.

This is...messy.

Really freaking messy.

"Taylor!" Coach snaps when a few seconds of silence tick by.

Theo's head hangs between his shoulders, his curly hair damp with sweat as he rubs his hand over it. "Yeah, Coach?"

"Answer me. And tell me why the hell Logan thinks it has something to do with Baby Thorne."

*Shit.*

I'd almost thought he'd forgotten. *Hoped.* Like maybe I could fly under the radar and pretend this never happened. My lower lip trembles, and I suck it into my mouth, biting the tender flesh to keep it from visibly proving just how much I'm freaking out at this moment.

Theo lifts his head and meets my gaze, making me feel exposed. Naked. Vulnerable. And I hate being any of those things. Especially around a guy who only slept with me because I forced him to. But there's so much in his gaze.

Resignation. Shame. Pity.

Like I'm a kicked puppy, and he's the one who delivered the blow.

Theo clears his throat and tears his attention from me to Coach. "Blakely has nothing--"

"Bullshit," Burrows interrupts, standing up from the bench in front of his locker. "The guys all made a bet to see who could sleep with her first, and Theo won by threatening to kick me out of his place if I didn't leave her alone with him." I gasp at how quickly he threw me under the bus. He turns to me, his eyes shining with regret. "But I swear, Blake. I didn't care about the money. I liked you before. You have to know I--"

"Fuck you, Burrows," Theo interrupts. He stalks closer to him, as if he's ready to go another round and start throwing punches. They're chest-to-chest, their brows pulled low and angry as Theo spits, "We both know you put cash into the pot because you were confident she'd let you touch her."

"Says the guy who was adamant he didn't even like Blake before giving me a hundred bucks under the bullshit excuse it was to support the rest of the team's endeavors." Burrows scoffs and shakes his head. They're in the center of the room now. Facing off with each other. Having a pissing contest in the middle of the locker room while a dozen spectators surround them as the intermission timer ticks away, counting down the seconds until the second period of the game begins.

The vein in Burrows neck throbs as he adds, "If you wanna see the messed-up person in this scenario, you should take a look in the mirror."

"Enough!" Sanderson yells.

Theo's chest heaves as he backs away from Burrows and cranes his neck toward Coach, fire and rage leaving his angry expression ablaze. I've never seen him this pissed off. This worked up. He's usually a pretty laid-back guy. Until I come into the picture. Then he turns into an angry caveman with a capital C. But against his own teammates? I never thought I'd see the day.

And it's all my fault.

"I really thought you dipshits could handle having a girl behind the bench," Coach says, his tone lethal. "But apparently, I was wrong."

My breath hitches, and I step forward, my footsteps sounding like they belong to a tiny mouse compared to the angry stomps the floors are accustomed to after today. "Coach, please. I need this internship."

"Coach," Russ intervenes. It's the first time he's said anything since I walked onto the ice at the beginning of the first period.

"Not now, Russ," Coach mutters.

Russ runs his palm over his soft gray hair and clasps his hands in front of him. Casually. Like we're discussing the weather instead of my future in LAU's athletic department. "I'm just sayin' you shouldn't ruin Blake's opportunity because the team's thinking with their dicks."

Sanderson's nostrils flare, his fingertips turning white as he squeezes the clipboard in his hand.

*Please don't make me lose this internship.*

*Please don't make me lose this internship.*

The mantra churns in my head over and over again as Coach glares at each of the players, one by one. And I hate how I'm out of control. That my future is in the hands of someone else. Someone who isn't too pleased with the effect my presence has on the team. I can't exactly blame him. What the Hawks were doing on the ice wasn't hockey. It was...ridiculous. Childish. Embarrassing. Not only for the players but also for Coach.

"Russ is right." Coach's voice cuts through the tension in the room like a sharp knife. "But from now on, LAU's team has a no fraternization policy. Effective immediately. And if I find out any of you are trying to date––let alone place bets on Blake or anyone else in this locker room––you're finished. We clear?"

"Yes, sir," the team murmurs.

Sanderson points his finger at me. "Same goes for you, Baby Thorne. I expect you to be professional from this moment forward. Understood?"

My heart feels like it's beating out of my chest as I force a nod. "Yes, sir."

"Good. Now, let's get back on the ice, and get our heads out of our asses. Go Hawks!" He pumps his fist into the air and heads toward the exit.

"Go Hawks!" the team yells.

I stay at the back of the room as the rest of the group files down the hall to the rink, preparing for the second period. When I'm the last one left in the locker room, I let the air whoosh out of my lungs and lean against the row of lockers, my mind spinning.

Drained. Exhausted. Relieved.

But the relief only lasts for a second, then my brittle future flashes in front of me, feeling more out of reach and unattainable than ever.

This is my future. My freaking career. And there's no way I'm letting anything get in the way of it. Not even Theodore Taylor.

## 22

# THEO

The final score taunts me on the scoreboard as I head back to the rink. Colt's still on the bench. He never left. Not after the last buzzer rang out through the arena ending the game and marking our first loss of the season. Not after the fans left. Not after the rest of the team showered and headed home, licking their wounds, ready to drown their sorrows at SeaBird.

Today's game wasn't exactly a great way to start our senior year or impress the first wave of scouts. It doesn't matter we've already received a few offers. The ones worth caring about were in today's stands. And we fucked up.

I adjust my baseball hat on my head, twisting it forward as I take a seat on the edge of the bench next to Colt. The bastard doesn't even acknowledge me. The space is charged. Tense. And I don't know how to fix it. To shift the balance back into our friendship. Not after the shit I pulled. Not after the way he found out about it.

I stare blankly at the scoreboard again. One to five. The only point scored was by Logan which only adds salt to the wound of defeat.

Fucking Logan.

I can't even be pissed he called me out in the locker room. No one forced me to touch Blake. That's on me. I wanted to touch her. To claim her. To own her. But I wasn't thinking about the aftermath. I wasn't thinking about Colt or our friendship. I was only thinking about her. The fucking *Thorne* in my side.

Tearing my attention from the score, I look at the chipped half-wall separating the benches from the rink instead, unable to face Colt head-on until I get this shit off my chest. "Listen. I––"

"I don't want to hear it," he mutters.

I tilt my head and force myself to look at him, my shame clawing its way up my throat. But this has to be done. Has to be said. Has to be heard. The question is…will Colt listen?

"Come on, man," I push.

His dead eyes turn to me. "Did you touch my baby sister?"

I hesitate, shoving aside the twist of guilt in my chest. It's the way he says it. With disgust. Resentment. Like I betrayed him. His best friend. What he doesn't get is this isn't fair for either of us.

If Blake were anyone else's little sister, I wouldn't feel bad. I'd fucking claim her. But she's Colt's family. Colt's baby sister.

There isn't anything that will change it.

He deserves the truth. And he deserves to hear it from me.

"Did you touch my baby sister?" he repeats.

"Yeah, man. I did." I squeeze the back of my neck, unable to look at him any longer. "But it wasn't because of a bet."

With a scoff, he rests his elbows on his knees and scratches his jaw, staring at the ice in front of us. "Then why'd you do it?"

Because I like her. Because I've wanted to touch her for

years. Because she knows how to get under my skin and make herself at home despite my best attempts to keep her at bay. But none of those reasons will be enough. I know Colt. He might not have cared if Blake and I were a thing before. But now? After how everything went down and the way Logan twisted it? There's no way.

He turns his dull gaze to me again. "I know I said she can handle herself. And she can. With anyone but you."

It would hurt less if he would've decked me.

"What's wrong with me?" I ask.

A dry, angry laugh slips out of him. "One and done, right?"

"Not with her," I argue.

"So, you guys are a thing now?"

"I…" I let out a sigh, replaying the night for the thousandth time. "I dunno. After it happened, she left."

He frowns. "You didn't go after her?"

"How could I? She's your little sister––"

"Yeah, and you fucked her," he reminds me, the callousness in his words feeling like sandpaper against an open wound. "You think I'd prefer you hit it and quit it, treating her like you would anyone else on campus? Like some puck bunny? Fuck that, Theo. I'm not blind. I've known you've had a thing for her since we were kids. Why won't you own up to it and date her for real?"

The idea of treating Blake like anything other than perfect leaves a sour taste in my mouth. "She isn't a puck bunny."

"Yeah, I know. So why'd you treat her like one?"

"I didn't," I argue. "Like I said. She left. I was gonna make things right. I was gonna tell you. I was gonna figure it out." I take off my hat, squeezing the brim with my hands. "Things just got…complicated."

"Have you talked to her since?" he asks.

I shake my head, defeat settling into my bones. "I dunno what to say. You know how she is. She's stubborn. And when she's decided something..."

"What do you think she's decided?" He glances at me again.

"That I look at her like she's a puck bunny." The words cause my stomach to roll, voicing Blake's and Colt's concern alike.

"And?"

"And you know I'd never look at her like that," I argue, offended he'd even assume such bullshit.

"How would you look at her?"

"She's a friend, Colt." The lie tastes bitter on my tongue, but I swallow it back. "She's always been a friend. I've always cared about her. Enjoyed spending time with her. It's like... she's one of the guys, I guess."

"Until her freshman year of high school," he clarifies. "Then you were an ass."

"I wasn't--"

"I know you were the one who beat the shit out of Tommy Thoreson for even thinking about asking her to prom."

"She deserved someone better than Tommy Thoreson," I defend.

"Someone like you?"

I sigh again and put my hat back on. "We both know I'm even worse than Tommy."

With a low chuckle, he mutters, "With everyone else, sure. But with Blake?" He shrugs. "I dunno, man. You've always looked out for her. Cared about her."

"That can't happen anymore."

"Why not?"

"Coach's no fraternization policy."

"So talk to him," he offers. "Or you can tell me the truth."

186

"Who said I'm lying?"

He tilts his head as if to say *stop being a dipshit*, then he says, "I know you, man."

*Fuck.*

He's right.

He does know me.

My head hangs between my shoulders as all the potential outcomes filter through my mind the same way they've been for days, and why I know a relationship with Blake would never work. Not in the long run. It'd be easier if I didn't know Blake so well. If I wasn't attuned to her wants and needs. To her hopes. Her dreams. How much they clash with mine.

It's bullshit.

And it isn't fair.

"Tell me," he pushes.

"Because I'll screw it up, and it'll put both our futures on the line. Besides, Coach heard from more than one source that the Rockies want me. I'll be across the country by the end of the year. Leaving isn't fair to her."

"Fucking her and pretending it didn't happen isn't exactly fair, either," he points out.

*Way to call it like it is, Colt.*

Another scoff slips out of me, and I scrub my hand over my face. "Good point."

"If she isn't some puck bunny, you shouldn't write her off under the guise of protecting her. She's a big girl. She can make her own decisions. And she'd be pissed if she found out you thought otherwise. You should call her."

"I've tried––"

"Call again. Show up on her doorstep. Meet her for a run. Do something to fix this mess. I don't care what it is, but I already lost Logan. I'm not gonna lose another friend because he couldn't get his head out of his ass."

He's right. He's been through enough shit over the last few months––hell, the last few years. He deserves a break. An opportunity to have things go smoothly for once. And I need to make it happen.

My phone rings in my pocket, and I pull it out, ready to silence the call when Colt and I see my mom's name flash across the screen.

"Answer it," Colt mumbles.

My thumb hovers over the red button, but he prods, "Seriously. If Mama Taylor finds out you ignored her call because of me, I'll never hear the end of it."

My mouth tilts up in amusement, and I slide my thumb toward the right side, bringing the phone to my ear. "Hey, Mom."

"Hello, my favorite Theodore."

I chuckle and scrub my hand over my face. "I'm your only Theodore."

"And my favorite," she repeats.

"Gee, thanks." Colt lets out a breath of laughter beside me. I add, "What's up, Mom?"

"Just wanted to know if you've heard from your brother."

My parents had Macklin when they were young while my dad was going to school to become a dentist. Ten years later, they had me. The age gap didn't exactly make us close, especially when he got a girl pregnant in high school and wound up marrying her by the time I was eight only for her to leave him years later.

I shake my head even though she can't see me and answer, "Not really. Why?"

"Because he moved into his cabin last month and is living like a mountain man. That's why."

"What's wrong with Mack living in the mountains, Mom?"

"Nothing's wrong with it," she argues. "I just want to make sure he's okay. He's seemed...guarded lately."

"Can you blame him? He just got divorced."

"It's been two years."

"His kids aren't talking to him."

"And he isn't talking to me," she huffs. The familiar rhythm of the KitchenAid flares to life, and I bite back my amusement. Mama Taylor has always been one to tune out her anxiety with baking. Apparently, today isn't any different.

"Please call him," she begs. "See if you can go see his new place. Maybe chat with him a bit? Ask how he's doing? He'll be more honest with you than he is with me."

"Mom," I groan.

"Please? I'll make cookies."

"You're already making cookies."

Colt snorts but doesn't look my way, attempting to give me privacy, though it's pointless. Clearly, he can hear the entire conversation.

I glance at him, let out another quiet laugh, and clear my throat. "Fine. I'll check up on him."

"Promise?"

"Yes. But only if you make enough cookies for Colt too."

"Oh, is he there with you?" she asks, her tone lightening.

Colt leans closer to the cell and calls, "Hey, Mama Taylor."

I put the call on speaker in time to hear Mom's voice. "Hey, my favorite Colt! How are you?"

"I'm good."

"Good. You should go with Theo to comfort Macklin. He had a messy divorce last year--"

"Two years," I correct her.

"Well, the paperwork wasn't signed until last year, but you're right. They've been separated for two years now," she

189

concedes, "and he needs some extra support. Do you think you could help Theodore?"

"Colt has enough on his plate," I deflect for him. "But I'll be sure to give Mack a call, okay?"

"Okay, honey. And, Colt?"

"Yeah?" he answers, leaning a little closer to my phone.

"Make sure Theodore gives you a plate of cookies when I drop them off later. All right? I know how you boys are. Always hoarding everything in your rooms instead of leaving it in the common area."

"I don't hoard," I start, but Colt cuts me off. "Sure thing, Mama Taylor."

"Love you, boys!"

"Love you too," we grumble in unison.

I hang up the phone and look at Colt again, refusing to hope for the best when I definitely deserve to have my ass kicked for the shit I pulled with Blake. We've been through a lot over the years. A lot of highs, and a few shitty lows too. Maybe this will just be another one for the books.

"So...are we good?" I ask, my voice gritty and unsure.

His chin dips. "Fix it with Blake, and we're good." He decks my shoulder, and pain radiates into my neck and down to my elbow almost instantly. "And don't lie to me again. All right?"

With a laugh, I rub at the sore spot on my arm, grateful it wasn't my face even when we both know I would've deserved it either way. "Yeah, man. I promise."

"And don't forget to give me some of your mom's cookies. Those things are the best."

Relief settles into my bones as I push myself to my feet and offer my hand for Colt to take.

When he does, I answer, "Deal."

## 23

## BLAKELY

I still haven't spoken to Theo. Other than the daily good morning and goodnight texts he's been sending—— though I still can't figure out why——he's been radio silent. Not that I blame him. I haven't exactly been chatty. Truth be told, I've been avoiding the bastard like a bad stomach bug. It hasn't stopped me from watching him on the ice, though. In a way, I'm afraid it's the only time I'm actually able to get away with it. Watching him. Studying him. Remembering him. His hands on my body. His breath against my neck. The way his full lips pull up, showcasing a soft, barely-there dimple etched into his right cheek anytime he's amused.

It's hard.

Not knowing where we stand.

Not knowing where I want us to stand.

Not knowing where he wants us to stand.

I don't do unknowns.

They're messy. A waste of time and energy.

Doesn't make it any easier to stop replaying what-ifs, though.

Nibbling on the inside of my cheek, I find his jersey number in the sea of players on the ice. The game's in the third period, and the teams are tied three to three. We're playing the Tornados who are currently number one in the nation. To be fair, it's still early in the season, but it didn't stop the Tornado's rank from riling up the team before today's game. The guys are amped up, and there have already been two fights. One between Depp and a left wing on the Tornados, and the other between Colt and their defenseman.

Things are heated, to say the least, and the timer is slowly ticking down, boosting everyone's adrenaline and testosterone until I'm pretty sure the bench is reeking with it.

"Come on!" Logan yells, pounding his hockey stick against the ground as two of the guys on the opposing team slam Theo against the glass. I cringe as he somehow passes the puck to Colt at the center of the rink. The guys who'd pinned Theo sprint after it like cats chasing a mouse.

Colt races toward the net but passes the puck back to Theo at the last second, confusing the Tornados' goalie as their defensemen scramble after it. Theo's in position on the right side of the ice and slaps the puck into the goal. The red light illuminates, confirming the point, and the Hawks go wild.

"Yeeeesss!" they scream, their enthusiasm seeping into the crowd as everyone chants Theo's name.

"Tay-lor! Tay-lor!"

The Tornados' defenseman, however, is less than amused. My breath hitches as he skates back to Theo and says something. Theo grins and makes a smart-ass comment back to him. Or at least, I assume it's a smart-ass comment. I can't exactly hear their conversation over the chanting crowd. But it doesn't matter because it must've had the desired effect. Theo looks arrogant as hell, and his opponent looks…pissed.

With a smirk, Theo winks at me, still riding the high from scoring. When the defenseman says something else, Theo's amusement vanishes into thin air. With a final look in my direction, he turns back to the opposing teammate, his upper lip curling as he spits something back and shoves at his chest.

*Shit.*

The angry defenseman slashes at Theo's face with his stick, and I gasp. The clang as it connects with Theo's helmet makes me flinch, but it must still connect with part of his face because a loud curse rings out through the arena as his head jerks back and crimson liquid spills onto Theo's white jersey. Like a rubber band snapping, Theo recovers and shoves the Tornado player, then throws off his gloves and skates closer, ready to rip the guy apart. Everything happens so fast. I'm not sure whose blood is who's before the teams are in an all-out brawl, and the referees are whistling to break it up.

My hands cover my mouth as I watch everything from the bench, unable to tear the players apart even if I wanted to.

A few seconds later, a referee is escorting both men to their benches, and I catch a glimpse of Theo. Blood is pouring down his nose, and his knuckles are raw as he steps off the ice, his eyes blazing with fury. They've both been kicked out of the game. Not that I even care. His wounds need to be examined. Now. Clearly, they're doozies.

Russ ushers me with him through the tunnel toward the locker room, trailing behind a very pissed-off Theo who obviously needs some medical attention.

"Ice pack," Russ orders me, then calls out, "Straight to my office, Taylor!"

Theo's shoulders are bunched, and his hands are clenched at his sides as he marches into Russ's office without a word.

He paces back and forth like a caged beast, muttering expletives under his breath as I race toward the massive ice machine at the back of the room and fill up a bag for his face.

Russ has medical gloves on by the time I return and motions to the black-cushioned table. "Taylor. Sit."

"That motherfu––"

"I know," Russ says. "Sit down and stop talking. I need to see if you're gonna require stitches."

Theo does as he's told, albeit grudgingly, and tilts his head, giving Russ the perfect view of the cuts on his nose and lip. They look nasty.

Russ inspects them for a second, then barks, "Thorne, get some gloves on and a wet washcloth. We need to clean him up."

I set the ice pack onto the bench next to Theo's thigh and slip a pair of gloves on, wetting a small white towel under the faucet.

"Russ!" Tukani yells from the locker room. "Graves did something to his shoulder. It's bad. Get out here!"

Russ curses under his breath and turns to me. "Take care of this the best you can. I'll be back in a minute." He races out of the room, leaving me alone with the *still* very pissed-off Theo.

*Great.*

My hands tremble as I take Russ's place in front of Theo, the air practically crackling with unsaid words and weighted tension. Nibbling on my lower lip, I touch his wound with the edge of the white washcloth. I know it will be stained red by the time I'm finished cleaning him up.

Theo winces but doesn't pull away, his gaze glued to my face. Curious. Frustrated. Anxious.

"Sorry," I mutter, trying to be more gentle as I go in a second time. "That was bad."

He sighs but doesn't say a word, his muscles softening slightly as the last of his adrenaline seeps out of him.

"Why was he so pissed at you? I mean, I know it's kind of a dumb question since you'd just scored and all, but..." My voice trails off. "That was over the top even by hockey standards. Didn't help how you shoved him when he was all riled up, though."

"So, it's my fault?" he counters.

"Down boy. I'm just saying––"

"When he saw me wink at you, he called you a puck bunny and said something about you sucking his dick, Blake."

With a frown, I fold the washcloth again and press a fresh corner to his nose. "And you didn't like his bullshit comment?"

"Of course, I didn't like it," he growls. "The disrespectful motherfu––"

"Language," I tease, cleaning him up a bit more.

It shouldn't make me happy he's hurting, or that he stepped in when he most definitely didn't have to. But it does. It's the sweetest, most neanderthal response Theo's ever had. And even though I'll most definitely be keeping the onslaught of butterflies to myself, the least Theo deserves is my gratitude.

"Well...thank you," I murmur. "For defending my honor. Even if it was one hundred percent unnecessary. I most definitely have thicker skin than that, but I still appreciate it. I *think*," I add with a smirk.

He chuckles but winces as the split on his lip opens slightly from his smile. It disappears almost instantly.

"Ouch." I tilt my head and examine the rest of his face, taking in the bruising beneath his right eye along with the red mark on his forehead leading to the bridge of his nose and the top of his upper lip.

Brushing my gloved hand against his forehead, I hold his hair back and take a closer look.

*Yikes.*

"That bad?" Theo jokes when he catches me staring. But there's amusement in his gaze instead of the angry, sailor-swearing left wing who came off the ice, and I'm grateful for it.

Pissed-off Theo is not for the faint of heart.

I definitely prefer my Teddy Bear.

I let out a breath of laughter, gently following the purple bruise across his nose and forehead with my forefinger. "It looks like he got you right here with his stick."

Again, he winces and leans into my palm. The wrinkles along his forehead soften as if my touch eases a bit of the pain, so I don't move away from him. I simply cradle his face. And it feels good to touch him. To hide it under the guise of work when I've been dying to be close to him since...forever. But especially since the sexcapade incident. I don't even know why I've been pushing him away anymore.

Actually, it's a lie.

I know exactly why I've been pushing him away. Because all I really want to do is pull him closer even when I know it's a mistake. So the easier option? Is to keep the distance between us. To tell myself it's necessary because I don't want to lose this internship, which I don't. But losing Theo after I've had a taste? The second option isn't exactly a walk in the park, either. The last two weeks have been brutal.

But this? Touching his face? Having him look at me like this? Like I'm more than a puck bunny. More than Colt's little sister. It's dangerous. For my heart. My hope. My future.

I bite my lip but don't pull away as I whisper, "You sure you're okay?"

"Yeah." He leans into my touch a bit more and closes his

eyes for a moment. Then, he opens them, pinning me with those dark, hypnotic orbs as if he can only show so much vulnerability before crumbling from it. "So much for my helmet, though. At least I was wearing my mouth guard. Pretty sure I would've lost a tooth otherwise."

"Yeah, I'd say so," I reply with a laugh, studying the damage to his lip a little more closely. It looks tender and sore. But it doesn't look like he needs stitches.

"Are you *sure* you're okay?" I ask.

"Fine."

"You're *sure*?" I repeat, unconvinced. I take a fresh corner of the washcloth and run it beneath his nose. At least it isn't bleeding anymore, but it'll definitely be swollen for the next few days. Poor guy.

"Yeah, Blake. I'm sure." He grabs my wrist and leans even more into my palm, soaking up my heat through the thin layer of nitrile of the glove separating us. I watch a drop of sweat trickle from his hairline down to his temple. It isn't fair. How attractive this man is. All stubbled jaw and surfer boy with a side of arrogance I most definitely should not find endearing or charismatic. But it is. *He* is. Even when he's covered in sweat and blood, he's still the most gorgeous person I've ever laid eyes on.

And those eyes?

Damn his eyes.

I swear they can see into my soul.

It isn't fair.

What he does to me.

How he makes me feel.

His gaze softens as if he can read my thoughts. "Blake, I'm--"

"You did really well out there." I murmur, desperate to temper our connection.

He chuckles. "Thanks. Now, if I could figure out how to do well in *here*, that'd be great."

I don't have to ask what he's referring to. I already know. Things have been weird between us, and it's been even more stilted and awkward since our little chat about the whore money in the locker room. But it isn't his fault. It's mine. He's been trying. He's been texting. He's been wanting to talk, and all I've done is push him away.

I close my eyes. "Theo…"

"I'm really sorry, Blake."

I meet his gaze and let out a sigh. "We've been through this. You have nothing to apologize for."

"I do," he argues. "Let me make this right."

"There's nothing to make right. I'm fine."

"Bullshit. Give me a chance. Let me make it up to you. To Colt."

"Is that why you're bringing this up?" My lungs constrict in my chest. "To make it up to *Colt*?"

"And you," he repeats softly. "Let me take you out. Let's get rid of this…awkwardness. It doesn't have to be weird between you and me."

"It's always been weird between you and me," I counter, biting back my annoyance. I try to move my hand away from his face, but he cups it with his own, forcing me to keep my hand in place.

"No, it hasn't."

"Yes, it has." The washcloth in my opposite hand lands on the cushioned bench with a wet plop, and he lets me go. But I'm done pretending. I'm done hiding away from the reality of our relationship, no matter how rocky it's been, just to keep up the ruse we're…what exactly? I think this is the problem. I don't know what we are. *Enemies?* Hardly. Sure, the bastard gets under my skin because he's so damn over-protective, but I've never hated him.

*Friends?* I guess it's closer, but I've never imagined any of my other friends naked. I've never wanted them to kiss me the way I want Theo to.

But *lovers?* I can't even think the word without wanting to laugh. Theo doesn't do lovers. Hell, I don't do lovers, either. But Theo? He *really* doesn't do them. Not that it matters. The fact is simple. It's always been weird between us, and I'm done avoiding the truth and how much it slays me.

Theo touches my chin and tilts my head up until our gazes meet. "Talk to me. Tell me what you're thinking. Tell me how I can fix this. Because seeing you all torn up inside? Seeing how you refuse to look at me or answer my texts? It's killing me, Blake."

"You want the truth, Teddy?" I whisper.

"Yeah."

"Fine." I lean away from his touch. "Ever since my fifteenth birthday when you saw me in a dress for the first time, you made our relationship weird and you started treating me differently. And how weird is it that I can literally pinpoint the exact moment when you stopped treating me like a friend?"

"I didn't--"

"Yes, you did," I argue, poking him in the chest. "Which is why I refused to wear a dress for the next four years until Mia twisted my arm for the party a few months ago where--*again*--you made it weird."

Desperate, he grabs my wrist to keep me from poking him and drags me closer, pulling me between his open thighs. He's so close I can taste his breath. Smell his sweat. The pheromones radiate off him, soaking into me, teasing my senses until I'm desperate for a taste. A reminder of what it feels like to have his mouth on mine. His hands on my waist as he grabs my hips and pushes into me.

My breath hitches, but I stay quiet, my attention slipping to his mouth. It's oh, so close. Oh, so tempting.

"Give me another chance to make it *not* weird," he begs.

With a scoff, I pull my hand from his grasp and cross my arms. But we're still close. Too close. If only I were strong enough to put more distance between us. But I've never been strong. Not when it comes to Teddy.

"Because it worked out so well all the other times," I remind him.

"If you won't do it for me, do it for Colt."

"We both know I'm not selfless enough for that."

His chuckle is low and throaty as he counters, "Yeah, I call bullshit on that too. But if you won't do it for him, do it for you. The old you. The new you. Whoever you want. Just... give me a chance to make shit not weird between us."

It's his eyes that do me in. The sincerity. It reminds me of when we were kids, and he stole the last can of Crush from the refrigerator, not realizing I'd been saving it. The next day, he delivered a whole two-liter with my name scribbled across the front in black Sharpie along with a warning: *That means don't touch this, Colt, Knox, or Garett! I know where you live.*

And even though it wasn't a bag of cinnamon bears, I'd savored the two-liter of Crush for weeks, refusing to share with anyone but Theo. Colt and Logan were pissed, which only made the soda taste *that* much sweeter. I loved it more than anything. The memory makes me smile as I peek up at Theo again, my heart fluttering in my chest like a dying hummingbird.

"Please, Blake?" he repeats.

It would be so easy to give in. To give him another chance. To fall for him. But I can't. Not without putting my internship in jeopardy. And I'd be insane to let a guy come between me and my future.

I pull away from his touch, choosing to stare at the split in his lip instead of his tempting gaze. But I stay quiet. Because I don't know what to say or how to be strong enough to pull away.

"Come to the Taylor House again," he murmurs.

I peek up at him.

"Come hang out. Sip a few beers. Play some pool. Let me make it up to you. Let me prove we can be in the same room together without me screwing it up. Please?"

*Damn his eyes.*

"What about Coach's rule?" I ask, but my mouth snaps shut when Russ enters the room.

"Graves dislocated his shoulder," he announces. "We're going to the hospital for some X-rays. Are you good here?"

I nod way too enthusiastically considering the circumstances, but I can't help it. "Yup. The bleeding has stopped. I don't think we'll need stitches or anything."

"Good."

Russ's attention shifts from me to Theo and back again. Like he's reading the room. Like he's been a fly on the wall all along, and it causes the hair along the back of my neck to stand on end.

*Are we that obvious?*

His jaw tightens, but he doesn't say a word, disappearing toward the exit.

With my anxiety caught in my throat, I open my mouth to call off our plans, but Theo cuts me off. "I'll pick you up at eight on Friday. As friends like you said. Besides, it'll save space for parking, and you can lessen your carbon footprint. You're welcome."

"Won't it still save car space and lessen my carbon footprint if I carpool with one of my friends?" I point out. "I could always catch a ride with Ash or something."

"You could, but you won't. I'm picking you up." He gives

me a look daring me to argue, but I keep my lips pulled tight as the rest of the team shuffles into the locker room down the hall.

The game must be over.

Taking the ice pack from the bench, Theo mutters, "Good girl."

Then, he stands up and walks away.

## 24

## THEO

**Me: Hey. We still on for tonight?**

I send the text and stare at my phone, anxious for Blake's reply as I stand on my brother's front porch. The message says it's been read, but the little blue dots don't appear. Which means she isn't answering me.

"Come on, Blake," I mumble under my breath as I stare at the screen.

When two minutes go by without a response, I let out an annoyed sigh, tuck my phone back into my pocket, and knock on the heavy oak door in front of me.

The hinges are smooth as butter as Macklin opens the front door to his new place. It's a cabin in the woods. There aren't any neighbors for at least a couple miles, and even those are recluses. Pretty sure it was the main selling point for Mack.

"You look like shit," he greets me.

I tug the bill of my hat a little lower and step inside his new place without waiting for an invitation. "Says the hermit. How's the drive to the hospital from here?"

"Not bad. Thirty minutes, give or take."

Mack became a paramedic after high school. He was always the one with the brains and had enough empathy to be a perfect fit in the medical field. Unfortunately, having a baby at sixteen can mess with long-term plans, including going to medical school. At least the bastard had the insight to buy some lottery tickets. It only paid out ten million, which, by lottery standards is pretty low, but he isn't one to complain. Not even when his ex, Summer, took her half and ran for the hills as soon as the money hit their bank account.

Tucking my hands into the front pockets of my jeans, I look around the newly-finished cabin. Mack built it with his own two hands while living with our parents after the divorce. It has three bedrooms, large glass windows along the walls, a massive fireplace, two bathrooms, and a kitchen with granite countertops and dark green cabinets. Most people would kill to live here, and Mack threw it together in his spare time when he wasn't in the back of an ambulance saving lives. All right, that's not entirely true. I know he paid to have a contractor do a few things, but overall, this place was his baby, and it turned out great.

"Looks nice," I add. "I haven't been here since the foundation was poured. You should've let me and the guys come help."

"It was good to be distracted."

I turn around and face him again. "And now that it's finished?"

With a shrug, he walks past me and into the family room. There's an L-shaped leather couch pushed up against one wall. It separates the kitchen from the massive fireplace on the opposite side of the large space. Mack collapses onto it and props his feet up on a dark, mahogany coffee table in the center of the room. A stack of logs sits next to the unlit fireplace, which I'm sure will be roaring as soon as the first snowstorm hits. Blue and gray stone make up the hearth which covers half the wall, and a huge TV hangs above the mantle. I lift my chin toward the stonework. "Did you put it in yourself?"

"It was a good distraction," he repeats. Not with pride, but with a sad humility. Apparently, Mom wasn't completely off-base sending me out here to check on him.

I clear my throat and look around the space again, unsure what to say. "It turned out good."

"Thanks. So." He scratches his jaw, then lets out a sigh. "Mom sent you?"

"She's worried about you."

"Why?"

I shrug and sit down beside him on the opposite side of the couch. "Probably 'cause you're shit at talking."

"What's there to talk about?"

"I dunno? What's new?" I ask.

"Nothing."

I scoff. "You gotta at least give me something. How're Hazel and Miley? Have you heard from them lately?"

"No. Summer keeps filling their heads with a bunch of shit since the divorce. They still don't want to talk to me."

*Bitch*, I think to myself, but I bite my tongue.

"And it's not like I can force it," he adds. "They're in high school now. They can make their own decisions."

He's got a point, but it doesn't make the situation any easier.

"That sucks," I mutter, thumbing the edge of my cell.

"I text them every week," he continues. "Ask about their day. If anything's new. Sometimes I send memes or funny TikToks I think they'd like. Usually, they don't reply, but every once in a while, I get a response."

"That's something at least," I offer.

"Yeah, I guess."

What it is, is depressing, but it's not like I have my shit together, either, so I'm not exactly one to talk. Actually, I'm not usually one to talk––period––and Mack's the same way, which makes this conversation about as easy as having a root canal.

Mom owes me big-time for this.

I set my cell on the coffee table, giving up on the idea of receiving a response from Blake and rub my hands against my jeans.

"How's hockey going?" he asks. "I was at the arena the other day when you played the Razors. Work had me on standby in case there were any major injuries during the game."

"If you were at the Razors' game, then you saw us play like shit," I point out.

"Come on, you weren't that bad."

I quirk my brow, daring him to lie again.

Hiding his grin behind his hand, he clears his throat, and concedes, "All right. Has the rest of the season at least been better?"

I motion to the damage on my nose. "I got a stick to the face and was thrown from our last game."

"So that's why you look like shit." He laughs and lifts his chin. "Bet you got a few good punches in though."

I flex my sore hand in my lap. "Maybe."

"See? So, you're fine."

With a scoff, I mutter, "Gee. Thanks for your concern, big brother. Next time you're at a game, we should grab a drink after."

"Yeah, that'd be good. You get any offers yet?"

"A few potential contracts. One with the Rockies."

"No shit?" His face lights up. "That's great, man. Seriously. You've always wanted to play for them."

He's right. When I was little, it was all I could think about.

Then Colt's dad died, and I didn't get the call from any decent recruiters like I'd been hoping for after high school graduation. So, I decided to get more playing time at LAU instead of going to the ECHL in hopes of getting picked up by the NHL. From the look of things so far, it's worked, but I'm not going to get my hopes up yet. There are still too many variables. And like our father says, there's no ink on the contract yet.

I shrug one shoulder and kick my feet onto the coffee table. "We'll see how it shakes out."

"Anyone else interested in recruiting you?"

"There are a few more but nothing solid yet. Some rich guy pulled a bunch of investors together and decided to form a new expansion team. They keep trying to get Colt and me to sign with them. It's closer to home but less money, and..."

"And it's not the Rockies," Mack concludes.

"Yeah. It's not the Rockies, so we'll see."

"How's Colt doing?"

"He's good. He and Blake are both at LAU now."

"I saw."

"When?"

"At the Razors' game. I ran into her. How is it having her around again?"

"It's, uh..." I take off my hat and rub my thumb against the brim, avoiding Mack's gaze from the opposite side of the couch. "It's interesting."

His face sparks with understanding. "Ah, so that's what it was about."

"Huh?"

"You still have a thing for her?"

"Who said I had a thing for her?"

"Come on, man. You can admit it now. We've all known you've liked her for years."

"Doesn't matter." I clear my throat and sit up a little

straighter, setting my feet back on the ground while refusing to acknowledge it's so I can escape faster if need be. "I've already pissed her off beyond repair."

The bastard doesn't even bother to hide his amusement as he stretches out his legs and folds his arms. "What'd you do?"

"Slept with her."

He laughs a little harder. "No shit? Does Colt know?"

"Yeah," I mumble as my phone lights up on the coffee table. I reach for it, anxious to see if the notification is from Blake, but it's Missy, one of the newer puck bunnies. Shit. Someone must've given her my number. It was probably Burrows. Or maybe Logan.

*Assholes.*

"Is Colt pissed?" Mack asks, bringing me back to the present.

"He was." I turn off my cell and set it back on the table. "Now, he just wants me to fix things."

"So, he's cool with it?" he prods. "You and Blake?"

"We aren't together."

He pulls back, even more shocked. "Why?"

"Because we aren't."

"That isn't an answer. Who's holding it up? You or her?"

"No one," I lie.

He laughs a little harder. "Okay, let me ask you this. Do you want to be together?"

I shift on the cushion, feeling more uncomfortable on the new leather couch than I should be. Then again, I'm afraid it might not be the furniture leaving me itchy. "Dating isn't really my thing."

"Why not?"

"I dunno."

"You've never had a girlfriend," he points out, though I'm not sure who he's trying to remind.

"And you've only had one." I stare back at him, not giving

a shit I'm about to hit below the belt as my jaw tightens. "Look how that turned out."

"Summer didn't want me anymore," Mack mutters, more resigned than hurt. Like he's learned to accept the truth, no matter how painful it is to admit out loud. "And maybe it's my fault. Maybe it's because we'd been together since we were kids and she wanted a chance to be free of relationships in general. But just because I had a shitty experience doesn't mean every relationship is doomed to fail."

I hang my head and squeeze the bridge of my nose, letting the pressure ground me so I don't spew any more bullshit I'll regret. "I'm not saying it is. I'm just saying––"

"You don't want to be rejected by the one girl you've always wanted," he clarifies. "Which is understandable. I still can't figure out why Blake has worshipped your ass since kindergarten. She's way out of your league. "

I scoff, biting back my chuckle. But I don't deny it. We both know it's the truth.

"So, why doesn't she want it? A relationship?" Mack pushes.

"I dunno?" I answer. When we were in the locker room, I could still feel the pull. The attraction. Like magnets pulling us together, winding their way between us like it's always been. She wanted me to kiss her. I could tell. Until she flipped, pushing me away.

"Want my two cents?" he asks.

Exhausted, I look at him and rub my hand over my face. "If I say no, will you still give it?"

He snorts. "Probably."

With a wave of my hand, I say, "Floor's all yours."

He tosses a pillow from the couch against my chest. "I think she knows you don't do relationships, so she's thrown herself into the same category as every other girl you've been with."

"But she isn't like every other girl."

"I know it. And you know it. The question is...does she?"

Putting my hat back on, I set the pillow under my arms and rest them against it, fighting every instinct inside of me to admit the truth out loud as I stare at the fireplace in front of us. "I dunno."

"Well, I think it's time you figure it out."

"And if I fuck it up again?" I ask.

He hesitates, resting his elbows on his knees and rubbing his hands together as if he's considering my question. A dry laugh escapes him. "Look at it this way. At least you didn't get your girlfriend pregnant in high school, then offer to marry her, settling for a job instead of your dream career and letting her take half your winnings from the lottery, leaving you high and dry."

"Way to set the bar real high, Mack," I return.

"At least the mess was good for something."

He turns on a football game, and we shoot the shit for a couple more hours when my phone lights up with another message. This time, it's from Blake.

**Blake: If I say no, will you show up anyway?**

I smirk and type my response.

**Me: I think we both know the answer to that.**

**Blake: Aaaand I guess I'll see you tonight.**

**Me: Looking forward to it.**

## 25

## BLAKELY

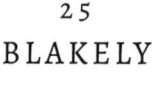

"Welp," I say, lifting my hands from my sides. The girls insisted on giving me a once-over before I walk out of the house. They're all lounging in the family room, watching the bachelorette passing out roses on the TV screen. When they see me, Mia mutes the show and checks me out.

"*That's* what you're wearing?" she asks with a frown.

I look down at my hoodie and jeans. "Uh, yes?"

"On a date?" Kate lifts her brows as if I'm a crazy person.

I shove my hands into the pouch of my red LAU sweatshirt. "It isn't a date."

"But you guys slept together," Ash reminds me.

"And?" I counter.

"And tonight, he's picking you up and taking you to a Taylor House party as his plus-one," she continues. "Kind of the definition of a date."

"It isn't a date," I argue. "And I'm not his plus-one. He's just…driving me so there won't be too many cars parked in front of his house."

Ash snorts. "And the fact you could've caught a ride with Mia and me?"

With a huff, I repeat, "It isn't a date," though I'm not entirely sure who I'm trying to convince anymore. It feels like a date, which is why I decided to wear the biggest, baggiest hoodie in my closet. When I caught a glimpse of my reflection earlier, I almost died laughing. The thing practically drowns me and almost reaches my knees. It belonged to Colt, but I stole it from him a few months ago, and it's perfect for tonight. Totally worth it.

"Okay, it isn't a date," Kate concedes, sharing a quick glance with Mia. "But let me ask you this. Do you like him?"

"I'm not allowed to like him."

"Why not?"

"Because he doesn't look at me like that despite us having sex"––Kate scoffs, but I ignore her––"*and* because Coach Sanderson put the kabosh on romantic relationships thanks to the first game of the season and how shitty the team played. Therefore, I'm not allowed to like him. It's as simple as that."

"One"––Mia raises her pointer finger––"he most definitely *does* look at you like that. We've all seen it firsthand, so don't even bother denying it. And two"––she adds her middle finger into the air––"Sanderson doesn't have eyes everywhere, so technically…"

Her voice trails off, and Ash pipes up, "Ooo, a forbidden romance. Colt and I did that once. It's hot." She winks at me. "This one time, we were at SeaBird––"

Nose wrinkling, I lift my hand and say, "Ew, stop. Colt's my brother, remember?"

Mia laughs and throws a kernel of popcorn at Ash and asks, "Do you trust us?"

"No?" I answer with a laugh.

"Oh, come on," Ash begs.

Mia stands up from the couch, loops her arm through mine, and drags me back to my bedroom without giving me a chance to argue anymore.

When I follow her without protest, she calls over her shoulder, "See, ladies? The trick is to *not* give her a choice. Come on. Let's get to work."

"Get to work on what?" I ask as we reach my bedroom. I have a feeling I know where this is going, and after the last makeover debacle, I'm a little hesitant. Especially if I wanna keep up the whole *just friends* parameters I'd originally set with Theo.

And I should.

Heaven knows I should.

Letting me go, Mia digs around in my closet like it's the most natural thing to do but doesn't bother answering me. I should probably be used to her behavior by now. All of them share clothes, makeup, and food like it's going out of style.

Which is the opposite of how I grew up.

Boys are so different from girls, it's not even funny. When you were raised with a bunch of older brothers, the lack of barriers between female roommates feels comical sometimes. It's like I've entered an alternate universe or something.

Kate sits next to me on the edge of my bed, probably to keep me from shoving them all out of my room, while Ash opens my dresser and pulls out a black, lacy bra, tossing it onto my lap. Meanwhile, Mia is still elbow-deep in my closet, searching for clothing options. Seriously. You'd think they'd orchestrated this whole thing.

"Put it on," Ash orders pointing to the bra with a look stern enough to make Professor McGonagall proud.

"But we're just friends," I remind her as I lift the bra into the air and examine it further. Don't get me wrong. My baby boobs look awesome in this bad boy, but that's beside the point, especially if I don't *want* Theo to notice my baby boobs.

*Right?*

"Just because you're lying to yourself by saying you're only friends with Theo doesn't mean it won't be fun to make him drool over you for the night," Mia returns without bothering to look at me. She slides the hangers in my closet from left to right as she checks out what she's working with. Clearly disappointed with her options, she says, "Ash, go see what you can find in our closets. All this girl owns are hoodies and workout clothes." As Ash scurries off, Mia turns back to my closet and continues rifling through everything.

"Besides, Blake. You like him. I know you like him. Ash and Kate know you like him. And even if you didn't--which we've already concluded you do--there's nothing wrong with wanting to be appreciated from afar."

"Especially with this hair," Kate admits, scrunching my messy curls in her hand. I'd left it down, letting it hang around my shoulders while refusing to acknowledge it's because I know how much Theo likes it this way.

"Do you have any idea how jealous I am of this?" she adds, playing with my messy strands.

"Says the girl with this gorgeous dark hair." I pick at the luscious locks flowing down her back like a damn waterfall to prove my point. "It's so thick and shiny it practically glows."

"It's also straight as a board," she finishes. "It doesn't even hold curls when it's caked in gel and hair spray."

"Still beautiful, though. I bet Wes likes it," I tease.

Her shoulders deflate as Ash returns to my bedroom with some clothes in her arms. She stops short, sensing the change in Kate. "Oh, no. What'd I miss?"

"Blake brought up Wes, and Kate got quiet," Mia explains.

The girl's more blunt than a Clint Eastwood cigar. She walks to Ash and filters through the clothing options, lifting a shimmery black top and a pair of low-rise jeans into the air. Satisfied, Mia hands them to me and turns her attention on Kate like she's Mia's next order of business. Poor girl.

"So, my dear Kate," she says. "What's up with you and Wes? And why haven't we heard about any of it before now?"

Tucking a few strands of dark hair behind her ear, Kate mutters, "Nothing's going on with us."

"Baloney. You've been out past 10:30 pm two times this week, and for you, that's saying something, my friend."

Kate rolls her eyes. "Okay. I like him. I don't know if he's the one or anything, but yes. I like him."

"And it's a problem because…?" I ask as I slip off Colt's oversized hoodie.

"Because of my…condition," she mutters, picking at a tiny piece of lint on her jeans like it's the most interesting thing in the world.

"What about it?" I prod.

"I haven't told him yet."

"Kate," Mia and Ash say in unison.

"I know, okay?" She flicks the lint onto the carpet. "I know I need to tell him."

"We've been over this," Mia scolds. "It isn't fair to keep him in the dark."

"Yeah, but it isn't fair to have my nose rubbed in the fact that as soon as he sees me as someone broken, he'll break it off, and I'll be all alone again."

Well, damn.

When she puts it that way…

Mia's attention shifts to Ash as I finish getting dressed, then sit back down on the bed and throw my arm around Kate's shoulders. I hate how insecure she feels about her epilepsy. I hate how it makes her feel different. Unwanted. Like she's a burden when she's the opposite. She's an asset, and anyone would be lucky to claim her. To have her in their corner. I know I am. But I haven't walked in her shoes. I haven't experienced the things she's experienced. And if she's too freaked out to tell him, she probably has a good reason. But it doesn't mean she should keep sticking her head in the sand. It can't be healthy for anyone, let alone Kate and Wes. It's a mess.

Squeezing her knee, I announce, "I have an idea. Let's mark our calendars for the night after you tell him. It can be tomorrow. It can be a week from now. It can be whenever you're ready. But you're going to tell him, and then you're going to come home, and you're going to tell us how it went. We'll be ready to congratulate you or mourn with you depending on how the night goes. Regardless, you won't be alone."

Ash plops down on Kate's opposite side. "Yeah. I'll make Colt buy some Ben & Jerry's."

"And I'll invest in a dozen eggs in case we need to throw them at Wes's house," Mia finishes.

I laugh and squeeze Kate's knee again. "See? It'll be perfect."

"Yeah." She sighs, looking less than convinced as she gnaws on her bottom lip. "Perfect."

"Now, time for your makeup," Mia announces. She grabs my hand and drags me toward the bathroom, the other girls trailing behind. "Let's see how Theo likes smokey eyes."

26

## THEO

**M**y blood rushes south as soon as she opens the front door.

*Fuck me.*

If Blakely wanted to mess with my head tonight, she's successful.

I clear my throat and tuck my hands into my back pockets to keep from pulling her against me and kissing the shit out of her when I promised myself I'd take things slow.

I bet she still tastes like cinnamon.

When she catches me checking her out, she gives me a knowing smirk. "You sure that's how friends should look at each other, Teddy Bear?"

"You sure that's how friends should dress around each other, Baby Thorne?" I counter.

Batting her long lashes, she quips, "Maybe I want you to play wingman tonight."

"And maybe you want me to snap and shove you up against the nearest wall like the last time you were all dolled up."

Her lips curve up even further. "Would you do that to Colt? Ya know, since we're just friends and all."

My gaze slides down her body again. "If he looked like you, I might."

With a light laugh, she steps onto the porch, closing the front door behind her. Her perfume hits my nostrils as she turns around to lock it. My mouth waters at the familiar scent and the soft brush of her hair against my chin. I step back and give her some space even though it kills me. I can barely control myself around her on a good day. But when she looks like this? I'm fucking doomed.

Once her keys are back in her purse, she turns around and catches me staring. Again.

Rolling her eyes, she explains, "Mia and Ash felt like using me as their own personal Barbie doll tonight." She waves her hand up and down her body to showcase her outfit. "Which is why I look like...*this*."

"You look beautiful, Blake."

A light blush spreads across her freckled cheeks, and she pushes her red hair over one shoulder. "Friends don't tell their friends how beautiful they look."

"Sure they do," I argue, guiding her to my car and opening the passenger door.

Her eyebrow arches as she gives me a look telling me she thinks I'm full of shit, while the dark makeup around her eyes makes the green color almost hypnotic.

Fucking beautiful.

"Oh, so Colt likes to compliment you on your outfit choices when you go out?" she challenges.

"Only if I'm wearing his favorite hat," I quip.

With a smirk, she twists in the passenger seat and grabs something from the back. A sliver of skin peeks from beneath her sparkly black top, showcasing her lower back and the tiny set of dimples playing peekaboo above her dark jeans. I grip the edge of the door to keep from reaching for her, well aware of how close I am to snapping when the night has only begun.

Something is in her hand as she turns back around and faces me. I'm still standing at the open passenger door, looking like a dumbass as she reveals my favorite baseball hat I'd tossed into the back of the car after practice yesterday.

"You mean like this one?" She puts it on and bats her lashes at me. "What do you think?"

I think she looks like a wet dream. Like she cherry-picked every single thing I love about her and created the perfect woman with one caveat. She's untouchable.

For now, anyway.

I slap the bill of the cap, and she laughs again, readjusting it, not giving a shit what it does to her recently curled hair. Or at least I assume she curled it. Her waves are less messy than usual. More tame. I'm not sure which look I prefer. She's beautiful either way.

But when she's wearing my favorite baseball hat?

Fuck me.

If the girl's trying to give me blue balls, it's working.

"Theo?" she prods.

Realizing I've been caught staring like a creep, I shake my head and close the passenger door, rounding the front of the car and climbing behind the wheel.

As the car rumbles to life, I can't help but glance at her again. The silky smooth skin along her arms and stomach. The freckles playing peekaboo on her shoulders, cheeks, and the bridge of her nose. Even with nothing but the glow from the dashboard, she's fucking perfect.

"Are we gonna go? Or...?" she prods.

I swear I'm losing my fucking mind.

Tonight isn't about lust. Or at least, it isn't supposed to be. It isn't about claiming her. Not yet, anyway. It's about making amends. It's about fixing what I'd broken by sleeping with her in the first place. It's about earning another chance and showing her she isn't like other girls. And she isn't *just* Colt's little sister. Not to me.

But if that's the case, why is the thought of getting her naked all I can think about? I want to drive somewhere quiet, lay the seats down, and teach her how to ride my cock while straddling me as I suck her tits into my mouth. I want to scream, "She's mine," from the rooftops without giving a shit about Coach's rule in regards to dating her. Without giving a shit about anything but the next time I can have this girl naked and under me. The next time I can make her smile or hear her laugh. The next time I can hold her hand or see her mouth, *vacuum beach* while wearing my hat just to get under my skin.

*But it's not why I'm here*, I remind myself.

I clear my throat and shove the car into reverse, backing down the driveway and pulling onto the street.

"So, uh, favorite song?" I ask. My knuckles are tight around the steering wheel as I fight for a distraction, for a normal conversation, though I refuse to look at her. I'm not sure I can.

"What?" she returns.

"I wanna know your favorite song."

"Oh." She pauses. "Anything by Broken Vows or Group Project. You?"

I glance her way. "Group Project?"

With a gasp, she says, "Tell me you've heard of Group Project."

I shake my head. She raises her hand, palm facing up. "Where's your phone?"

"My phone?"

"So I can play a song on Spotify, Teddy." Impatient, she reaches into my jeans' front pocket and pulls it out, barely grazing my dick––that's now standing at full attention–– with her dainty little fingers.

*Yup. She's trying to kill me.*

Once a song is playing through the speakers, I try not to stare as she sings along. The girl's terrible and can't sing for shit, but the confidence emanating from her tiny frame as she dances in my passenger seat is the sexiest––and most awkward––thing I've ever seen.

As the song ends, she turns down the volume and asks, "So? What'd you think?"

"I think it's adorable you know all the lyrics."

"Damn straight, I do. Now, show me a song where you know all the lyrics."

I smirk as she hands me my phone, my choice already locked and loaded. When the introduction to "We Didn't Start the Fire" by Billy Joel plays through the speakers, she laughs and joins in, spouting off the lyrics word-for-word.

Macklin used to drive Colt, Logan, Blake, and me to school when we were kids. He always had a thing for old music. Most of it would make us cringe, but there were a few songs we couldn't get enough of. This was one of them. I'm not sure what it was about being able to keep up with the legend himself, but we used to love blasting this song and calling out the other person when they got the lyrics wrong.

My grin widens as I catch Blake jamming out to the chorus, and when the song ends a little while later, she turns down the volume, adjusts my baseball hat on her head, and asks, "So how's Mack doing? I ran into him at one of your games, but he was kind of stand-offish. Last I heard he was married––"

"Divorced, actually."

She grimaces. "Aaaand that explains so much. *Ouch.* They were together forever. What happened?"

"I dunno. I guess even people who get together in middle school can change over the years."

"Yeah, but…it's rough. How are Hazel and Miley?"

"They're all right, I guess. It's been almost two years since the fallout, so I think they're getting used to it." I tap my thumb against the steering wheel and add, "Hazel's graduating from high school this year."

"No freaking way."

"Yeah."

"Dude. Time flies," she says. "I remember when you became an uncle, ya know."

"You do?"

"Yeah. We all thought it was weird because our uncles were all old, but you were what, six?" She motions with her hands like her head is exploding. "Crazy."

"I guess so," I reply. "I never knew anything different. Did you know Mia's like Hazel? Her aunt's only six years older than her too. Or…something around there, anyway."

"Yeah, her aunt's dating Fender from Broken Vows, right?"

I nod. "Yeah. I actually met him a little while back. Mia introduced us at SeaBird before Ash and Colt started dating."

"Ah, that's fun. I've heard he's a pretty good guy. Did you know he set up a charity recently for kids from broken homes and stuff?"

"No shit?" I ask.

She nods. "Yeah. It's actually really cool. If I had more time, I'd volunteer, but with the internship and school, it's been kind of crazy."

"I get it," I reply, checking my blind spot and merging into the left lane. "But it sucks. I think you'd be good at it. Hanging out with kids and shit."

Her laugh makes me smile. "Mia said the same thing.

Maybe in a few years. We'll see. I'll have to think of someone to set Mack up with."

I snort. "Yeah, I'm sure he'd love it."

"What? He isn't a fan of blind dates?" she questions.

"Do you know anyone who *is* a fan of blind dates?"

She shrugs. "I dunno, maybe?"

"Name one," I challenge, barely withholding my laugh.

With another shrug, she says, "I've been on a couple that were fun."

A bark of laughter slips out of me as I flick my blinker on again and turn onto my street. "I call bullshit."

"What? It's the truth!"

"Who set you up on a blind date?"

"I don't know? My mom once?"

"And? How'd it go?"

"He was nice."

I scoff. "Nice. Sure."

Reaching over the center console, she smacks my shoulder. "What? He was!"

"Did you go on a second date?" I challenge.

Her straight white teeth dig into her bottom lip as she pulls the brim of my hat a little lower to hide herself and looks out the window. "Maybe?"

"Bullshit," I repeat. "Did your mom meet him at church? I bet she did, huh?"

"Theee-ooo," she groans, smacking my shoulder. "Okay. You win. Enough with the interrogation."

"I'm just sayin'," I argue. "No one likes a blind date."

"Fine. We won't set up Mack on a blind date with anyone. Happy now?"

"Maybe."

Crossing her arms, she looks out the window and mutters, "Party pooper."

As I pull up to my house, trepidation pools in my stomach. Cars are already littered across the driveway, preventing me from pulling into the garage, so I shove my car into park a hundred feet down the street. I rest my forearm on the steering wheel and stare up at the house, unable to move. It's dark out, but the lights are on inside, casting a glow along the front lawn. The music is thumping, ringing loud and clear through the windshield, and there are people scattered around the front, talking and laughing and kissing.

I don't move. I don't climb out. I just stare. At the life I used to crave. The highs I used to chase. The women. The alcohol. It looks so empty from the outside.

"There a problem?" Blake asks.

"Speaking of party poopers," I mutter, tearing my attention from the house to Blake. "You sure you don't want to get out of here?"

She laughs and motions to the party in front of us. "We haven't even gotten *into* here yet."

I scratch my temple but stay put behind the wheel.

With a smile, she reaches for my knee and squeezes playfully. "Come on, Teddy Bear. Don't tell me you hate your own parties."

I look down at her hand on my thigh. The way her long fingers barely reach from one end to the other. The way her nails are free of polish and her fingers free of jewelry. She's so effortlessly beautiful. So quietly gorgeous. It's the little things. The subtlety. The way she stands out because of it, even though she has no idea.

"Dude. You okay?" she asks.

I clear my throat and look at her, meeting her gaze. "I'm good."

"You sure?"

I nod. "Yeah."

"Should we go inside?"

"Sure."

She reaches for my favorite hat still on her head, ready to take it off, but I tug at her wrist and stop her. "Leave it on. You look good with it."

*Incredible, actually.*

The fire in her eyes sparks, like she wants to fight me on it, but she decides against it, letting her hand rest in her lap. "Only 'cause I'm feeling generous." She climbs out of the passenger seat, and I follow behind her, locking the car once the doors are closed.

The bass is thumping, practically shaking the windows as we walk up the driveway. Tukani is on the front porch with Depp. When they see us, their eyes heat with interest and roll over an oblivious Blake.

With a glare in their direction, I press my hand to Blake's back and lead her up the steps to the front door.

"Hey, Baby Thorne!" Tukani calls.

"Hey, Tsunami!" she returns.

The Tongan grins and pulls her into a hug, winking at me over her shoulder when he catches my scowl.

Chuckling, Depp steals Blake from Tukani and squeezes her against his side. The gesture is more friendly than annoying as if he doesn't feel like having his ass kicked tonight. He lets her go and takes a swig of his beer.

"What're you doing here?" he asks her.

"Just stealing some free booze. You?"

Lifting the beer bottle in a cheers motion, he answers, "Same."

"Ah, and here I'd been hoping for another game of Strip Pong," Tukani chimes in.

"Since you put up such a good fight the first time," Blakely jokes.

A rumble of laughter echoes from Tukani as Depp adds, "Bet Burrows would love to have another stab at—"

"Aaaand we're going inside," I interrupt, pressing my hand

225

to Blake's back again. It takes everything inside of me to keep from tossing her over my shoulder and racing back to my car, but I control myself. For now, anyway.

"See you later, guys!" Blake calls over her shoulder and peeks up at me as we step inside the house. "Is there a problem, Teddy?"

"No problem."

"You sure?"

"What makes you think I have a problem?"

"You're being particularly pushy tonight."

"I'm always pushy," I remind her.

She hesitates, considering my comment, then letting out a soft laugh. "Good point. We should––"

"Theo!" a high-pitched voice interrupts, hitting a frequency sounding almost like nails on a chalkboard, only worse.

My expression falls as I catch the culprit striding toward us on stilettos. Missy Beckman. One of the bunnies. She rises onto her tiptoes and kisses my cheek, the sour scent of alcohol on her breath. "Why haven't you called me lately, Theo? I've missed you."

"And on that note," Blake interjects. "I'm going to grab a drink." She slips through the crowd, heading toward the kitchen without a backward glance. It's like the first night she came to the Taylor House all over again.

*Thanks a lot, Missy.*

## 27

## BLAKELY

I pour the Crush and vodka over ice into the red plastic cup, hating the jealousy as it crashes through my system like a massive wave, especially when it's so damn unwarranted.

What? He isn't allowed to say hi to the opposite sex anymore?

*Come on, Blake. Take a chill pill.*

I go easy on the vodka, adding another splash of Crush to balance out my drink and head outside, dodging around a couple going at it like rabbits in the kitchen. Suddenly, the party ambiance feels overwhelming, and the idea of some fresh air sounds like heaven. I leave a wide berth between me and the Beer Pong tournament on the back patio. Burrows is in his element beating Austin, but I ignore the look he gives me and keep walking, grateful for my insistence on wearing sneakers instead of the heels Mia suggested when dressing me up like a Barbie doll tonight. At least my shoes won't get caught in the grass.

I snort at the idea of me in heels and bring the cup to my lips, taking a small sip. Ash and Colt are talking near one of the large maple trees in the side of the yard, and I stop short when I see them. She looks sad, wiping at her cheeks as Colt pulls her into a hug. She lets him and rests her head against his chest.

Yikes.

*What's going on?*

I'm most definitely intruding, though I don't want to turn around and walk inside, either. But sticking around doesn't exactly sound like my cup of tea at the moment. Tiptoeing a few paces back, a stick cracks beneath my shoe, and I freeze.

*Dammit.*

As if they can feel my stare, Colt lets Ash go and walks toward me, a frown marring his features.

"Hey, big brother." I give him a tentative smile. "Everything okay? I swear I wasn't snooping, but––"

"Keep an eye on her. It's getting cold. I'm gonna get a blanket." He heads toward the house without another word, and I rock back on my heels, turning to Ash.

With a pathetic smile, she gives me a wave from beneath the massive maple tree.

I step closer, unsure what to say. Whatever I just walked in on? It looks messy. And I already have enough on my plate.

"Hey," I offer weakly.

"Hey." She sniffs and wipes under her nose with the back of her hand. "Where's Theo?"

"He's...around," I mutter, taking another sip of my drink.

Ash nods but doesn't say anything else, too distracted by whatever I've walked in on to ask me for details.

Clearly, something's on her mind. I've never been good at girl talk, but my instincts are telling me it's exactly what she needs.

*Where the hell's Mia when I need her?*

I glance at the house and scan the patio, but she isn't anywhere in sight.

*Here goes nothing.*

"Everything okay?" I ask carefully.

Rubbing her hands up and down her bare arms, Ash mutters, "I think so?"

"You think?"

She rolls her watery eyes and folds her arms, looking oh, so small and oh, so fragile. "I love your brother, Blake."

"Well, duh," I tease. "He kind of loves you too."

"I know." She licks her lips and lets out a sigh. "But it's hard to know if it's enough. If *I'm* enough."

My lips pull into a frown. The idea of Ash and Colt not working out feels like a sucker punch to the chest. "Ash, what are you saying?"

She shakes her head. "We're fine. It's just...he's getting all these offers, and I'm seeing how overwhelming it can be to date a famous person. Not that he's crazy famous yet, but the writing's on the wall, ya know? He's the real deal. And the future ahead of him? It's insane. And awesome. And...kind of terrifying." She sniffles and lets out a heavy breath. "He invited me to go with him. To wherever he wants to go, since almost every team in the NHL is chomping at the bit to get him to sign with them, but..."

"But what?" I ask.

"I don't know. Is it too soon? We haven't even been dating for a year. But the idea of a long-distance relationship? Of him leaving without me?" She bites her bottom lip, fresh tears flooding her watery eyes. "It feels terrible, Blake. Unimaginable. It feels like I'm ripping off a limb or something, which I know is ridiculous, but I can't help it."

My attention shifts to the house, an image of Theo coming to mind as her words wash over me. When he left for college, I was a mess. And that was before we kissed. Before we slept together. Before I felt an ounce of the connection we've shared since transferring to LAU. The idea of being in a full-blown relationship with the bastard, of being in love with him and knowing he loves me while also knowing there's potentially an expiration date on said relationship? Yeah. It would suck big-time. I can only imagine what Ashlyn's going through. How she's feeling. How she's processing everything.

"He doesn't want to leave you, though," I remind her, hoping the positive words will be enough to shake her out of the sad little bubble she's found herself in.

"I know," she clarifies. "He's amazing like that."

"He is," I agree. Colt's head over heels for her. He has been since they first met.

"But these are big decisions, Blake," she whispers. "Massive ones. Decisions that can and will affect the rest of our lives. It's...scary, isn't it?" Pushing her hair away from her face, she shakes her head again. "I mean, I know it's quick. And it is. But I love him. Seriously, Blake. I love the shit of your brother."

"I know you do."

"I do," she repeats. "I really do. It's just...overwhelming. And I hate how I've been acting like a crazy person lately."

"It's a tough decision. Anyone would act crazy if they were in your shoes." I offer my drink to her and point out, "But it does sound like you need a drink."

"Ain't it the truth." She takes a sip and hands it back to me.

I squeeze her hand. "It's okay to be overwhelmed. But don't let it ruin what you and Colt have. You two are perfect for each other, Ash. Like seriously. Nauseatingly perfect."

She laughs and wipes beneath her eyes. "You're right. I'm being––"

"Cautious," I finish for her. "Which makes sense, considering your past with Logan. Putting all your eggs in one basket burned you the first time. Or so I've been told," I add with a smile.

She glances at the house, searching for my brother and pushing her blonde hair over her shoulder while kicking the small patch of dirt beneath our feet. "Colt isn't anything like Logan. He's never been anything like Logan."

"You're right. He isn't," I agree. "Which means if you decide to stay back, and you guys do the long-distance thing for a little while until you're ready to move across the country, he'll be okay with it. He'll wait until you *are* ready. I know it."

"You think?" she whispers, looking over at me with those big doe eyes, the moisture clinging to her lashes.

"Yup. And if he even thinks about breaking your heart, I'll neuter him for you. Future nieces and nephews be damned."

She laughs and wipes at her tearstained cheeks as footsteps sound from behind us.

Colt returns with a thick comforter and wraps it around Ash until she's basically a burrito. With a soft kiss to her forehead, he turns to me and says, "Thanks for keeping her company."

"Always," I answer, adding, "But treat her right, okay?"

"Don't worry, Blake." Colt smiles down at his girlfriend. "Ash is stuck with me."

Squeezing her eyes shut, she snuggles into his chest but doesn't say a word.

Feeling like I've been excused, I saunter off, letting the chilly air ground me as I lift my head toward the sky in search of quiet. Stars twinkle in the distance, the dark blues and almost black atmosphere reminding me of how small and insignificant my problems really are. I lay back on the ground and pull my jacket a little tighter around me, balancing my cup on the grass beside my hip.

KELSIE RAE

The music is still blaring from the Taylor House, but it's quieter out here. More peaceful. Less...chaotic. Crickets are singing their nightly lullaby among the trees. The cadence is soothing. Hypnotic. Addictive. And I let it roll over me, easing the jealousy in my chest while hoping it'll be enough to quiet the what-ifs filtering through my mind.

Is Theo sleeping with her right now?

Did he take her to his room instead of using the spare one in the basement? Did he worship her the way he worshipped me?

My phone buzzes in my purse, but I ignore it, searching for the Big Dipper constellation hidden in the sky instead.

I don't know how long I stay out here soaking up the comfortable ambiance before footsteps rustle in the grass behind me. And even though I don't need to look to see who it is, I do. Because I'm a sucker for the bastard.

Twenty bucks says it's Theo.

## 28

## BLAKELY

Against my better judgment, I roll onto my side and search for the culprit in the darkness. The silhouette moves closer, but the darkness around us hides the majority of its features. Not that I need them. I could pick Theo out in a lineup while blindfolded.

"You," I accuse, giving him my back and pushing myself to a sitting position.

"You," he returns, the same accusing note to his voice.

"You should get back to the party."

"I don't want to be at the party."

"Then why do you throw them?" I counter.

He shrugs and plops down beside me, resting his arms on his bent knees. "Habit, I guess."

"Is that why you sleep with puck bunnies too?"

He stays quiet for a beat, then drops his head back to look at the sky. "Slept. Not sleep."

From the corner of my eye, I glance at him and twist back to the stars.

"Past tense, Blake," he clarifies when I've been silent for too long. "Past tense."

I dig my teeth into the inside of my cheek, annoyed with myself more than I am with Theo. Because I shouldn't be annoyed. I shouldn't care who he sleeps with or what he does in his spare time.

But that's the thing.

I *do* care. I cared in high school. I cared while he was away at college. I cared before he touched me for the first time. And I sure as hell care now.

Sensing my frustration, Theo tears his attention from the sky and looks at me. Then, he stands up and slaps the bill of the baseball hat I'd stolen from the back of his car.

I jerk in surprise and glare up at him. "What was that for?"

"Let's play Horse." He motions to the basketball court on his neighbor's property.

It's a full-size court, complete with outdoor lighting, fresh paint on the asphalt, and a small bin with a lid set back behind the hoop. It looks super nice, and since there aren't any of our college friends hanging out on the premises, I assume it's because the place is off-limits.

"Are we *allowed* to play Horse?" I ask.

He offers his hand and challenges, "Since when has obeying the rules held you back?"

I roll my eyes but take his hand and let him help me up, ignoring the heat seeping into my palm and causing goosebumps to race up my arm. I shouldn't be surprised. I've always had this reaction with him, and after our little rendezvous in his spare bedroom, it's only gotten worse.

Theo guides me to the basketball court and flips a switch on an outlet box beside the hoop. Outdoor lighting illuminates the painted asphalt. There's a small bin on the outside perimeter of the court, and Theo opens it, tossing a basketball to me. I catch it on reflex, glancing at the darkened house on top of the sloped hill.

"Are you sure we won't get in trouble?" I ask.

"They aren't home. But even if they were, Mrs. Norman loves me and wouldn't care."

"You're positive?" I reiterate.

He laughs and lifts his hands, gesturing for me to pass him the ball. "Yeah, Blake. I'm positive."

The ball bounces once between us as I toss it to Theo. We take turns shooting it around the key. I'm a little rusty, but it doesn't take long to find my rhythm, and soon, we're hitting shots left and right.

After ten minutes or so, the tension from earlier starts to dissipate, and I'm reminded of how easy it is to be with Theo. How comfortable the silence is. How playful the banter can be. Well, at least when one of his previous conquests doesn't interrupt.

It's addictive.

"Man, I haven't played basketball in forever," I say.

"You've still got it," he notes, watching me dribble the ball, pull up, and take a shot.

It swishes through the net with a satisfying whoosh.

He rebounds it before doing a layup, his arms flexing as he tosses the ball into the basket.

"You're not too shabby yourself," I reply. "Tell me. How does it feel to be good at everything you do?"

"I'm not good at everything I do," he argues.

"Uh-huh. Sure. How many offers have you gotten for the NHL so far?"

"Before Colt came back to play again? Zero."

"And after?" I prod, well-aware of how great his stats looked last season, let alone how good they're looking with Colt back on the ice. Those two are like bread and butter together. Sure, before college, things took a bad turn when my dad died. His death didn't only throw off Colt, causing him to spiral and quit the sport altogether. It also messed with Theo and everyone else on the team. After all, not only had Theo lost his coach, he'd lost his best friend too. The combination sent Theo's stats into a nosedive right before the NHL's draft.

And he wasn't chosen.

Even from a distance, it killed me to watch him lose all he'd been working for. So he opted to go the NCAA route, instead. Now, things are back on track, and his dreams are actually reachable. The guy should be freaking out, not hiding behind his insecurities. To be honest, even with his history, I didn't know he had insecurities. The guy's a force to be reckoned with on *and* off the ice. He's always been this way.

The bastard shoots me a look that makes my insides squirm but doesn't answer my question, chasing after the basketball while choosing to ignore me.

"Oh, is someone being humble?" I tease. "It's okay to admit you're the cat's pajamas, Teddy Bear. I just ran into Ash who confirmed Colt's already received plenty of offers. I'm sure you have too."

He shoots the ball from the side of the court but stays quiet.

"Honestly, it's probably a good thing you're anti-relationship," I add. "Apparently, Colt and Ash have been trying to figure out how to do the long-distance thing next year or if they're ready to jump in with both feet and move in together. It's put Ash through the wringer. Has he talked to you about it at all?"

He moves to shoot the ball but stops short and looks at me, joking, "Did Ash send you to get information from me?" There's a tightness in his expression making me pause.

"No?" I step closer and strip the ball from his grasp, demanding his full attention. "Is there any information I *need* to get from you? 'Cause so help me, if Colt ruins his relationship with Ash—"

"Colt would do anything for Ash," he interjects, "including taking a smaller contract to be with her if she wasn't interested in moving far away. She has nothing to worry about."

He steals the ball from me and takes a shot. Nothing but net.

I sigh, surprised by the tension that has worked its way into my shoulders. I force myself to relax. "I kind of told her the same thing. Doesn't make it easy for Colt, though. Especially when he's seeing all those salary and bonus numbers. It's a lot to give up to be close to the woman he loves."

"I guess so."

"Is it why you keep women at a distance? So you won't have to leave anyone behind when you go and become a big, famous hockey player?" I ask as he pulls up for another shot.

The ball arches through the air and bounces off the backboard, missing the basket by a millimeter.

He doesn't chase after it. Instead, he turns to me and frowns. "Who says I won't have to leave anyone behind?"

I jog toward the ball and rest it against my hip, more invested in our conversation than the game, but I don't show it. This feels too personal. Too intimate somehow. Like we aren't discussing hypotheticals. We're discussing...more.

"Don't get me wrong. I know you're close with your parents and Macklin, but you guys still have your own lives, and they've known what your future was likely going to be after graduation since you were what? Twelve? With Ash, it's a little different. She didn't plan on falling for a guy who could up and move or be traded at any second. It's a little tougher to wrap your head around, ya know?"

"I guess so," he repeats. "How would you feel? Falling for a professional athlete?"

I shoot the ball, and it drops into the hoop with a swish. "You mean knowing I was always going to come second to his career?" I cut him off before he has a chance to answer. "Depends on how he handles it."

"Like what?" Theo asks.

"Like…does he talk to me before making decisions? Is he open and honest? Does he look at opportunities like they're his future or *our* future? That kind of thing. Not that it matters," I rush out, hoping he isn't getting the wrong idea or thinking I'm still fawning over the bastard. I force a smile and tear my attention from him and back to the basketball hoop.

"Why doesn't it matter?" he pushes.

"Because I'm not dating an imaginary professional hockey player?" I laugh but avoid his gaze. "Besides, Colt's most likely moving away, and my brothers are already halfway across the country. I'm not gonna leave my mom. She's already alone enough of the time anyway. Instead, I'm going to focus on non-relationship things. Like school. My internship. My friends. Those kinds of things."

The silence that follows is heavier somehow. More charged. Less easy. He passes me the ball, and I take another shot, but it doesn't even reach the hoop. I'm distracted. Unsure.

As he rebounds the ball for me, he asks, "So, care to make it interesting?"

My attention flicks from the basket and back to Theo, grateful for the distraction. His nose is still a little swollen from his fight, and the bruise on his forehead isn't as dark as it used to be, but even now, the memory causes my heart to twinge, despite my gratitude for the subject change. "Depends. What do you have in mind?"

"A bet."

My mouth twitches. "You sure it's a good idea?"

"I mean, unless you're too chicken," he challenges.

I grin. "I think we both know I never back down from a friendly game or competition. What are the stipulations?"

"First,"--he passes me the ball and steps closer--"you can't back out if I win."

"I would never--"

"Promise me."

With less than a foot between us, I take in the little laugh lines framing his eyes and the way the outdoor lighting casts shadows on his face while highlighting his strong jaw and sexy smirk. I swear, the guy's too attractive for his own good. Cocky. Confident. Playful. It's like he's baiting me. Like he's already playing a game, though I haven't quite figured out the rules yet. And damn him, he knows me too well. He knows I'm curious. He knows I'm never one to back down from a challenge. He knows he has me right where he wants me.

"Okay, I'll bite." I cross my arms, grateful for the basketball keeping Theo from coming too close. "What do you want if you win?"

"If I win, I get to kiss you."

# BLAKELY

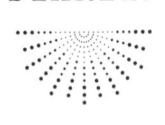

I feel like my heart is about two seconds from pounding out of my ribcage it's beating so hard. But after our conversation about relationships and hockey and hypothetical futures, it's a lot. The idea of kissing Theo. Of letting him kiss me. Especially when it's under the guise of a freaking bet.

Tugging the brim of his hat a little lower on my head while praying it'll hide my blush, I say, "Friends don't kiss friends."

"I don't want to be friends, Blake."

My eyes widen in surprise, the memory of Missy's lips against Theo's cheek still fresh in my mind.

"Teddy," I warn.

"Just calling it like it is, Blake."

My breathing is shallow as I try to get a grip on what the hell is going on between us. The silence only heightens everything else. How close he's standing. How sweet he's been today, despite our run-in with one of his past conquests. How good he smells. What I bet he'd taste like if I rose onto my tiptoes and pressed my lips to his. Like Orange Crush, probably.

His attention drops to my mouth, and I bite the inside of my cheek. "I--" The words catch in my throat. I don't know what to say. Because this is dangerous. My feelings for Theo. His feelings for me. Especially when my internship's on the line.

Shifting the ball from my stomach to my hip, I ask, "And if I win?"

He steps even closer. My chest brushes against his, causing my nipples to tighten as I peek up at him.

"What do you want?" he murmurs, his voice low and throaty while still managing to be playful and...

*Is he baiting me again?*

Oh, how weighted the question is.

I want a lot of things. I want to read Theo's mind. I want to know if he's seeing the real me or how many different ways this scenario could play out. I want to know if he's really thought this through or if he's being impulsive. I want to know if he's delusional or if I'm delusional for even considering agreeing to kiss him.

Yeah. I want a lot of things.

"Blake?" he prods, his hand slipping around my waist, the same confident smirk teasing the corner of his lips.

"I don't know what to say. We agreed--"

"I lied."

"Theo--"

"I want more than friends."

"But Colt--"

"I've already talked to him. He's okay with it."

"And Coach--"

"He'd get over it," he answers, his arrogance wafting off him in waves.

241

"And me?" I challenge.

For once, he doesn't already have his answer locked and loaded. His brows furrow as he looks at me. *Really* looks at me. Gone is the confident hockey star everyone knows and loves. Gone is the partier, laid-back, whatever-floats-your-boat senior at LAU who's on the fast track to the NHL.

Instead, he's replaced with the boy I fell in love with. The boy who bought me a two-liter of Crush. The boy who would tug on my messy ponytail. The boy who let me steal cinnamon bears from his bedroom and would let me watch movies with him. The boy who won me over so many times, I've lost count while hating how much I'd look forward to every single moment he'd grace me with.

I lick my bottom lip, sucking it into my mouth as I search for something to say. Something to either break the spell or give me the courage to take what I want without any more reservations. Because this push and pull? It's going to obliterate me.

"If you win, I'll back off," he murmurs, taking my silence as a rejection. "I'll be okay with just friends. I'll stop being overprotective. I'll stop calling and texting. I'll"––he clears his throat and lets me go––"I'll do whatever you want me to do."

*Whatever I want?*

A breath of laughter slips out of me. If only I knew the answer.

I step to the top of the key and dribble the ball. "Are we playing Horse or Pig?"

"Pig," he decides. "Not sure I can wait to collect my winnings in the time it would take for Horse."

*Aaaand, cocky Theo is back*, I mentally note as he moves into position beside me and waits for me to take the first shot.

The rules are simple. If I make a basket, Theo has to take

the shot from the same spot on the court. If he makes it, I take another shot somewhere else on the court. If he misses, he earns a P. If I miss, he takes the lead.

The first one to spell PIG loses.

Simple.

Unless you're playing with your childhood crush and a kiss is on the line.

Digging my teeth into my bottom lip, I bend my knees, then flick my wrist. The basketball arches through the air, bounces off the backboard, and lands in the hoop.

*Swish.*

Theo rebounds the ball and dribbles it toward me, positioning himself at the top of the key and shoots the ball.

*Swish.*

I grab the basketball and head behind the three-point line.

*Swish.*

He heads to where I'd been standing and takes a shot. It bounces off the rim and *barely* misses.

With a smirk, I call out, "P."

He rolls his eyes, runs for the ball, and tosses it to me. I shoot again but miss, giving Theo the opportunity to take the lead. He heads to my weak spot at the edge of the court and shoots. It bounces off the backboard and falls in for another point. I glare at Theo as I take his place and shoot the ball from where he'd been standing.

It misses.

"P," he returns.

We continue playing and are neck-and-neck until we're both P-I. Thankfully, I'm the first to shoot and have the advantage, but I miss the basket by an inch.

"Dammit," I curse under my breath.

Looking sexy as hell, Theo jogs toward the ball as it rolls across the court and picks it up. He crosses the half-court mark, pulls up, and extends his arms, flicking his wrist as he shoots the ball.

I don't even have to look at the hoop to know he makes it. His form is *that* perfect. *That* drool-worthy.

"Swish," he murmurs. Pointing at the ground, he commands, "Right here, Baby Thorne."

My lips flatten, but I take up my position and wait for him to retrieve the ball. He passes it to me.

"I don't know why you're looking so cocky, Teddy Bear," I quip. "We both know this is my sweet spot."

He scoffs but walks closer, letting the heat from his front melt into my back until my knees feel like Jell-O. "If you miss, I get to kiss you."

"And if I hit it?"

"Don't hit it."

I turn my face toward him. Only a centimeter of space is between us.

So. Damn. Close.

I tear my attention from his lips and stare up at him. "But we both know how much I like to win."

"Even if you miss, I think we can still consider it a win."

The man has a point.

Way more amused than I should be, I pull up to take the shot, but at the last second, Theo grabs my waist and tugs me to one side. The ball rolls off my fingers at an awkward angle, missing the basket by a solid three feet as my jaw drops and I twist in Theo's arms until I'm facing him fully.

With an outraged laugh, I smack his chest. "You cheated!"

"You really think I'm gonna let you go, Blake?" Theo's lips lift on one side, his grip tightening around my hips as he quirks his brow and bends closer. "Now, I believe it's time to pay up."

"And I believe you cheated," I repeat.

"And I believe you should've been more specific with your stipulations," he argues.

"Oh, really? What stipulations?"

"We never said in the rules we couldn't touch each other."

I laugh again, blown away by the guy's audacity. "Didn't think I'd have to spell it out for you."

He twists the hat I'd stolen from his car around until the brim is facing backward, leaving him plenty of room to kiss me without any obstructions.

*Sneaky, my friend. Very sneaky.*

But I don't pull away. Don't twist it back. Not when he's looking at me like this. Without reservations. Without any hesitation. Simply…everything a girl dreams about.

His grin tugs at my stupid heart as he plasters himself against me, and I swear I can feel his heartbeat. The way it kicks up a notch when I spread my fingers against his broad chest. The way his breath becomes more shallow and his nostrils flare, breathing me in. The way his gaze is playful but almost nervous too. Like he's anxious. Hopeful. Curious to see how I'll play this moment out. If it'll be in his favor, even though he's done everything in his power to line it up exactly the way he wants while still giving me the final say.

"You gonna pay up, Baby Thorne?" he rasps.

*Baby Thorne.*

If my internship wasn't on the line, I'd be all over this moment. But I'm not an idiot. And I'm not going to put everything I've worked for in jeopardy for a guy who loves the chase but hates the follow-through. Especially when I know he isn't sticking around for the long haul.

*Don't be stupid, Blake.*

I bite my lip but rise onto my tiptoes, holding his gaze for the longest of seconds before twisting my neck and grazing his cheek with my lips.

My heels hit the ground again, and his jaw drops.

"That wasn't a kiss," he growls, reaching for me.

I dodge his greedy hands and shrug one shoulder. "Yes, it was."

"I meant on the lips."

"Should've been more specific with your stipulations," I quip, turning on my heel toward the Taylor House. I peek over my shoulder with a cheeky grin and ask, "You comin'?"

## 30

# THEO

After the run-in with Missy, Blake and I had fun tonight. Talking. Flirting. It was natural. Easy.

Until it was hard.

Like keeping my hands to myself. Or the way my dick's been throbbing in my jeans. Or the way I had to stop from demanding to know what she wants from me or if I even have a chance after everything we've been through.

Sometimes I feel like I'm dealing with a fragile piece of glass, while other times she proves she's stronger than steel. It leaves me off-kilter, unsure where we stand or where she even *wants* us to stand.

But I do know what I want.

The question is…is patience the key to winning her over? Do I need to play *friend* until she can learn to trust me again? Maybe I should push her to face what she wants the same way I always have? The same way she pushes me?

I don't fucking know.

The lights in front of her townhome are on, illuminating the empty porch as I pull into her driveway and put the car in park.

"I had fun tonight," I tell her.

She turns in her seat and faces me fully, the glow from the dashboard illuminating her soft features. "Me too. I think we needed it."

I nod. "I still think you owe me."

"You think I owe you?"

I nod again, my attention dropping to her mouth.

With a laugh, she shakes her head. "I already paid up, remember?"

"On the cheek."

"You really think you can handle anything more?"

The challenge in her gaze lights a fire inside of me. It spreads from my stomach and down into my groin, leaving my balls aching as I lean across the console to see what she'll do. How she'll react. If she'll back away from me, or if she'll finally give in and let me kiss her again.

Her lips tilt up in a smile, but she stands her ground. Watching. Waiting to see if I'll really cross the line again. I don't know why I'm surprised. It's Blake. The girl has bigger balls than most of the guys on the team.

But she doesn't get it. This is what I want. Screw Coach and his bullshit rules. Screw my own reservations that've been holding me back for way too long. Screw all of it. Anything keeping me from Blake is bullshit anyway. I see it now. And it's time Blake recognizes it too.

When I get close enough to taste her breath as it slips from her parted lips, she whispers, "This is a bad idea, Theo."

"Why?"

"Because it isn't you." She peeks up at me through those thick, dark lashes.

"Who says it isn't me?"

Her smile turns sad. "Every person you've ever come in contact with."

"What's that supposed to mean?"

248

"It means you like the setup of *one-and-done*, remember?"

"And?"

"And you've already gotten it from me." She forces the same sad smile and shrugs one bare shoulder. The combination hits me straight in the chest.

Mack was right. Blake's assuming she's like every other girl, when it couldn't be further from the truth.

I give her some space and lean back in my seat, resting my head against the headrest. "What if I want more?"

"You don't want more, Teddy. It's not you, and there's nothing wrong with that. You like having your options open. You always have."

My nostrils flare, but she doesn't give me time to defend myself. She barrels forward, wrecking our night with a sledgehammer. "Don't get me wrong. I honestly wouldn't have had my first time with someone else, but I'm not stupid. And I'm not going to fall for a guy who can't give me what I want."

"Who says I can't--"

"Stop," she interrupts.

"No. I'm not gonna stop. I like you, Blake. We get along. There's chemistry here."

"Yeah. There is," she agrees. "But for how long? And at what cost? You don't exactly have a strong track record for following through or settling down, let alone the fact you're leaving. You might not have any offers yet, or maybe you do and you don't want to tell me about them, but I can still see the big picture, Teddy. I'm not in it. And it's okay."

"Don't call me Teddy," I growl. It's stupid, and I know I'm picking a fight over bullshit to distract us from the real issue, but I can't help it. I feel like I'm being backed into a corner, and I can't do anything to stop it.

"What was your goal tonight, Theo?" She scrubs her hand over her face. Remembering her makeup, she tucks her hand under her thigh to keep from ruining it further. "Was your goal to win me over and make me yours, or was it to make up for being an ass in the first place? Because if it's the latter, you're doing a bang-up job."

She pushes the passenger door open, ready to escape, but I reach out and grab her wrist, keeping her in place.

"Stop," I order.

"Why?"

"I already told you I like you, Blake."

"So?" She laughs, but there isn't any humor in it. "You like a lot of girls. You've *always* liked a lot of girls."

"Not like this."

"Then prove it," she goads. "Because from my perspective? All I've ever been is the girl you took for granted, so why should I start taking your feelings seriously now?"

"That's how you think I look at you?" I rasp. "I never took you for granted, Blake. I just didn't want to fuck it up. You're my best friend's little sister. I was scared."

"What do you have to be scared of? I've always been here. Rooting for you. Watching you. Loving you." She laughs. "Why do you think I never lost my v-card, Theo? Are you really this dense?"

My teeth clench together, but I stay quiet.

"It always belonged to you. *I* always belonged to you." She lets go of another slow, unsteady breath. "But seriously. Look at this from my perspective. You're asking me to put my internship and future career on the line for a guy who's never had a real relationship in his entire life. A guy who's most likely going to be in another state after this season. A guy who has never seen me as anything but his best friend's little sister until someone else showed interest in me."

"That's bullshit, Blake," I rasp.

She's killing me. Fucking twisting the dagger in my chest

as I watch the only thing I want slip through my fingers. And there's not a damn thing I can do about it.

"Is it, though?" She tugs her arm from my grasp and climbs out of the car, slamming the door behind her and marching up the stairs to her porch. I follow her, my feet pounding up the concrete steps until her back is to my front and she's pinned between the door and my chest.

The position brings a swell of memories to the surface. We've been here a time or two. Me pinning her against a wall. In the bathroom. Before I kissed her for the first time. In Burrows' room. Before I slept with her. Before I pulled a few barriers between us down and caught a glimpse of the girl I've been lusting after for way too long. The girl I couldn't bring myself to claim until now. Until it's too late.

I lean closer and breathe her in. Her familiar scent clings to her red hair. It tortures me. The urge to take this a step further is overwhelming. I want to push her against the door and kiss her until she can't even think straight, let alone hide behind some bullshit excuse as to why we can't be together.

"Blake," I murmur against the crown of her head. A few wisps of hair stir from my breath. But I don't say anything else. I can't.

She leans against me, letting her muscles melt ever so slightly into my warmth as I crowd her against the door. I drag my hand lower and squeeze her waist. It's painful to be this close to her without giving in and kissing her the way I want. Holding her the way I want. Fucking driving into her the way I want.

"I want you, Blake. I care about you--"

"Then prove it," she interrupts. "And I mean in a way that's bigger than asking me out under the guise of making it up to my older brother, or coming up with a stupid bet so you can have the excuse to kiss me again." She leans her forehead against the door and lets out a shuddered breath. Like I've finally pushed her past the edge.

"Prove it in a way that's real, Theo," she challenges. Her voice is stronger. More determined. She isn't begging me. She's goading me. Daring me. "A way that makes me different than all the other girls I *know* you've been with. A way that puts me first and gives me a reason to do the same for you."

"And if I do?"

She shrugs one shoulder but doesn't answer me.

And she won't. I know her better than that.

She's stubborn.

And she's done talking about this. For now. Her skin is warm against my lips as I lean down and press a kiss to her bare shoulder, unable to help myself. She tastes like sunshine and spice. My fingers dig into her waist again, and she arches her back, rubbing her ass against my groin as if to prove what my prize will be if I can beat her challenge.

And fuck me, do I want to win.

"Are you teasing me, Blake?" I rasp.

She peeks over her shoulder. "Are you finally realizing what's at stake, Theo?"

I force myself to let her go, missing the feel of the curve of her hip against my palm. But I refuse to torture myself any longer. Not when it won't get me anywhere. Not tonight, anyway. Not until I can prove she's the real deal.

"Goodnight, Blake."

With a coy smile teasing her lips, she holds my stare. "Goodnight, Theo."

Suddenly, she turns around and grabs my bicep, keeping me in place while looking up at me with those bright green eyes one more time.

"One more thing," she whispers.

My attention slides to her mouth. "Yeah?"

Her lips flicker with a ghost of a smile. "Good luck."

Then she lets me go.

My footsteps feel heavy as I walk back to my car. But I don't pull out of the driveway until she's safely inside.

When the door closes behind her, I can't help but smile as I shove my car into reverse.

*You want me to prove it, Blake?*

You won't know what hit you.

## 31

## BLAKELY

There's a bag of cinnamon bears on the hood of my car along with a two-liter of orange soda. No note. But I don't need it. Clearly, Teddy Taylor has struck again.

Grabbing the goodies from the top of my car, I put them on the passenger seat and drive to the rink. I'm still not sure if it was a good idea to throw down the gauntlet like I did, but I was tired of being tired. Tired of holding back. It isn't like me. I'm the girl who goes after what she wants, and despite my best interest, I do want Theo. I've always wanted Theo. But I need to know he wants me too. And not only for a night. For the long run.

Don't get me wrong. I'm not convinced we'll wind up married with two babies and a white picket fence or anything. But a solid relationship lasting longer than a weekend would be great. Especially when my internship is potentially on the line.

When I arrive at the rink a few minutes later, I stare at the stupid snacks for a solid thirty seconds, unsure if I should send Theo a thank you text or let the bastard sweat a bit more.

*Nah. He can wait.*

I tuck my phone into my purse and head to Russ's office.

"You're early," he notes without bothering to look up from the sports section of the newspaper.

"Didn't know they still printed those." I motion to the gray recycled paper in his hands.

"Only the big papers. Everyone else has gone digital." He says the word like it's a curse and folds the newspaper onto his desk. "You ready to help with today's game?"

"Always. Anything I need to do beforehand?"

"Burrows will need a rubdown after. Graves is still having shoulder issues, but I'll deal with him."

"Okay."

"You good with Burrows?" he prods, his sharp gaze pinning me in place.

"Why wouldn't I be?"

"Because of the bet."

"It's not an issue."

He holds my stare for another beat, then nods. "All right. Anything else I need to know about? Maybe pass along to Sanderson?"

I know what he's referring to. What he's insinuating. He's talking about what he saw when he interrupted me with Theo in his office not so long ago. I can only imagine how we must've looked. Me tucked between Theo's legs. Theo grabbing my wrist. Our hushed voices. I've never been very good at hiding my feelings for the bastard––or at least it's what Mom tells me––so, I shouldn't be surprised Russ is asking me this. Especially when we both know what's on the line if I slip up and give in to LAU's hockey captain's advances.

A weaker person would cave under Russ's scrutiny, but I

keep my head held high and lie straight through my teeth. "Nope."

His eyes narrow for a split second. "Fine." He opens up the newspaper again. "You can sanitize the equipment in here. Once the game starts, we'll stay on the bench. Hopefully there won't be any more brawls."

"I mean, it's hockey," I remind him, my lips lifting in the corners.

He smirks but doesn't comment, so I get to work.

Fifteen minutes later, Russ and I join the rest of the team in the locker room. Sanderson gives a quick speech, and everyone heads to the rink. Even though there's plenty of room in the tunnel, it still feels like being packed into a can of sardines thanks to the boys, their gear, and the extra four inches of height their already massive bodies are taking up due to their skates. Yeah, it definitely feels like I'm being squeezed between a group of amped-up hockey players as we walk toward the ice. But I'm not complaining. In a way, it almost feels like home.

"Did you get my present?" a deep voice murmurs beside me.

I glance to my left and find Theo towering over me. Somehow, he managed to slip beside me in the sea of players.

*Sneaky, Theo.*

I try to act casual, ignoring the spike of adrenaline and the knowledge of how close we're standing. It doesn't matter if Tukani's on my other side because Tukani doesn't give me butterflies. Theo on the other hand...

"I meant the cinnamon bears," he clarifies when I don't answer right away.

"I know what you meant," I answer, glancing at an oblivious Tukani and peeking up at Theo again. The guy's tall on a good day, but with his skates and pads? He looks massive.

Untouchable. And so damn sexy in his hockey gear it's not even funny. I know what it's like to have his mouth on mine. And after his declaration last night?

I shake off the thought and add, "If you're not careful, I'm gonna send you my dentist bill."

He chuckles. "Pretty sure Papa Taylor would be happy to take care of your cavities for free."

"Is that how you get away with it?" I quip. "Eating all the sugar?"

"To be fair, I used to have a different diet. It was boring. Everything tasted the same. Like shit," he adds, driving his point home. Clearly, we aren't talking about his eating habits anymore. "But after a taste of those cinnamon bears the other day?" He smirks down at me, his eyes heating a fraction. "Gotta say, I don't think I could quit, even if you asked me to."

"Hmm," I hum.

His eyes drop to my mouth as he asks, "You gonna wish me luck in today's game?"

"Yeah, you gonna wish us luck, Baby Thorne?" Tukani interjects, bouncing his eyebrows up and down.

Apparently, my conversation with Theo is over. For now.

Feigning annoyance, I shove Tukani toward the ice and order, "Get out there, Tsunami."

Throwing his head back, he laughs as the announcer says his name over the speaker, leaving me with Theo.

"Good luck," I add.

Softly checking me with his shoulder, he slips on his helmet and steps onto the ice. Not gonna lie. I can't help but fall for that cocky look as he skates toward a few of his teammates lined up in the neutral zone, his hockey stick raised in the air while the announcer calls his name over the speakers.

Burrows' name is called next, and he slips past me, his

eyes holding mine for a split second too long as he joins the rest of the players on the ice.

I should feel guilty––and in a way, I do––for hurting Burrows. For pushing him away at the party, only to sleep with Theo. But even if I could go back, I wouldn't.

I should be thanking him. Burrows. For pushing Theo to see me as someone other than his best friend's little sister. Not that I was using Burrows or rubbing him in Theo's nose. Still. We haven't really talked since everything happened. Even the massages have been practically silent thanks to Russ's proximity. They've felt forced. Awkward. Tense.

I watch as he skates toward the opposite side of the lineup, leaving plenty of space between him and Theo, which only adds another block of guilt to my shoulders. I'll need to fix it soon. Talk to him, maybe. I just don't know what to say.

Russ clears his throat beside me and folds his arms when he catches me staring. "Everything good?"

"Yup," I answer, though he doesn't look convinced. Apparently, I'm batting a thousand today.

～

THERE ARE ONLY THREE MORE MINUTES IN THE FIRST PERIOD of the game, and we're down two to zero as the seconds tick by on the clock.

"Come on, guys!" I yell, cupping my hands around my mouth as Depp and Graves fight with the opposing team's center for the puck.

Depp steals it and passes it to Theo at the center of the ice. Theo chips it off the board toward Colt. Charging the goalie, the defensemen hot on his tail, Colt slaps the puck into the left corner of the goal and the crowd goes wild.

"Go Hawks!" they chant.

The team lifts their hands into the air and skates around the rink in a victory lap, Theo leading the charge.

It's funny. How something as simple as Theo looking at me while skating on the ice can bring back a memory. Or memories, to be exact. Like all the times I'd come to Colt's games and cheer on the team. Like all the times Theo would find me in the crowd and give me a glimpse of his cocky smirk or a frustrated scowl when the game wasn't going the way he wanted it to go. Like all the times he'd score a goal and search for me in the stands, tossing me a wink like the arrogant sonofabitch he really is.

And today isn't any different. When his attention catches on me, I give him a thumbs up, a soft smile teasing at my lips.

With a mock glare, he yells back, "What? No *vacuum beach*?"

My teeth dig into the inside of my cheek as I fight back my grin and give him the bird instead. He throws his head back and laughs––hard––and skates to the blue line to finish off the first period.

And just like that, a swell of hope spreads in my chest, and it's too late to reel it in, no matter how much I want to. Then again, I guess I shouldn't be too surprised. It's Theo, for Pete's sake. The man knows what he's doing, no matter how oblivious he might seem.

Clearly, I'm playing with fire.

And the candy on my car this morning, combined with the familiar ambiance that brought us together in the first place along with a look hot enough to melt a glacier in a snowstorm?

*Swoon.*

Colt manages to slip in a final goal before the buzzer rings out in the arena, tying the score at the end of the first period.

After a quick break, the rest of the game passes by in a whir, and LAU wins, four to three.

As the team celebrates in the locker room, victory music blaring from a set of black speakers, Theo approaches me. His hair is damp with sweat from the game, but his pads and jersey are missing, giving me a delicious view of his abs.

*Hey there.*

I tuck my hands into my elbows, crossing my arms to keep from running my fingers against his six pack as I force myself to hold his gaze instead of ogling him the way I desperately want.

"Hey, Baby Thorne," he greets me, looking as cocky and drool-worthy as ever. I blame the endorphins from winning, but the bastard's a hockey player, so part of me thinks his arrogance is just ingrained in his DNA.

"Good game, Teddy," I tell him.

"It wasn't bad." He steps closer, his height still intimidating despite losing his skates and opting for a pair of Nikes. He smells like sweat and sex. So good. So tempting. I lean a few inches away in hopes of breathing in some non-orgasm inducing air, but it's useless. My back hits the cinderblock wall behind me with a quiet thud.

*I am so out of my league.*

"Only scored one goal this time, though," he informs me as if I wasn't given front row seats to the game.

"*Only* one." I scoff. "You also assisted twice. Did you forget that part?"

"Must've slipped my mind. Guess I was too busy stealing glances your way."

*Stupid butterflies.*

I tilt my head to one side. "And why's that?"

"You had me waiting for my *vacuum beach*. Which I never received, by the way."

With a laugh, I argue, *"Vacuum beach* is all it takes to distract you from the game?"

"If it's coming from you? Yeah. You're quite the distraction, Baby Thorne. Consuming my thoughts. My time. My imagination." He rests his forearm against the wall behind me, just above my ponytail. He's caging me in, his hot gaze dancing with amusement. It would be so easy to let him kiss me right now. To let him lean a little closer and——

I look around his chiseled body, realizing how close we're standing.

*Shit. How did that happen?*

The warning bells are going off inside my head as I peek around him and search for Coach or Russ or anyone else who might notice our friendly banter is borderline flirting. Thankfully, they're too distracted by Tukani who's standing on one of the benches, thrusting his little heart out in rhythm to the rap song pulsing through the speakers.

It doesn't mean Theo should be standing over me like this, though. Not when we're in the middle of LAU's locker room. Not when his coach specifically mentioned no fraternization with me and the players. Not when I warned him to prove he likes me before I even think about coming out and telling the world——and Coach Sanderson——about my feelings for the guy.

But the bastard knows what he's doing. He knows how to flirt. How to look effortlessly sexy without a shirt on. How to push my buttons and make me cave. And boy, do I want to cave.

*Stay strong, Blake,* I remind myself.

Sucking my lips between my teeth, I challenge, "So, I'm a distraction, huh?"

"Yeah."

"And when you find a new distraction?" My eyebrow arches.

"What do you mean?"

With a shrug, I taunt, "I guess I'm curious how long it'll take for the right puck bunny to come along, mouth *vacuum beach* at the right moment, and snap you out of whatever funk I've seemed to put you in with the ladies."

He scratches his jaw, cocking his head and looking down at me with those damn soul-piercing eyes. They're sharp and hard and unyielding as they see past my snark, revealing my insecurities one by one. "Do you want me to snap out of this *funk*, Blake?" he finally asks.

I gulp. "I want––"

"Thorne!" Russ yells.

"Yeah, Russ?" Colt calls back.

Russ stops short and corrects himself. "*Baby* Thorne. Come on. Let's get Burrows' recovery started."

*Shit.*

Did he see how close we're standing? Does he see how pissed Theo is? Can he see how close I am to letting him kiss me in front of everyone after two tiny interactions?

*Get a grip, girl.*

I move to slip out from under Theo's arm but catch Burrows watching me and freeze. His attention shifts to Theo, his jaw clenching as he looks at the ground and walks past us.

"I'm gonna talk to Coach," Theo tells me.

My heart picks up its pace, and not in a good way. More like a your-butt-is-about-to-be-smacked kind of way.

Again, *not* the pleasant kind of smacking.

I shake my head and try to focus.

It's a mistake. He shouldn't talk to Coach. Not yet. Not until I'm sure. Not until *we're* sure. About us. About whether or not this chemistry is long-lasting. About whether he'll grow bored or distracted as soon as we come out as more than friends.

Keeping my voice low, I glare back at him and warn, "There's nothing to talk about. Not yet."

"Yeah, well, for me, there is."

Losing my bravado, my eyes plead with his. But I don't know if it's because I'm scared of pissing off Coach or if it's because I'm scared of making this thing with Theo real. Tangible. *Boring*.

For him. Not me.

What if he does grow bored? What if, once he's gotten what he wanted, he doesn't care anymore? He goes back to his old ways? It would wreck me beyond repair, and witnessing it firsthand during my internship? It would kill me.

I don't want him to talk to Coach. I don't want him to open a can of worms I'm not sure I can handle. I just want... Shit, I don't know.

I don't know. I don't know what I want. I want confidence in my relationship––or whatever the hell this is–– with Theo before I put my internship on the line. I want *all* of Theo. And I want it for the long haul. I don't want to worry about puck bunnies or contracts with the NHL or anything else getting in the way of the happily-ever-after I've been dreaming about since I was a little girl.

And what I *really* don't want? Is the possibility of making decisions when they're too early. When this relationship is too early. It's risky. Terrifying. And I'm afraid I'll end up caught in the crosshairs because of it.

"It's a bad idea, Theo," I tell him.

"It'll be fine. Coach is a good dude."

I glance around the locker room, but everyone's still too amped up on their win to notice us talking, let alone hear our conversation over the music blaring. Shifting my attention back to Theo, I whisper, "I don't want to put my internship on the line yet. Will you please listen to me and wait? I'm not ready——"

"Baby Thorne!" Russ barks, his voice echoing from down the hall.

"I need to go. We'll talk later, all right?" I slip out from beneath his arm without bothering to wait for his response and walk toward Russ's office.

## 32
### BLAKELY

Russ is already working on Graves' shoulder as I walk into his office, my body still trembling from my interaction with Theo. When Russ sees me, he tilts his head toward Burrows resting on the cushioned black table in the corner of the room.

"Start with the foam roller. I'll be over in a few."

I grab the gray foam roller from the cabinet, giving Burrows a tight smile.

*Stupid Graves and his stupid shoulder.*

With one hand on the back of his neck, Burrows squeezes, his eyes glued to me. But he doesn't say a word. I guess I'm not the only one who doesn't know what to say.

"So…," I drag out, my voice tight. "Should we get started?"

"Sure."

He lays down, lifting his leg so I can put the foam roller beneath it, and I get right to work. Other than a low groan, Burrows stays quiet as I start the techniques Russ had walked me through when I first started shadowing him. And it's nice. Cathartic almost. Getting lost in my work. Letting the quiet wash over us. A few minutes later, Burrows sits up, and we do a few more stretches, working on his thighs and calves as well as his knee.

"So," he grunts, "I looked for you the other night. At the party."

*Welp. So much for the comfortable silence.*

I offer him a tight smile and mutter, "Oh?"

"Where'd you go?"

"Nowhere in particular."

"I wanted to talk to you."

"No need," I mumble under my breath.

"Do you hate me?"

*Fuckity, fuck, fuck, fuck.*

My nose scrunches up, and I finally give in and groan, "Burroooows. Let's not make this a thing, okay?"

"Look, I wanted to apologize."

"I don't care."

He pulls back, surprised. "How can you *not* care?"

"Because I don't," I offer weakly. "I know it's stupid, but what's done is done. I've moved on and let it go, so you should too."

I glance at Russ who's still helping Graves on the opposite side of the room. The celebratory music is blasting from down the hall, and I'm grateful for it. Grateful for the way it's covering our conversation and how personal it might get if Burrows keeps blabbering his big fat mouth.

Propping himself onto his elbows, Burrows brings himself a little closer to me as I stand next to the cushioned table he's lying on.

"But I fucked up."

"Everyone fucked up," I clarify. "It was a stupid bet made by a bunch of stupid boys. That's it. But I'm not holding onto it, and neither should you."

"Yeah, well, I am holding onto it," he announces.

"Yeah, well, you shouldn't be."

I dig my fingers into the muscles on either side of his knee, hoping it'll shut him up and I can get this thing over with as quickly as possible. His expression pinches in discomfort, and he hangs his head, letting out a slow breath.

*Oh, physical therapy, you heartless bitch. I kind of love you right now.*

"Helps that I get to take it out on you," I joke, hoping my sarcasm will lighten the mood.

With a low chuckle, he looks up at me again, and his dark eyes pin me in place. "I still like you, Blake."

"Nope." I shake my head and keep my attention on his leg while avoiding his gaze at all costs.

I really don't want to have this conversation.

"I'm serious," Burrows says. "I like––"

My gaze snaps to his. "I'm going to stop you right there."

He frowns. "Blake––"

"Seriously. Stop," I beg, continuing the massage. The sooner I finish, the sooner I can escape this conversation. And boy, am I ready to call it a day.

"Is this about Theo?" he demands, keeping his voice quiet.

My hands freeze, and my spine straightens. "What?"

"I wanna know if this is about Theo."

"It's none of––"

"It is. Isn't it?"

"There's nothing going on between me and Theo," I lie.

He shakes his head as if he can't believe I'm such an idiot.

*Neither can I, buddy.*

"Theo's bad news, Blake," he reminds me. "The parties he throws? You've been there. It's like some freakin' orgie or some shit."

My fingers hesitate against his skin as a dry laugh escapes me. I'm blown away by the audacity of this guy. Seriously, he can't be this dense. Even if I want to personally strangle Theo half the time, it doesn't mean I won't stand up for him when he isn't around.

"*That's* the tactic you're gonna go with?" I ask him. "Theo's a bad guy?"

Pinching the bridge of his nose, Burrows mutters, "He isn't a bad guy, he's––"

"And now you're not even going to stick with it?" I tsk, more amused than annoyed. "Come on, man. I expected more from you."

I can almost taste his exasperation on my tongue as he shakes his head and asks, "What do you want from me, Blake? How can I convince you to give me another chance?"

I glance at Russ again, my spidey-senses tingling, but he isn't listening. He's too engrossed in the x-rays Graves' doctor sent earlier this week.

"I'm not looking for a relationship right now," I whisper, my thumbs moving from his knee and down to his calf.

"Not even with Theo?"

"*Especially* not with Theo."

"I saw you looking at him on the ice."

"I was looking at everyone on the ice," I lie. Truth be told, the guy managed to steal the show, but I'm not about to admit it to Burrows. "And even if I was looking at him," I add, "we're just friends."

"So, you aren't dating him?" he challenges.

"I'm not dating anyone. *Especially* anyone on the team."

"And if I weren't on the team?"

"I still wouldn't be interested."

He grabs my wrist, sitting up fully until we're far too close for my comfort. "Why? Because you want someone else?"

"What I want is to keep this internship."

"Then let me talk to Coach. I'll explain––"

"I don't like you like that," I tell him. "And I know it isn't what you want to hear, but I don't see my feelings changing anytime soon, if ever. The you and me ship?" I wiggle my finger between us. "It sailed a while ago, Burrows. To be honest, it's long gone. Like over the horizon never to return kind of gone."

His fingers graze along the inside of my wrist, but the butterflies I know should be present are missing. It's like when Colt touches me. All I feel are calloused hands. No zing. No goosebumps. Nothing.

For some reason, it only aggravates me more. It'd be easier if I liked Burrows. If I was able to compare what I feel for Theo to someone else and to have it hold a candle to my feelings for the bastard. But the truth is? There is no comparison. There's *never* been a comparison. With anyone.

"Why?" Burrows whispers, bringing me back to the present.

I shift my gaze from his touch to his brown eyes and pull my hand away from him. "Do I need a reason?"

"No, but if you have one, I think I deserve to hear it. Especially if it involves someone else."

"I already told you--"

"I know what you said. But I think you're full of shit."

"I'm not full of shit," I argue. "And even if I was--which trust me, nothing will come of it--I can't help it if I have feelings for someone else."

"Especially when that someone doesn't deserve you," he mutters.

With a laugh, I nod and get back to massaging his legs. "On that, we agree."

"You gonna do anything about it? Let him do anything about it?"

I shake my head again. "What's the point? Like I said, I need this internship. I need the future it'll bring me if I don't screw it up. I like the people I get to meet and the things I get to learn. I'm not going to give it up for a guy like *him*, as you so eloquently reminded me a few minutes ago."

"Yeah. Well. Good. Because he doesn't deserve you," he repeats.

"Again. On that, we agree," I quip.

"You gonna come to the Taylor House tonight?"

"And witness said reasons why a certain someone doesn't deserve me?" My nose wrinkles. "No, thank you."

"Come on. We'll go together," he suggests.

My gaze narrows.

"As friends," he clarifies.

*Friends.*

Sure.

Been there. Done that. It was not successful. So, nope. No, thank you.

Patting his thigh, I reply, "Unfortunately, I have plans. But thanks for the offer. Now roll over. We're going to do a few more stretches."

And even though he grumbles something under his breath, he does as he's told, and I'm left feeling lighter than I've felt in weeks.

## 3 3

## BLAKELY

**B**ig Red cinnamon gum is sitting on my windshield along with a Vitamin water. I bite my lip to keep from smiling as I pick them up and put them onto my passenger seat.

No note.

Again.

Not that I need one this time, either.

My phone dings with a text, and Theo's name lights up on the screen.

Apparently, I spoke too soon.

A photo of Colt giving me two thumbs up while rolling his eyes appears along with a message.

**Theo: Colt gave me the green light to date you. Just so you know.**

I shouldn't find the photo endearing, but I do. I also shouldn't think it's cute how Theo went out of his way to get my brother's permission, even when we both know I'm a grown-ass woman who can do whatever she wants. The fact he asked? It's kind of adorable.

The problem, however, is Theo knows it.

And I refuse to let him win.

**Me: See? Here's the thing. You think he's the gatekeeper to my heart, but he isn't. He knows it. And I know it. (Hence capturing his eyes mid-roll in the picture.)**

**Theo: And who is the gatekeeper? Coach?**

**Me: Is this you trying to prove you like me?**

**Theo: One cinnamon treat at a time 'cause my girl likes to keep things spicy. ;)**

I snort and drop my phone to my lap. But I only make it out of the driveway before I pick my stupid cell back up again. I can't help it. The guy's too addictive. Too enticing. And the way I crave every single encounter with the bastard? It isn't fair. Especially when he says things like *my girl*.

Praying for strength, I type out my response.

**Me: I'm not sure if you've been hit in the head one too many times, but I'm not your girl.**

**Theo: You've always been my girl. Sorry it took me so long to see it.**

Well, shit. If the guy wanted to make his point clear, he succeeded. My phone buzzes with another text.

**Theo: I'll see you in a few, Baby Thorne.**

My heart pinches, and I type my response.

**Me: See you at the game, Teddy.**

$\sim$

Spicy cinnamon explodes across my taste buds as I chew the gum Theo left on my car. I shove the rest of the pack into my purse, well aware how long the flavor lasts. I'm going to need another dozen pieces to make it through today.

The locker room is bustling with players. It's a big game today. Clearly, everyone can feel it. The energy. The anticipation. They're putting on their gear while I hang out by the empty showers, waiting for Russ to finish a private phone call in his office.

"Hey," Colt greets me, looking like a badass hockey player in his full get-up as he walks toward me. "Did you get the picture?"

"Of you looking like a jackass?" I quip. "Why, yes. Yes, I did."

"Good. I already told him you don't give a shit about whether or not I approve of who you date, but I want you to know…" He smiles a little wider. "I do approve."

"Well, it's a moot point, anyway."

"Why?"

"Because he's Theo."

"So, what?"

"So, he's Theo," I reiterate. "Everyone knows he has the attention span of a gnat on crack. Honestly, I'm surprised he even bothered to mention his feelings. They'll be gone in a week."

With his hands folded across his LAU jersey, he moseys closer like he has all the time in the world while his amused gaze never leaves me. "You know Theo better than anyone, Blake. Do you really believe it?"

"That he has the attention span of a gnat on crack? Yes."

"I meant the second part," he clarifies. "Do you really think his feelings for you will be gone within a week?"

"I…" My mouth closes, the words clogging my throat.

"Pretty sure you know him better than that, Blake."

"All right, everyone!" Coach yells, stepping out of his office. "Let's get the game started."

"I have an announcement I'd like to make, first," Theo interrupts. The guy looks right as rain with a cocky grin plastered across his face as he waits for Coach to give him the go-ahead.

Coach crosses his arms, bracing the clipboard against his chest. "Where are your skates, Taylor?"

"I'll get them on right after the announcement."

His teeth clench, but Coach gives Theo a sharp nod. "Make it quick. We have a game to play."

Clearing his throat, Theo steps forward and waits until he's sure he has everyone's attention. Burrows looks annoyed as his focus shifts from Theo to me. Depp is too busy texting on his phone to pay attention. Tukani is playing with a fidget spinner, his locker still wide open. And Logan and Graves are both huddled together but aren't saying a word.

It's still weird sometimes. To see Logan. He was practically the third amigo in Colt and Theo's friendship. But after everything went down with Logan, Colt, and Ash, they split like a couple of atoms, and I still can't decide if he's over it or if he's only biding his time.

Once the locker room is relatively quiet, Theo jumps onto one of the benches, giving him an extra two feet of height while commanding the room with his presence. Not gonna lie. He looks like a god among men with his dirty blonde wavy hair and piercing eyes. The way he holds himself with confidence, demanding the attention of everyone around him while managing to wield said attention with perfection. Pretty sure he could be a politician if he wanted. Hell, he'd have my vote for sure.

"I'm gonna make this quick, 'cause we have a game to win," Theo starts. "As you guys know, Coach decided to put a no fraternization policy into place a few weeks ago." He tosses me a wink. "But he didn't give my heart the memo."

My heart falls to my stomach as everyone's eyes find me in the room.

*This is...*

Untucking my wavy hair from behind my ear, I drop my chin to my chest and whisper under my breath, "What's he doing?"

Colt glances at me and steps closer, sidling up next to me while keeping his voice low. "I think he's trying to prove his feelings."

"I don't want him to prove his feelings. Not like this."

"Don't worry, man," Tukani quips, oblivious to the sidebar I'm having with my older brother. He sets his fidget spinner back into his locker and slaps it closed. "We all know you're in love with Colt. No need to make a big deal out of it."

The team laughs, and Theo joins in. But Coach? He looks on edge. Suspicious. My anxiety spikes, and I fold my arms, watching the scene unfold like an impending car crash.

This is a *bad* idea.

"Colt, make him stop," I breathe out, my tone laced with desperation.

With a careful smile, Colt murmurs, "Give him a minute."

But I can't. I can't give him a minute. Not when I told him I didn't want to put my internship on the line until I knew he wanted me for the long haul. Is that what he's trying to do? If it is, he's screwing it up royally. I can see it on Coach's face.

In the hardness of his features. The way he's folding his arms and digging his fingers into the clipboard. The guy's seconds from throwing down the gauntlet. I can see it clear as day, so why the hell can't Theo?

"As you all know, I've had a thing for Blake since we were kids," Theo continues. He turns slowly on the bench, confirming he still has everyone's full attention.

Coach's nostrils flare.

"Seriously." My hands shake as I grab Colt's jersey and tug him closer. "Make him stop."

Theo grins down at me like he's on top of the world, oblivious to the ticking time bomb with the clipboard standing a few feet away from him.

"Stop," I mouth at him, but he only winks at me and continues. "She's one of the most amazing people I've ever met."

"Careful, Taylor," Coach warns.

Theo chuckles and waves him off. "Yeah, Coach. I know you don't want us dating, but I really think if you gave us a chance--"

"I have my rules for a reason, and you know I'm not afraid to enforce them," Coach barks.

"Shit," I whisper.

Raising his hands in defense, Theo says, "And I get it, Coach. You've always ruled with an iron fist, and it's brought our team to victory time and time again. But what I feel for Blake? It won't affect the game or the team." Theo looks around the room. "Right, guys?"

The team stays quiet, their attention shifting from Coach, to Theo, to me, to Colt, and back again.

Coach's knuckles are white as he throttles the clipboard, his stance less than accommodating. "There's a reason I put the policy in place, Taylor."

"I know, but--"

"While you and Blake are on this team, dating is off-limits," Coach orders. "I'm not going to budge on this."

Theo's eyes widen in surprise. He glances at me again and jumps off the bench, stepping closer to Coach. This time, his voice is quieter but still plenty loud for the rest of the team to hear. "Come on, Coach. We're fine. I really care about her."

"Enough," Coach snaps, his tone brooking no argument. "This is *not* negotiable."

As if Theo can feel the shift, he scrubs his hand over his head. But instead of looking contrite, Theo looks more determined than ever to make me his. "That isn't fair. You were fine with it before the bet."

"Yeah, and the rest of the team went and pissed on the situation, and look how it turned out. It affected how you and everyone else on this team played on the ice. I'm not going to allow--"

"Then, we won't let it affect how we play."

"I'm not going to discuss this, Taylor."

"But it's bullshit," Theo argues, his voice rising. Clearly, he didn't expect his little announcement to be taken this way. Everyone is being given front row seats to the conversation, and it isn't exactly painting him in the best light.

He's...pissed.

And with the way he's going head-to-head with Coach, getting right up in his face?

He isn't the only one who's frustrated.

This is bad.

*Really* bad.

How the hell can Theo not see he's proving to Coach why the no fraternization policy needs to be in place at this very moment? It's causing friction in the locker room. And we're all witnessing it right in front of our eyes, minutes before a game.

*Fucking hell.*

My stomach rolls, and my fingers dig into the sleeve of Colt's jersey even more as I pull him closer. "Colt. Fix this."

Colt steps forward, but his hands are just as tied as mine.

"Coach," he starts.

"Not now, Thorne," Coach barks, glaring at Theo. "Get your skates on, and get your ass on the ice, Taylor. We'll discuss this in private."

"Bullshit," Theo spits. His skin is mottled with red, and there's a vein in his forehead throbbing as he curls his upper lip, refusing to back down. "Me dating Blake isn't a big deal. Why won't you––"

"Blake, you're fired!" Coach snaps. His words wash over me like a vat of acid, but I'm too stunned to speak, let alone register his words.

*What did he say?*

I'm…

I blink slowly, convinced I've heard him wrong.

*Wait, what? I'm fired?*

There's no way this is happening.

I've done nothing wrong. This internship means *everything* to me.

Is the room spinning? Why does it feel like the room's spinning?

Maybe I'm dreaming. This isn't real.

I can feel everyone staring at me. As if I really am in a dream. One where you're naked in front of a group of people. And everyone's watching you. Waiting for you to realize how bare and vulnerable you really are.

And I am. I've been stripped bare, and I'm so freaking vulnerable, I might actually puke. My short fingernails dig into my palms as I fist them together. But the familiar bite of pain doesn't wake me up. It only confirms my greatest fear.

This is real.

This is happening.

And Coach's threat? It officially came to fruition. In front of everyone.

"What the fuck, Coach?" Theo yells. "I didn't want––"

"Coach, you can't kick her off the team," Colt argues, snapping out of the same haze I'd been lost in. He leaves me alone at the edge of the room and goes head-to-head with Coach Sanderson, flanking Theo's side.

"You wanna blame someone?" Coach asks my brother. "Blame Theo for not following the goddamn rules."

*This can't be happening.*

I shake my head and step forward, desperate to fight for what I want despite the insane circumstances. "Coach, I didn't do anything."

Theo talks over me, anxious to fix the shitstorm he's created. "They're bullshit rules, and you know it."

Ignoring him, I hold Coach's gaze and beg, "You can't fire me. I obeyed the rules. I told Theo no."

"Unfortunately, your position can be filled in an instant," Coach grits out, glaring at Theo again. "Finding a new captain or left wing isn't so easy."

I pull back, a gasp slipping out of my parted lips as the truth hits me square in the chest.

He's serious.

I'm––I gulp––finished.

In the blink of an eye, everything I've worked for is gone.

But Coach is right. I'm a dime a dozen. I'm at the bottom of the food chain. Hell, I'm a nobody on this team. Theo, however, is irreplaceable. He's one of the stars. One of the top scorers who's being recruited by multiple teams across the country. Who knows? He's so coveted, he might already be signed with one of them.

That's the problem though, isn't it? He knows how important he is to this team and thought it would give him free rein to get what he wants. Instead, it backfired in *my* face.

I can feel his gaze on me, branding the side of my cheek as the realization finally settles into Theo's bones the same way it's settled into mine. He reaches for me, but I step back, keeping distance between us. And I need it now more than ever.

Theo glares at Coach, his upper lip curling in disgust. "Fine. I quit the team."

A few murmured *oh shits* echo around the room, but they're drowned out by the whoosh of my heart drumming in my ears.

He can't be serious.

He can't quit.

He loves the game.

He loves everything about it.

It's what he was made for the same way Colt was.

Coach's face is red with fury as Theo leans closer to him without an ounce of self-preservation. He's being so reckless. So disrespectful. So freaking stupid. This is his future on the line. What the hell is he thinking?

This has gone too far.

Convinced there are going to be blows within the next two seconds, I march toward Theo, grab the collar of his jersey, and force him to look at me. "Stop talking, and get your ass on the ice."

His face twists with disgust, though I'm not sure if it's directed at Coach or himself. He grabs my face and rasps, "I'm gonna walk, Blake."

"No. You're not."

"Blake," he begs.

I pull away from him, the truth settling heavily on my shoulders. If I don't remove myself from this situation, it could cause permanent damage to Theo's career, and I can't let it happen.

"You've done enough," I murmur. My chest heaves as I turn to Coach, praying I have enough strength to keep my emotions in check until I can get to my car. "I'm really grateful for the opportunity I had to shadow Russ. It was a great experience, and I"––I swallow back my tears––"I can't thank you enough." Choking back the lump in my throat, I head toward the exit without another word as Theo yells after me.

I ignore him.

I ignore everything.

The way I'm dizzy with anger. And resentment. And hurt. I ignore it all, shove my key into the ignition, and pull out onto the main road. It only takes two seconds for the realization to hit like a ton of bricks.

I just lost everything I've been working for.

And it's all Theo's fault.

3 4

BLAKELY

I turned off my phone after silencing it for the tenth time. Between Colt and Theo, the thing vibrated for a solid two minutes until I put it out of its misery. If only I could so easily quiet the replay from the locker room. It's been running in a constant loop in my head.

The door slams behind me as I step over the threshold and into the house, desperate to block out the world.

"What the--?" Mia's head pops through the doorway of her room down the hall. She frowns. "What are you doing home? Aren't you supposed to be at the game? Ash already left and is sitting with your mom in the stands. Is everything okay?"

A sardonic laugh bubbles out of my throat as I toss my keys onto the kitchen counter like they're a grenade. "I just got fired."

Her frowns deepens. "What?"

"I just got fired," I repeat, hoping if I say it enough times, it'll take away the sting.

Without a word, she walks down the hall toward me and opens her arms wide, taking me in for a hug.

Squeezing my eyes shut, I hold her close, unable to swallow back the lump in my throat any longer as the tears finally slip past my defenses.

I don't know how long she hugs me, how long she lets the recent events settle into my bones. But the silence does shit to quiet my racing thoughts. I'm so overwhelmed. So frustrated. So...blown away by the entire situation.

"What happened?" she murmurs. Her voice is nothing but a breath in the otherwise quiet room.

My shoulders slump in defeat. "Theo thought it would be a great idea to prove he cares about me by making some big gesture in the locker room. Unfortunately, it blew up in his face, and Coach fired me."

"No," she murmurs in disbelief.

I squeeze her a little tighter. "Everything I worked for, Mia. It's all gone."

"Shhh... " She guides me to the couch. I collapse onto the cushion, and she joins me, her expression pinched with concern. "Tell me everything."

By the time I'm finished, I'm a blubbering mess with a wad of tissues in my hand. I can't help it. I'm tired of being strong. Of getting back up again and fighting for a future I'm not even sure I want anymore.

"Fuck him, Blake," Mia announces as I wipe beneath my nose with a tissue. "You should've let the bastard quit."

"I couldn't do that to him. He loves hockey."

"I don't care. He screwed you over."

I bite my tongue to keep from defending Theo, especially when we both know he doesn't deserve it. But it still hurts. My feelings for him. The loss of my internship. The sweetness of his insane gesture, no matter stupid it was. I told him. I told him it was a bad idea. I told him to wait. But he didn't listen. Didn't care enough about my opinion to take it seriously. And look who's face it blew up in.

Sniffling, I suck my lips between my teeth and try to steady my breathing as I shrug one defeated shoulder. Because I don't know what to say or what to do. Not anymore. Nothing will fix this.

I don't know if I should be mad at Theo or flattered or––

A loud pounding against the door echoes throughout the townhome, followed by a deep voice. "Open the door, Blake! Open it right now."

My head falls in my hands, and I rub at the moisture clinging to my cheeks.

"I'm serious, Blake. Open the damn door. Now!" Theo yells.

Mia touches my knee and squeezes softly. "Do you want me to answer?"

I nod, then shake my head before nodding again.

*I have no idea what I want.*

"I'm going to answer it," she decides for me. "What do you want me to say?"

"I dunno." I sniffle again. "I can't talk to him right now."

With a sad smile, she pats my knee and stands up, heading to the door.

The hinges squeak softly as she opens it, but I lay on the couch in the fetal position to keep out of sight. I don't want to face him. I don't want to see him or talk to him. I'm too hurt to do anything but sit here on the couch and cry.

I can still hear him, though.

"Where is she?" he demands. Desperation taints his voice, making my heart squeeze in pain.

"She doesn't want to talk right now."

"Let me in, Mia," he begs. "I need to fix this."

"How?" she asks. "How do you think you can fix this?"

There's a pause, and it acts like a knife in my chest. I don't say a word. I don't peek over the edge of the couch. I don't do anything. I just sit here. Listening to the pain in his voice.

Waiting for a solution that'll fix this. There's only one problem. I don't know what the solution is. And I'm afraid Theo doesn't, either.

"I'll do whatever she wants," he pleads.

"I'm not sure she knows what she wants right now. Aren't you supposed to be at the game?"

"I don't care about the game."

I sit up and get to my feet, walking toward the front door like a woman on a mission, even though I have no doubt he can see the evidence from my breakdown written across my tear-streaked face. It's probably all blotchy and shit, but I don't even care anymore. Let him see my pain. My frustration. I'm done hiding it from him. It's all I've done for years. I'm sick of it.

When Mia sees me approach, she rocks back on her heels and steps away from the door, leaving it wide open. "I'll, uh, be in my room." Her bare feet scuff quietly against the hardwood floor as she walks away, leaving me alone with Theo.

"Fuck, Blake," he chokes out, taking in my tear-stained cheeks. "You're killing me."

"You shouldn't be here," I whisper.

"Baby--"

"I'm serious. You should go. You have a game to play. It's already started. You're going to be in so much trouble--"

"Don't do this, Blake."

"I'm not doing anything."

"Bullshit."

I glare back at him, the curse spreading a fire through my veins. And I'm grateful for it. The anger. The rage. I'll take anything other than the helplessness I've been drowning in.

"You know what? You're right," I tell him. "I *am* doing something. I'm pushing you away. I'm pushing you away because I asked you to not approach Coach, but you did it anyway."

"I was trying to prove—"

"Yeah. I know," I spit. "You were trying to prove you could get anything you want without any repercussions to you. And look who got burned for it."

Pain slashes across his features as he shakes his head and balls his hands into tight fists. "You know I'm sorry. You know I'd do anything to go back and change it."

"Yeah, well, you can't."

"Blake, I care about you."

I laugh and shake my head, wiping away another stupid tear on my cheek. "Yeah. And that's the shittiest part about all of this. Because I care about you too." I suck in a shallow breath. "I've always cared about you. For so long, Theo. For so long, I've cared about you." I squeeze my eyes shut, the ache in my chest more than I can bear. "But right now, I'm a little preoccupied because I have to figure out what the hell I'm going to do with my life now that my only option has been ripped away from me."

"It wasn't your only option."

"What else do I have, Theo? Nothing. I have nothing."

"That isn't true."

"Says the guy who has his entire future ahead of him," I spit. "Tell me. Have you signed with a team yet? After college? Every time I ask, you dodge the question. So, I wanna know. Are you leaving? Does our relationship have an expiration date before it's even begun? Did I lose my internship for a guy who's going to leave me anyway?"

"I'm not going anywhere."

"You should get back to the game."

I close the door without waiting for his response, but his hand slaps against the wood, stopping my success.

"I'm here, Blake. I'm here, and I'm fighting. Can't you see it?" he spits. "I want you more than hockey."

"For now," I clarify, my heart breaking with every word.

"Sure. But what happens when you get bored? Whether it's five days from now or five years? Hell, maybe it's fifty." I bite my lower lip to keep it from quivering and shake my head, shoving down my stupid emotions and how much they're threatening to choke me in this moment. I can't look at Theo. Not when I'm so close to breaking. I stare at his hands and the way they're gripping the door. Is it weird that I love his hands? That I miss the way they feel against my body? That I want to hold them? I want to entwine our fingers. I want to bring them to my lips. I want to hold on. Oh, how I want to hold on.

But it isn't that easy.

And I'm tired. Tired of seeing what we could have slip through my fingers no matter how tightly I've tried to hold onto it.

Instead, I let him go.

Squeezing my eyes shut, I whisper, "What happens when you look back at your life and realize you had to give up something you love to be with the person you care about? It isn't fair, Theo. It isn't fair to you, and the resentment you'll inevitably feel isn't fair to me. So what, then? Where does it leave us?"

"Blake…" The pain in his voice rivals my own.

"You should go." I shake my head and close the door.

This time, he lets me.

And it hurts even more than I could've imagined.

## 35

## BLAKELY

"This is a bad idea," I mutter as I stand on one leg while bending my opposite at the knee and pressing my foot to my butt in a quad stretch. I haven't exercised in almost a week which is saying something considering I've been addicted to endorphins since I was a toddler. But I haven't been able to get out of bed, let alone find the energy to run or lift weights or do anything but the bare minimum. Other than school, I've been sulking in my room. So much so, this afternoon, Mia, Kate, and Ash bombarded me after my last class and dragged me to LAU's soccer field. It's getting a little chillier, but the grass is still green, and there isn't a cloud in the sky.

It's almost peaceful. Or at least, it would be if it wasn't for the little voice in the back of my head telling me I should be spending my time finding a new job instead of soaking up what's left of the sunshine before winter is upon us. Then again, the stupid voice has been saying a lot of stupid things lately. Like how stupid I am for letting Theo go. How stupid I am for ignoring his texts. How stupid I am for avoiding Colt just because he's associated with Theo.

Yeah. Lots of stupid going on lately.

I just don't know how to stop it.

"First, it's an excellent idea," Mia announces, pulling her long blonde hair into a ponytail. "And second, you needed to get out of the house and think about something else for a few hours anyway. Why not do it while hanging out with little kids?"

"Mia," I groan.

"Blake," she mimics using a whiney voice.

"Come on. It'll be fun," Ash quips as she stretches her arms over her head. She's wearing a blush pink sports bra and spanx set with a pair of Colt's black joggers hanging low on her hips. The sweats practically swallow her whole, but Colt insisted she steal them from his gym bag when he dropped her off at the field, convinced the preteen boys wouldn't be able to concentrate with her butt on full display. After rolling her eyes, Ash obliged.

"I can't believe Mia wrangled you into volunteering too," I tell her.

"To be fair, the hours count toward my teaching degree, so..." She winks, then bends down and touches her toes.

The girl has a point.

I join her, glancing at the parking lot between my legs. "Way to kill two birds with one stone. Wish I had the same luxury."

"You could," Mia reminds me. "Don't get me wrong. Being outside while exercising and teaching kids how to do something you love sounds like a few birds with one stone, but being paid to do it?" She bounces her eyebrows up and down. "Sounds like the trifecta, don't you think?"

"How come she gets paid?" Ash demands, though there's humor in her voice. She stands up and bounces from one foot to the other in a stationary boxer jog. "You said I had to do this for free."

With a grin, Mia tells Ash, "The *experience* is your payment because you get to use it for your degree. Blake, however, could make a little moolah. If she's interested, there's still a full-time position needing to be filled and since the internship fell through..."

*Fell through.*

I'd laugh at her stretch of the truth if it weren't so pathetic.

Ignoring the familiar pang in my chest, I twist at the waist, keeping my feet planted and stretch my lower back as I ask, "Fender hasn't found anyone yet?"

"He's a little busy touring the country and asked if I could take care of it. When Theo made an ass out of himself, and you got fired, I figured I'd hold out for a few more days. See if I could convince you to do this instead." She picks up a brand new soccer ball from the lime green mesh bag lying on the grass and tosses it at me. When I catch it, she grins. "See? You got this."

I open my mouth to argue with her but decide against it.

She's right. I do need a distraction. And running around on freshly-mowed grass while teaching kids how to kick a ball seems like the perfect way to do it. Add in the prospect of making some money while figuring out what I want to do with my life or how the hell I can potentially land a new internship this late into the season is the icing on the cake.

Besides, it's not like I'm doing anything else with my life.

"Okay," I announce. "But only until I find something else."

Mia and Ash share surprised looks as Mia says, "Deal."

"Deal."

~

LAU WAS KIND ENOUGH TO ALLOW THE CHARITY TO USE THEIR soccer field for the day. It doesn't hurt that a few of the professors like to hang out at SeaBird after a long week, and Mia knows most of them on a first-name basis. One of which is the sexy statistics teacher, Professor Buchanan. He's also the guy who convinced Ash to tutor Colt when he first transferred and has connections like nobody's business. Connections that led to us using the field today. It's the perfect place to teach a bunch of kids how to kick a ball and what good sportsmanship is.

There are six volunteers scattered around the trimmed grass, including us. Most of them are like me and have a history in athletics. Some even managed to make it a few years playing professionally. The rest of the volunteers have zero experience, like Ash and Mia, but agreed to help out anyway. There's something about coming together and teaching kids––especially the ones who come from not-so-great home lives––and I'm glad I was dragged here to do exactly that.

As I juggle the ball on my knees, trying to keep it in the air for as long as possible, the parking lot behind the goal begins filling with cars.

I'm not as good as I used to be, but I can still hit ten before the ball is knocked out of reach, and I have to chase after it. Mia laughs and takes a turn juggling the ball but only hitting it twice before it bounces away from her. Meanwhile, Ash takes pictures on her cell and squeals when the ball ricochets off Mia's foot, almost hitting her in the forehead.

Kids are dropped off one by one, and once they've been separated into groups, Mia hands me a whistle and tells me to have some fun.

The kids look at me with wide eyes, hanging on my every word as I teach them how to stretch properly and explain some of the basics.

But the craziest part? It's the most fun I've had in years. And passing along knowledge I've somehow picked up along the way is the most rewarding thing I've experienced since blowing out my knee in high school.

Seriously. It feels good. Really good.

To be seen.

Appreciated.

Hell, these kids practically worship me. And by the time their caregivers come and pick them up, Mia's grinning from ear to ear.

When I catch her staring, I point my index finger at her. "Not one word."

"Not even I told ya so?" she quips.

"Those are four words."

"*You're a genius, Mia* is four words too," Ash interjects as she gathers the balls on the grass.

I snort and toss a soccer ball at her as Mia leaves me with a knowing grin and starts collecting the orange cones from around the field.

*Maybe they're right.*

*Maybe I'll be okay after all.*

# 36

## BLAKELY

"**D**ude, great job," I say, hip-checking the cute little eleven-year-old named Bridger.

His cheeks turn pink as he drops his gaze to the ground. "Thanks."

The rest of the group was picked up over an hour ago. And now, it's only me and Bridge. Well, Mia's sitting on the grass near the parking lot with her phone pressed to her ear trying to figure out how to get ahold of Bridger's foster mom, but she doesn't really count since she's a little preoccupied.

We've been passing the soccer ball back and forth across the field for the past twenty minutes, but it's easy to see how uncomfortable the kid is from being the last one here. In fact, it breaks my heart. How could someone just forget to pick him up? Like, come on, lady. Have a heart, would ya?

When Bridger catches me glancing at Mia and the nearly empty parking lot, he mutters, "Sorry she's late."

"It's okay. Gives us more time to practice."

"I can wait by myself," he offers, kicking at the grass with his hands tucked in his pockets.

"No deal. I'm having too much fun." I jog a few feet away from him and kick the neon yellow ball at him again. We've been working on ball control for the past forty-five minutes, and the kid's legitimately talented.

When he passes the ball back to me, I ask, "Seriously. Have you played a lot of soccer in the past?"

He shrugs. "My dad would play with me sometimes."

"Well, you're a natural," I tell him.

Another shrug.

"Want to play another round? Maybe practice hitting toward the goal? Or we can try to see how many times we can juggle it before the ball hits the ground?"

His little shoulders bounce up and down again.

"Or we could just sit and chat while we wait," I offer.

Sucking his bottom lip into his mouth, he kicks at the grass. "Whatever you want, Miss Blakely."

My eyes crinkle in the corners.

*Miss Blakely.*

This kid is way too adorable.

"I'm a sucker for twenty questions," I murmur. "Wanna play?"

He peeks up at me, his brown eyes tugging at my heartstrings. "Sure."

"Alrighty, then." I plop onto the grass and cross my legs in front of me, patting the ground beside me.

Cautiously, he sits down and cradles the soccer ball in his lap.

There are so many questions I'd love to ask, but I refuse to let him get lost in his own head when it's clear he lives there far too often.

I start the game. "Favorite candy?"

"Snickers."

"Ooo, those are good. Personally, I'm a sucker for Take 5s."

"What's a Take 5?" he asks, looking up at me.

I gasp and clutch at my chest. "You don't know what a Take 5 is?"

Shaking his head, he says, "No?"

"Dude. You gotta try a Take 5. I'll see if I can bring some to the next practice."

"You don't have to," he mutters. He looks back down at the grass, picking some of it with his fingers.

I nudge his shoulder with my own. "I want to. I'll even bring a bag of Snickers, and we can compare with the rest of the group. Does that sound okay?"

His shoulders lift in another shrug, but his cute little lips tilt up in the corner, too, and the sight gives me hope. Like maybe he'll be all right after all.

"Okay, what's your favorite soda?" I prod.

"Orange Crush."

"Shut up! Orange Crush was my best friend's––" I snap my mouth shut, surprised by the declaration and how much it hurts to think of Theo or the fact that I look at him like my best friend instead of my brother's.

"Your best friend likes Crush?" Bridger asks.

I clear my throat and clarify, "Technically, he was my brother's best friend before he was mine. But yeah. Crush was his favorite growing up. He used to have it all the time."

"I only get it on special occasions or if I save up enough allowance," Bridger admits.

*Oh, my heart.*

I continue asking him questions, and he continues answering them for another few minutes when a familiar red Toyota truck pulls into the parking lot.

It takes me a second to place it, but when I do, the hair rises on the back of my neck.

"What about you, Miss Blakely?" Bridger asks me.

I tear my gaze from the parked truck and back to the little

boy beside me. "I'm sorry. What was the question?"

"What's your favorite sport?" he repeats.

"Oof. Tough question." My lips purse as I weigh my options. "Not gonna lie. I kind of love hockey, but you can't tell anyone."

"Hockey?"

"Yeah. My brother's a hockey player, so I was kind of raised watching him play."

"My brother's in prison," Bridger mumbles, his lips pulling into a frown.

*Shit.*

I'd done my best to stay away from anything family related, but apparently, I slipped up. It's like the kid's a minefield. I wrap my arm around him and pull him into a side hug without saying a word.

But the silence only spurs him on.

"He was dealing drugs. Ended up in juvie."

Damn.

I didn't even know what juvie was at his age, let alone how to get drugs.

My throat constricts, but I clear it. "I'm…I'm sorry, buddy."

"It happens."

My heart pinches, but I bite my tongue to keep from arguing with him. Because he's right. It does happen. But it shouldn't. Especially not with kids.

"Trudy's here," he mutters, pushing to his feet while still cradling the soccer ball to his chest. I'd been so focused on our conversation, I hadn't noticed the seafoam green van pulled up next to the curb. The windows are rolled down, and Mia's talking to the driver, though they're too far away for me to hear what's being said.

As I stand up and wipe off my butt for any dirt or pieces of grass, he offers the ball to me, but I shake my head. "Keep it, Bridge. You can practice juggling and show me your progress at the next get together, okay?"

He shakes his head. "I can't take––"

"Dude," I scold with a smile. "Take it."

He frowns and looks at the ball in his hands, then glances at me again. "You sure?"

"One hundred percent. Like I said, my brother's a hockey player and is going to be big and famous one day. I think he can afford a ball." I wink at him and add, "I'll see you on Thursday, okay?"

His chin dips in a tiny nod. "Okay."

"Bye, buddy!" I wave my hand.

As he walks back to the parking lot, a car door squeaks open before closing with a solid thud, and I turn to see Russ striding toward me with his hands in his front pockets.

I knew I recognized his truck.

Part of me wants to run in the opposite direction, another wave of embarrassment flooding my system for how things turned out, but the other part is too curious to leave. Too *bitter* to leave.

*Why the hell is Russ here?*

With my hand propped on my hip, I wait for him to walk closer and keep my head held high despite the voice inside begging me to tuck my tail between my legs and get the hell out of here.

But I refuse to give in. To let him and Coach and everyone else on the hockey team win.

*I did nothing wrong*, I remind myself.

When he is close enough to hear me, I call out, "Fancy seeing you here."

"Baby Thorne," he greets me. He looks tired. Remorseful. Almost uncomfortable, which is saying something. The guy doesn't give a shit about what other people say or think. He's a military man through and through. He's also a man of few words, and right now, he isn't saying shit. Before, it was something I genuinely liked about the guy, but in this moment, I kind of want to smack him for it.

"Can I help you?" I prod, my tone syrupy sweet but laced with a sharpness I can't hold in despite my best effort. The truth is, he kind of betrayed me. Coach betrayed me. I was tossed aside so easily. So quickly. It hurt like a bitch.

He looks up at me, unphased by my prickliness. "We want you back."

"We?" I ask.

He nods. "Sanderson wanted me to reach out."

I almost choke on my snort but swallow it back as I rock on my heels and fold my arms. "He did, did he?"

"Wanted me to see if you're still interested in the internship."

My teeth dig into my tongue to keep from lashing out from the balls on this guy. I want to remind him I was fired. It's not like I left because I was bored or uninterested in the opportunity.

*Duh.*

But still. He wants me back? *Coach* wants me back?

"Did Theo put you up to this?" I demand.

"Taylor wasn't involved in this decision. You're talented, Blake. Genuinely. And I don't blow smoke up anyone's ass unless they deserve it."

I dig my fingernails into the inside of my crossed arms, confirming I'm very much awake, but keep my expression indifferent. Part of me wants to say yes. To beg him to let me come back and finish out the season.

If he'd shown up thirty minutes earlier, I would have.

But that was before my conversation with Bridger. Before I met a little boy who'd never had a Take 5. The boy with the broken family and a penchant for soccer. Before I felt needed. Before I felt like I could truly make a difference. An impact reaching a hell of a lot further than athlete recovery and injury prevention. Don't get me wrong. Those things are still important, but in all my studying, all my experience from shadowing Russ, I never felt needed in the way I did with Bridger. Never felt important in the way I did with Bridger. The realization is staggering.

Trudy's van pulls out of the parking lot, and I watch the brake lights disappear down the street.

"Blake?" Russ prods.

Holy shit, am I really doing this? Am I really giving up my lifelong dream despite the second opportunity to have it? Am I letting it go *willingly* instead of having it ripped from my fingertips?

Am I crazy? Am I going to regret this?

An image of Bridger rises to the surface, followed by a dozen more faces belonging to the other kids I met today. They were all so sweet. So desperate for affection. My heart cracks, and I rub at the ache, indecision threatening to tear me in two.

"You're going to say no, aren't you?" Russ murmurs. I can feel his stare on the side of my face.

I blink and tear my attention from the empty parking lot. "I appreciate the offer, Russ. I really do. But I think I'm where I'm supposed to be."

The bastard doesn't even look surprised.

"The kid looked up to you. I could see it from my truck."

"He's a sweetheart," I say.

"Seemed like it." Russ pats my shoulder. "If you ever change your mind, you know where to find me."

"I'll keep that in mind."

He turns toward the parking lot but stops and looks at me again, his gaze filled with pride. "You ever need anything... you call me."

He heads back to his car, and I'm left reeling.

With a deep breath, I tap my knuckles against Coach's office door. It's propped open with an old puck shoved beneath it, but Coach is reading something on his desk, too engrossed to notice me.

I clear my throat. "Coach?"

He looks up. "Yeah?"

"Can we talk for a sec?"

Motioning to the chair opposite his desk, he replies, "Take a seat."

I collapse into the chair as if my body weighs a thousand pounds and rest my elbows on my knees.

"So?" he prods, when I've been quiet for too long.

"I want to date Blake."

Leaning forward, Coach steeples his fingers in front of his chin. "You made it clear at last week's game."

"I know. And I was wrong to ask your permission in front of everyone."

As stoic as ever, the bastard stays quiet but continues staring at me, making me squirm.

"And I'm sorry I went about it the wrong way," I add.

"Apology accepted." He looks down at the paperwork in front of him. "You're dismissed."

I stay seated, my annoyance simmering just beneath the surface, but I force myself to keep it in check. I didn't come back to the arena after talking with Blake. I was too frustrated. Too amped up. To be honest, I was afraid I'd lose my shit on Coach and wind up spending the night in jail for assault. So instead, I visited Mack. He let me drown my sorrows in the beer in his fridge and forced me to spend the night to sleep off my hangover on his couch.

The next morning, we talked, finally opening up to each other. And even though it almost killed me, I told him everything, including how I'd screwed up with Blake. He's the one who convinced me to come back here. To Coach's office. He's the one who convinced me to fight for my future––both on *and* off the ice––and to apologize for being an ass.

And so, even though the words taste bitter, I clear my throat and say, "I'd like to come back and play on the team. I shouldn't have walked out."

Coach looks up at me again, his expression unreadable. "You're right. You shouldn't have. It wasn't fair to me, and it wasn't fair to the team."

My molars grind against each other. "You're right. It wasn't."

"Glad we can agree. You also shouldn't have missed the last few practices."

"You're right. I shouldn't have."

"Good. You're benched for one more game, but if you can make it to all the practices, I'll let you start against the Wolverines."

It sucks being benched, but after the shit I pulled, it feels more like a slap on the wrist than anything else.

"Thanks," I tell him.

His chin dips in acknowledgement, and he repeats, "You're dismissed."

"I'm not finished."

He drops the pen onto his desk and leans back in his chair, crossing his arms. "Fine. Finish."

"I want you to give Blake her job back. I'm the one who screwed up. Not her. She deserves to be on this team. I'll stay away from her if that's what it takes. But it isn't fair she was fired because of me."

"You're right," he replies. "It isn't."

I lean further into my chair, surprised by how easily he conceded. "So...will you give her back the internship? Will you let me fix this?"

He sighs, his attention dropping to the paperwork on his desk before snapping back to me. "Russ already tried. She declined the offer."

Confusion swirls in my lower gut as I lean forward in my chair. "What?"

"She declined," he repeats.

"Why?"

"By the time I cooled down and asked Russ to reach out--which he'd been chomping at the bit to do--she'd already found a new position with a charity. Something involving teaching kids sports. Despite the information, Russ tracked her down and invited her to come back, but she said no. Seeing how happy she was, he didn't fight her on it." Coach's mouth lifts slightly. "He actually thought it was an even better fit for the girl, and I have to agree."

"So, she isn't coming back?"

"She declined," he reminds me. "It's out of my control."

"Then..." My voice trails off as the questions filter through my mind, one after another, leaving me more clue-less and lost than I'd been *before* working up the courage to sit in Coach's office with my tail tucked between my legs.

"You look lost," he notes.

"If she doesn't want the internship anymore, I don't know…" My voice trails off, and I wipe my palms on my jeans.

"You don't know how to make it up to her if you can't help get her job back?" he finishes for me.

I nod and squeeze the back of my neck.

"Good question. If I can help, let me know."

I nod again but stay quiet. Because I don't know what to do or say. Not anymore.

"Did you decide on the contracts?" he prods, changing the subject.

I shake my head. I've been too distracted by Blake to even read over them.

"Have you talked to anyone about your options? Your parents? Colt? You know he signed last week."

"Yeah, I know," I mutter.

It's funny. When his dad died, he dropped out of the NHL draft, even though he probably would've ended up being picked in the first round. But with him back on the ice, they were all anxious to sign him. I decided to wait and get some more playing time before making any decisions, slipping past the ECHL and choosing the NCAA instead. I had no idea how lucrative of a choice it would play out to be until my personal life became more complicated too. It muddied the waters.

When Colt first transferred to LAU, I was the one with my head on straight. The one with my future laid out. The one with all the plans and all the dreams, and I put in the hard work to fulfill them.

Now, the idea of leaving––of playing for my favorite team across the country––feels like torture. Like it's too far away from the life I've built. Like it's making me give up more than I want. And in exchange for what, exactly?

I don't even know anymore.

"You need to decide what you want, Theo," Coach warns.

"I know what I want," I argue.

And that's the problem.

As if he can read my mind, his brow arches, and he checks the time on the clock hanging next to his office door. "Russ found her at the field yesterday but said she likes the track too. Might wanna start your ass-kissing there." His gaze flicks back to mine. "I'll see you at practice tomorrow."

"Yes, sir."

"You're dismissed."

## BLAKELY

With my feet propped up on the coffee table, I ignore Colt and Ash making out at the front door. They've been saying goodbye for the past ten minutes, and I kind of want to smack them for it.

I hate being jealous. But I am. I can't help it. They're just so cute together. No drama. No fighting. No miscommunications or misunderstandings. Or at least, none I've heard of since interrupting their little conversation at the Taylor House not so long ago. They're freaking perfect for each other.

And it's annoying as hell.

Especially when I've been avoiding the guy I thought was perfect for me. I've been ignoring his texts. And I feel guilty for it. I know how much he wants to talk. To make things up to me. And I've been... What exactly? Too stubborn? Too hurt?

Honestly, I don't even know anymore.

Part of me wonders if I did this to myself.

But relationships and me? We aren't friends. I learned it a long time ago and was reminded of the sad truth after I was fired. The sooner I accept it, the sooner I can enjoy what I *do* excel at.

Like my new job. And helping kids. Helping them fall in love with being outside. Helping them fall in love with running, and jumping, and throwing, and kicking, and moving their bodies because it's fun to move their bodies. Helping them see how beautiful they are on the inside and out. Helping them fall in love with being active and how important it is——not only physically but mentally and emotionally too.

It's what I'm good at. And that's what I need to focus on. Not relationships. Not Colt and Ash. And definitely not Theo.

"Go," Ash tells my brother with a laugh. "Seriously."

"Yes, please go," I chirp from the couch. "You two are disgusting."

"Disgustingly sweet," Mia interrupts as she walks down the hall from her bedroom. "Seriously. Colt, if you ever manage to figure out cloning, can you please make another of yourself? Some of us have crappy luck with love."

Ash snorts, and Colt laughs, dropping another quick kiss to Ash's forehead.

"Speaking of which. Have you heard from Shorty?" he asks.

Her eyes widen like a deer in the headlights as her phone dings with an incoming text and she wiggles it back and forth. "Sorry, it's work. Gotta go. We'll catch up later. Byeeee." She turns on her heel and heads back to her room, leaving me——yet again——with the two love birds.

*Great.*

"Is she doing okay?" Colt asks Ash, his eyebrows pinched.

"She's...being Mia." Ashlyn wraps her arms around Colt's waist and leans her head against his chest. "But I definitely think we should figure out how to clone you, so she can see how awesome relationships can be when you're with the right person." Her lips tilt up in a rueful smile, and she lifts her head, looking up at him. "Actually, never mind. Even if you had a clone, I'd still be jealous seeing you with someone who isn't me."

"Doesn't matter, Ash. Each and every one of them would still pick you." He leans in for another kiss, and she sighs against his lips.

"Love you," she whispers.

"Love you too, Sunshine." Colt turns to me, his expression still soft and sweet from his little exchange.

*Gross.*

"Listen, Blake. Whenever you're ready––"

"I'm not," I sing.

"So…you're still ignoring me?" Colt asks.

With a huff, I twist on the couch, using the back as a cushion for my elbows so I can face him fully. "I'm not ignoring you. I've been…busy."

"Busy ignoring me."

"Busy with my new job," I clarify.

Despite his accusation, I've seen the bastard almost daily, thanks to his relationship with Ash. Not that I can complain. I love my brother. But I also know he lives with Theo, and plays hockey with Theo, and talks to Theo every day, and when I'm trying to avoid all things *Theo*, it makes our relationship a little stickier than I'd like it to be.

"You've also been ditching my games," he reminds me.

"Again. I've been busy. Between classes and organizing activities for the charity, it's kind of chaotic."

He shakes his head softly, and I know he wants to argue, but the bastard's nice enough not to. "I'll let it go. For now," he clarifies. "But I expect you at some of my next games, all right?"

I stick my tongue out at him and flop back onto the

couch, facing the darkened television screen.

"Love you, sis," he calls.

I ignore the pinch in my chest and how desperately I want to ask about his stupid best friend. But I don't. Because I can't. Even thinking Teddy's name is enough to break me. Actually having a conversation where he's the main talking point? Nope. No, thank you.

With a quick blind wave at Colt from behind the edge of the couch, I say, "Bye, big brother."

I hear another lip-smacking kiss behind me as Ash says goodbye to Colt. I catch Kate's reflection in the black television screen as she slips through the door before Ash can close it. Then, she slams the door behind her. I jerk up and look behind me.

*Uh, this can't be good.*

Kate is never frustrated. She's basically the nicest person on the planet and doesn't have an angry bone in her body.

Until today.

Ash and I exchange worried glances as Kate marches into the family room and drops her backpack onto the floor. It lands with a solid thunk next to the couch as she collapses onto the ugly-ass recliner in a heap. But the girl doesn't say a word. She just sits there, staring blankly at the window in the opposite direction of Ash and me.

"So...," Ash drags out the word, eyeing Kate warily while rounding the arm of the couch and lowering herself onto the edge of the cushion next to me. Like she's sitting on pins and needles. Then again, so am I.

Kate shakes her head but *still* doesn't say a word. Not a damn one.

Footsteps echo from down the hall as Mia approaches the family room, her eyes glued to her phone.

"Good news. Ashton texted me. I don't have work at SeaBird tonight. Hallelujah. We should––" Her heels digs into the floor when she sees all of us sitting in silence. Slipping her phone into the back pocket of her jeans, she tiptoes into the room and sits on the edge of the couch between Ash and me, mirroring our position.

"What'd I miss?" she whispers to no one in particular.

*Good question.*

"We broke up," Kate replies. She isn't crying. She isn't angry. She isn't relieved. She's…numb.

"Oh, honey," Mia starts, but Kate lifts her hand and stops her.

"It's fine."

"Kate," I say because obviously, she is *not* fine.

"Seriously. It's fine," she lies, scratching at her temple while keeping her blank stare zeroed in on the window. "I knew it was going to happen. I knew he'd only see me as a problem. A girl who couldn't give him what he wanted in the long run. I knew it."

"But it isn't true," Ash murmurs.

With a dry laugh, Kate shakes her head and finally looks at us. "If it weren't true, Wes wouldn't have broken up with me fifteen minutes ago."

"I thought you told him about your…" Mia hesitates, the word *epilepsy* catching in her throat. "I thought you already talked to him a little while ago?"

"I did. And he said it was fine. Didn't even really bat an eye about it. Which only made it worse." She wrings her hands in her lap, anxiety twisting her gorgeous features.

"What changed?" I prod.

"If I had to guess, he finally gave in and Googled it. Stupid Google," Kate mutters under her breath, shaking her head again. "I swear, that *thing* is the bane of my existence."

Ash grimaces. "You don't know he Googled––"

"What else could he have done? Everything's been great. Perfect, actually. He even told me he loved me." She laughs again and wipes under her eyes with her index finger, a chink in her armor finally showing. "Can you believe it? I told him about my condition, he pulled me into a hug, kissed the top of my head, and said it was okay. But it wasn't okay. Obviously," she adds, her tone laced with sarcasm.

"Then, he's an ass," I announce.

Ash nods and walks to the kitchen, grabbing a pint of cookie dough ice cream from the freezer and a spoon from the cabinets, handing them to Kate.

With a tight smile, Kate lets the only comfort we can give rest in her lap. She looks more exhausted than I've ever seen. And that's saying something. The girl works harder than anyone I know. Her semester is packed, and when she isn't studying, she's working or visiting her parents.

"You know what's really stupid about it all?" she asks. "I haven't had a seizure in a year. I've been taking my medication. I've been studying. I've been doing everything a perfect student has to do to succeed in life, and I *still* get the shaft."

"He's an immature asshole, Kate," I argue. "Seriously. You deserve someone so much better than Wes."

Another snide laugh bubbles out of her as she wipes beneath her nose with the back of her hand. "Sure, I do."

"I'm serious, Kate. He doesn't deserve you," I tell her.

"And who does?" she challenges. "Santa Claus? The Easter Bunny, maybe? Ooo, how about a fae lord in need of a human princess?"

Mia frowns. "Kate––"

"I've tried looking for someone who accepts me in all my less-than-perfect glory, but the guy doesn't exist. And every time I think he does, he finds out about my condition or sees me seizing firsthand, and poof. That's it. He's gone. And I'm not enough."

"Kate," Ash scolds.

Kate sets the untouched ice cream and spoon on the

coffee table and pushes to her feet. "I'm going to study for a test in Professor Buchanan's class. I'll talk to you guys later."

"Kate," Ash tries again, but Kate ignores her and slips down the hall, closing her bedroom door with a quiet click behind her.

We sit in silence, none of us knowing what to do, or what to say, or how to act after everything Kate just unloaded. Because she's right. It isn't fair. She's amazing. The fact Wes couldn't see past her disease and left her high and dry? It's bullshit. Of course, the girl has trust issues. She deserves to have those trust issues. But what she doesn't deserve is to be punished over something she has zero control over. Actually, scratch that. What little control she does have, she's utilizing to the best of her ability. She stays away from alcohol. She stays away from drugs. She goes to sleep at a decent hour and even wakes up early to make sure she doesn't throw off her sleep schedule. The girl takes her medication at the same time every day and even puts up with her overbearing parents. She's mature. Thoughtful. A go-getter. And the shit Wes pulled? It's ridiculous.

But is it his fault? At least he didn't string her along once he realized he couldn't handle her disease. That has to count for something, doesn't it?

Ash picks up Kate's ice cream, puts it back in the freezer, and sits down on the cushion beside me, twisting her hands in her lap as she stares at the hallway leading to Kate's room. Like she's itching to comfort her.

We all are.

"Well, that sucks," Mia mutters, putting her feet on the coffee table and settling back into the couch.

"Yeah," I breathe out.

*It really does.*

"She needs someone older," Ash decides. "Someone who doesn't run at the slightest inconvenience, ya know?

Someone who isn't afraid to take on the hard shit because he knows Kate's worth it in the end."

"Right?" Mia adds. "All these college boys are pansies."

"Except Colt," Ash gushes shamelessly.

I roll my eyes. "You two make me sick. You know that, right?"

"But the good kind of sick." Ash winks. "Speaking of which, how are...things?"

With a scoff, I mutter, "Subtle, Ash."

"I'm just saying..." Her voice trails off, and she lifts her hands in defense.

Mia and Ash exchange glances and Mia announces, "I'll get the alcohol. You ask the questions."

"Mia," I whine.

"Hush." Ash pats my knee. "Now, where were we? Oh. Right. Colt may have mentioned how miserable––"

"Stop," I beg. "Seriously, I can't hear about him."

"He misses you," Mia interrupts from the kitchen. "Even stopped by SeaBird so he could ask me how you're doing."

"He did?"

"Uh, yeah," Ash answers. "And it was super adorable and pathetic all at once."

I nibble my lower lip. Finally giving in to my curiosity, I ask, "And what'd you guys say?"

"I lied and said you're doing awesome," Mia replies, setting down a trio of wine glasses onto the kitchen counter and searching for the wine opener in the drawer. "Although, I have a feeling Colt might've spilled the beans about your misery 'cause he didn't look too convinced. But Ash is right. He looked miserable when we saw him."

"Good," I decide. "He deserves to be."

"Just tell me this," Ash starts. "Is there a world where you'd forgive him? Where you'd give him another chance?"

It's a question I've been asking myself since I closed the

door in his face. But it's hard. Complicated. And even if I did overreact, the idea of starting a relationship that already has baggage and tacking on long-distance? It sounds miserable.

But I'm already miserable, so…

I sigh and puff out my cheeks, unsure how to answer. "I don't know."

"It isn't a no," Mia quips, pouring dark red wine into three goblets on the kitchen island.

"It isn't a yes, either," I mutter.

"I think you should," Ash decides. "I saw the spark between you two. And even though you've been keeping yourself busy with school and the charity, we've still noticed how down you've been."

"We've also noticed how few parties have been happening at the Taylor House since Theo had his heart broken," Mia chimes in.

"He was an asshole," I tell them, but I'm not sure who I'm reminding anymore.

Especially when I found a career path I love *so* much more than anything I'd been doing before the charity fell into my lap. It's crazy. How quickly my world was turned upside down, and I can't help but feel like it was for the better, despite my fear when letting it go…in every way except for one.

"All men have their moments," Ash says, bringing me back to the present. "It's whether or not they can make up for their assholery and make the changes to *not* let it happen again that makes them worth it."

Balancing three filled-to-the-brim glasses in her hands, Mia walks over to us and gives a goblet to me and Ash, then lifts her own into the air. "To assholes."

Ash and I join her, clicking our glasses together. "To assholes."

Then, I drink the whole thing down.

313

## BLAKELY

There's a track next to the gym at school. I have weights at home, and usually, I'm a sucker for running around campus instead of the monotonous loop a track provides, but sometimes, I crave it. The monotony. The way I can push myself, timing each lap until my muscles are spent and my lungs are aching.

And today, it's exactly what I need. A distraction. Something I can focus on. Something I can lose myself in. And since we haven't covered running or any other track and field games, I figured it wouldn't hurt to get in a quick run before introducing the kids to the track field. They should be here any minute.

I've been here for almost an hour and take another cool down lap, letting my Nike's pound against the asphalt in rhythm to my steady heartbeat until I round the last corner and pause. It isn't for long, barely a millisecond, but it's enough to throw me off. To bring me back to reality. To erase the distraction running usually gives me.

I keep my gaze glued in front of me, ignoring a stupidly attractive Theo who's stretching his quads next to the track.

314

His red and black joggers match his LAU T-shirt as he watches me from the edge of the grass. Since his navy blue eyes are partially hidden beneath the brim of his baseball hat, it only showcases his strong jaw even more.

I guess I shouldn't be surprised he finally managed to track me down. He's been texting at least every hour and even cornered me at The Bean Scene yesterday, offering to walk me to my car. I looped my arm through Colt's and said he'd take care of it. Thankfully, my brother was a gem and didn't bat an eye.

Today, however, is a different story. The one and only cherry-popper is here in the flesh. And he's looking at me. Despite my best effort at pretending he doesn't exist, I can still feel it. His gaze. His hesitancy. His remorse.

Which is ridiculous.

We're cool. So, we slept together. Big deal. I asked him to take my v-card, and he ruined my career by trying to claim my heart in front of everyone. It's *super* great. But I've moved on, or at least, I'm trying to. Okay, it's a lie. I haven't moved on. I'm not sure I *can* move on. Not when it comes to Teddy. But crawling back to him after everything that happened? I can't exactly do that, either.

I glance at him again, my heart rate kicking up a notch. I have a feeling it has nothing to do with the exercise.

Why is he here? I know for a fact how much he hates running. Did he know I'd be here? And if that's the case, should I be flattered or would it make me feel even more desperate? I stare at the white painted lines separating the lanes on the track and try to get a grip on my emotions before it's too late. But it still doesn't make sense. Why hasn't he given up yet when I know he has the attention span of a gnat and I've already made my stance very clear?

My stance I've been regretting as soon as I slammed the door in his face, but still.

When I don't slow down as I run past him, Theo curses under his breath and jogs after me.

"Blake, wait," he calls.

The rhythmic thump-thump of his feet against the pavement rings in my ears as he runs after me, so I pick up my pace. My lungs are screaming at me since I've already been working them for the past hour, but the bastard doesn't slow down. He doesn't quit. He keeps pushing.

So, I do too.

Pumping my arms back and forth, I speed around the final turn while trying to block out his pounding feet acting like a soundtrack in a horror movie or something. Which is an insane analogy. He would never hurt me.

At least, not any more than he already has.

Once he finally catches up to me, he matches my pace and stays glued to my side.

*Bastard.*

Despite the stitch in my ribs, and the lightheadedness making me dizzy, I run two more laps until I finally give in and slow down.

"Thank fuck," Theo mutters beside me as he catches his breath.

It's kind of adorable. Or at least, it would be if I wasn't so pissed at him.

With my hands on top of my head, I breathe in deep and attempt to slow my heart rate as I ask, "What are you doing here?"

"Wanted to talk."

"Well, I'm finishing up my run, so…"

"Yeah. Caught that. Guess it means I'm running, too, until you're ready to talk."

"Since when do you run?" I challenge.

"Since"––*deep breath*––"recently, apparently."

"You don't run," I remind him, my breath slowly steadying as the seconds tick by.

He takes another deep breath and rolls his eyes. "Special circumstances, I guess."

"Like what? Your puck bunnies aren't available?"

His brows furrow. "Huh?"

"When I was moving in with the girls. You said fucking was your favorite form of cardio," I remind him. "Guess I figured if you're at the track, they must be busy or something."

It's a low blow, but I can't help myself. He hurt me. More than once.

He grabs my bicep to keep me from darting off but continues catching his breath. And I hate how good it feels. His hand on me. The way I want him to wrap it around my waist and just...hold me.

*Snap out of it, Blake.*

His heated gaze burns the side of my face as we stand in silence at the edge of the track, but I don't look at him. If I do, he'll see how much I'm hurting. How much I miss him.

"I wouldn't know if the bunnies are busy," he says. "I haven't talked to them in months."

I scoff and tug my arm away from him. "Sure, you haven't."

"I'm serious, Blake."

"Not sure why you're telling me about your sex life, Teddy. It's not like it has anything to do with me anymore."

Frustrated, he twists his baseball hat backwards and asks, "Look. Can we talk?"

I glare at him. "There's nothing to talk about."

"Come on, Blake."

"I'm serious. What's done is done, okay? No hard feelings. Let's just...move on and go our separate ways. And since you're leaving at the end of year, anyway, it's what's best for both of us, right?"

"Blake," he repeats. There's an edge to his voice causing me to pause.

I suck my lips between my teeth, look up at him, and wait.

"Give me another chance."

I laugh. "You're joking, right?"

"I meant what I said to Coach. I care about you. I could fucking love you, Blake. And I was wrong for putting your job on the line. It's not what I meant to do."

"We've already covered this," I remind him. "Besides, I'm…" A beat-up red and rust minivan pulls into the parking lot and seven kids pile out of the back, racing toward me with giant grins. Theo follows my gaze and tucks his hands into his pockets.

"I can't talk about this right now," I seethe under my breath through a fake-ass smile directed at the kids.

"Then when can we talk about it?" he asks.

"Never?" I offer, taking a step away. He grabs my arm and twists me to face him.

"You know, for a girl who's convinced I'm gonna leave, you're doing a hell of a lot of running from me."

I gasp, blindsided.

But I don't have time to argue with him. Not when the kids are arriving, and I have a class to teach.

"Hey, Blake!" one of the kids calls. His name is Billy, and he's one of the sweetest little boys I've ever met. He's also in the foster care system and has a twin brother and a little sister. Both of whom are trailing behind him.

Billy stops short when he sees how tense I look, and I hate the fear flashing in his eyes. "I-is everything okay?"

"It's fine," I promise, giving Theo my back as I group a few more kids together on the grass surrounding the track loop. "We're having a little bit of an argument, but I promise Theo's a nice man, okay? I'm sorry if we scared you."

"Yeah, buddy. We're good," Theo calls from behind me. "I just asked Miss Blakely to race me, but she's too afraid I'll win, so…"

I stop short, convinced I've heard him wrong as a few of the kids around me "*ooo*" like we're on the playground and a fight could break out at any second.

"I'm sorry. What did you say?" I ask, facing him again.

The bastard's cocky smirk does annoying things to my insides as he says, "I said…you're too afraid to race me."

"Who says I'm afraid?"

His gaze softens, and I know he isn't thinking about the race anymore. He's referring to something bigger. Something more.

With a shrug, he rasps, "Guess it's just a hunch."

Refusing to let him see how close he hit home, I demand, "What are the stipulations?"

His biceps bulge as he crosses his arms, considering his options as the kids wait with bated breath.

"If I win, you give me another chance to make it up to you for being an––" He hesitates, remembering our current audience is all under twelve, and clarifies, "A *jerk*."

"No thanks," I deflect, ignoring how much it feels like ants are crawling beneath my skin. I never turn down a bet. *Ever.* And oh, how I would love to beat Theo's ass today. But accepting his challenge would open the door for more communication. More feelings. And I'm not sure I'm strong enough to keep them in check. Not when I'm so close to caving already.

Stepping closer, he pushes aside his amusement and drops his voice low until only I can hear him. "I messed up, Blake. And it's been killing me. I should've listened to you and taken things slower. I shouldn't have ruined your trust."

He scrubs his hand over his face. "But I'm here. And I'm not done fighting for this. Fighting for us. Give me a chance to do it differently. Please."

*Damn those eyes.*

"Come on, Miss Blakely," Billy interjects. "You can totally beat him."

Theo's mouth lifts in a smirk, his eyes shining with sincerity. "He's right. You *can* totally beat me."

"Glad we're finally in agreement," I quip.

"Yeah," he chuckles, and the sound makes my stomach somersault. "It's a pretty rare thing with us, isn't it? We should probably work on that."

"And what if I win?" I continue, ignoring his assumption we have anything to work on in the first place because we aren't a *we*. Not anymore. Not ever, actually. The realization stings.

"I'll give you whatever you want. Space. Dinner," he teases, though I can see the worry in his eyes.

Because he knows I'm faster than he is. But he's desperate. And his desperation is about to bite him in the ass.

"You're not worried?" I ask.

"Scared as hell." His dry response makes my mouth twist up in a ghost of a smile before I bite it back.

At least he's honest.

As if he can't help himself, he trails his fingertips along the shell of my ear, tucking my hair behind it as he looks down at me with so much want, so much need, I'm afraid my legs might give out at any second.

*Stay strong, Blake*, I remind myself.

"But I'm not afraid to make a fool of myself or fight for the things I want. Besides, you aren't the only competitive one around here." He drops his hand to his side as if remembering I'm not his to touch. "One lap. Then, I'll either leave you alone...*for a week,*" he clarifies, "or you'll give me a chance to make it up to you tonight. Deal?"

"A week?" I ask with a laugh, my heart twinging. But I can't help it. The guy is hands down the most stubborn person I've ever met.

He brushes his fingertips against my arm but drops his hand to his side again. "You really think I'd let you go forever, Baby Thorne?"

Stupid heart. And his stupid proximity.

"Yeah, come on, Miss Blakely!" Bridger calls. I'd been so distracted by my conversation with Theo, I hadn't realized we'd collected quite the crowd. Almost everyone's here. Even a few of the other volunteers are watching.

*Great.*

"I'm not sure it's a good idea," I hedge, and it isn't because I'm afraid of losing. It's because I'm afraid of winning. We've played this game already. Put our hearts on the line under the guise of a bet. And so far? It hasn't exactly worked out in our favor. He's been on my mind constantly since the blowup with Coach. And even though I've ignored his texts, even though I've avoided all things cinnamon and every Adam Sandler movie on the planet, none of it has made me feel better. I've still missed him. I've still read his text messages. I've still thought about him. More than I'd like to admit. The idea of him giving up under the guise of it being what I want, even if it's only for a week? In reality, it sounds pretty terrible.

So where does it leave me?

Honestly, I have no idea.

"You can do it, Miss Blakely!" Billy's little sister calls. Her name's Hailey, and she has the darkest, curliest hair I've ever seen. She also looks at me like I'm a warrior goddess, practically worshipping the ground I walk on since the moment

321

we first met. The idea of letting her down pushes me forward.

I give her a smile and turn back to Theo, crossing my arms and popping out my hip. "All right, Teddy Bear. I'll play."

"Oh, you will, huh?"

"Mm-hmm." With a bow, I motion to the starting line a few feet away. "Ladies first."

He chuckles, lining himself up with the starting line and bending into a runner's stance. "On the count of three?"

I stand beside him, mirroring his position. "One."

"Two."

"Three."

# THEO

*S* *hit, this girl's fast.*

We take off from the starting line, pumping our arms back and forth. She's on the outside of the track, giving me the smallest advantage, and even though I don't want to admit it, I'm gonna need all the help I can get if I want to beat her.

She's right. I hate running. But I've also been doing it more often lately to blow off steam before and after practices. Guess I'm a sucker for beating myself up, and today isn't any different.

She laughs as she passes me. The tiny wisps of red hair that've fallen from her ponytail trail after her in the wind. Her ass looks great in her black shorts. Her lean stomach and muscular back pull and stretch as she takes the second turn around the track.

*Fuck, what I wouldn't give to hold her again.*

Forcing myself to focus, I dig deep and push a little harder, knowing full well it might actually kill me. The distance between us is smaller now, but she's still a foot or two ahead. Such a small distance, but it feels like a mile as my heartbeat thrums in my eardrums.

Ba-dum. Ba-dum. Ba-dum.

*Come on, asshole.*

Our feet hammer against the track as we take the final curve, Blake's heavy panting spurring me on. The kids are cheering next to the finish line, their tiny hands waving in the air as they scream their lungs out.

At least they find this entertaining.

I'm so close.

*So. Fucking. Close.*

But it isn't enough.

I cross the finish line right behind Blakely, and I collapse onto the grass, rolling onto my back. There isn't a cloud in the sky as my chest rises and falls in a chaotic rhythm, proving just how shitty I am at pacing my breathing while running. It's a bitch to recover from.

Blake collapses next to me on the field, a wide smile of satisfaction stretched across her face. Our past doesn't matter in this moment. The shit I put her through doesn't matter. Nothing does. Because she's riding the high from beating my ass fair and square, and we both know it.

"You won, Miss Blakely! You won!" the kids cheer, surrounding us on the grass.

"Miss Blakely's still got it," Blake says as she catches her breath. "Everyone take a victory lap so I can have a little chat with my friend."

*Friend.*

I'll take it.

The kids take off at a sprint while the volunteers give us a wide berth, leaving us alone, and I savor the moment, hoping it won't be our last.

With her hands cupped behind her head, Blake stays quiet and catches her breath.

In. *Hold.* Out. *Hold.*

I can't help but picture her naked as she pants, her skin still glistening with sweat. I've experienced it firsthand. The way her tits fit perfectly in my palm. The way her strong legs feel around my waist. The way she felt breathing against my neck as she came around me. Sometimes I feel like it was a lifetime ago. And then there are moments like this, when I swear I can *still* feel her.

"You cheated," she pants, snapping me back to reality.

I laugh and push myself to a seated position, propping myself up with my hands behind me and my legs stretched in front of us. "No, I didn't."

"Yes, you did!" she argues, taking another deep breath. "You've been practicing."

"Practicing isn't cheating."

"It's withholding information. Same thing." She glares at me, but there's amusement too. *Pride.* It's the sexiest thing I've ever seen.

I shrug off the thought and argue, "I don't know why you're complaining. You still won."

"Yeah, but you made me work for it. Not cool." Her lips purse, barely hiding the smile I know is simmering right beneath the surface.

I take in the slight crinkles at the corners of her green eyes showcasing her sense of humor and the way her mouth is tilted up into a smile. She looks so carefree. So perfect.

"I always said you needed someone who could push you," I remind her.

She gives me the side-eye and mutters, "Didn't think you'd take the responsibility on yourself."

"I've always taken that responsibility on." I reach for her hand and rub my thumb against the back of it. When she doesn't pull away, I inch closer. "Let me pick you up at eight o'clock tonight, Blake."

"You lost, remember?" She tilts her face up toward the cloudless sky, and her amusement slips into something more somber. More guarded. She isn't staring up at the sky because she finds it mesmerizing or beautiful. It's because she's avoiding me. I can feel it. And I hate it. The space I put between us.

"Throw me a bone," I beg. "Let me make it up to you for being an ass. Please?"

She turns and faces me again, a cloud of vulnerability and indecision tainting her emerald gaze. It reminds me of the night we slept together. The night I crossed a line and ruined our brittle friendship, even though she begged me to. The trust she wants to give that she's holding back out of fear.

I put the fear there. I hurt her.

Fuck, I hurt her, and I'd do anything to take it back.

"Baby, I'm sorry," I rasp, scooting closer and tilting her head until I have her full attention. Until she can't turn away from me. Not anymore.

Peeking up at me, the pain clear in her eyes, she whispers, "I can't be hurt by you again."

"I won't hurt you, Blake."

"Promise?"

My chest aches, and I brush away the strands of hair sticking to the side of her cheek. "Yeah. I promise."

"Okay." Her gaze drops to my lips before she sits up, tangles her fingers in the hair at the nape of my neck, and tugs me closer to her as she falls back onto the grass. "You should kiss me now."

I chuckle but follow her lead, balancing on my elbows to keep from crushing her as we lay on the grass. "I thought you'd never ask."

When our mouths connect, she opens wide, letting me dip my tongue between her lips. If we weren't in public and surrounded by kids she'd been tasked with watching, I'd climb on top of her, bury myself inside her, and refuse to stop. But I've already made her lose one job. I'd prefer to keep it from happening again. Doesn't mean I won't push our luck, though. I kiss her softly, nibbling her bottom lip as she tangles her fingers in my hair and lets out a soft moan when––

"Yo! You're in public!" a voice yells.

Twisting beneath me, Blakely breaks the kiss and looks at Mia, her face heating with embarrassment.

Mia walks toward us with her arms folded, giving us a look that would make any strict mother proud.

"Oops?" Blake grimaces.

"Yeah, yeah. Get out of here, Theo." She waves her hand at me like I'm a pesky fly in need of shooing. "She'll call you later."

With a groan, I stand up and offer my hand to Blake, pulling her to her feet.

"I'll see you tonight?" I ask.

"Unless I come to my senses before then," she quips, rising onto her tiptoes and kissing my cheek.

I snake my arm around her waist and tug her closer. "See you tonight, Blake."

# 41

# BLAKELY

"**Y**ou nervous?" Mia asks, resting her shoulder against my bedroom doorjamb.

I paint some tinted chapstick onto my lips and take another once-over of myself in the mirror. Clicking the cap back on the tube, I turn to Mia. "Is it weird if I say no?"

She laughs. "No, it isn't weird. You guys have known each other forever. You've been dancing around a relationship for years. I think, if anything, it'd be weird if you *did* feel weird."

"That's a lot of weird," I joke.

"You're a lot of weird," she returns quickly, her lips stretching into a smile.

Grabbing a leather jacket from my closet, I slip it on and tug at the hem of my black tank top. Mia helped pick out my outfit, and I have to say, the girl has skills. With her help, my face looks fresh and dewy, my makeup looking natural and flawless. I braided my hair over one shoulder, leaving it loose and messy around my face while my freckles play peekaboo on my cheeks and the bridge of my nose. The combination feels like me. The real me.

The me I'm hoping to reintroduce to Theo tonight.

Without any barriers. Or shitty history. Just the good. And there's so much good.

"Seriously, you look gorgeous," Mia notes. "He's going to lose his shit."

"I hope so," I say dryly. "Do you work tonight?"

"Yup. Sammie's been showing me how to make a few drinks. Hopefully, I'll have a little more time behind the bar."

"Ooo fun. I'd say I'll come visit so you can make me a drink, but since I've been flagged and all..." I roll my eyes, the memory of Theo turning me in more amusing than infuriating since the dust has settled.

With a laugh, Mia says, "Good times. Good times. Do you know what you're doing tonight with Theo?"

"No idea. He only told me to be ready by eight, and he'll pick me up."

"I think this is good," Mia decides. "Healthy."

"Me too. Can I ask you something?"

"What?"

"You haven't really dated since Shorty..." The comment hangs in the air, but I don't know what to say.

"I've been too busy being your fairy godmother," she quips.

"Do you want to? Date anyone?"

"I think relationships and me are...not a good fit. Really me and men in general." She avoids my gaze, picking at her cuticles. "I mean, look at my history, Blake. Male number one. My dad, who was a drug addict before being murdered after borrowing money for my education. You know, that was fun. Male number two. Shorty, who was pretty much the furthest person from Prince Charming on the planet, and was not only a cheater but also an abusive stalker." She finally looks at me and gives two thumbs up. "A real keeper, that one. Even my date with Colt, who, for all intents and purposes, is guy number three in my examples for today. He was the *one* guy who had his head on straight that I'd ever really hung out with, and it was clear he was in love with Ash as soon as he laid eyes on her when picking me up for our first date. Also, to clarify, I'm not into Colt or anything, I'm just saying…"

"I get it. Go on. You can make your point."

She pushes herself from the doorjamb and moseys into my room, checking her perfectly drawn eyeliner in the mirror hanging on my wall. "My point is…I guess I don't know how to pick 'em. Which is fine. I know how to be on my own. Honestly, I'm an expert at it. It's probably better this way."

"You sound like Kate."

"And you sound like someone who has a date to get to," she deflects. Clearly, she's finished with this conversation. "Have fun, okay? I'll see you later." She clicks her dark manicured fingernails against the doorjamb in goodbye, then heads down the hall, grabbing her purse from the kitchen counter and closing the front door behind her.

*Weird.*

~

THE NIGHT FEELS A BIT LIKE DÉJÀ VU WHEN THEO PICKS ME UP a few minutes later. He compliments my outfit. I blush. He touches my back, guiding me to the car. I follow his lead on wobbly knees.

It's like a dance.

One I'm all too familiar with.

Except this time? This time, there's an undercurrent pulsing between us. Okay, there's always an undercurrent pulsing between us. But tonight? It's different. More charged, maybe?

I legit don't even know, but there's definitely…something.

Like my body already knows where tonight could end up. And for once, I'm not fighting it, and neither is he.

The heat from Theo's palm disappears as he opens the passenger door, and I peek over at him.

"Thank you," I murmur.

His wrist is casually resting on top of the door as he smiles down at me. The moonlight highlights his sharp features. But it's the hat that really does me in.

Like he's in his element. Like opening my door is the most natural thing in the world. Like looking good enough to lick is as easy as breathing to the bastard.

And for the first time ever, there's something I can do about it.

This is a date.

A real date.

I'm allowed to touch him. To kiss him. To go home with him. I can do whatever I want. And the best part? After his little declaration at the track earlier, I know he wants it too. There's nothing holding us back. Not anymore.

The realization is...mind-blowing.

When I don't get in the car, the side of his mouth lifts in amusement, and he challenges, "There a problem?"

"No problem."

He cocks his head, his smile falling slightly. "You having second thoughts?"

Holding his gaze, I shake my head.

"Then, what is it, Blake?"

"Do you know how unfair it is?"

"Unfair *what* is?" he asks.

"The fact you get to walk around looking like"—I wave my hand at him—"this, and I had to spend years just... watching. And yet I had no idea I was allowed to touch."

That same sexy grin reappears with a vengeance, turning my insides into mush as he steps closer, pinning me between

331

the car and his own hot chest. I grab the edge of his leather jacket for balance, using my opposite hand to twist his hat around until the brim faces backward.

So. Damn. Sexy.

"And now?" he challenges.

"Now…" I tug him closer, loving our height difference more than ever. His lips are almost on mine. But he doesn't kiss me. He's letting me take the lead. And I'm not ready to put us out of our misery. Not yet.

My tongue darts out between my lips, wetting my bottom lip and pulling a low groan from Theo. I whisper, "Now, I'm going to touch you as much as I want, and there's nothing you can do about it."

His laugh is low and throaty. The sound shoots straight to my core. "Not a thing, huh?"

"Nope." I pop the 'p' at the end, closing the last bit of distance as I rise onto my tiptoes and press my lips to his.

His mouth is hot. Minty. Addictive. He drags the tip of his tongue against the seam of my lips, urging me to open for him. But instead of obeying, I settle my heels back onto the ground and give him a coy smile.

"There." I pat his chest. "That'll hold me over."

I start to slip into his car, but he grabs my waist and spins me around, pushing my back into the closed rear door.

"I think the door swings both ways, Baby Thorne. If you get to touch me whenever you want, I should be allowed to do the same, right?"

He grabs my wrists and twists them behind me until they're resting between my lower back and the car's cold metal frame. The stark contrast is dizzying, heightening my nerves and adrenaline. If Theo were anyone else, I'd knee him in the balls, but this? This game? This teasing? Especially when it's combined with the years of pent-up lust and attraction I've been fighting? It's the hottest thing I've ever experienced.

"Are you pushing me, Theo?" I ask.

"Do you like being pushed, Blakely?"

I bite my lower lip. My attention slides from his dark blue eyes to his mouth only inches from mine. So. Damn. Close. I can almost taste him. Maybe it's the lingering mint on my tongue from moments ago. Maybe it's his breath swirling with my own in what little space is between us.

Regardless, I want it.

His mouth on mine.

His hands on my wrists.

Arching my back, I press into him, and his hard length grazes my stomach, causing my breath to hitch.

Yeah.

I want it all.

All of him.

He slips his thigh between my parted legs, pressing it against me. Against the ache in my core. I nearly buckle from the pressure, but Theo keeps me pinned in place. Like I'm weightless. I roll my hips slightly. Hell, it's barely even a roll. More like a tiny shift. But it's enough. Enough to steal my breath. Enough to light the spark between us. Enough to give me the friction I crave.

Growling low in his throat, Theo lets go of my wrists with one hand and grabs my throat. Then his mouth is on mine. Taking. Owning. He swallows my moan as he presses his knee against me again. My clit throbs with the friction, and I open my mouth wider, letting Theo fuck my mouth with his tongue. But it's good. Oh, so good. I grab his ass and pull him closer, my desperation making me way too needy on my own freaking driveway. But I don't care. Not anymore. Not when I've spent years holding back. Years telling myself I don't want Theo. I don't need Theo. I don't crave Theo.

*Bullshit.*

Theo's grip on my throat squeezes for a split second as if he can't help himself. He lets me go and cups my breast over my shirt, but it isn't enough. I need more. I need him.

"Theo," I whimper, grabbing his wrist and pushing my boob into his hand like I can't get enough.

And I can't.

Not when it comes to him.

He swallows my voice with his mouth, kissing me harder as his opposite hand unbuttons my jeans and slides down. When his hand cups my sex, I moan, well aware of how drenched I must feel. Hell, I'm soaking. He rests his forehead against mine, his breathing more staggered as he slips his index finger inside of me.

I gasp.

"Shit, Blake," he rasps.

With a grin, I bite my lower lip and roll my hips against him. "You should keep doing that."

"Like this?" He crooks his finger inside of me, and my jaw drops.

"Yeah," I breathe out. "Just like that."

His finger pumps inside of me a few more times, then he adds a second finger. The stretch feels amazing, and my eyes roll back in my head as I savor the feeling. The connection. The fucking pressure. It's building. I can feel it. The ever-elusive orgasm. I grind against the heel of his hand, goose-bumps spreading across my skin.

"Yes, baby. Chase it."

I grab his wrist, and he thrusts his fingers inside of me again despite the lack of room to work with thanks to my jeans.

"Take it," he orders against my lips. He slides down my throat and nibbles softly.

*Shit, I'm close.*

"Ride it out, baby." He scissors his fingers back and forth and pushes his hand up against my clit a little harder, rolling his hand against me. And it feels good. So fucking good. My knees shake, and a cool sweat breaks out along the back of my neck. But I chase it. I take it. I ride it out.

Then, I come.

Holy shit, do I come.

Bending forward, I rest my head on Theo's shoulder as my muscles tighten around him. My heart is racing as the orgasm washes over me. It starts in my core, spreading to the top of my head and down to my toes. And I don't want it to be over. To lose the connection between us like the last time we were intimate.

When I'm finished, Theo slips his hand out of my pants and licks his fingers, his hot gaze on mine. I grab the waistband of his jeans and trail my hand down to the ridge in his pants, but he stops me.

Looking up at him, I quirk my brow. "Theo…"

"You think this is the first time you've given me blue balls, Blakely?" He chuckles darkly, kissing the tip of my nose. "Get in the car. You can make it up to me later."

## 42

## THEO

I was right. My balls ache. But it was worth it. To see Blake come. I hadn't planned to finger her in her drive-way, but I think she was just as pent-up as I am and needed the release.

Now, she's chattier. Less stressed. More animated. Like the Blake I used to know. And it's been nice. Natural. Like the good old days.

Checking the GPS on my phone, I pull into the parking lot of our final destination a few minutes later. I've never been here, but the reviews online were decent, and there wasn't anything similar for at least another ten miles, so it will have to do.

Curious, Blake leans forward in her seat and looks out the windshield, checking out the old, decrepit building. "Where are you taking me?"

There's a pink and blue neon sign hanging from the gray brick. It reads *Flannigans*, and a few bunches of matching balloons frame the entrance. She's never been here, either. The realization makes me smile as another wave of anticipation floods my system. Shit, I haven't been this excited in years.

"Remember during the summers?" I ask. "When you'd want to come with Colt, me, and Logan to the arcade?"

"And you guys were jerks and always said no?" She tears her attention from the entrance and scowls at me. "Yeah. I think I recall."

"To be fair, it was your mom's fault, not ours, but––"

"But I'd still mouth *vacuum beach* through the window when she'd drop you guys off."

With another laugh, I turn off the car and pull the key from the ignition. "Yeah. I remember. Classy, by the way."

She perks up in her seat and flicks her thick braid over her shoulder. "Classy's my middle name."

I almost snort but don't call her out. "Yeah, well, the arcade we used to go to as kids is closed now, but this place has good reviews online so…"

Her smile softens as understanding washes over her. The hope in her eyes reminds me of a kid on Christmas morning. "So, you're taking me to an arcade?"

"Yeah." I lift my ass from the driver's seat and pull out the wad of money from my back pocket, slapping it on the center console. "After all, we've got some cash to waste."

The light from the dashboard makes her green eyes glow as she stares at it, though I can't tell what she's thinking. I knew it'd be a risk to bring it up. But the money has been taunting me for weeks, and I didn't know what else to do with it. Besides, if we want a chance to start fresh, we might as well face our demons, including the bills in front of us.

"Is that my virginity money?" she asks.

I scratch my jaw, unsure how she's going to react. "Uh, yeah."

Those same eyes flick to mine. But instead of the hesitation or hurt I'd expected, they're filled with mirth. She grins, easing the knot in my chest and the guilt I've been carrying since the moment Austin shoved the money against my chest in LAU's locker room. Hell, even before.

"You, my dear Teddy," she leans across the center console and kisses my cheek, "are a genius."

## 43
## BLAKELY

A thousand dollars can buy a shit ton of arcade coins. Okay, it's more like nine hundred and seventy-three dollars can buy a shit ton of arcade coins. We saved the rest for cotton candy, a couple bottles of water, and a large pizza. Now, our bellies are full, and I'm pretty sure I haven't laughed this hard in years.

We've been wasting money, earning tickets, and giving handfuls of coins to every little kid we pass. It's freaking perfect.

"Did you think of this all on your own?" I ask, pulling off a cloud of blue cotton candy from the white paper tube in my hand.

"Think of what?"

"Coming here."

He plucks the candy from my fingers and pops it into his mouth, letting the sugar melt on his tongue. "Maybe," he answers.

"Aaaand?" I prod. "What made you think of it? I haven't been to an arcade in forever."

"Neither have I." Another cloud of candy disappears from

339

the white stick as he reaches over and pinches some between his fingers. "I thought of it when we were talking about *vacuum beach* and *olive juice* in Russ's office a while ago."

"Ah." I steal the cotton candy from Theo's hand and put it in my mouth. His eyes stay glued to my lips as my tongue darts out and licks the excess sugar from them. Ignoring the onslaught of butterflies in my stomach, I clear my throat and keep walking through the arcade littered with different games.

*Wait.*

Why am I ignoring those butterflies?

I stop and face him again because I'm allowed to kiss him, dammit.

When I peck a quick kiss against his lips, I smile and take another bite of cotton candy. "So *vacuum beach* sealed the deal, huh? Noted."

"Want to know a secret?" He grabs my hip and pulls me against him like he can't help himself.

*Aaaand there are the butterflies again.*

"Yup. Let's hear this secret," I answer.

"Colt used to always grumble about it when we'd get inside."

I bite back my laugh and shake my head because there's no way this is true. "No, he didn't."

"It was the only time you didn't mouth, *olive juice* to him."

"You guys got to go and be big kids, doing your own thing and spending your allowance on games, while I had to stay at home and hang out with my mom 'cause I was *too young*," I explain, mimicking my mom's stern voice. "I was jealous. So sue me."

"Yeah, well, I was jealous too," he counters.

I frown, pausing before hooking my arms around his neck, being careful to keep the cotton candy from touching the back of his head as we sway slightly back and forth. "And what were you jealous about?"

"That I got *vacuum beach* all the time while your brother got *olive juice* mixed in."

"Friends don't get jealous over *olive juice*."

"This friend did," he says. His swaying slows as his grip around my waist tightens.

I still can't believe how long we've been fighting this. This pull. This attraction. I bite my bottom lip and whisper, "Why?"

"Because I liked you, Blake. Even back then, you managed to get under my skin in a way no one has. Ever."

The words hit like a strong shot of whiskey, leaving me warm and light. It'll never get old. Hearing those words. Admitting our childhood feelings. Feeling safe enough and brave enough to admit it out loud. I'm left reeling.

"You managed to get under my skin too," I breathe out. "And no matter what I tried to do, I couldn't get you out of my system."

"I guess you're stuck with me, huh?"

"I hope so."

He tilts my head up and kisses me, tasting like cotton candy with a side of Theo. It's heady and addictive, and the only thing keeping me from having a full-blown make out session in the middle of the arcade is a crying toddler screaming at the top of its lungs for more popcorn.

I pull away and let out a laugh, wiping at the edge of my mouth with my thumb as reality crashes into me.

"Keep it in your pants, Blake," Theo teases.

"Says the guy who was grabbing my ass."

"Language," he scolds, not even bothering to hide his cocky smirk as he tilts his head toward the game in front of us. "We should play." The game has two basketball hoops set up side by side and is surrounded by nets.

"You looking for another rematch?" I ask.

He grins and puts two coins into the machine. "Nah. I already got what I wanted."

"Oh, really?"

"Yeah."

"And what's that?"

His smile softens, but the crinkles around his eyes make my heart pitter-patter away. "You."

## 44

## THEO

After the arcade, we made out in the car for a while, and I drove us to my place where we finally made it to my bedroom. I thought it would've been weird. Having Blake stay the night. I wasn't kidding when I told her I don't sleep with girls. But it's Blake. Things have always been different with her.

The morning light filters through the window as she drags her fingers along my bare chest, snuggled against me beneath the gray comforter.

It's peaceful.

Quiet.

"Is it weird that I'm already going to miss this?" she murmurs.

With a frown, I lift my head from the pillow and look down at her. Her mess of waves frame her freckled face as she stares blankly at the wall, lost in her own thoughts.

"Miss what?" I ask, my voice still gritty from sleep.

"This." She peeks up at me. "When you graduate this spring and leave me for the high life."

"Who says I'm going anywhere?"

That same sad smile greets me. "Don't tell me you're sticking around after graduation. If you haven't already gotten a shit ton of offers yet, they're gonna come, Theo."

She's right. They've already come. So many it makes my head spin most days, but I haven't signed any contracts yet. I haven't been able to. I've been too focused on Blake. On us. On the future I want to build and how much it doesn't align with the future I've been building since I was a kid.

It fucking sucks.

Dragging my finger against her bare arm, I murmur, "So, what?"

"So, I think it's awesome, and I couldn't be more excited for you. Doesn't mean I don't get to be sad every once in a while too."

"You have nothing to be sad about, Blake."

Her lips purse as if she wants to argue, but she only hums. "Hmm."

"I'm serious. I'm in this for the long haul."

"I know you are. And I am too. Trust me. I've literally never been happier. But..." She sighs and burrows into my chest a little more. "I'm also going to take advantage of soaking up every moment before you go." Her hot breath tickles my bare peck as she rests her forehead against it, shielding her expression with her messy hair. "God, I don't want you to go."

"Blake––"

"Blah. Enough sad talk."

"Blake," I repeat. Tangling my fingers in her hair, I force her to look at me.

"I think your future's awesome, Theo. Seriously, I couldn't be happier––"

"Stop."

She sucks her lips into her mouth but stays quiet, her

bright green gaze hitting me like a sucker punch to the gut. The vulnerability. The sadness.

"I want it to be *our* future. You and me."

A spark of hope ignites, but I can tell she's fighting it. Fighting the idea of us being together long-term. Not because she doesn't want it. But because she's scared. Scared of letting me in. Scared of falling for me the same way I've already fallen for her. Especially when our future is so precarious, so unknown. I guess I don't blame her. It's why I haven't signed any contracts. Why I haven't asked if she'd be willing to move across the country for me. Why I haven't asked if she'd even want to. The answer? It could break us.

"You want it to be our future?" she whispers.

"Yeah, Blake. I really do."

She settles her head against my chest. Her breath tickles my bare chest as she lets out a soft sigh.

"Okay."

45

# BLAKELY

Things have been perfect lately. I go to Theo's games. He volunteers at the charity whenever he has time. We meet up between classes for coffee and have sleepovers almost every night. Literally, it's perfect with a capital P.

And since it's my day off, and Theo doesn't have any practice tonight, we're snuggled on the couch at my place, watching *Big Daddy* when the front door opens with a quiet squeak. I glance over the edge of the couch and find Mia with a box tucked beneath her arm.

When she sees me, she pulls back, surprised. "Oh. Hey."

"Hey," I greet her.

With a tight smile, she repeats, "Hey." Her attention darts to Theo. "Sorry if I interrupted."

"You're not interrupting," I reply.

"I'll just..." She grabs the scissors from the junk drawer and opens the box on the kitchen island, more tense and elusive than usual.

"Ooo, what'd you buy?" I ask, standing up and rounding the edge of the couch in hopes of making her feel more included. After all, I've been on the single train, and while it has a few perks, being surrounded by love-birds like Ash and Colt, or Theo and me has to be exhausting.

When Mia sees me approaching, she grabs the small tube from the packaging and slips it behind her back. "Oh, I didn't buy anything exciting." Gathering the garbage, she throws it in the trash bin and adds, "I'm gonna go study in my room. Have a fun night."

"Dude," I say when I catch a glimpse of the pepper spray in her hand. "Is that––"

"It's for running. You've been busy lately, and I've been going alone more," she clarifies, cutting me off. "Better to be safe than sorry, right? Not a big deal. Good night, guys."

She heads to her room without a backward glance, the tube clutched tightly in her palm.

My lips press together as I watch her leave, then I head back to the couch.

Reading me clearly, Theo hooks his arms around my shoulders and tugs me against him. "Everything okay?"

"Mia bought pepper spray."

With a frown, he looks toward the empty hall. "Hmm."

"It's weird, right?" I ask.

With a shrug, he offers, "Usually, I'd say no. But with her history with Shorty and how quickly she left…" He lifts his chin toward the empty hallway as if to prove his point. "I dunno."

"Shorty's gone, though. He was drafted to the Tumblers in Ohio last year. Wasn't he?"

Theo nods. "Yeah. Started playing for them this season."

My lips pull into a frown. "Then, why would she be freaking out?"

"I dunno," he repeats.

Ash and Colt come bounding through the front door,

snapping me from my thoughts. I shake off the dread in my stomach and greet them. "Hey, you two."

"Hey," Colt answers, and Ash adds, "Are you guys busy for dinner tonight?"

"Tonight?" Theo and I exchange glances. He shrugs and says, "Nah, I don't think so. What do you guys have in mind?"

"We want to go to La Tavola Della Famiglia and celebrate."

"Celebrate?" I ask.

With a slight shake of his head, Theo clears his throat, and Colt stares at him, his gaze narrowing when he says, "We'll, uh, we'll tell you tonight. What do you say we leave in an hour or so?"

Ash nods. "That should work. I'll text Kate."

"Sounds good."

"You should invite Mack too," Colt tells Theo. "Mama Taylor will appreciate it."

Theo snorts but pulls out his phone and sends a text to his brother. "Always kissing my mom's ass, man."

"And I always will," Colt jokes.

Checking the time on my phone, I tuck it back into my jeans and tangle my fingers with Theo's, tugging him down the hall. "Come on. Let's shower."

Colt's nose wrinkles. "Really, Blake? Gross."

Ash laughs and rises onto her tiptoes, kissing Colt's cheek. "Come on. I'm sure we can find a way to distract you in my room."

It's my turn to make a face. "Colt's right. *Gross.*"

"So...no sex when we're in the same house?" he offers.

I nod and let Theo go like he has cooties. "Deal."

"Come on," Theo argues. He grapples for my waist and tugs me against him again. "Colt's my roommate, and Ash is yours. We'll never get any alone time."

"Sorry, Teddy," I pat his chest and laugh at his mock frown, "but we've gotta draw the line somewhere."

"Yeah. You should just be happy I'm cool with..." Colt's nose scrunches again as he looks between Theo and me. "*This.*"

Stealing the keys from Colt's hand, Ash tangles their fingers together and leads him to the front door. "We'll see you at the restaurant."

"Bye!"

As soon as the door closes, Theo pounces on me like a damn cheetah and drags me toward the bathroom. "They're out of the house. That means we can do it."

With a laugh, I lock the bathroom door behind us, stripping my clothes off like they're on fire. "We've got one hour. Let's put it to good use."

The restaurant is fancy-schmancy with a side of caesar dressing. With low lighting and a menu just for wine, it's official. Either Ash is pregnant or they're getting married. Hell, maybe both. I fidget with my napkin, but Theo grabs my hand and rests it on the table while the scent of garlic and parmesan makes my mouth water as the waitress sets down a basket of garlic bread.

*Come to mama.*

I rip off a corner of the loaf and nibble on the goodness, letting the butter and salt melt over my tongue.

So. Freaking. Good.

Theo chuckles beside me, cutting off a slice for himself.

As Mia smooths down the napkin in her lap, she asks, "So? What's the special occasion?"

Ash turns to Colt and squeezes his hand resting on the white tablecloth. "Do you want to wait until everyone gets here or do you want to tell them right now?"

Shaking his head, Colt mutters, "I already feel weird making it a big deal by coming out to dinner. Let's just...tell them, I guess."

"Come on, it's something to celebrate," Ash argues as if none of us can hear their conversation.

"Okay, what's going on?" I interject. With my elbows on the table, I lean closer and steeple my fingers in front of me, the bread forgotten. For now, anyway. "You guys are talking all cryptically and shit. Are you pregnant or something?"

Ash's eyes nearly pop out of her head, and she reaches for her glass of water, chugging it down while Colt belts out a laugh, finding way too much amusement in Ash's response. "Now, *that's* a reason to celebrate. Right, Sunshine?"

Elbowing him in the ribs, Ash says, "No, we're not pregnant. Colt finally decided where he wants to go and sent the papers this week."

"No way," I gush. "Where did you pick?"

"I, uh," Colt glances at Theo, then back to me. "I decided to sign with the Lions. They're a new franchise. It's going to be a lot of work, but I'm excited to help build the team from the ground up and should get a lot of playing time."

Practically brimming with pride, Ash grins and adds, "It's seriously going to be perfect."

My jaw drops. "Why didn't you tell me?"

She hooks her arm into the crook of Colt's elbow and rests her head on his shoulder. "He didn't want to stress you out."

"Why would it stress me out?" I stand up and pull Colt into an awkward hug since the bastard's still sitting. "I'm so happy for you, Colt!"

His chest rumbles with amusement as he hugs me back. "Thanks, Blake."

"So when did they reach out to you?" I pull away from him and return to my seat. "I know Theo's been dying to hear from some of the teams."

Colt frowns and looks at Theo, whose eyes are practically bulging from his skull.

"I, uh," Colt clears his throat. "I don't know?"

"Sorry I'm late," Kate apologizes, interrupting our conversation.

She isn't. The waitress has barely delivered our drinks, and we haven't even ordered our meals yet, let alone the fact Macklin's still a no-show. The girl looks like a jittery ball of nerves with a side of exhaustion. Not quite sure how she's able to pull off two contradictory emotions, but she's doing it in spades. Her hair is a mess, and her shirt is slightly skewed as she unzips her jacket and collapses into the chair across from me like a sack of potatoes while bouncing her leg up and down beneath the table like the Energizer Bunny.

"You're totally fine," Ash replies.

"Actually, scratch that," I interject. My gaze narrows, and I study her carefully as I sit back in my chair. "*Are* you totally fine?"

She rolls her eyes and reaches for the glass of wine in front of Mia. Once she swallows half its contents, she sets it back on the table without bothering to apologize for stealing Mia's drink.

"Sure. What's mine is yours," Mia jests.

But it's as if Kate doesn't even hear her. She's too busy chewing on her thumbnail.

"Okay, seriously. What's wrong?" Mia demands.

"I ran into Wes," Kate mutters.

With a grimace, I exchange worried glances with Ash and Mia as Ash prods, "And?"

"And he was on a date with someone else." She sniffles, then clears her throat. "I got to serve him and his new...*girl* for the last forty-five minutes. Needless to say, it wasn't exactly comfortable."

"Yikes," I mutter.

Leaning toward me, Theo keeps his voice low and asks, "Who's Wes? What'd I miss?"

Mia asks another question, but I don't hear what it is as I answer Theo, "I'll tell you later."

"At least he tipped me well," Kate mentions, her tone laced with acid. "The jerk owes me that much."

Her fidgeting grows more frantic, her eyelids fluttering as she stares at the white linen napkin in front of her.

"You...sure you're okay?" I prod.

But she doesn't answer.

"You guys," I whisper, my gaze darting around the table as a rush of adrenaline floods my system.

Something's wrong.

"Kate? Honey?" Ash tries to get her attention. She touches Kate's arm, her worry heightening and matching my own.

"Shit," I whisper.

"What's going on?" Theo asks. He can feel the tension swirling the same way my roommates and I can.

"Kate?" Colt demands sharply, as if he hopes a stern voice will be enough to snap Kate out of whatever she's going through.

But Kate's shaking only gets harder. More chaotic. More terrifying. With her back as stiff as a board, she slides off her chair and onto the floor, convulsing in a way that shakes me to my core.

I cover my mouth, my fear taking over.

"What the fuck?" Theo growls as he jumps to his feet.

"She's having a seizure," I explain, though I've never felt more helpless in my entire life. "What do we do? I don't––"

"Do we call an ambulance?" Ash asks as she slides onto her knees next to Kate. She reaches for her but pulls back at the last second. "I don't––I don't know what to do."

"Give her space," a low, strong voice commands. My head snaps up to find Macklin barreling toward us from the entrance, his phone pressed to his ear. I turn to Theo and find him tossing his phone onto the table. He called his brother. Thankfully, Mack was already on his way and must've been parking or something, but it doesn't erase the helplessness drowning out my senses. I feel like my hands are tied. Like I'm paralyzed. Helpless. Like I can't fix a damn thing. I can only watch. And it's the worst feeling in the world.

Shrugging his arms out of his jacket, Macklin squats next to Kate and shoves his coat under her head, ordering Ash to back up.

Ash jumps back, giving Mack and Kate plenty of room as her eyes well with tears, the same helplessness blanketing her.

"Was she eating when it happened?" Mack demands.

We shake our heads as he pushes away a few of the chairs close to them.

"N-no," I answer. "She'd had some wine, but that's it."

"Good." He nods, internalizing the information before ordering, "Someone time it."

"Th-the seizure?" Ash asks. Her voice is nothing but a whisper.

Mack nods again. "How long has she been seizing?"

"Th-thirty seconds or so?" Mia offers, looking just as confused, just as overwhelmed, as the rest of us while Ash pulls out her phone and starts the timer.

"Does she have a history of seizures?" Mack asks, his eyes never leaving Kate's shaking body.

"Epilepsy," Ash answers. Her eyes are even glassier now. She blinks, and a drop of moisture glides down her cheek and drips off her chin. "But I've never…" Her breath hitches, and she covers her mouth.

"We've never seen her have an actual seizure," Mia clarifies. Her voice is numb. Almost distant. Like she isn't here anymore. She's absent. Disconnected. In shock.

With another nod, Mack demands, "What's her protocol?"

"Protocol?" I ask.

"Usually, people with epilepsy have a protocol in place in case of a seizure. Some request an ambulance. Others ask to wait it out, especially if it's the norm for them. Do any of you know what she'd prefer?"

"She's pretty private," Mia offers. "Sh-she doesn't like to talk about it, so we don't really know."

Mack's jaw ticks as his attention flicks to Ash. "Time?"

"Thirty seconds," Ash replies. Colt's behind her and pulls her against him, wrapping his arms around Ash's waist and pressing her back to his front.

I turn to Theo, my lower lip trembling, and he pulls me into his embrace, anchoring me.

"Theo, call an ambulance," Mack orders. "If she won't tell you what to do when she has a seizure, we'll decide for her."

"She won't want to make a big deal," Ash murmurs. "And if she can snap out of it––"

"This is a big deal," Mack grits out. "Theo. Now."

Letting me go, Theo grabs his phone from the table and dials 9-1-1. I'm pretty sure he's never felt more terrified in his entire life.

Then again, neither have I.

After Theo called the ambulance, Kate woke up groggy and disoriented. When she realized she was on the ground and we were all standing around her, the blood drained from her face and she tried to get up. But Mack held her back, telling her to stay calm and the ambulance would be at the restaurant any minute to take her to the hospital.

She was furious.

But the worst part? She wouldn't stop apologizing. Hell, she couldn't. It broke my heart. We followed in our own cars to the hospital, but she refused to see any of us. It's like she was ashamed. And I hate how she felt ashamed.

Honestly. It broke my heart.

Staring out the passenger window, I replay the night all over again, chewing on the pad of my thumb and glancing at Theo, his wrist resting against the steering wheel.

"You think she'll be okay?" I whisper.

He squeezes my knee and pulls into his garage. "Yeah, Blake. I think she'll be okay. Mack's staying with her despite her wanting to be left alone. He said he'd text us if there are any more updates, but remember. Seizures are kind of par for the course with epilepsy."

"I know." I let out a breath. "But knowing it and seeing it firsthand are two different things."

"Yeah."

"Thanks for letting me stay over tonight."

"You think you even have to ask?" he volleys back, lifting our entwined fingers and bringing them to his lips. His kiss is soft. Gentle.

I smile. "I believe you were the one who pointed out you don't sleep with women," I remind him.

He chuckles and kisses my fingers again. "You're always the exception, Blake. *Always.*"

We head into his house, but the place is surprisingly quiet on a Saturday night. I look around the empty kitchen and ask, "Where is everyone?"

Theo hasn't really thrown a Taylor House party since I was fired from the team. However, the lack of roommates or normal hustle and bustle usually present in the house is missing.

Right now, it's only us.

"Logan's throwing a party at his place," Theo explains as he shrugs off his jacket.

"Oh."

"Yeah."

"How are things on that front, anyway?" I ask.

"Unless we're on the ice, Colt and I stay out of his way, and he stays out of ours."

"Do you think you guys will ever be able to smooth things over?"

Theo scratches his chin but stays quiet for a minute before muttering, "Doubt it. Come on. Let's go upstairs. I'm exhausted, and I'm sure you are too."

He's right. I am exhausted. My limbs feel like they weigh

a hundred pounds as I walk up the stairs to his room. Theo gives me one of his shirts to sleep in and disappears into the bathroom to brush his teeth. As I run my fingers over the black cotton material, a memory resurfaces from dinner.

"Question," I say when Theo enters the room.

He smiles back at me. "Answer."

"When Colt brought up his signing with the Lions, you made a face at dinner."

He squeezes the back of his neck. "What?"

"At dinner. You made a face. What was that about?"

"What face?" he counters, though he looks nervous. On edge.

"When I said you're still waiting for offers, Colt looked at you and made a face. Like I was the crazy one or something."

"Blake…"

"I didn't want to make a big deal about it at the restaurant, especially after everything happened with Kate, but…" My voice trails off, leaving him plenty of time to fill in the blank, though he doesn't say a word.

The silence only fans my curiosity. My hesitation grows with every passing second.

"Did you lie to me?" I ask. "Have you received any offers?"

He sticks his tongue against his cheek then runs it along his teeth. Looking antsy. Nervous.

"Theo, answer me," I demand.

"It's complicated."

"How, exactly?"

Jaw tight, he motions to his desk in the corner of the room as if it holds all of the answers.

My brows furrow as I walk closer to the dark lacquered desk, warning bells ringing loud in my ears.

There's a manilla folder lying on the back corner of the desk. Everything else is neatly tucked away in the drawers.

"This?" I ask, my attention darting to it, then returning to Theo.

He hesitates for a brief second, then dips his chin. Like he can't even look at me. Can't talk to me. Like the words are lost, and he doesn't know what to say.

My hands tremble as I open the folder and read the top page, flipping faster through the stack of papers. The words jumble together, but it doesn't take a genius to piece together what it is or who it's for.

Contract. Rockies. Bonus. Sign Here. His name is scrawled along the dotted black line.

"What is this?" I whisper, scanning the paperwork for the hundredth time.

"Blake−−"

"I just…" I set the papers down. Slowly. Carefully. Like they're laced with poison, and even the tiniest paper cut could leave me destitute. "I need to know what these are. Actually, scratch that. What I need to know is when you signed with them. Because I've asked multiple times if you've received any offers, and you said you hadn't."

"I never said I hadn't−−"

"Don't hide behind a technicality," I warn.

His expression falls. "Blake…" Theo reaches for me, desperate to hold me against him, but I step back.

Shaking my head, I pull away from his touch no matter how much it kills me. "Are you going to leave, Teddy? Have you already decided? Is that why you didn't want to tell me?"

"I wanted to tell you, I just…didn't know what to say." He scrubs his hand over his face, defeated.

"What you're supposed to say is, *Hey. I've gotten an offer from the Rockies, my dream team as a kid. How cool is that? Yeah, they're a couple thousand miles away, but this is something I really want. What do you think, Blake?* That's what you're supposed to say."

He stays quiet, his gaze dropping to the ground as he shifts from one foot to the other. Sheepishly. Shamefully. His silence only kills me more.

"Do you want to know what I would've said back to you, Theo? I would've said, *Hell, yes! This is amazing, Teddy. I'm so excited for you.* But instead you kept me in the dark," I tell him. "Which leaves me...where, exactly?"

"Blake," he rasps. His voice is thick with pain and regret.

I lift my hand and cut him off. "I know I should tell you to chase your dreams. I know I should tell you I'm willing to do the long-distance thing––and I am––but not like this. Not when I'm expected to just...tag along. Unless you were planning on ending things with me before you left?"

"That's not what I want!"

"Then, why didn't you tell me?" I demand. "If you want there to be a you and me, I need there to be an actual you *and me*," I explain, fighting between numbness, hurt, and absolute fury. "I need us to be equals. I need us to communicate. I need us to talk about things like adults instead of finding out about a pretty fucking huge decision like *this*"––I wave my hand toward the stack of papers––"like it's a dirty secret. Like it's something that deserves to be kept from me when we both know I have a right to know about it. Or at least, if you looked at me like a partner, I would."

"I *do* look at you like you're a partner." His face twists in pain and fear. Fear that I'll leave him. Fear that I'll walk away. That I'll push him away, the same way he's clearly pushing me.

"Do you?" I ask. "Do you look at me like a partner, or do you look at me like I'm some...some little girl you need to protect? Because I'm stronger than you think, Theo."

"Baby..." He reaches for me but stops himself and scrubs his palm from his forehead to his chin, his fingers digging into his skin. Like this is killing him.

Fun fact, Theo: it's killing me too.

"Why didn't you tell me?" I push. "I've been asking for weeks about offers, and you've always deflected. But this?" I pick up the papers and shove them against his chest. "This isn't some verbal agreement. This is binding."

"I haven't sent it yet," he rushes out, fumbling with the papers. "Where do you want me to go? I'll do whatever you want, go where––"

"Don't you get it?" My voice cracks. "Where you go isn't the issue."

His shoulders deflate. It makes him look more lost than ever.

I let out a shaky breath and step closer to him, touching his forearm and dragging my fingers down his bare skin to his fisted hands. "This is why I was upset about the whole Coach firing me situation. Because you didn't listen to me. You didn't communicate with me. You didn't respect my opinion."

"Blake, I––"

"Let me finish," I beg.

He stays quiet, his gaze glued to the ground.

"You made a decision without even bothering to talk to me about it, even though you knew it could potentially affect me. That's why I was mad before, and it's why I'm mad now. I need us to be a team. And in order to do that, you need to stop jumping into things without discussing them with me. I'm not trying to be controlling. I'm trying to be seen as an equal in this relationship instead of some girl who's just... tagging along while you follow your dreams. Does that make sense?"

His frown almost kills me as he tears his attention from the carpet and looks me in the eye, his gaze swirling with regret. "Yeah, Blake. It makes sense."

"Okay." I sniff, my emotions clogging my stupid throat as

I pull out my phone and send a quick text to Colt. "I'm going to have Colt drive me home tonight."

"Babe——"

"It's okay. And we're okay, all right? I just...I need a minute to wrap my head around..." I wave my hand toward the stupid stack of papers. "Your future."

"You mean *our* future."

"If you want it to be *our* future, you need to work on letting me build it with you instead of expecting me to be cool with whatever you decide. That's not how a relationship works, Teddy." I bite my lip to keep from rambling more.

I need to back off for now. I need to rein in my temper. I've already proven my point, and no one likes listening to a broken record. But holy hell, it's hard right now.

"Don't go." He grapples with my hand, refusing to let me go while also refusing to acknowledge why I'm frustrated in the first place.

A breath of air whooshes from my lungs as I fight the urge to run like last time. To hide from our problems instead of fighting through them. But even though I'm determined to make our relationship work, this still hurts.

It hurts a lot.

*Breathe, Blake,* I remind myself.

"Do you understand what I'm saying?" I ask. "Because I need to know. I need to know if I'm getting through to you. If you can see why I'm upset right now and how it has nothing to do with where you sign and everything to do with your lack of communication."

His head hangs. "I should've told you. I'm sorry."

He's right. He should've. But rubbing it in his face won't get us anywhere.

The scruff of his jaw tickles my palm as I cup his cheek. "I know."

Leaning into my touch, he offers, "Let me drive you home. You don't need to call Colt."

"I already texted him. He's on his way."

"Blake––"

"It's okay. I think this whole contract thing combined with the Kate scenario from earlier drained me more than I realized. I just want to go home and go to sleep." I nod to myself. The idea sounds better and better the longer I let it settle. "We'll talk later, okay?"

I turn toward the hall, but he grabs my wrist and spins me around until I'm facing him again. "When? When will we talk?"

I lick my lips, unsure what to say. "I-I don't know. Later."

"That isn't an answer."

"I don't have one."

"Are you coming to the next game?" he pushes.

I shake my head. "I can't."

"Blake––"

"The kids have an activity that day," I explain. And it kills me. The pain in his eyes. The hurt. The distance I can feel growing between us with every passing second.

"Promise me we're okay," he growls.

My eyes flick to his. "We're okay."

"Okay." With a sigh, he lets me go.

I head out of his room and down the hall, taking the stairs one at a time, and feeling...sluggish. Like I'm not even in full control over my own body right now, let alone my emotions or relationship. Once I reach the front door, I pull my jacket close around me, but it does shit to keep the evening chill from seeping into my bones like a sponge in ice water.

Colt's truck is already parked in the driveway with Ash in the passenger seat. They must've been close by when I texted. Without another word, I climb inside and rest my head against the window.

Well, it's official.
Today was shitty.
I hope tomorrow will be better.

# 48

## BLAKELY

"So...you still pissed at Theo?" Colt asks. Ash invited him to watch *The Bachelorette* with us before their fancy date night, and the bastard brought ice cream, so I couldn't exactly kick him out. Not that I wanted to. But seeing him being all sweet and adorable with Ash only made me miss Theo more, which I didn't even think was possible.

"I'm not pissed at Theo," I lie.

Actually, it isn't a lie. I'm *not* pissed. I'm hurt that he kept something so important from me. There's a difference. Don't get me wrong. I'm trying to get over it. But it still takes time. I'm almost glad he's helping Macklin with a few things at his cabin and can't hang out tonight. And the fact I'm helping with the charity and missing Theo's game tomorrow? Talk about a happy coincidence.

"So, you're *not* pissed he kept the negotiations with the Rockies from you?" Colt pushes.

My lips flatten.

"Look, it was a dick move, but--"

"We've both been busy," I interrupt. "But we're fine. I'll see him...later."

The word haunts me like an order of bad sushi. Because I might have been the one to throw out the term when I left a few nights ago, but he's the one who's embraced it whole-heartedly. The bastard hasn't even reached out to me. Not really. Other than a quick text here and there...nothing. He hasn't asked to hang out. He hasn't asked if he can come over. Just good morning and good night texts. That's it. And I want to hate him for it.

"Hmm," Colt grunts, unconvinced. "Are you coming to the game tomorrow?"

"I'm busy."

"With what?"

Annoyed, I pull up *Doodle Jump* on my phone and attempt to look occupied as I mutter, "I'm teaching Bridger and the rest of the kids how to play basketball on Saturday. Happy now?"

"What if they came to the game, instead?"

My cell lands with a soft thump in my lap, and I give him my full attention. "Like, the *hockey* game?"

Colt smiles. "Yeah. This way, you can come to a game, support your big brother, and expose the kids to another sport, which––from what Ash explained to me—is kind of part of the job. It's a win-win, right?"

Except for the little tidbit about me potentially running into Theo at the game after our little blowup. But hey. Who's stressing over something like that?

Me. I'm stressing.

So much so, I've been avoiding anything and everything to do with hockey, the Taylor House, and even SeaBird.

I shouldn't.

I know I shouldn't.

Sure, it's only been a couple days since I saw him last, but it feels like a lifetime.

I promised I wouldn't run. And I'm not. But facing him? It

doesn't exactly sound like a picnic, either. Not when it seems like he's avoiding me too.

*Why does this have to be so complicated?*

"Come," Colt pushes, bringing me back to the present. "It'll be good to clear the air."

Scooting further into the cushions, I clutch a pillow to my chest and huff out, "I don't need to clear the air. Theo and I are fine."

He scoffs but doesn't call me out for it as Ash walks into the room in a white dress showing off her curves. The girl's hot with a capital H, and I glance at Colt, catching his jaw almost unhinged as his gaze slides up and down her body.

I shove at his shoulder. "Gross. Get a room."

But the bastard doesn't even acknowledge me. He's too focused on his girlfriend. Standing up, he wipes his hands against his jeans, strides toward her, and pulls her against him, kissing her softly. His fingers play with the ends of her curled blonde hair as he murmurs, "Like your dress, Sunshine."

She smiles back at him and presses her lips to his. It isn't lewd or over-the-top.

It's sweet.

And makes my stupid heart ache.

I tear my gaze from the sight in front of me, picking at my cuticles while cursing that it isn't enough to distract me from the love emanating from the opposite side of the room.

It isn't fair.

How cute they are together or how I've been given a glimpse of what it feels like to have their kind of love. The kind you can feel from the top of your head to the tips of your toes. The kind of love that's all-consuming.

I don't want to give it up.

"Blake," Colt says.

I clear my throat, force my hands to stop twisting in my lap, and look up at him. "Yeah?"

He pulls out a folded envelope from his back pocket and shows it to me. "Here are the tickets to Saturday's game. There are forty––"

"Forty?" I gawk. "Dude. That's way too much."

"Too late." He sets the envelope onto the counter next to a box of Lucky Charms. "There are vouchers for ice cream too."

"Kate said she'll help with face paint before the game," Ash adds, hooking her arm through Colt's.

"You talked to Kate about this?" I ask.

"Yup." Ash smiles. "We figured it'd be a good distraction for her too."

*Amen to that.*

Kate's been hiding away ever since her seizure, refusing to open up to us or anyone, for that matter. She's gone into full-blown recluse mode, and it doesn't matter how many roommate meetings we've thrown together in search of a solution. None of us can figure out how to snap her out of it.

"Mia took the day off at SeaBird too," Ash adds, "so, we'll all be at the game and can sit together."

"That actually sounds great," I grudgingly admit.

"Right?" She kisses Colt on the cheek and drags her hand from his shoulder to his chest, tugging softly on his dark, cotton T-shirt. "Hey. Can you give me and Blake a minute?"

"Sure thing."

The door closes with a quiet click behind Colt. Then, it's only me and Ash.

My nose wrinkles, sensing a not-so-subtle shift in the air.

"Want to talk about it yet?" she asks as she moseys toward me on the couch, her heels muffled by the plush carpet.

"We've already had this conversation," I remind her.

And we have. In the car after Colt picked me up at Theo's.

The next morning when I was a lazy lump in my bed and ditched my morning run with Mia. Yeah. We've had this conversation lots of times, and it still isn't my cup of tea.

With a huff, Ash collapses onto the couch next to me and folds her arms. "Look. I know I'm not Mia, and I'm not as good at prying info from my roommates, but seriously. I'm right here, *and* I'm dating a hockey player just like you. We kind of have a thing or two in common, Blake. You can talk to me."

I want to laugh at her assumption, but I hold it back. Ash is too sweet to handle my sarcasm, and in this moment, I want to sprinkle it on everything like confetti.

"Talk to me," she prods, squeezing my knee.

"No offense, but you and Colt are *nothing* like me and Theo."

Her eyes widen. "Ouch."

"I'm just saying… It's different with me and Theo. That's all."

She quirks her brow, unconvinced. "How?"

"Because Colt talks to you. He values your opinion. He asked you to come with him after graduation. Theo doesn't do any of those things with me. It's different."

With a sigh, she tucks her hair behind her ear and asks, "Did you ever think he hesitated in asking you because you're not graduating this year?"

"So?"

"So, he had a hard enough time convincing you to give him a real chance in the first place. Add another barrier like long-distance, and maybe he's afraid you'll run for the hills."

I pull back, surprised. "I've already transferred from one college. It's not like I can't do it again."

"And if he gets traded halfway through his first year? What then?"

"Your point?" I snap.

369

"My point *is* that you're right. You have a good reason to be frustrated. He should've talked to you and made his feelings clear as well as his plans. But he's right too. He has a good reason to be scared you'll run at the drop of a hat, which, despite your promise to keep fighting for your relationship, is exactly what you're doing."

If she'd slapped me, I would've been less offended.

With a glare, I argue, "I'm not running."

"Then, what are you doing?"

"I'm...waiting."

"For what?" she asks.

It's an excellent question. I'm waiting for a lot of things. I'm waiting for Theo to show he cares. To *prove* he cares. To prove he wants this. Wants us. To prove he wants to communicate and grow and fight for our relationship. Is it too much to ask?

Nibbling on my thumbnail, I shake off the thought and ask, "Have you decided what you're going to do with Colt? Are you moving with him? Are you staying here?"

"It's still up in the air. Part of me thinks it's why Colt chose the Lions. Because they're close, and I won't feel any pressure to follow him across the country until I'm ready."

"And you aren't ready?" I prod.

"Part of me is. The other part is still terrified."

"What do you have to be scared of? You and Colt are like...the dream team of relationships."

"He's pretty perfect," she admits with a laugh. "Relationships are never easy, though, Blake, even if they are worth fighting for. Especially when you find someone as awesome as your brother...and *Theo*." She nudges her shoulder with mine.

"I'll keep it in mind," I mumble. "Now, get out of here. You're keeping my brother waiting. Have fun on your date."

"We will."

With a half-assed wave, I watch her close the front door and walk toward the kitchen, picking up the thick, worn envelope.

My name is scrawled across the front. And if I didn't know any better, I'd say the font looks a hell of a lot like Theo wrote it.

Or maybe I'm imagining things.

I set the envelope down and puff out my cheeks.

Damn him.

My phone buzzes with a text, and I pull it out of the front pouch of my black hoodie.

**Theo: Miss you.**

*Speak of the devil.*

My chest pinches as I read his message. That's all he has to say? No, *Can I come over?*

Or, *Can we talk?*

Or how about, *Hey, I was thinking about the contracts, and I'd love to hear your opinion.*

I let out a sigh and type my response.

**Blake: Miss you too.**

**Theo: I'm thinking about you.**

With a dry laugh, I fight the urge to roll my eyes even though he can't see me.

**Blake: Obviously, since you texted. I'm thinking about you too, though. I don't like how we left things.**

**Theo: Neither do I, but I'm not going anywhere, Blake.**

I fight the urge to both laugh and cry as I reread his message over and over again. What the hell am I supposed to say? Because it feels like he's running. Like he's avoiding me. Like we're riding out the last stretch of our relationship by steering clear of each other when all I really want is for him to hold me, to talk to me, and tell me I'm loved.

I stare at my phone screen, but the words blur together as my conversation with Ash rises to the surface. The one about how I'm running from my relationship with Theo even when it feels a hell of a lot like Theo's doing the same, despite his text. I blink away the glaze in my eyes, bringing the message back into focus and hit reply.

**Blake: Neither am I, Teddy. I'm not going anywhere.**

I hit send despite the fissure it causes in my heart. Because that's the problem, isn't it? I'm not the one going anywhere. Theo is. And he hasn't even bothered to tell me where or asked if I'm willing to tag along.

**Theo: Good. Be patient with me for a little longer, okay?**

I'd laugh if I wasn't so close to crying. Heading back to the couch, I collapse onto it and tuck my feet beneath my butt, trying to dig up the courage to respond, especially when I have no idea what to say. After a few minutes, only one word shines back at me on the screen, and I hit send before I can talk myself out of it.

**Blake: Trying.**

**Theo: We're gonna get through this. You and me, Baby Thorne. It's always been you and me.**

I set my phone face down on the coffee table and turn on *Happy Gilmore*.

Apparently, I'm a glutton for punishment.

Then again, I'm in love with Theodore Taylor, so I guess I shouldn't be surprised.

## 49

## BLAKELY

The place is thumping with people. Like seriously. You'd think it was a championship game or something. Not that I'm complaining. The exposure is great for LAU's hockey program and the players in general.

Colt supplied matching LAU T-shirts for the kids. The bright red makes it easier to spot the group in the crowd. I do another head count, confirming we have all of them and breathe a sigh of relief.

A few ushers are set up near the tunnel leading to our seats, and they help us find them, making sure everyone is situated where they're supposed to be. Ash and Mia are on the far side of the row, and Kate, my mom, and I take up the side closest to the area where the team sits.

When the Hawks skate onto the ice, the crowd starts clapping, and so do the kids. True to Ash's word, Kate spent the last hour painting their faces, and even my lifeless heart couldn't help but fall in love with how adorable they all look. She even managed to paint a black hawk silhouette with a red background on my face along with Theo's jersey number on my cheek. I look ridiculous, but I love it nonetheless.

"He was really sweet for putting all of this together," Mom comments, leaning closer to me so I can hear her over the deafening chants of the people around us.

I nod. "Yup. Colt's a sweetheart."

With a look full of confusion, Mom asks, "Colt?"

"Hey, the game's about to start," Kate interrupts and places her fingers into her mouth, blowing a loud whistle that makes my ears ring.

"Yowza, Kate," I return, shying away from her.

She simply grins and turns back to the game, so I do the same, grateful for a glimpse of the Kate I've gotten to know since moving in.

A few minutes later, the referee drops the puck at the center of the rink between the Hawks and their opponents, the Warriors. Then, they're off.

I can't focus on the game. I'm too distracted by my thoughts. The what-ifs and what-should've-beens roll around in my head like a carousel of unfinished business. I used to love coming to hockey games. I used to love cheering for Colt and his friends. I used to love the slight chill in the air. The clang of the cowbells in the crowd. The familiar ring of the red alarm whenever a goal is made. Even the hot dogs from the stands were a familiar tradition. One I've loved for as long as I can remember.

But will I still love it? If hockey turns out to be the cata-lyst ending my relationship with Theo?

*It isn't over*, I remind myself, but it doesn't erase the rush of anxiety at the thought of losing him.

I focus on Theo's last name stitched onto the back of his jersey and frown. I've missed him. More than I can even acknowledge to myself, let alone admit out loud. When he left for college after high school, I stuck my head in the sand and signed up for two marathons, a volleyball recreation league, and a full-time load of courses at my community college. And it worked. Distracting myself. I was able to focus on everything and everyone outside of my feelings for a guy who didn't know I existed. It was great. Until I saw Theo again.

Now, even the distance from the past four days hasn't been enough to curb my feelings for the guy. It doesn't matter that I've been throwing my time into work, school, and Netflix. I've missed him more than anything else in the world.

And it's been less than a week.

Which is ridiculous. And stupid. Because it's the littlest things that make my heart ache the most. Like a silver Big Red gum wrapper. Or an old song on my playlist. Even driving makes me think of him. The roads running past SeaBird. The track where we raced. Everything reminds me of Theo. And nothing is putting a dent in my feelings for the guy.

What am I supposed to do when he leaves for real? Do we try the long-distance thing? Does he even want to try the long-distance thing? He didn't tell me, so how the hell should I know?

I didn't bother Googling the Rockies team. I didn't need to. I know where they're located. I know how busy their schedule is. I know how quickly Theo will be thrown into the deep end, and how little we'll be able to talk when we're thousands of miles apart once the season starts.

*Don't go, Theo.*

The buzzer rings, signifying the end of the first period, and the team heads through the tunnel beneath the arena seats. Theo follows slowly behind Colt toward the locker room but stops and looks up, finding me in the sea of people without a blip of hesitation. My breath hitches as our gazes connect. He takes off his helmet and balances it on his hip, mouthing *olive juice.*

Then, he slips out of sight, leaving me even more raw and lonely than ever.

～

BY THE TIME THE SECOND PERIOD IS OVER, THE SCORE IS FOUR to one for LAU. I don't see a single goal, though. All I see are Theo's lips mouthing *olive juice*, and I'm not sure how much longer I can sit here without losing my shit.

We're in the middle of the third period, and my knee won't stop bouncing as anxiety sweeps over me. I need to get down there now. I need to talk to him. To apologize for being so cold this week. To tell him I love him and need him and want him.

*Man, I'm a mess.*

A few minutes later, Mia and Ash stand up on the opposite side of the row, motioning for the kids to follow. My brows furrow as I watch them start to round up the kids.

"What's going on?" I ask Kate.

"I think they're going on a big bathroom break before the game ends."

"Oh." I start to stand up, but Kate stops me.

"Stay. We've got this covered."

"I think I can help––"

"Seriously, Blake," Mom interjects, grabbing my hand and keeping me in my seat. "They can take care of it."

Kate smiles back at me, ushers the last of the kids from our row, and heads up the stairs.

The alarm buzzes with another goal scored by Colt, and the audience starts cheering. Another ten minutes go by, and I look over my shoulder toward the tunnel leading to the bathrooms and snacks. It's empty.

Not a single kid has returned.

Patting my knee, Mom says, "They're fine, Blake."

"They've been gone forever. What if they--"

"The girls can handle it. Relax. Here." She digs into her purse and pulls out a package of Big Red gum. "Take this."

Confused, I stare at the package in her hand, pointing out, "You hate Big Red."

Her smile tightens, making her look guilty as hell as she shoves it into my lap. "Oh, baloney. Take some. It'll keep you distracted."

Convinced she's acting like a crazy person but too over-whelmed to call her out for it, I take the gum, open it up, toss a piece into my mouth, and chew furiously. Unfortunately, it doesn't do shit to distract me from Theo and how good he looks in his jersey.

How can I be so mad and so in love with one person at the same time?

As the final seconds tick down on the clock, I pull out my phone to text Ash, but Mom grabs it from my hand and tucks it under her thigh. "No. No phones."

"Mom, I gotta find out where they are. It's been forever--"

"They'll be fine. Promise."

Unconvinced, I take in her not-so-well-hidden mischie-vous look and demand, "Okay, seriously. What's going on, Mom?"

"Watch the game, honey." She grabs my chin and pushes it back toward the rink.

I wiggle from her grasp and turn toward her again. "Mom--"

"Watch," she orders, barely withholding her smile.

Yeah. Something is definitely up.

I study the players on the ice, but there isn't anything out of the ordinary. It's like every other game I've ever been to. Thirty seconds later, the buzzer sounds, signifying the end of the game, and the announcer's voice rumbles throughout the arena.

"And the final score for today's game is LAU five points and Minnesota University three points. However, for those who would like to stay, please remain seated. There's a bonus piece of entertainment beginning any moment."

Minnesota University disappears through their tunnel leading to the away team's locker room while the LAU team skates back onto the ice. Most of them are holding hands with little kids in red LAU shirts.

*Shut. The front. Door.*

The players skate slowly as the mini-people shuffle into place, and my jaw drops as I recognize the children.

"Did you know about this?" I breathe out, unable to tear my attention from Ash, Mia, Kate, and the rest of the kids on the ice.

Mom squeezes my knee again. "Told you they were fine."

"What is this?"

"It's a surprise."

"Did Colt––"

"Honey." She chuckles softly. "I love your brother, but do you really think he'd plan this whole thing for you?"

My attention flicks to her for a split second. I stand up to get a better view of the ice. The kids are spread out, forming a small circle around the center of the rink. Each is holding a small basket of rose petals and scattering them along the ice. The contrast between the red from the petals and the white from the ice is staggering but absolutely beautiful, especially from this distance. It's like I'm given a bird's-eye view, and the sight makes my knees weak. She's right. There's no way Colt would do this. But Theo?

I fold my arms and dig my fingers into the soft cotton of my sleeves. My heart rate picks up its pace, pitter-pattering faster and faster as every second ticks by while I search the rink for Theo.

But he isn't here.

*Where is he?*

Doing my best to hide the onslaught of anticipation thrumming through my veins, I remind myself, *Don't get your hopes up, Blake.*

But I can't help it.

I've never been able to help it when it comes to Theo.

It doesn't matter how many times I've gotten my hopes up or how much it hurts, I keep coming back for another hit of Teddy Taylor. Why would today be any different?

The main lights switch off. Only a few spotlights illuminate the ice. My skin prickles with awareness as the majority of onlookers sit back in their seats, their curiosity getting the best of them.

A few seconds later, a man appears from the tunnel and heads onto the ice, his shaggy blonde hair on full display. It's Theo. A very dapper Theo. He touches the buttons on his navy blue suit and runs his fingers through his dirty blonde hair while balancing a bouquet of red roses in one hand and a microphone with his other one. His signature hat is missing, but he still looks sexy as hell as he faces the crowd. He searches the stands, finding me transfixed beside my seat.

With a smirk, he lifts a microphone to his lips and murmurs, "Blakely Thorne. Do you mind coming down here for a minute?"

## 50

## BLAKELY

A rush flows through the arena as the crowd searches for the elusive Blakely Thorne.

"Oh my gosh. Is he going to propose?" a lady asks from a few rows behind me.

With a glare, I look back at her and snap, "He's not going to propose."

*Or at least he better not.*

Mom touches my back and pushes me gently toward the stairs. "Go on, Blake."

With wide eyes, I turn back to her. "Mom––"

"Go."

This can't be happening.

Like for real.

This. Can't. Be. Happening.

I fist my shaking hands at my sides and walk down the steps, careful not to fall flat on my face as everyone watches me. Some people cheer while others stare curiously, and it takes everything inside of me not to tumble down the steps.

When I reach the bottom, Colt's already there with one hand outstretched. He helps me onto the ice, skating slowly so I can keep up with him in my Nikes as we make our way toward Theo in the neutral zone.

The crowd hoots and hollers as Theo strides closer. When he reaches me, Colt lets me go with a warm smile and takes Theo's microphone. Apparently, Theo doesn't need it anymore.

Yeah. Colt most definitely helped set this up, but I can't decide whether to smack him or hug him for it.

*Probably both*, I decide. But I'll deal with him later.

Besides, I'm a little preoccupied by the bastard in front of me.

Ignoring the ever-excited crowd surrounding us, I tell Theo, "Ya know, when I said we'd talk later, I didn't exactly mean in front of an audience after a week of you giving me the cold shoulder."

"I wasn't giving you the cold shoulder."

I glare back at him. "I mean..."

"I asked for your patience, remember?" Theo offers me his hand. "I needed some time to set a few things up. Come here."

I look around the chaos surrounding us, but stay still. "*This* is what you were setting up? It's insane!"

"Figured you deserved a grand gesture after the shit I pulled." Theo reaches for me again, balancing the bouquet with his opposite hand. "Come here, Blake. Please?"

Grudgingly, I grab Theo's hand as the crowd goes wild around us. His fingers are warm despite the chilly atmosphere on the ice, and he brings my knuckles to his lips, kissing them softly. And I hate how I can feel it everywhere. The brush of his lips. The memories they evoke. It's...consuming.

"Thanks for coming," he murmurs.

"Like I had a choice. You thought of everything, didn't you?"

His mouth lifts. "Maybe."

Scanning his sexy outfit, I ask, "Why are you in a suit?"

"'Cause I should've asked you to prom."

I snort. "And you thought today was the day to make up for it?"

"I have a lot of ground to make up for. Might as well start with my fuck ups in high school."

"If we're gonna play that game, you should probably start in elementary when you stole the last can of Crush."

He smirks and shuffles closer. "I thought I already atoned for that one by buying you a two-liter with my allowance."

*The man has a point.*

"Well, you could've at least told me to dress up," I argue, fighting off the urge to tug at his lapel and drag him closer. "I'm in jeans and a hoodie, for Pete's sake, and my face looks like I could've starred in Carrie." I motion to the black and red face paint.

His chuckle is warm and so are his calloused fingers as they tickle my skin, brushing my hair behind my ear. "You look beautiful, Blake."

"I look like I'm ready to watch a hockey game. Unlike you," I note. "How'd you get changed so fast?"

"That's what you want to know?" He laughs again, a little harder this time.

To be fair, I want to know a lot of things. Like why he went through all this work setting everything up for me. I want to know if he honestly thinks we can find a way to make this work. I want to know if he still loves me as much as I love him, and if he's going to finally learn how to communicate with me instead of keeping me in the dark.

And those questions are only the tip of the iceberg.

Yeah. I have a *lot* of questions.

"Actually, yes. Let's start with that." *After all, it's the easiest of my questions.* "How'd you get changed so fast?"

"I'm a guy," he answers. "I always get ready quickly. It helped that it took a few minutes to get the kids in place, so they gave me some time."

"Oh."

"I also planned a little speech and convinced the audio guys to play a few songs for us. Not to mention the Big Red." He leans closer and smiles, letting my cinnamon breath fan across his cheeks. "Smells good, by the way."

I ignore the compliment and blow out a big bubble with the gum. He pulls away, lets out a chuckle––which shoots straight to my core––and waits for it to pop.

Once it does, he grabs my waist and tugs me closer to him. "Dance with me?"

"And where would we put the roses?" I challenge.

They land with a soft woosh next to our feet as he pulls me against him again. I bite my lip to keep from grinning and roll my eyes, ignoring our audience in the arena and how adorable the kids are as they cheer their little hearts out.

"How'd you convince the kids to act interested in my love life?" I ask. "Some of them were even bored while watching the game. It's not like this can be any more interesting to them."

"Colt promised I'd pay them all a quarter for every time you roll your eyes––or laugh––and a dollar if you let me kiss you."

"You're joking."

Theo chuckles. "Not in the slightest."

"He offered up your money?"

"Yeah. I told Colt to figure out how to keep them engaged so they don't get bored on the ice. Bribing them was his solution."

"To be fair, it's a solid strategy," I note.

"You're not wrong. They're also some of your favorite

people. I needed to make sure they were here when I won you over."

I snort, my amusement shifting to something heavier. "Isn't that the problem, though? You always win me over, and I always cave to whatever you want."

"And that's a bad thing?" he teases, but there's still hesitancy in his gaze. Like he knows he's on thin ice. Like he knows he screwed up. Like he knows he hurt me.

"Not if you learn from your mistakes," I murmur. "But I need to know you're willing to cave for me too. To compromise. To look at situations from both perspectives before you just do whatever's best for you without considering how it affects me." I bite my tongue, my humor dissipating. "Blah. I'll stop. I know we've already talked about this, I just…"

"I know, Blake," he rasps. "Actions speak louder than words, right?"

I dip my chin. "Yes."

"Hence the grand gesture. It's also why I should've told you how beautiful you looked in a dress the first time you wore one. And every time after that," he clarifies with a smile. "It's why I should've taken you to prom. Why I should've told you how I felt after we kissed for the first time. It's also why I should've told you about the contracts. I've messed up so many times with you, Blake. I froze instead of acting. But it wasn't because I wasn't willing to compromise. I froze because I was scared. Scared to be vulnerable. Scared to let you in, when you'd already wiggled your way under my skin. I froze because I was terrified I'd lose you. I'm *still* terrified I'll lose you." His warm gaze rolls over my face, taking in every tiny detail as if committing them to memory. "But you were right. You *are* right. We're in this together. And I'm done fighting it or running from it, just because I'm afraid I'll mess it up again. I'm going to put us first. Which is why I want to propose..." His voice trails off, the words hanging in the air.

*Propose?*

Did he just say *propose*?

"Theo," I warn. Don't get me wrong, I love the bastard, but if he honestly thinks a proposal is going to fix this, he has another thing coming to him.

With a wry grin, he repeats, "I want to propose... that I take the Lions contract.".

My eyes widen in surprise, my heart galloping in my chest as I register his words before I smack his shoulder. "Not funny, Teddy."

He laughs, but keeps his grasp firmly around my waist. "It was a little funny."

"Uh huh. Sure. Way to scare the crap out of me," I reply, rolling my eyes while earning the kiddos another quarter for good measure. "But why would you choose the Lions over the Rockies?"

"It's closer to LAU. My parents. Macklin. *You.*"

"You know I would move if you simply *asked.*"

"I know, baby. I know." He runs his hands up and down my spine. "But I don't want you to uproot your life for me. To give up on your dreams so I can pursue mine. I want us to build our dreams together."

"But you've always loved the Rockies," I remind him.

"And I always will. But I love you more. I think the Lions contract is a better fit for *us.* Not me."

My gaze feels glassy, but I blink the moisture away. Because he's trying. He's talking. He's learning from our past mistakes. He's doing exactly what I asked, and I kind of want to kiss him for it.

"But I didn't send the contract in yet," he adds. "I wanted to talk to you first."

"Theo." I roll my watery eyes. "You don't need my

permission––"

"I know I don't. And I know you would've done whatever I wanted if I had only told you about it first." He grabs my chin and tilts my head up, making sure he has my full attention. Joke's on him. He's always had my full attention.

"I want to do this for you, Blake," he continues, his voice soft and raspy and oh, so sexy I can't even handle it. "Besides, if you agree the Lions are the best fit for us, I'm gonna play with Colt next season. That was one of my childhood dreams, too, remember? It's what I want. *You're* what I want."

He starts swaying us back and forth as "My Endless Love" by Diana Ross filters through the speakers.

When I recognize the song, I nearly buckle over and laugh harder than I have in years. Theo's grip tightens around my waist, keeping me from falling on my butt as I wipe the happy tears from my eyes and catch my breath through bouts of laughter. "You didn't."

"Is there something wrong with 'My Endless Love?'" He cocks his head, daring me to disagree.

I cover my mouth, but I can't stop cackling, the shift in emotions making me feel like I'm on a rollercoaster. "It's from *Happy Gilmore*."

"And?"

"And…" I practically melt in his arms, sliding my hands over the navy lapel on his suit and smoothing out the silky fabric. "You once told me you wouldn't be caught dead professing your love like Happy did."

"Apparently, the right girl can make a guy do just about anything."

"You also said it's probably the corniest scene in the entire movie," I remind him, fussing with the button on his white dress shirt.

Pulling me against him again, he sandwiches my arms

between us but doesn't bother to argue as he continues swaying us back and forth to the music.

"It made you smile," he murmurs.

With my head against his shoulder, I close my eyes. "And that was the goal?"

"Yeah, Blake. That was the goal."

"Mission accomplished," I whisper, peeking up at him. "Although, if I remember correctly, there weren't roses in the scene."

"Thought I'd add my own Teddy flare." He leans a little closer, his breath tickling my cheeks.

"I thought you didn't like to be called Teddy."

"Guess it's grown on me."

"Oh, really?"

"Mm-hmm," he hums, the sound low and throaty and oh, so hot it makes my knees weak.

"Has anything else grown on you?" I ask.

His mouth twitches, but the bastard still doesn't put me out of my misery, refusing to kiss me as his warm gaze bounces around my face. It's like he's memorizing it. This moment. Me. Everything.

"Just my best friend's annoying little sister," he murmurs.

If anyone else had said it, I'd be offended, but as the words slip past Theo's lips, I can barely withhold my laughter—or my love. Hell, it feels like it's bubbling up inside of me, clogging my throat and every ounce of logic and self-preservation. Instead, I just want to fall for the man in front of me. Let him love me the same way I love him. The same way I've always loved him. For years. But for the first time, the fear accompanying the thought is absent. If anything, I feel peace. He's asking for my opinion. He's learning to compromise. He's communicating—even if it is in front of a shit ton of people. He's doing everything I asked and more.

I love this man.

We're barely moving now. There's only so much coordination a girl like me has, and dancing on the ice without skates——and on top of roses——is quite the test.

Theo has me, though. Like an anchor, he keeps me grounded, his firm grip around my waist more than adequate to keep me from falling. Well, physically, anyway. Emotionally? I'm a goner.

Resting my head against his chest, I let the cheesy song wash over us and dance with Theo as our audience finally grows bored enough to file out of the arena. When the song ends, it's replaced with an instrumental Taylor Swift song. Gotta give the guy credit, he definitely has an eclectic taste, and I hum the melody as the team shuffles out, along with Mia, Ash, Kate, and the kids, leaving us alone on the ice.

As the song ends, and it's only me and Theo surrounded by roses, I look up at him. "Thank you."

His soft smile makes me melt.

And when he whispers, "Olive juice, Blake," my breath hitches at the words more potent than I love you could ever be. Because it's Theo. And what we have? It has depth. History. So much history, it's daunting sometimes, but there's a comfort in it too. A knowledge that we've been through so much together. Seen so much. Endured so much. And if we could conquer all of our past bumps along the road to being together, maybe we can get past our future hurdles too. Maybe we have a chance.

I don't say it back.

I'm not sure if I can.

Thanks to the thoughtful bastard, my voice is too busy choking on my own emotions to make a peep.

But my heart? It's fuller than ever.

My tongue darts out between my lips, and his attention drops to them before I mouth *olive juice*.

His lips are on mine in an instant. One hand cradles my

face while the other snakes around my waist and tugs me closer, melding me to him. But it isn't enough. Even our clothes are too much of a barrier. I want to feel him. I need to. It's like the final stupid rift between us is gone. And now that I have him? All of him? There isn't a chance in hell I'm letting him go. Nope. I'm gonna get lost in his kiss. In his taste. In his presence. Because I'm allowed to. Because I trust him. And I know he won't let me down. He won't hurt me. He won't push me away. Not anymore.

He drags his tongue along my bottom lip, and I whimper softly.

More.

I want more.

Tilting my head, I kiss him harder, my fingers tangling in his jacket and tugging at the fabric, anxious to rip it off. To connect with him.

He pulls away, allowing us a second to breathe, my chest rising and falling in heavy pants as I mumble, "You couldn't have chosen a less public place to make it up to me?"

"You told me to prove I care about you."

"And trust me, Teddy, you've proven it in spades. Now, if only we could find an ounce of privacy so we could make up properly…"

His gaze darkens, and he nips at my bottom lip, lacing his fingers with mine. "Come on. I have an idea."

## 51

## THEO

She deserves a bed. I know it. She knows it. But she also deserves to be worshipped, and I've spent way too long with my head up my ass to postpone it for another second in search of a comfortable mattress.

Tugging her down the tunnel and into a broom closet, I push her against the wall and breathe her in, resting my forehead against hers as my cock strains against the zipper of my slacks.

"You sure you want this here?" I rasp, peppering kisses against her throat before she tugs me up to meet her mouth with mine.

She smiles against my lips. "For the first round. Yes."

"And the second?"

"I'm thinking the car ride home."

I laugh. "And round three?"

"We might make it to the bedroom?" she answers thoughtfully. "But it might only be the couch."

"And the one after that?"

She squeezes my cock through my pants, dragging her

palm from the base to the tip. "I'm sure we'll think of something."

*Fuuuuck.*

Grabbing her wrist, I pull her away from me and tug her hands above her head. I hold them in place with my right hand as my left rips at the button on her jeans. Then, my mouth is on hers. Drinking in her whimpers. Her tiny moans. I find her slit and rub my finger against it, nearly coming on the spot. She's wet. So damn wet, I can hardly control myself as I slide my thumb to her clit and draw small circles around the little nub.

Her breath hitches, and her hands tug against my grasp, but I keep her pinned in place. Torturing her the same way she's tortured me for years.

"Theo," she whimpers.

"Shhh... " I dip my finger inside of her, and her hips thrust forward in the smallest of movements. But it's there. Her want. Her need for me. For this. For us. I let her ride my finger for a few more minutes, savoring the tiny sounds in her throat and the way she grows more desperate with every touch of her clit.

"Theo," she repeats. "If you don't push me over the edge--"

"Keep your hands up," I order. "If you touch me, I stop. We clear?"

"Theo," she warns, her bright green eyes practically glowing in the dark closet. I cup her cheek, running my finger over my jersey number painted on her skin.

"I like my number on you," I note as I slide down her body and tug her jeans down. There's a metal shelf above her head, and she tangles her fingers through the woven pieces, balancing herself as I strip her bare.

And fuck me, she's the most beautiful thing I've ever laid eyes on.

My tongue runs along my bottom lip as I grab her leg and hook it over my shoulder.

"One of these days, you're gonna let me repay the favor," she murmurs, watching me while I lean closer to her center and breathe her in.

Looking up at her, I kiss her pubic bone and counter, "One of these days, I'm gonna stop fucking up and will feel like I actually deserve your mouth on my dick."

Her chuckle turns into a moan as I spread her folds and slip my tongue between them. I swear the girl smells like cinnamon, but maybe it's my fantasies clashing with reality bringing the spice to the surface. Regardless, she tastes just as delicious as I remember. Better even. My mouth waters, and I dip my tongue into her center, tasting her.

With a gasp, her thigh clenches against my ear, and she arches her back, her knuckles white around the metal shelf.

"Fuck, Theo. Fuckity, fuck, fuck, fuck."

I laugh and squeeze her leg to keep from suffocating as I glance up at her. But she isn't looking at me. Her eyes are closed, and her lips are parted as the curses flow out of her like a geyser. My teeth graze against her clit in the softest of nibbles. Her jaw drops even further, and she looks down at me, her legs trembling.

"So help me, Teddy––"

Her words end in a jumble of more expletives as I bite a little harder and thrust two fingers inside of her.

Three pumps later, she comes, her knees going weak, and her hands slipping from the shelf above her. She weaves them into my hair and pulls me closer. I can't breathe. Not that I want to. No. This is a much better way to go than the suffering I'd been dealing with since I lost her the first time.

Or the second.

But air? I guess it might be nice in the next thirty seconds or so. I continue licking, biting, and sucking until the muscles in her thighs turn to mush around my neck, and she comes back down to earth. Her chest heaves from exertion as she wipes her forehead with the back of her hand, a dazed smile on her lips. I unhook her leg from my shoulder, making sure she can stand on her own. I get to my feet and slide my hand to her throat, squeezing softly as I lean in for a kiss.

Her eyes are still glazed from her orgasm, but she smiles a little wider and bites my bottom lip. My dick jumps in my pants, practically weeping for attention as her hand trails down my chest.

"Blake," I murmur.

Just like before, she squeezes me through my slacks, and I jerk in her grasp. The friction––no matter how little––is too good. Too promising. Too consuming.

I squeeze her throat again in warning, and her smile widens as she holds my gaze hostage.

"I believe you've earned my mouth, Teddy. The question is…what are you going to do with it?"

*Fuuuuck.*

## 52

## BLAKELY

"On your knees, Blake," Theo orders, his tone laced with a sexy raspiness that shoots straight to my core, despite my recent orgasm.

I lick my lips and slide to my knees, peeking up at him through my lashes.

He likes this. The control. It isn't something I would usually hand over. But for Theo? I can't help but make an exception.

"Unzip my pants," he demands. His eyes are hot with lust.

The metallic zip from the zipper echoes throughout the otherwise silent closet, and I wait for his next order.

"Take it out."

With a coy smile, I slip my hand into his dark boxers and slide my thumb against the head of his erection as I pull it free. The guy's big. And freaking dripping.

I look up at him and wait for his next command, his hard shaft barely an inch from my lips as I continue rubbing it softly with my palm. Up and down. Back and forth. Oh, how I want to tease him. To push him over the edge the same way he pushed me.

His jaw tightens as he watches me. He drags his hand against my cheek, pushing my hair away and gripping the side of my face. Then, he pulls me closer to him. It isn't painful, but there's a force behind it. A desire. It makes my mouth water and my insides clench with anticipation as I take him into my mouth.

His dick is hot against my tongue, the saltiness from his precum dripping onto my tastebuds. I take him deeper, savoring his little groans of pleasure and the way his hips thrust forward as if he can't help himself. He flexes his fingers against my scalp and drags me closer, his dick hitting the back of my throat.

I gag slightly, and he pulls back, dropping his hand from my head.

"Fuck. I'm sorry, baby--"

Wrapping my hands around the base of his cock, I dive in again, massaging the underside of his head with my tongue as I pump around him faster.

He groans again and gives in, pumping into me over and over again in tiny thrusts. The familiar spurt of cum hits the back of my throat, and I swallow it down, gulp after gulp, as he throws his head back and curses under his breath, his hand cupping the back of my scalp like he can't help himself.

And it feels good. To watch him like this. Satiated. Without a care in the world. Free. Happy. Content. I want to do it again and--

Three loud knocks shake us from our high, making us flinch at the obtrusive sound. Theo shoves himself back into his pants while stepping in front of me to keep me out of sight in case someone opens the closet door. With my heart in my throat, I slip on my jeans and clutch at the back of Theo's suit, praying whoever's on the opposite side of the door didn't hear us going at it like a couple of bunnies--and we hadn't even gotten to the good part.

"I have rules for a reason," a low voice yells through the door before slamming his hand against it again. "Now, get out of here and go find a place to hook up that I *don't* have to sanitize afterward, will you?"

I jerk back at the sound and cover my face. It's Coach Sanderson. And he's definitely not naive enough to think we were chatting about the weather in here. Especially not after Theo's not-so-discreet declaration of love after the game.

With my forehead pressed to Theo's spine, I let out a breath of laughter and squeeze my eyes shut.

Theo looks over his shoulder and down at me, his voice laced with amusement. "Is something funny?"

Footsteps echo from the opposite side of the door as Coach retreats.

"This is why Coach has the no dating rule," I tell him with a grin. "So his players wouldn't be hooking up in the janitor's closet."

Theo laughs and turns around, plastering me against him in a full-body hug. And it feels good. Comforting. Like I'm coming home.

Rubbing his hand up and down my back, he mutters, "We should probably get out of here.".

I nod against his chest as the day, and the roller coaster of emotions that came with it, finally siphon the last of my energy. "Probably."

"We'll have to do the walk of shame."

"And what do I have to be ashamed about?" I look up at him, my eyes shining with mirth. "I just got off on the hockey captain's mouth. And after your little declaration on the ice? Pretty sure I'm gonna be walking on cloud nine for the rest of the week."

Throwing his head back, Theo laughs even harder. "Glad I can be of service." He hooks his arm around my shoulders and guides me out of the closet.

And I feel lighter somehow. Lighter and happier than I have in who knows how long. It's perfect. I smile and snake my arm around his back, leaning into Theo and breathing him in like he's my own personal lifeline.

And in a way, I guess he is.

∼

THE DRIVE BACK TO MY PLACE IS SHORT, BUT I STILL MANAGE to get Theo off with a solid hand job as we weave through the side streets and pull up to my place.

"That's two," I quip as we head inside.

Theo's laughter drowns out the slight squeak from the front door as I push it open. Ash is at the kitchen table with a pint of ice cream in front of her and a shit-eating grin practically splitting her face in two.

"Can I help you?" I ask.

"So?" She bounces her eyes up and down. "Did you guys get it on at the rink?"

My jaw drops, and I shake my head while ignoring the way my cheeks heat. Like seriously. Did she really just ask me that?

Recovering from my embarrassment, I point out, "You sound like Mia."

With her hands raised in the air, one of which is still holding the ice cream spoon, Ash argues, "Hey, I'm just asking."

"Oh, come on," Mia interjects, her light footsteps echoing from the hallway. "Obviously, they hooked up. If they hadn't, they wouldn't be"––she checks the time on her phone––"forty-five minutes later than the rest of us."

I snort and fold my arms. "You two are nosy nellies."

"*Correct* nosy nellies," Mia points out. "You totally got laid."

"I knew it!" Ash gushes. "Colt will be so happy."

Theo and I exchange worried looks as he asks, "Why would Colt be happy about me sleeping with his little sister?"

"Cause now you owe all the kids fifty bucks each," Mia explains. She collapses onto the kitchen chair next to Ash and steals her spoon, scooping up a bite of ice cream from the cardboard container.

I scratch my temple, convinced I'm hallucinating. Either that, or my hearing is out of whack. "I'm sorry, what?"

"Colt said Theo would pay each of the kids fifty bucks if you and him 'scored' after the game," Mia explains with a wry grin, using her fingers as air-quotes.

The blood drains from my face. "He did not."

"Oh, he most definitely did," Ash informs me, shamelessly.

The toilet flushes from down the hall, and Colt steps into the hallway. When he sees us, he turns to Ash and raises his brows.

With a laugh, she nods, and Colt jerks his elbow back, his hand fisted, and bows his head in triumph. "Yes!" Then he turns to Theo. "Dude, you're out like six hundred bucks. Hope it was worth it."

Theo rolls his eyes but looks down at me still pressed to his side and drops a kiss to my forehead. "Worth every penny, man."

Sometimes, it's a little weird how cool Colt is with the whole *me dating his best friend* thing, but in a way, it's kind of awesome too. At least he was one barrier we didn't have to hurdle to find our happiness, even if it did just cost Theo six hundred bucks.

Then again, maybe we can pay the little monsters with our leftover arcade money.

"We're gonna head to Colt's tonight," Ash says as she pushes the almost-empty ice cream carton toward Mia and stands up. "But we need to catch up––and soon––because a little bird told me Theo may or may not have chosen the Lions' contract but wanted to run his decision by you before he turned in the contract, which means…" Her voice trails off, and she gives me a pointed look.

"Which means we need to buy some new Lions' merchandise," I finish for her.

She squeals and pulls me into a hug. "So, you guys talked about it? And you're both on the same page?"

I nod, digging my teeth into my lower lip to keep from grinning like a loon. But I'm so damn happy, I can't help it.

"Yay!" She lets me go and threads her arm through Colt's. "Okay. We'll definitely be talking later about this, but we kinda have to go."

"Sounds like a plan," I reply. "Bye, guys."

As they head out the door, Theo grabs my waist and pulls me against him. "Hey, Blake?"

"Yes?"

"Is this going to be a normal thing? Where you talk about me like I'm not in the room?"

"Is that a problem, Teddy Bear?" I challenge, hooking my arms around his neck.

He rolls his eyes and drops a kiss to my forehead, slowly swaying us back and forth in the center of the family room. And I love it. The ease. The comfortable silence.

"You're always gonna be a Thorne in my side, aren't you?" he murmurs.

"Would you have it any other way?"

His smile softens. "Nah. I wouldn't change a thing."

"Oh, really? Not even my bossiness?" I bat my lashes up at him with the most syrupy sweet smile I can manage.

He grins. "Nope."

"How about my addiction to cinnamon?"

"Gonna buy stock in McCormick and Big Red as soon as I get my bonus."

I laugh and drop my forehead to his strong chest. "And my obsession with bets?"

His hands slide down my waist, and he squeezes my ass. "How do you think you won me over in the first place?"

"And the way I call you Teddy Bear?" I quip, looking up at him again.

"We can put it on my tombstone."

"And my need to come out on top in everything I do?"

"I'm a sucker for a girl who knows how to bring her A-game."

My cheeks pinch from grinning so much. But I can't help it. The guy makes me laugh. It's one of my favorite things about him. "I'm pretty sure I can think of a way or two to bring my A-game right now," I mention. "You know, if you're interested."

His eyes heat. "Yeah?"

"Mm-hmm." I slip my hand down the front of his slacks and brush my palm against him. He's already hard and jerks slightly in my grasp as I tease him shamelessly. And it's crazy. How effortless this feels. How natural and perfect and *real*. It's more than anything I could've imagined when I was growing up and crushing on my brother's best friend.

It's better.

So much better.

And yeah. We've had our bumps along the way, but getting Theo to let me in, to take a chance, to stay and fight for our relationship––to convince *me* to stay and fight for our relationship––we're the luckiest people in the world.

He leans forward, resting his forehead against mine and closing his eyes. Despite his hard length in my hand, he doesn't look horny. He looks…relieved. And in love.

"Olive juice, Blakely."

My heart swells in my chest. "Olive juice, Teddy Bear. Forever and ever." I squeeze him softly in my palm. "Now, let's go find my bedroom."

"I thought you'd never ask."

# EPILOGUE

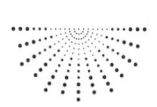

## BLAKELY

"It just had to be Lions, didn't it?" I mutter as I slide the hangers from left to right in the closet, perusing the new Lions merchandise I'd purchased as soon as they opened their online store in preparation for the season. I may or may not have bought every shirt, hoodie, and tank top in my size. If only they weren't covered in my least favorite animal.

With his hands behind his head, Theo chuckles on the bed, cool as a cucumber despite his first professional hockey game tonight.

"Is there a problem with Lions, Baby Thorne?" he asks.

I glance over my shoulder and roll my eyes. "I'm just saying, they could've picked a better mascot, thank you very much."

"I thought you liked lions."

"I like lion*esses*," I emphasize before grabbing a brand new black and gold hoodie from the hanger. It also happens to have the smallest lion head emblem of the bunch. "And don't play dumb with me, mister," I add. "We've had this conversation before, ya know."

"Yeah, I think you've made your stance pretty clear." Rolling off the bed, he grabs my hips and pulls me into him until my back is plastered to his front. With a quick tug, he snags the hoodie from my hands and throws it onto the bed.

I laugh and turn in his arms until I'm facing him fully. "I'm trying to get ready for your game."

"I think I should help." His calloused fingers slip beneath my——well, technically it's his, but I stole it——sleep shirt and brush against my sensitive skin. Goosebumps race up my spine.

"Oh, you think you should help, do you?"

He pulls the cotton fabric over my head. My hair hangs in a mess around my bare shoulders as my sleep shirt falls at our feet. His hungry gaze slides over my mostly naked body. Then, he cups my breasts.

As I watch his massive hands practically swallow my boobs, I challenge, "This is you helping me get ready?"

"It's me helping you relax. I thought I was supposed to be the nervous one today, Baby Thorne." He tweaks my nipple, grabs my hips, and pulls me against him.

"I'm not nervous. I just…want you and Colt to play well and kick ass during your first game, which, by the way, is why I still stand by my idea for you guys to petition Buchanan and convince him to change the mascot to the lionesses."

Henry Buchanan is the new owner of the Lions hockey team. Apparently, the guy likes to dabble in a little bit of everything. Either that, or his attention span is as bad as Theo's. He started out as the prince of the massive software company his father created before he decided to use his knowledge and teach students at LAU. Now, he's spending his inheritance on forming a new hockey team.

The guy's well-rounded. I'll give him that much.

Theo's chest rumbles with amusement as he laces our

fingers together and drags me to the bed. I follow him, reaching for the hoodie on the gray comforter, but he slaps my hand away.

With a gasp, I clutch my hand to my bare chest. "Excuse me!"

"Calm your perfect tits. I bought you something for today. Wait here."

He grabs a large square box from the top shelf in the closet and orders, "Sit."

It's bigger than any kind of jewelry box, but it isn't an average clothing box, either. My eyes narrow in suspicion as my butt hits the mattress.

Satisfied, he sets the box on my lap. "Open."

"Someone's bossy," I note, lifting the lid off. I set it on top of my discarded sleep shirt and the hoodie I'd planned to wear today. Gold and red tissue paper covers whatever's inside, so I add it to my stack of abandoned items. When Theo's gift comes into view, I gasp and cover my mouth.

It's a white and gold jersey, identical to the players'. But instead of a lion emblem on the front, a proud lioness is stitched into the fabric along with Theo's jersey number. She looks fierce and proud, her mouth open wide in a snarl. The colors are bold and vibrant against the white background and makes the fearless animal practically pop off the polyester. Carefully, I brush my fingers over the custom jersey, unsure what to say.

The mattress dips as Theo sits beside me and murmurs, "Do you like it?"

"Where did you get this?" I whisper. There isn't any lioness merchandise. Trust me. I've looked. But this? It's perfect.

"I knew I probably couldn't convince a bunch of grownass men to wear lionesses on their jerseys, so I didn't bother to petition Buchanan. *But* I figure you deserve to be recognized."

Tearing my gaze from the most thoughtful gift I've ever received, I look at Theo and bite my lip. "Theo…"

"You're right. Lionesses don't get enough credit, Blake. Lions wouldn't be the kings of the jungle if it weren't for their badass women by their side. I wouldn't be where I am today if it wasn't for you. Your support, your love and example, they've meant more to me than anything else in the world. And I can guarantee none of the lions on the ice tonight would be there if it wasn't for their badass lionesses who have their backs, either. So, thank you. For being you." He kisses my temple, and I lean into the simple show of affection, soaking it up until I feel like I'm glowing.

*How did I get so damn lucky?*

"Ya know, I guess lions aren't too bad," I murmur.

He pulls away and cocks his head. "You think?"

"Yeah. Especially when they take care of their lionesses."

"We take care of each other, Blake. Always." He kisses me again but snakes his hand around my shoulder, copping a feel of my bare boob one more time and squeezing it like a squeaky toy. "Now, get dressed. I have a press conference to get to."

He lets my breast go, but I grab his wrist, twist on the mattress, and straddle his waist with my thighs.

With a surprised grin, he grabs my upper thighs and asks, "What are you doing?"

"Oh, nothing." The proud lioness is on full display across my chest as I slip it over my head and move down a few inches, pulling his hardening erection from his basketball shorts.

"Blake," he warns, but he lifts his hips and helps me scoot them down. "We gotta get ready."

His cock jerks in my palm, and I rub my thumb over the

head. "You really think you could get away with giving me the most thoughtful gift on the planet and *not* give me an orgasm as a cherry on top?"

He chuckles and grabs my hips, his fingers flexing beneath my new jersey. "Two minutes, Baby Thorne. You take any longer, and I might have to spank you."

Pushing my underwear to the side, I line us up and mutter, "Tease," as I slowly lower myself onto him. His groan mingles with my own as he stretches me. I feel so full. So loved. So cherished. With my arms wrapped around his neck, I ride him. And when we're both close to the edge, I bite his earlobe and whisper, "Olive juice."

And I know without a doubt, those two words will only ever feel right when I'm with him.

I guess it's a good thing I'm never letting him go.

The End

### Prologue
Kate

MY HEAD IS POUNDING. NO, IT FEELS LIKE IT'S BEING SLICED IN half. Scratch that. It feels as if someone is stabbing it over and over again with little razor blades, leaving ribbons of brain instead of a single mass. Yup. That's how it feels. Which means one thing.

I had another seizure.

I blink slowly, taking in my surroundings. But I don't know where I am. I know it isn't home. It's bright, though. The ceiling has thick wood beams and gold fixtures. And there are people. So many people.

The restaurant. I'm at the restaurant. With Ash. And Mia.

And Colt. And Theo. They invited me to celebrate. I remember now.

It's okay.

It's going to be okay.

Okay, maybe it isn't, but things haven't felt okay for a while now, so I'm not sure why I'm surprised.

The restaurant is quiet as I open my eyes again, blinking slowly. A stranger is next to me. Brown, wavy hair cropped short on the sides and longer on the top. Kind eyes. Worried eyes. A strong jaw. And pretty, full lips pulled into a frown. I don't recognize him. And it isn't the seizure misplacing my shitty memory, either. Not this time, anyway. I would've remembered him. I know I would have. Maybe he's come into the restaurant before? The light blue eyes like the sky on a sunny day. The yummy full lips. The soft hair.

Whoa, girl. You're going in circles here.

Where am I again?

"Hey," the stranger murmurs, pushing my hair away from my forehead as his pretty blue eyes bounce around my face, assessing me.

Such pretty eyes.

With dark lashes and little flecks of navy spread throughout the sky blue color.

Blue. Blue. Blue.

"You okay?" he asks, his brows pinched in concern.

I laugh, nearly choking on the lump clogging my throat and the guilt squeezing my chest. "I'm sorry."

His pretty lips pull into a frown. "You have nothing to apologize for."

"Debatable," I argue, my head throbbing and my muscles already sore. I try to sit up, but the room feels like it's spinning. Strong, warm hands grasp my arm and back as the stranger helps me sit up. Somehow, I'm on the ground, though I guess I shouldn't be surprised.

It's usually where I end up when a seizure hits.

Everyone's standing around me.

Looking down at me.

All of my roommates are here. Ashlyn, Mia, Blakely. Theo and Colt are here too. Theo's dating Blake, and Colt's dating Ashlyn.

Dating.

The word brings a memory to the surface. A shitty one. Wes. My ex. He'd brought a girl to the restaurant where I waitress. I had to serve the bastard before coming here. It's why I was stressed. Why I downed Mia's wine without giving a shit it could trigger a seizure.

It's my own freaking fault.

I know better.

Ash's eyes are rimmed with redness, hinting she's holding back tears as she stares down at me. Colt's holding her against his chest the same way Theo's holding Blakely.

But none of them say anything. They're just watching me. Waiting to see if I'll start shaking again. If I'll have another episode.

It must've been a bad one.

Seizure, that is.

The word alone is like nails on a chalkboard but combined with the evidence surrounding me and how uncomfortable I must've made everyone feel? It might as well be… What's worse than nails on a chalkboard?

Man, I can't even think of a solid metaphor right now.

My head is throbbing.

I press my hand to my temple and close my eyes.

Kill me now.

"Are you strong enough to sit up on your own?" the stranger asks. His hands are still on me. Like everyone else, he's worried I'll collapse again, so he's reluctant to let me go.

I turn and look up at him again.

KELSIE RAE

He really is good-looking. A little older, though. Maybe thirty? Thirty-five? Definitely not anyone from my classes at LAU. I would've remembered him. Maybe he's come into my restaurant before.

Gah. I'm still going in circles.

I squeeze my eyes shut and try to shrug out of his grasp, but he doesn't let me. "I'm fine."

"Give yourself a minute," he suggests.

"I'm fine," I repeat.

"Kate, are you sure you're okay?" Ash asks. She squats down beside me and the stranger, her sweet expression filled with concern.

She's never seen me have a seizure. And clearly, now that she has, she'll never let me live it down. The girl's a mother hen on a good day. Now that she's seen me at worst? She'll never let me out of her sight again.

"I'm fine, Ash," I mumble. "Can we...not do this? I just want to go home––"

"The ambulance will be here any second," Mia chimes in.

My eyes widen in surprise as I register her words.

Ambulance?

Noooo.

"You called an ambulance?" I choke out, blinking back tears. "Why? I'm fine. This isn't a big deal. I'll just go home, and..." My voice trails off as the pounding in my skull heightens, drowning out my thoughts or whatever I'd been rambling about.

Shit, why is the room still spinning?

"Breathe," the stranger reminds me.

I let out a shuddered breath and close my eyes, letting a single tear slide down my cheek while attempting to block out my friends' faces. The pity. The concern. The fear.

Don't they get it?

It's just another day in the messed-up life of Kate

410

Winchester.

Lucky me.

### Chapter One
Macklin

MY BUDDY, FELIX, WAS ON DUTY AND TOOK KATE'S VITALS AS soon as he arrived on the scene with Remi, his girlfriend and a fellow paramedic. Felix didn't care that I insisted on riding with Kate to the hospital, but the bastard did shoot me a look when she told him it wasn't necessary. Mia offered to take my place as her plus-one in the back of the ambulance, but apparently, Kate was even more anxious about a friend joining her than a stranger. When her friends told her going by herself to the hospital wasn't an option, she chose me instead.

After a quick conversation with Theo, my little brother, I promised to text him with any updates, and we were off.

It's funny. How quickly an evening can turn upside down. Theo had invited me to join him and his friends who were celebrating…something. My guess is Colt, Theo's childhood best friend, asked him to extend the offer to me. Or our mom intervened. She's been worried about me since the divorce, calling in favors and asking anyone and everyone if they know any young women who'd agree to go on a blind date with a recently divorced man. Or if they could swing by and bring me some cookies she'd made earlier in the day in hopes of cheering me up.

I can't even begin to count how many strangers have shown up on my front porch in the middle of the fucking woods with cookies all because Mama Taylor asked them to. I gotta give the woman credit. She's a stubborn, convincing lady when she wants to be.

The blind dates, though? Well, I had to put my foot down somewhere.

Hanging out with Theo and his friends, however, I could swallow.

And even if it was a pity invitation extended by my little brother, I knew I needed to get out of the house. It's my oldest daughter's birthday, but she doesn't want to see me. Didn't even bother to reply to the happy birthday text I'd sent. She's avoiding me, convinced the bullshit my ex is spewing about me is true when it's the furthest thing from it. Don't get me wrong. I'm not a saint, but Summer's the one who called off the marriage and tore our family apart. Then again, maybe it was my fault. As soon as my winnings from the lottery hit our joint bank account, she took half of it, packed her bags, and sent me a text, informing me her lawyer would be in touch.

I didn't even bother to fight her.

We were both done with the marriage.

Done fighting for something neither of us wanted anymore.

But I wouldn't have called it quits if she hadn't pulled the plug. Because I'm not a quitter. Never have been. Not when she showed up on my front porch when we were practically kids with a positive pregnancy test in her hand. Not when she convinced me to use my college fund to pay for the new two-bedroom apartment in the city since I could only afford a studio in the suburbs.

If anything, it's the saying *no* part I suck at. Like when she took the house and convinced our two girls I'm bad news.

The ambulance hits a minor bump, and Kate winces, yanking me back to the present. Remi and Felix are in the front of the rig since I'm a trained paramedic and told them I'd keep an eye on the patient until we arrived at the hospital.

Doesn't mean she's said a word to me, though.

In fact, the girl looks pissed.

With her arms crossed and a nasty scowl marring her pretty face, she stares blankly at the back of the ambulance. Like I don't exist.

"How you doin'?" I ask her.

*Silence.*

I clear my throat and shift on my seat. "I should probably introduce--"

"Don't bother."

A scoff slips out of me as I tilt my head to the side. "I'm Theo's--"

"Were you the one who told them to call an ambulance?" she interrupts, finally gracing me with a look. Those gray eyes are stormy. Even stormier than in the restaurant when she'd first woken up. Like it's my fault she wound up on the floor. My fault she's in the back of an ambulance. My fault she can't ignore the entire situation and go about her day as if she didn't have a seizure in the middle of an Italian restaurant.

Leaning forward, I rest my elbows on my knees and hold her turbulent gaze. "Yeah. I was."

Her frown deepens. "Why?"

"Because your friends didn't know what to do, and someone needed to take charge."

"And you thought it was your right?" she demands.

"Yeah, I guess so. Ya know since you were a little preoccupied and all."

"You had no right to make that call."

She's seriously pissed right now, and I don't have the energy to fight her on something so small in the big picture.

"Look, it's not that big of a deal," I tell her. "They'll check you over. Make sure everything's okay. Call your doctor. Your parents--"

"They can't call my parents," she rushes out. The blood

drains from her face, making her already pale skin even whiter.

Hell, you'd think she just got caught with drugs on her and will be locked up for the rest of her life.

"Why?" I ask.

"Because."

I scoff and pinch the bridge of my nose. This girl really is a piece of work. "Gonna need more to go on than that."

"Because I don't want them to worry."

"They're *parents*," I tell her with a laugh. "It's what they do."

"Then why feed the fire, right? I'm fine."

I shake my head, fucking flabbergasted. Why is she fighting me on this? Why are we even having this conversation? Why do I even care what she does? Scratch that. I know exactly why I care. Because I have a kid who's avoiding me like I'm a criminal or some shit. And I know it isn't about me, and she can do whatever she wants on her birthday, but I'm still her dad. And if Kate can be so dismissive of her parents, so can Hazel. Which is exactly what she's doing with me. Not her mom. The woman's a damn saint in my daughters' eyes, but me? Their terrible father? Yeah, it's a bitch.

Shoving my own shitstorm of a life into the back of my mind, I tell Kate, "Look. Your parents care about you. They have a right to know––"

"I'm over eighteen. Well over eighteen," Kate spits. "They don't have a right to anything anymore. Not if I don't want to tell them. And since I'm conscious and coherent, I can make the call for myself."

She's serious. I pull back, surprised by the acid on her tongue and how determined she looks right now despite the splitting headache I know is cracking her skull in two.

"Fine," I concede. "Then, I'm staying with you."

"What?" she screeches.

"I'm staying with you."

"You don't know me."

"You're right. I don't. And we can keep it that way if you want, but I know proper protocol after someone with epilepsy has a seizure, Kate."

She flinches as the word epilepsy slips past my lips, but I don't call her out on it. Instead, I continue, softening my voice. "You're not supposed to be alone. And since you don't want your parents around, I'll be by your side until the doctor gives you clearance to go home. Then, I'll drive you, confirm one of your roommates is around, and leave you in their care."

"I'm not a baby––"

"And I'm not treating you like a baby."

"That's exactly what you're doing."

"No, I'm treating you like you have epilepsy, Kate." She squeezes her eyes shut, the word hitting her like a lash from a whip. I take a deep breath, adding, "And there isn't anything wrong with it, but there are good days and bad days. And if I had to guess, today's a particularly bad one, considering how your roommates responded. So yeah. We're going to treat it like a bad day. And we're going to acknowledge it. And we're going to get through it."

She shakes her head before pressing the heel of her hand against it and wincing.

My frustration dissipates instantly. But I don't reach for her. I don't offer any comfort. She doesn't want it, anyway.

With a sigh, I murmur, "Headache?"

She drops her hand back to her lap and stares blankly in front of her again. "I'm fine."

Sure she is.

"You know it isn't a weakness, right?" I mutter, scrubbing my hand over my face and spreading my legs wide in front of me as the ambulance pulls up to the emergency room.

"Asking for help. Acknowledging that you have a battle most people wouldn't even dream of fighting."

Her nostrils flare, but she doesn't look at me.

"You're a badass, Kate," I add as Felix puts the ambulance into park. "But even badasses have bad days sometimes."

Without another word, we head inside the hospital, and the doctors run a bunch of tests, asking Kate questions and confirming I'm allowed to stay in the room with her. She tells them it's fine but doesn't bother acknowledging me for the rest of the visit. And when I drive her home, thanks to Theo dropping my car off at the hospital after he and Blakely parted ways, Kate slams the car door behind her, folds her arms, and walks toward the townhome she shares with her roommates, not bothering to look back at me.

The front porch lights flicker on as Kate reaches the steps and walks to the front door. It opens, revealing one of her roommates, who pulls her into a hug almost instantly. We haven't been introduced, but she has a sleeve of tattoos on one arm and piercings along the shell of her ear as she meets my gaze over Kate's shoulder, dipping her chin in gratitude before guiding Kate inside.

Kate's right about one thing.

She's definitely well over eighteen. My guess is closer to twenty-five or so. Not that it makes it okay for me to be attracted to her. She's still young. Too young for a guy like me.

I shake my head and shove my car into reverse.

Guess my job here is done.

Read Now
Don't Let Me Break

# ALSO BY KELSIE RAE

Kelsie Rae tries to keep her books formatted with an updated list of her releases, but every once in a while she falls behind.

If you'd like to check out a complete list of her up-to-date published books, visit her website at www.authorkelsierae.com/books

Or you can join her newsletter to hear about her latest releases, get exclusive content, and participate in fun giveaways.

*Interested in reading more by Kelsie Rae?*

**Don't Let Me Series**

(Steamy Contemporary Romance Standalone Series)

Don't Let Me Fall - Colt and Ashlyn's Story

Don't Let Me Go - Blakely and Theo's Story

Don't Let Me Break - Kate and Macklin's Story

Don't Let Me Down - Mia and Henry's Story

**Wrecked Roommates Series**

(Steamy Contemporary Romance Standalone Series)

Model Behavior

Forbidden Lyrics

Messy Strokes

Risky Business

Broken Instrument

**Signature Sweethearts Series**

(Sweet Contemporary Romance Standalone Series)

Taking the Chance

Taking the Backseat - Download now for FREE

Taking the Job

Taking the Leap

**Get Baked Sweethearts Series**

(Sweet Contemporary Romance Standalone Series)

Off Limits

Stand Off

Hands Off

Hired Hottie (A *Steamy* Get Baked Sweethearts Spin-Off)

**Swenson Sweethearts Series**

(Sweet Contemporary Romance Standalone Series)

Finding You

Fooling You

Hating You

Cruising with You (A *Steamy* Swenson Sweethearts Novella)

Crush (A *Steamy* Swenson Sweethearts Spin-Off)

**Advantage Play Series**

(Steamy Romantic Suspense/Mafia Series)

Wild Card

Little Bird

Bitter Queen

Black Jack

Royal Flush - Download now for FREE

**Stand Alones**

Fifty-Fifty

Sign up for Kelsie's newsletter to receive exclusive content, including the first two chapters of every new book two weeks before its release date!

Dear Reader,

I want to thank you guys from the bottom of my heart for taking a chance on Don't Let Me Go, and for giving me the opportunity to share this story with you. I couldn't do this without you!

I would also be very grateful if you could take the time to leave a review. It's amazing how such a little thing like a review can be such a huge help to an author!

Thank you so much!!!

-Kelsie

# ABOUT THE AUTHOR

Kelsie is a sucker for a love story with all the feels. When she's not chasing words for her next book, you will probably find her reading or, more likely, hanging out with her husband and playing with her three kiddos who love to drive her crazy.

She adores photography, baking, her two pups, and her cat who thinks she's a dog. Now that she's actively pursuing her writing dreams, she's set her sights on someday finding the self-discipline to not binge-watch an entire series on Netflix in one sitting.

If you'd like to connect with Kelsie, follow her on Facebook, sign up for her newsletter, or join Kelsie Rae's Reader Group to stay up to date on new releases, exclusive content, give-aways, and her crazy publishing journey.